GRAVEYARD SHAKES

LAURA TERRY

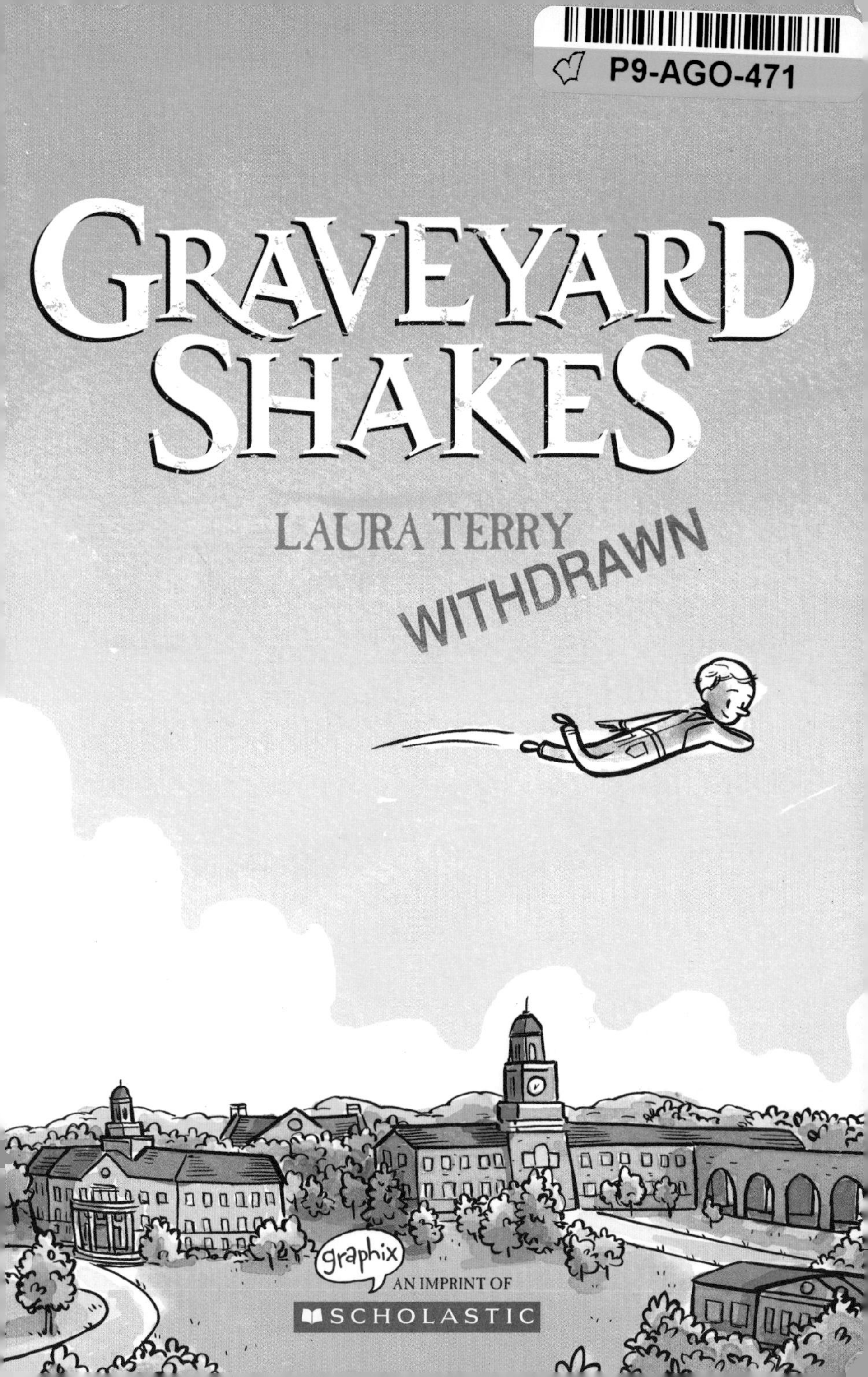

graphix
AN IMPRINT OF
SCHOLASTIC

Graveyard Shakes was painted using a combination of hand-painted and digital watercolor. The hand-painted watercolor was done on Saunders Waterford 140-pound cold-press paper and quinacridone rose, Prussian blue, and cadmium yellow pigments. The digital art was created using Kyle T. Webster brushes.

Library of Congress Control Number: 2016960079

ISBN 978-0-545-88955-1 (hardcover)
ISBN 978-0-545-88954-4 (paperback)

10 9 8 7 6 5 4 3 2 17 18 19 20 21

Printed in China 38
First edition, October 2017
Edited by Cassandra Pelham
Book design by Phil Falco
Creative Director: David Saylor

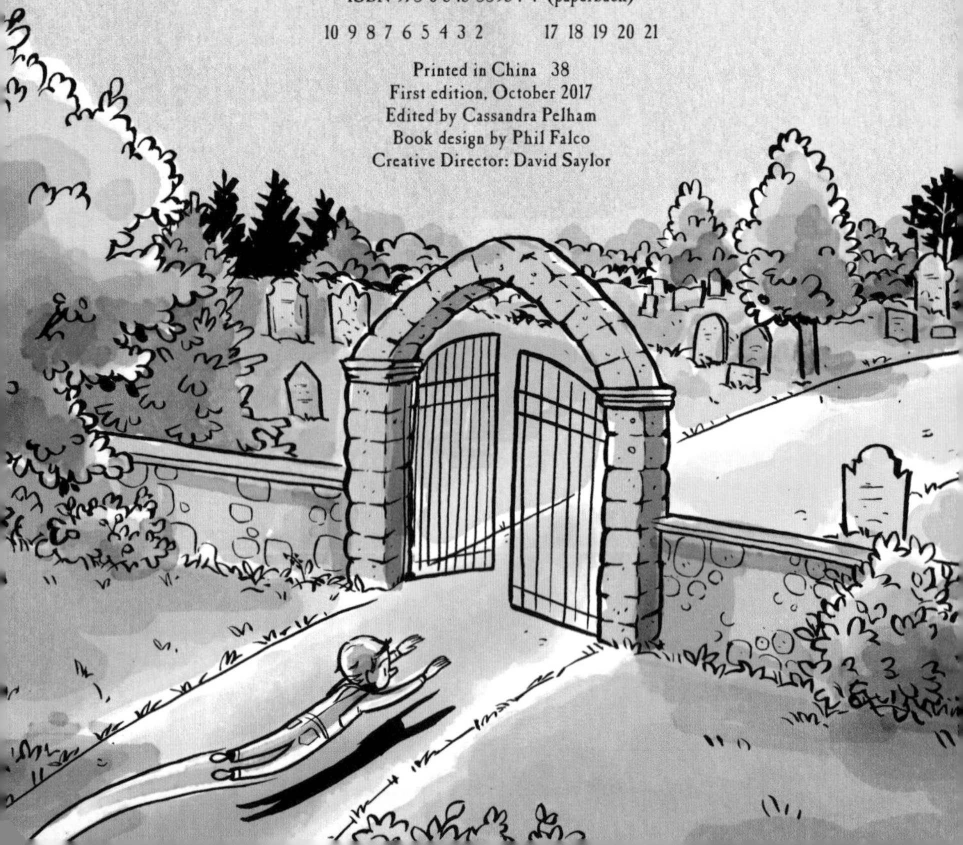

For my dad, Tommy Frank, and Casper

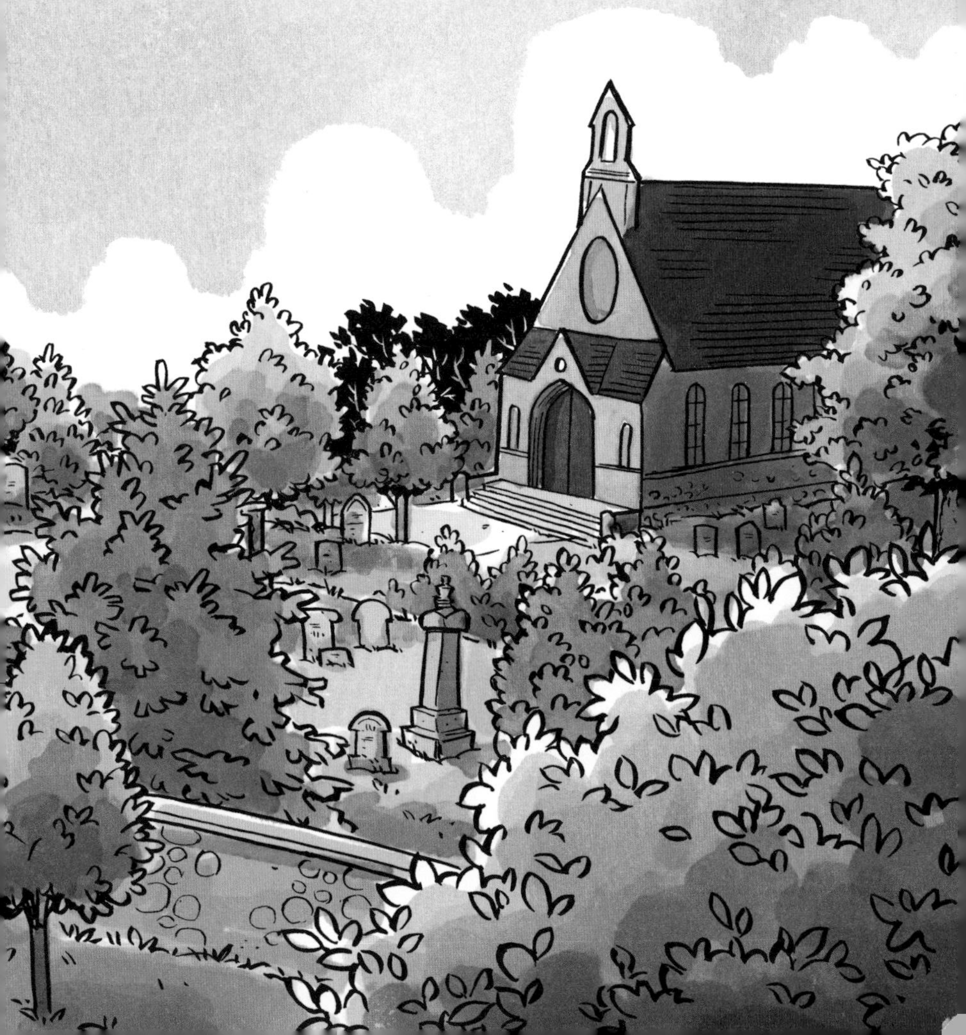

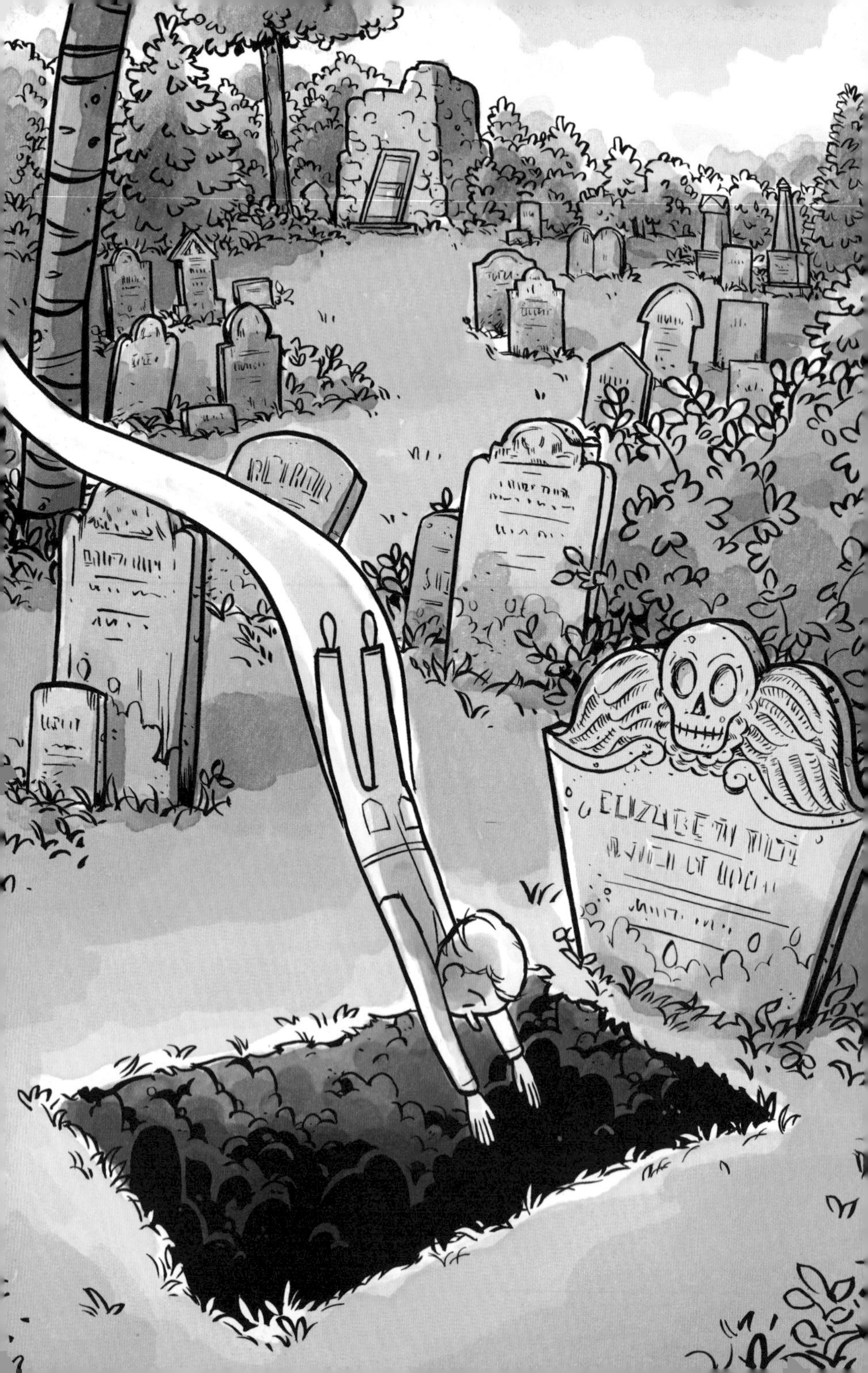

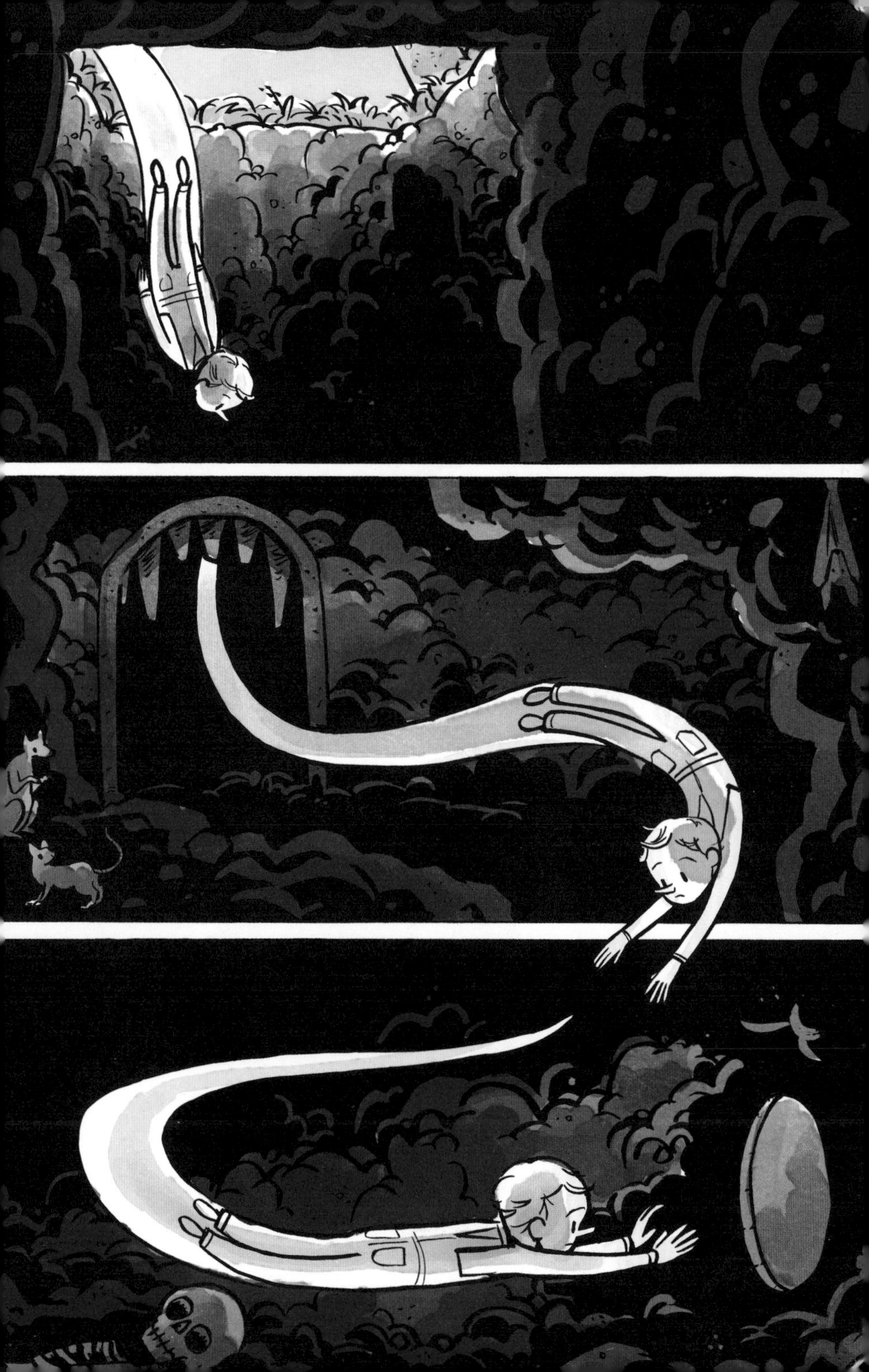

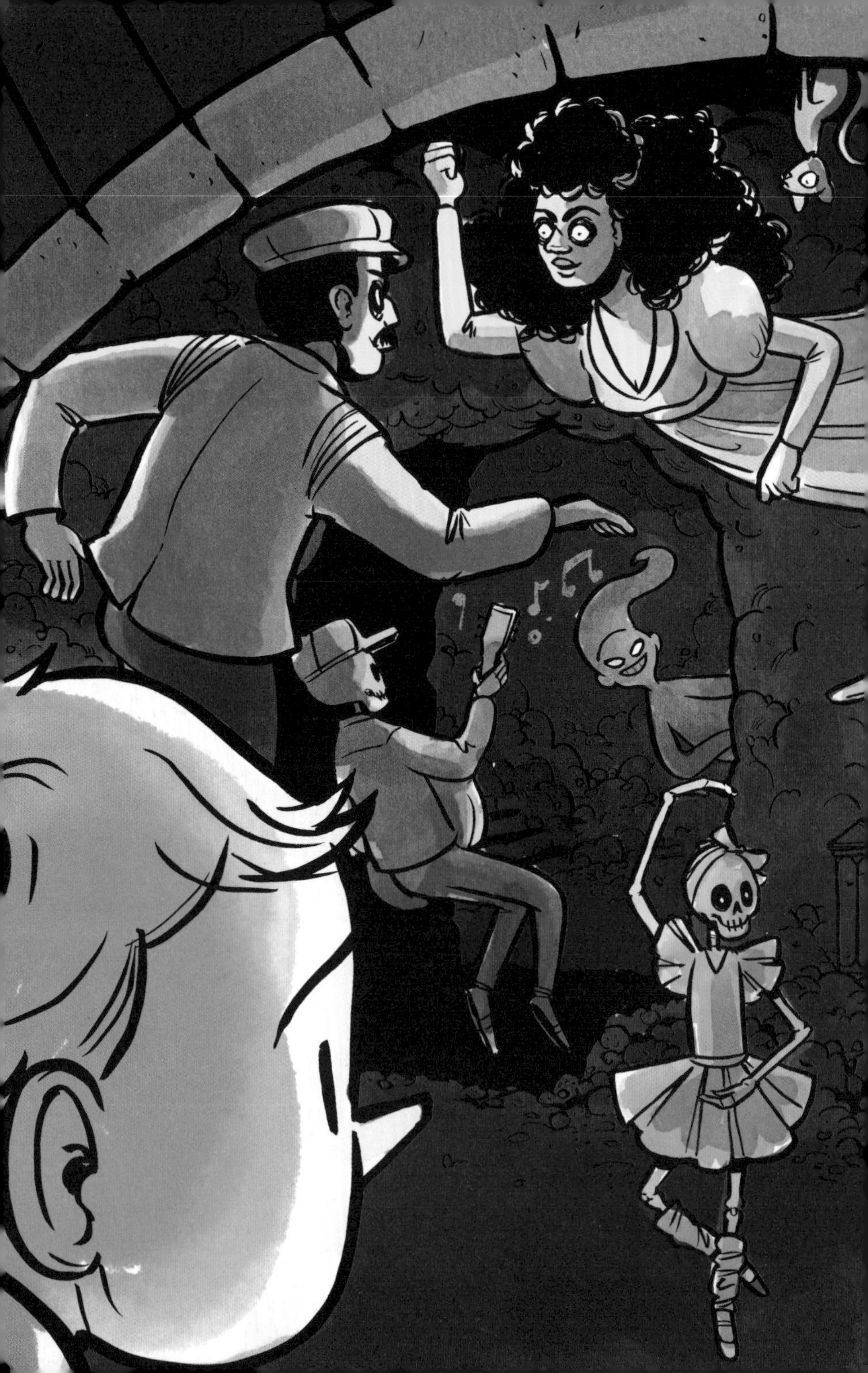

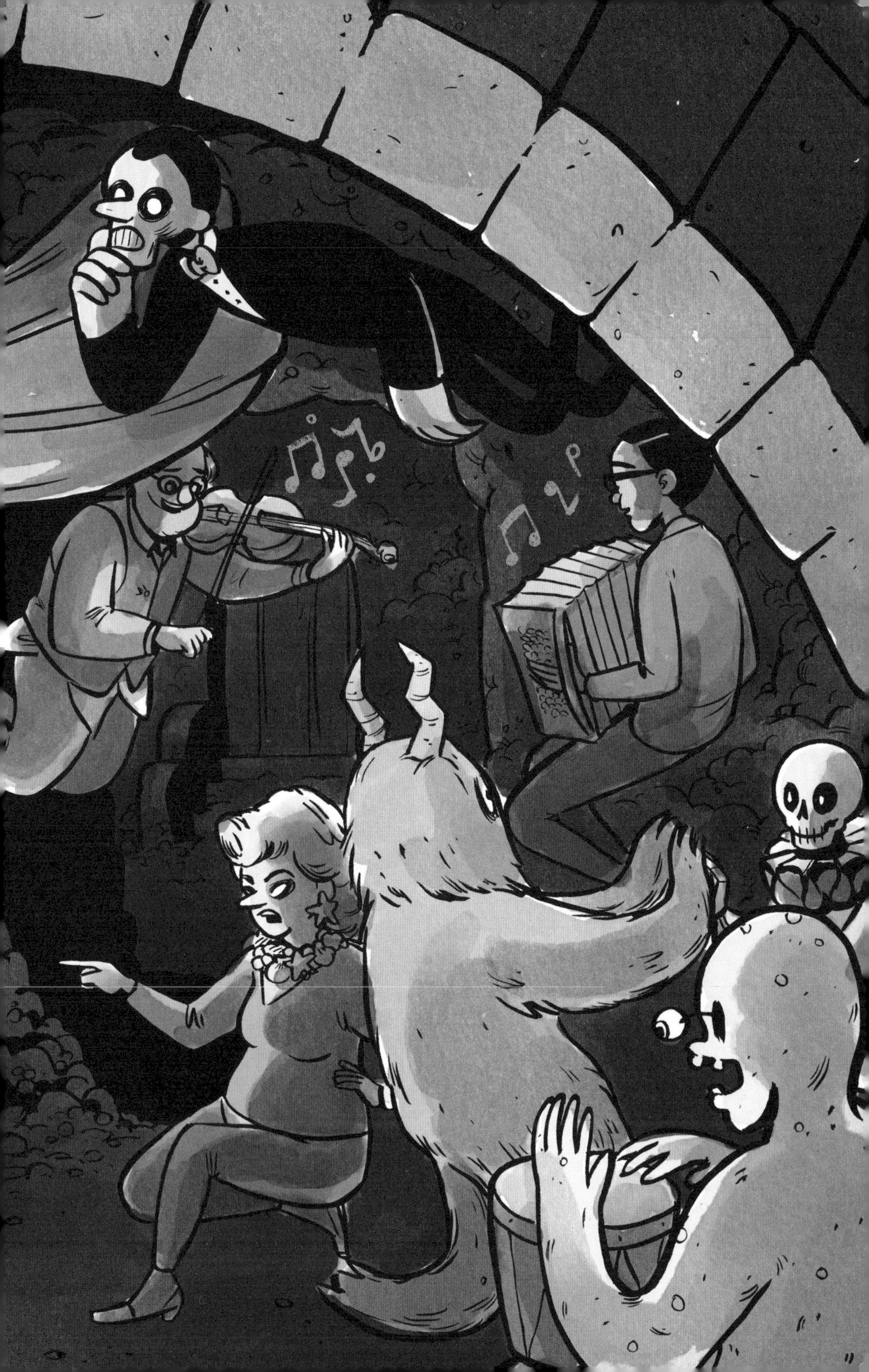

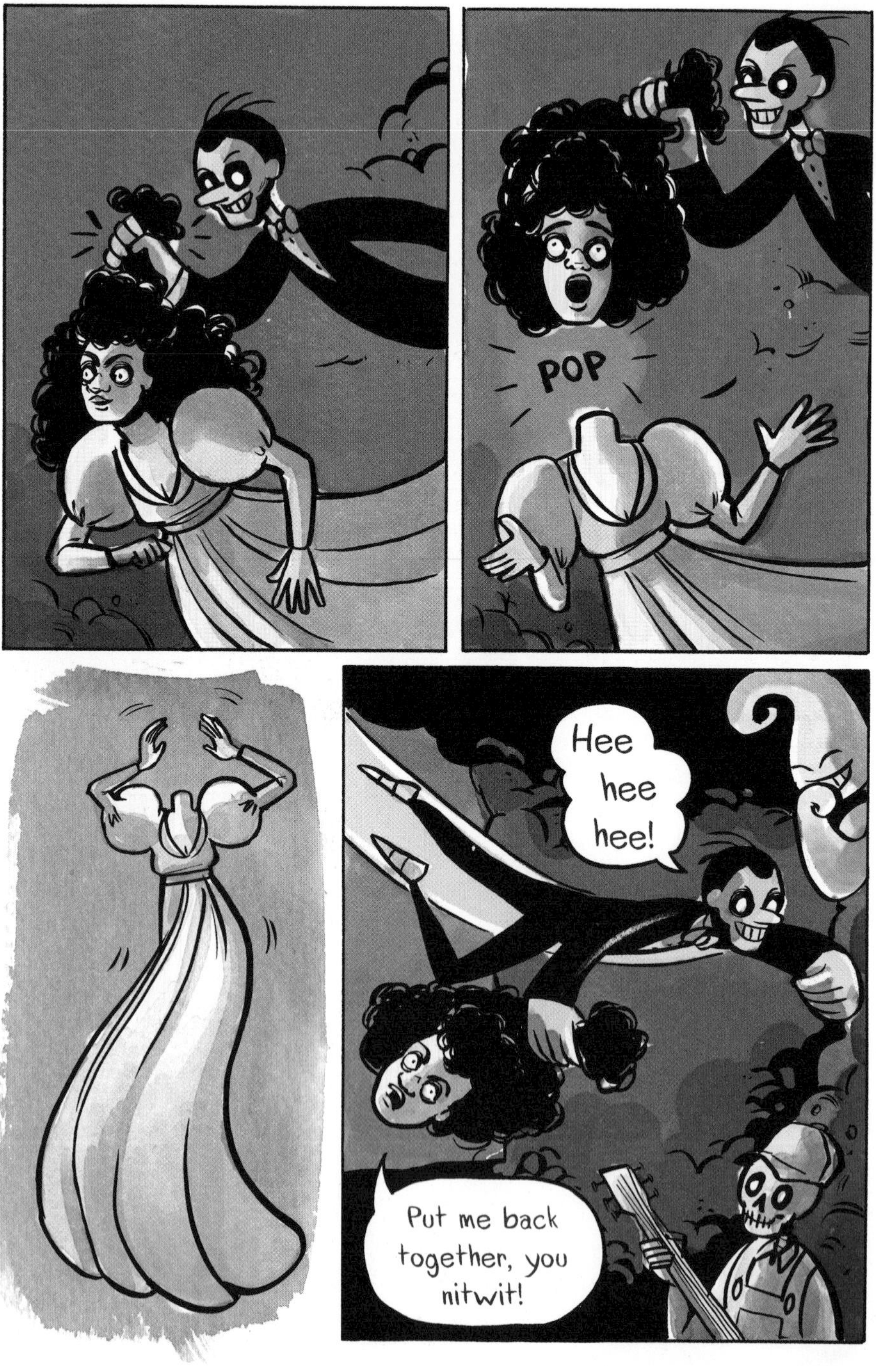
POP
Hee hee hee!
Put me back together, you nitwit!

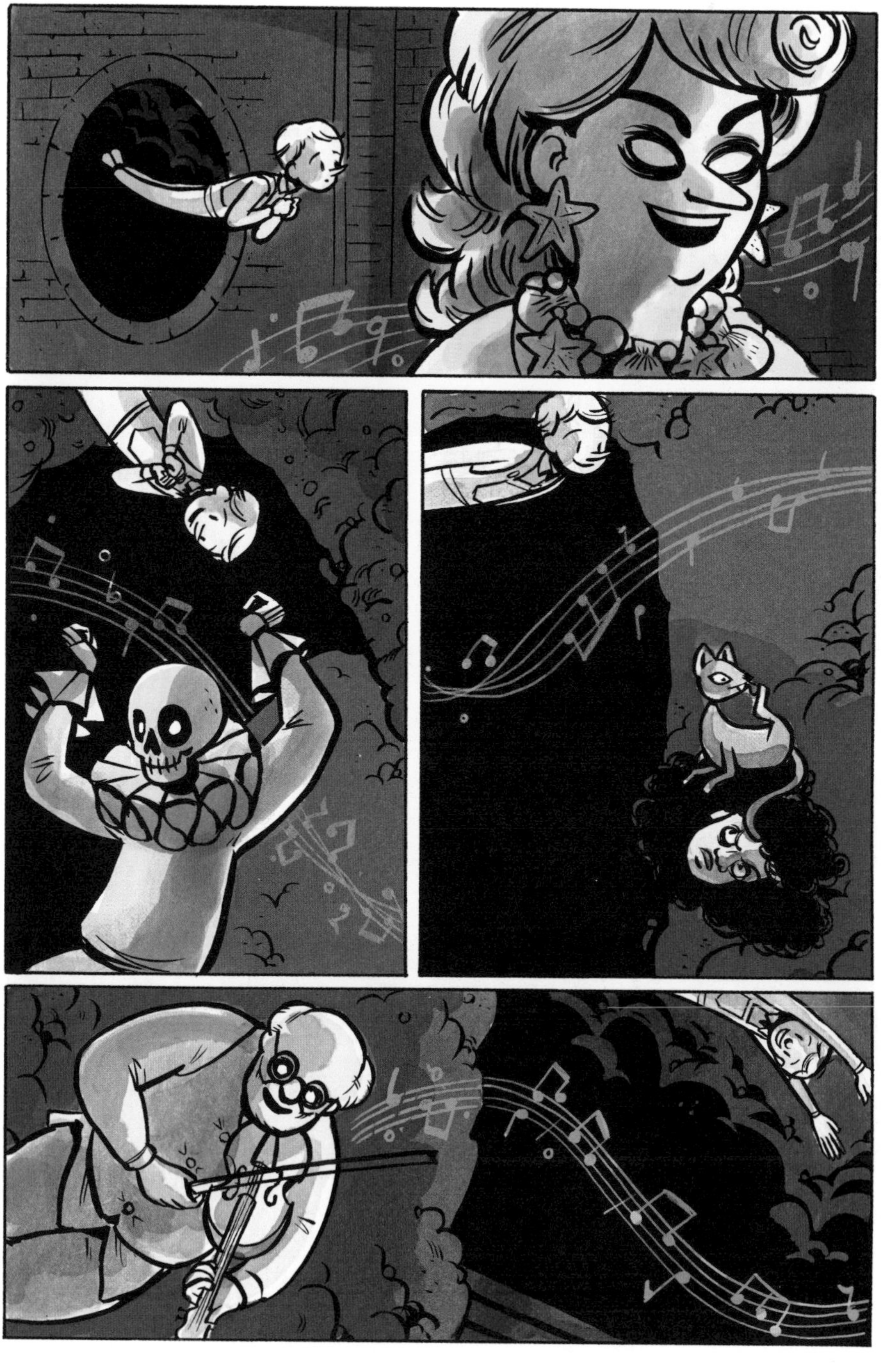

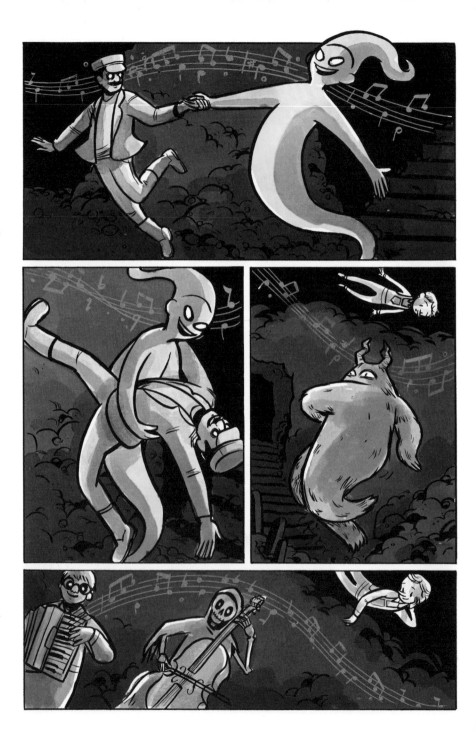

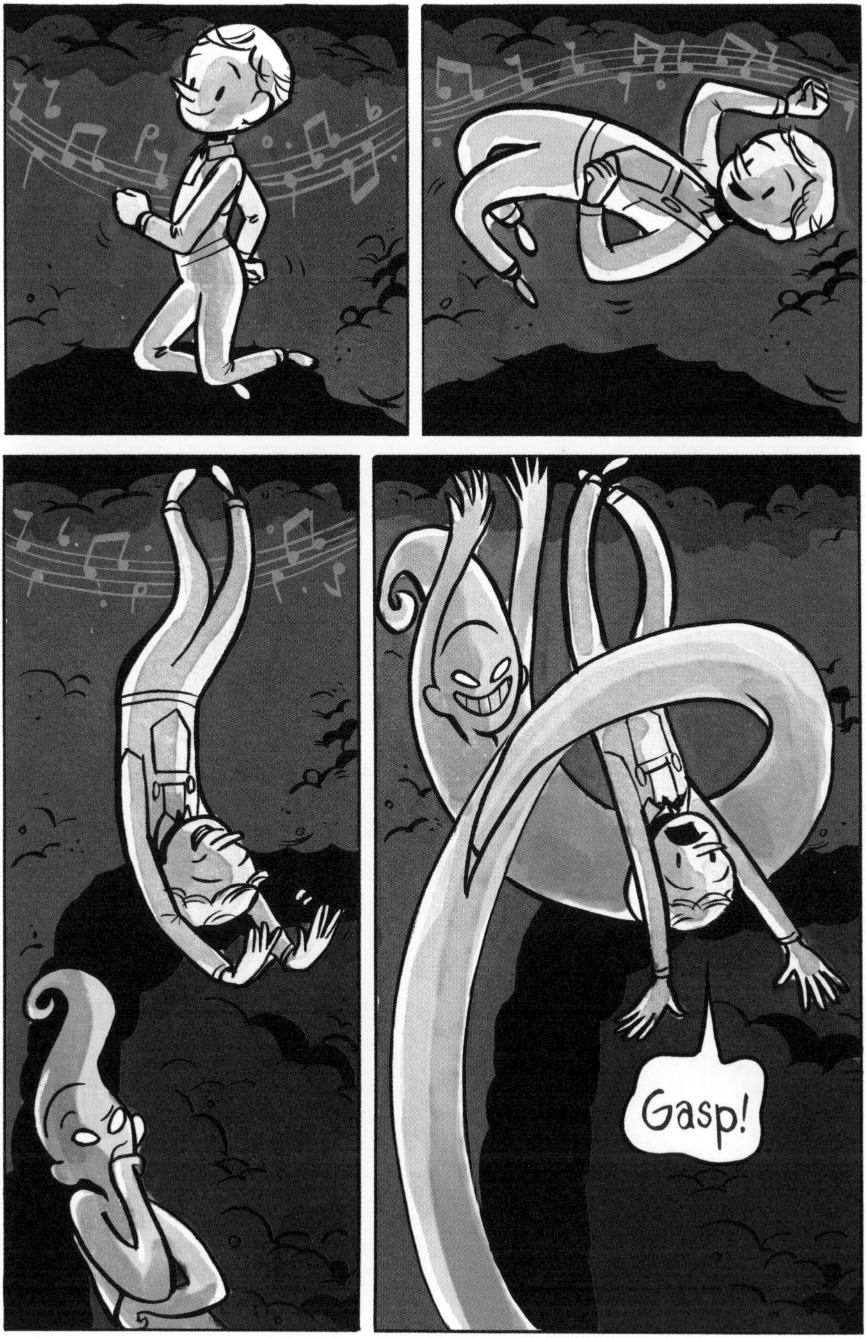
Gasp!

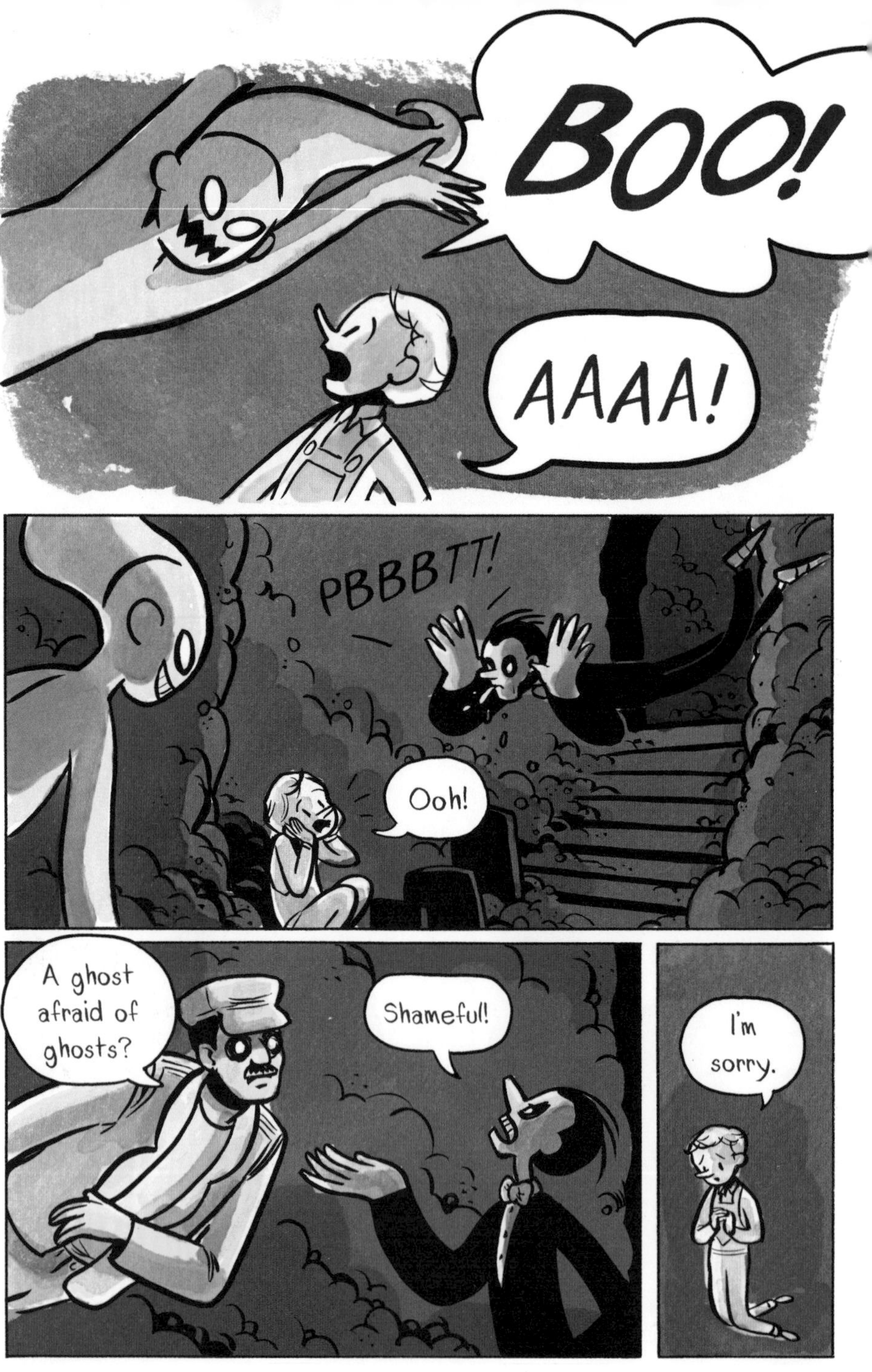
BOO!
AAAA!
PBBBTT!
Ooh!
A ghost afraid of ghosts?
Shameful!
I'm sorry.

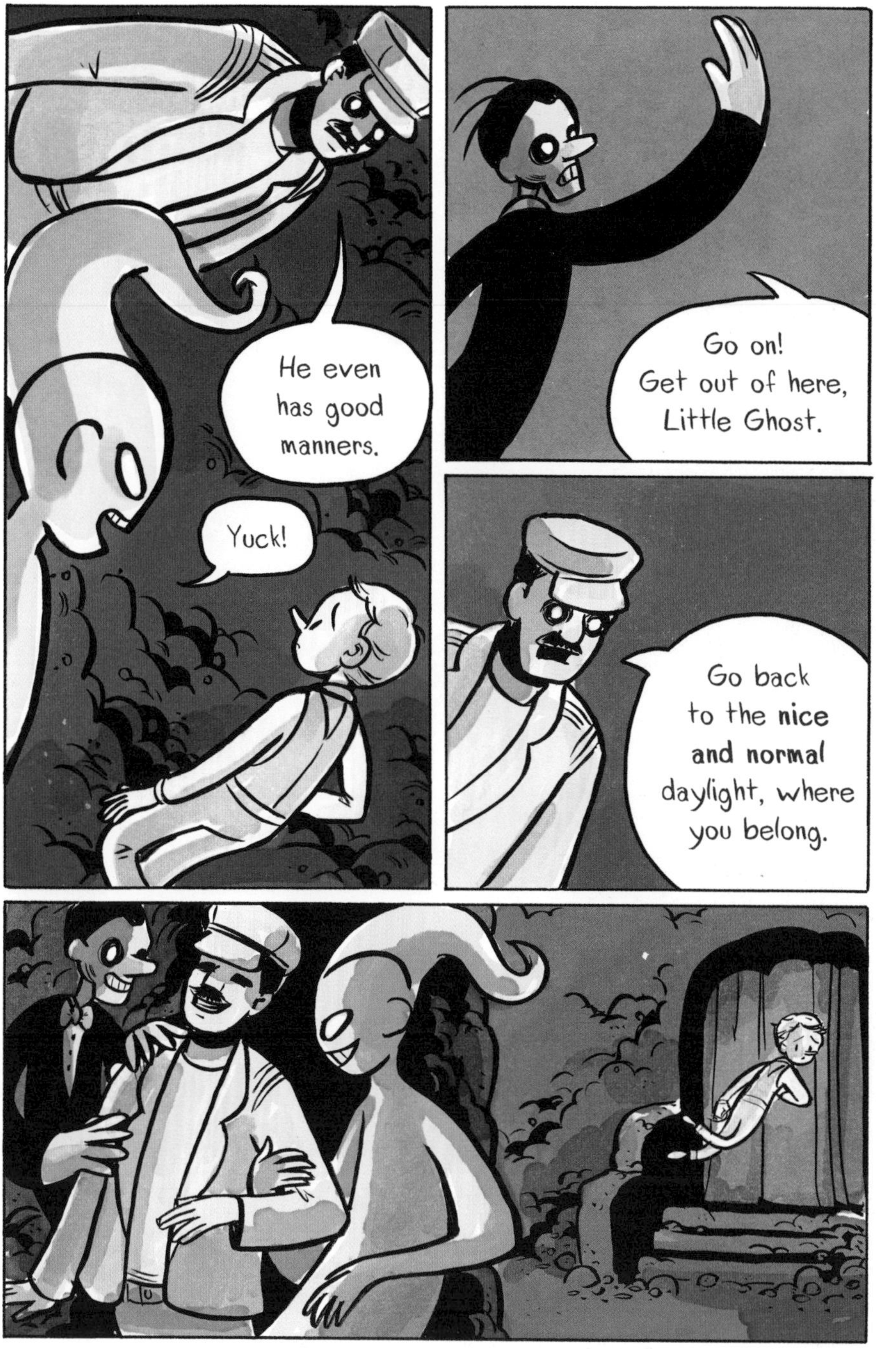
He even has good manners.
Yuck!
Go on! Get out of here, Little Ghost.
Go back to the **nice and normal** daylight, where you belong.

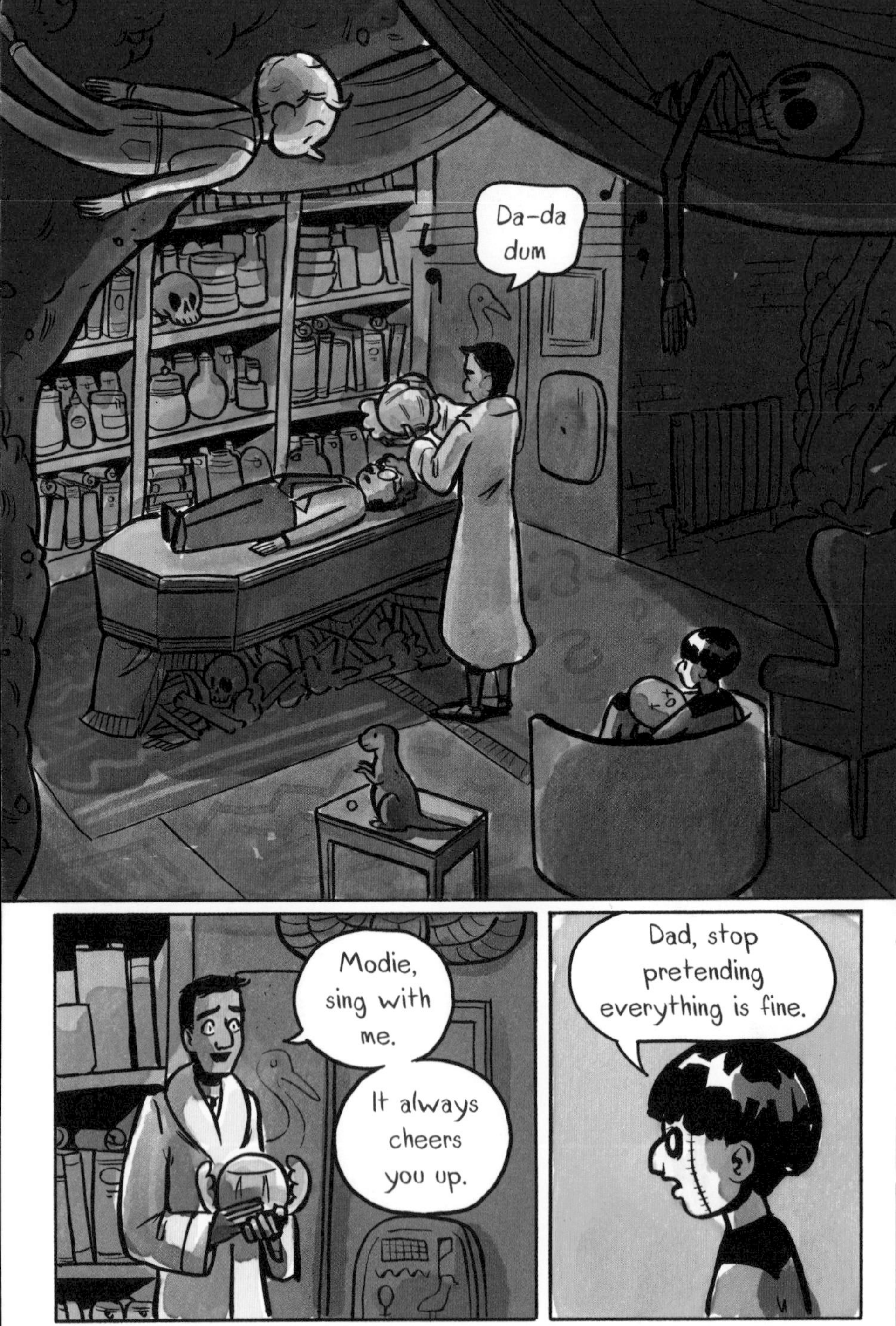
Da-da
dum
Modie, sing with me.
It always cheers you up.
Dad, stop pretending everything is fine.

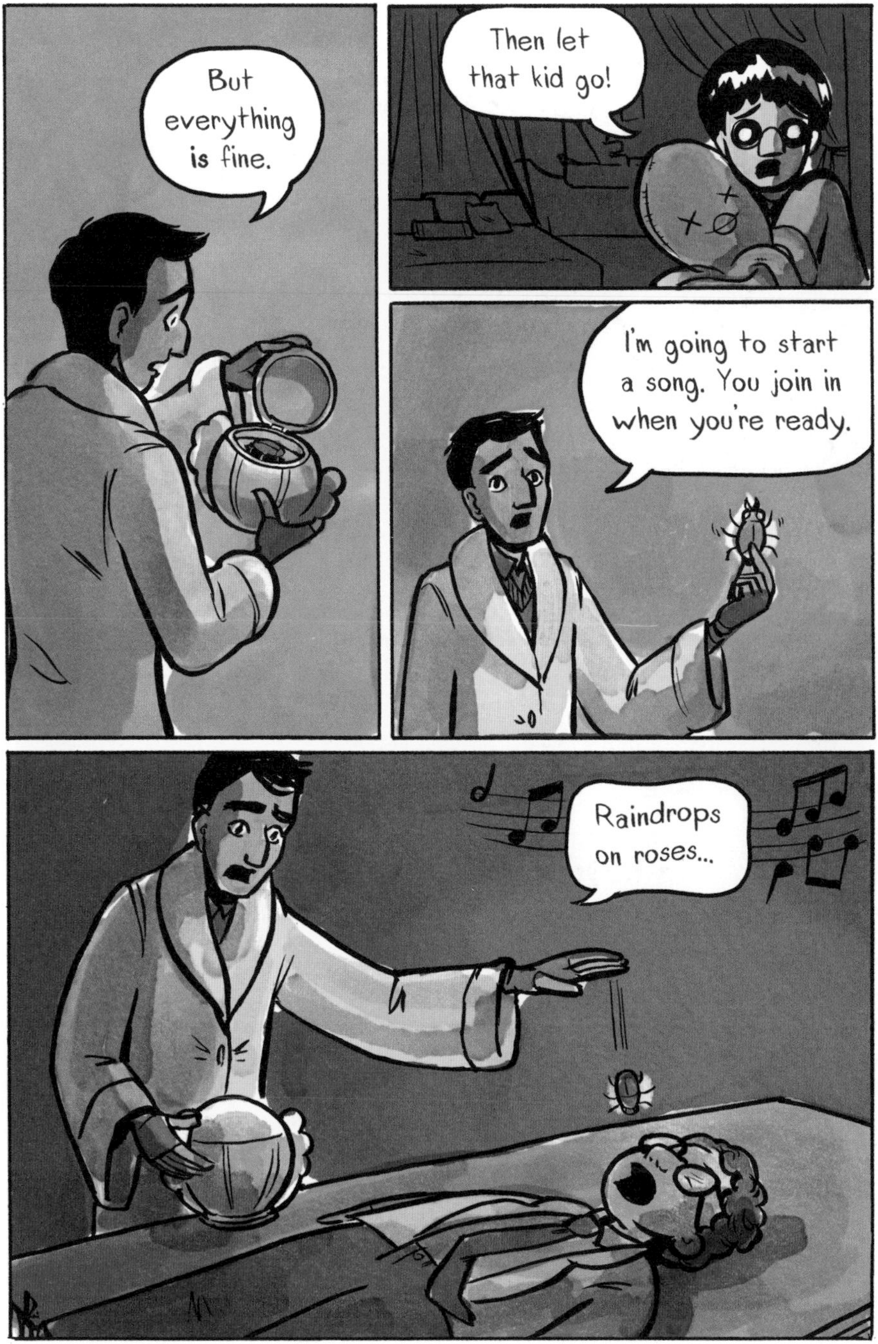
But everything is fine.
Then let that kid go!
I'm going to start a song. You join in when you're ready.
Raindrops on roses...

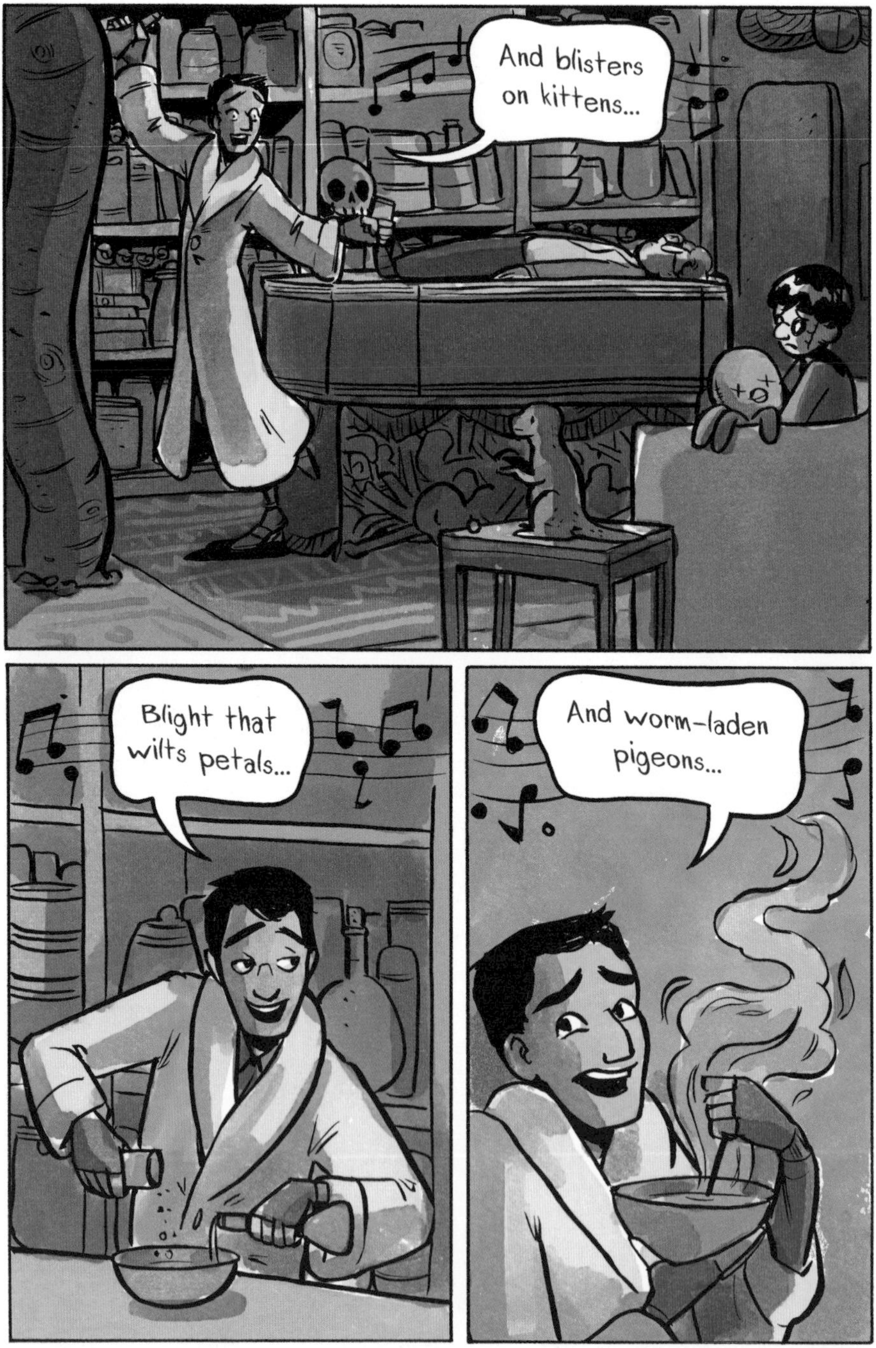
And blisters on kittens...
Blight that wilts petals...
And worm-laden pigeons...

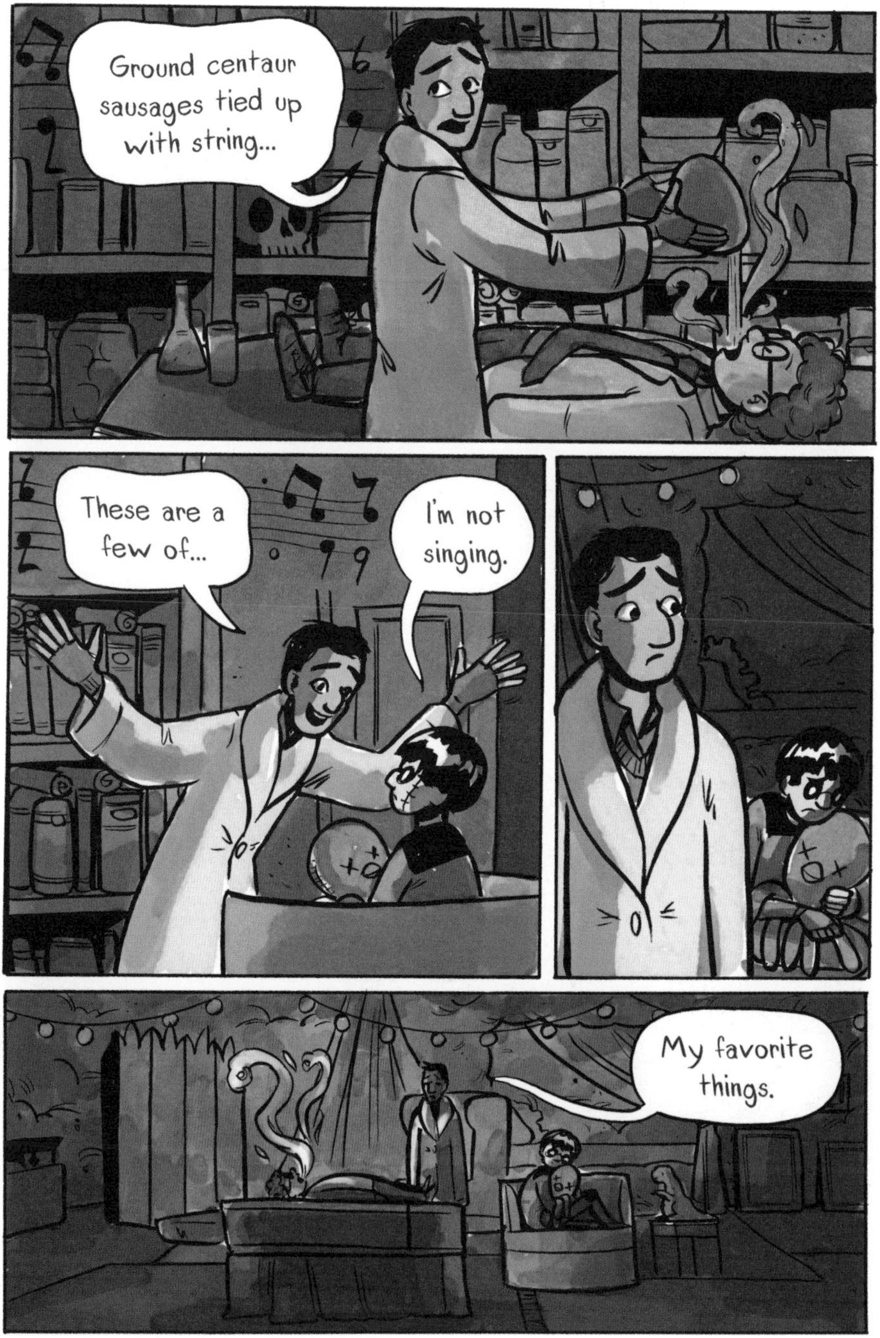
Ground centaur sausages tied up with string...
These are a few of...
I'm not singing.
My favorite things.

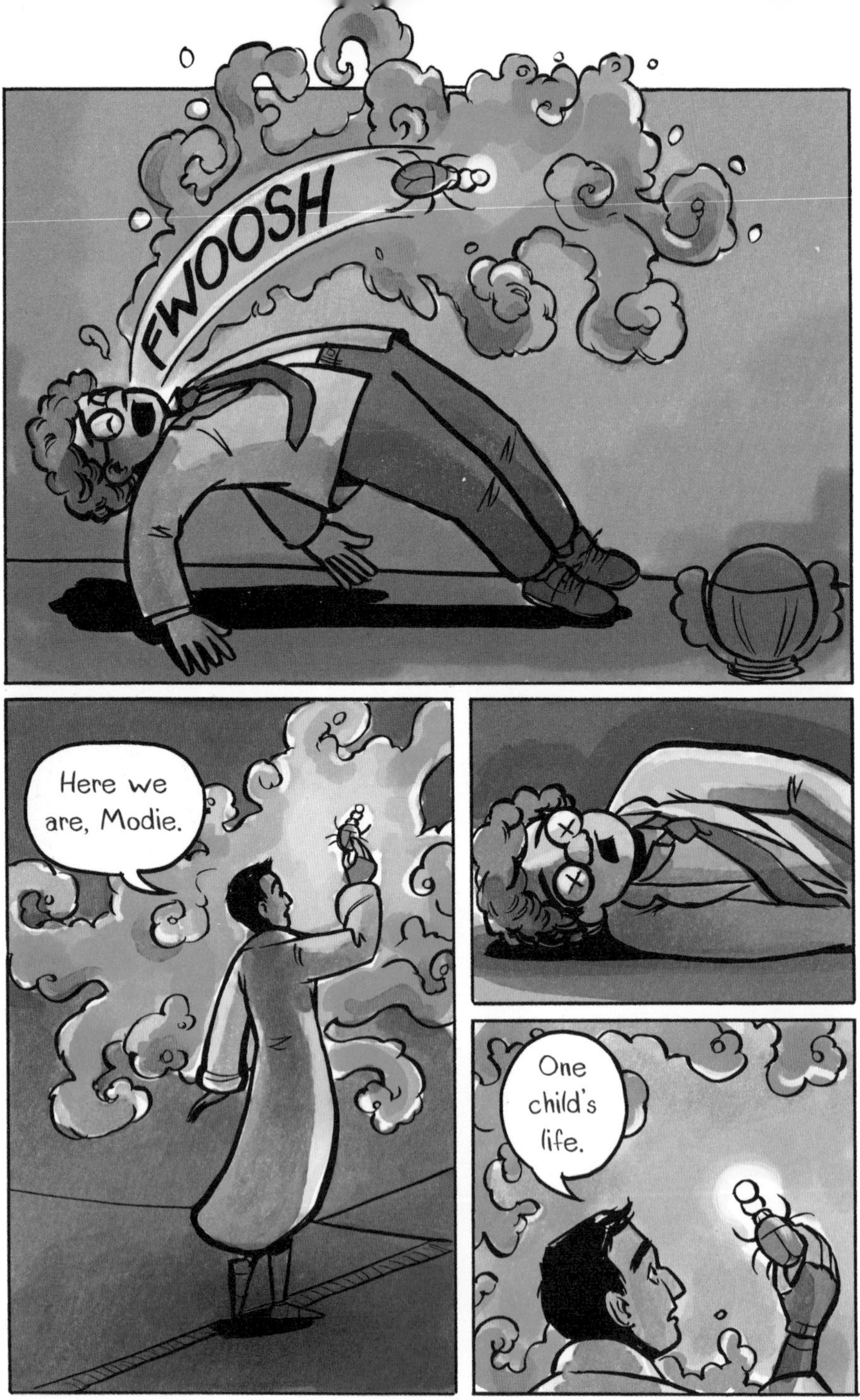
FWOOSH
Here we are, Modie.
One child's life.

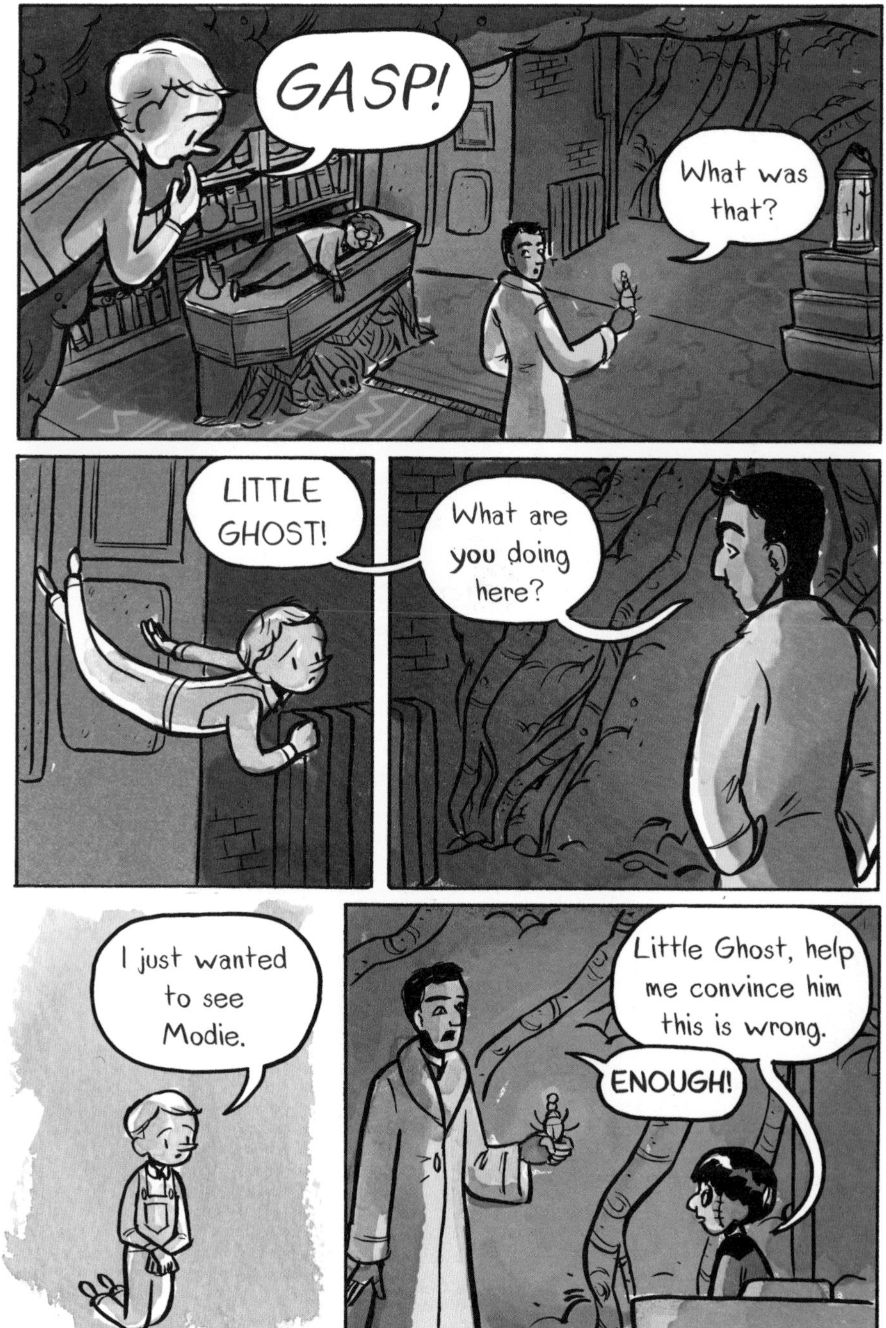
GASP!
What was that?
LITTLE GHOST!
What are you doing here?
I just wanted to see Modie.
Little Ghost, help me convince him this is wrong.
ENOUGH!

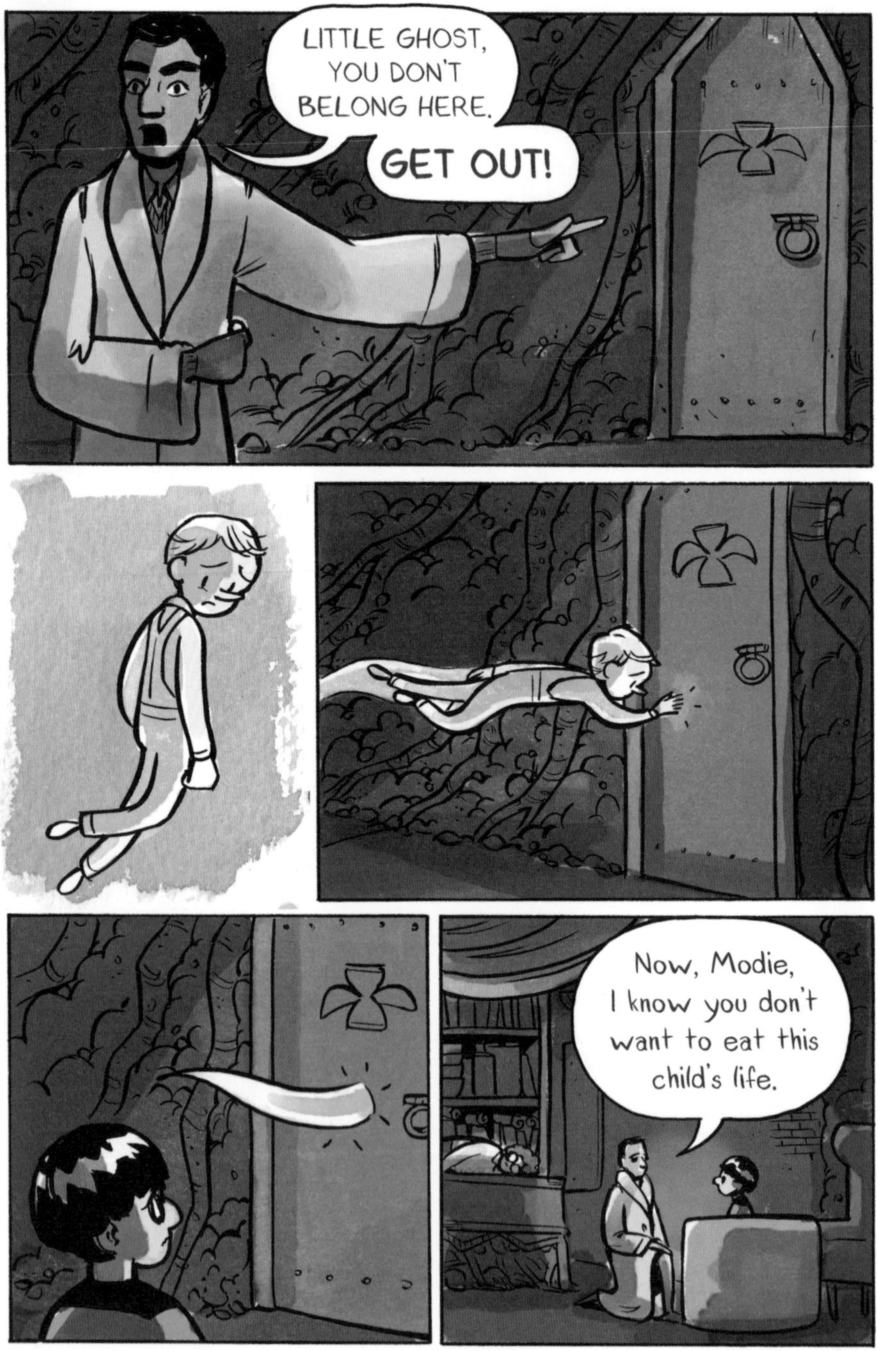
LITTLE GHOST, YOU DON'T BELONG HERE.
GET OUT!
Now, Modie, I know you don't want to eat this child's life.

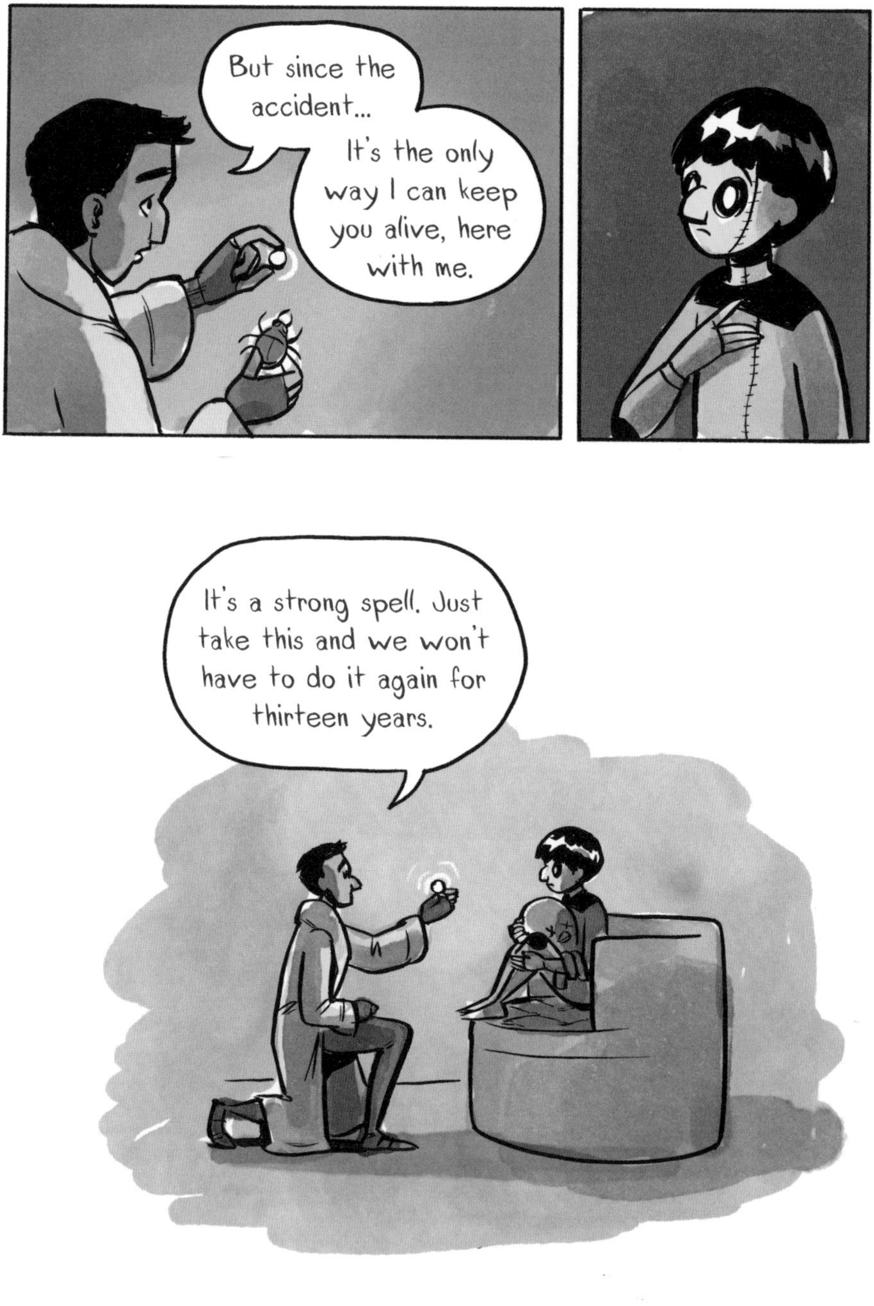

But since the accident...
It's the only way I can keep you alive, here with me.
It's a strong spell. Just take this and we won't have to do it again for thirteen years.

Twelve years and eleven months later . . .

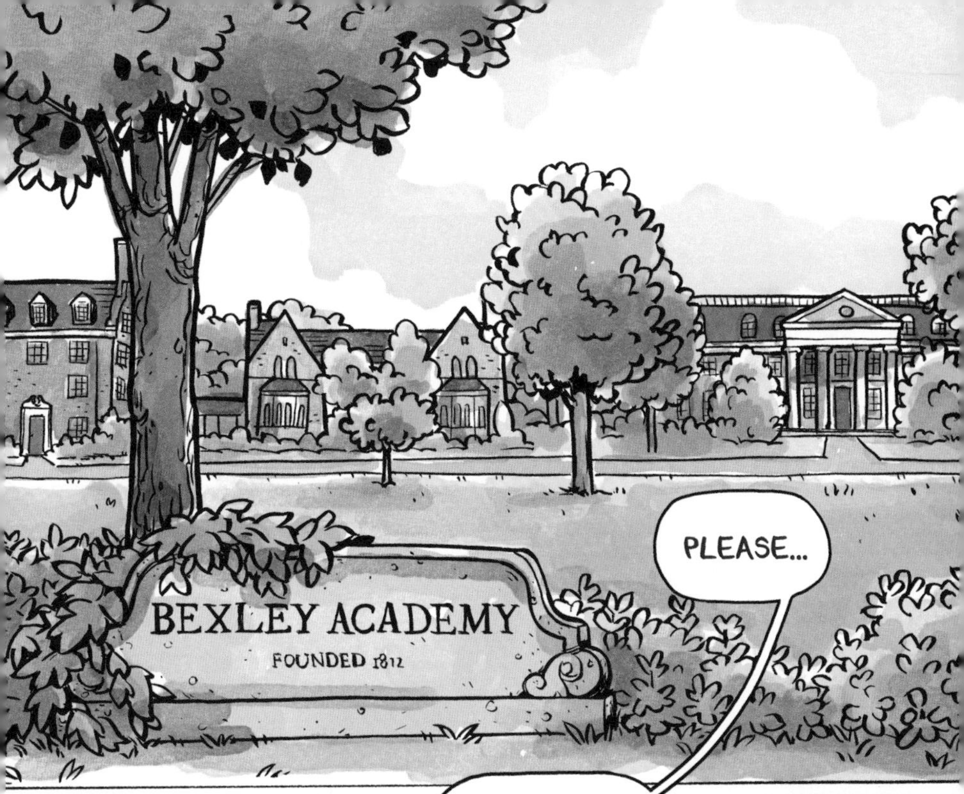
BEXLEY ACADEMY
FOUNDED 1812
PLEASE...

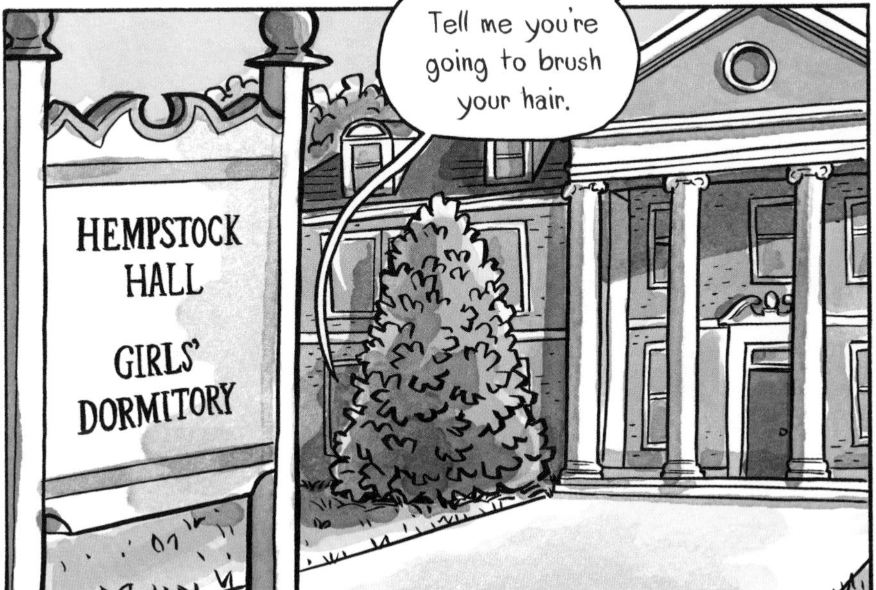
Tell me you're going to brush your hair.
HEMPSTOCK HALL
GIRLS' DORMITORY

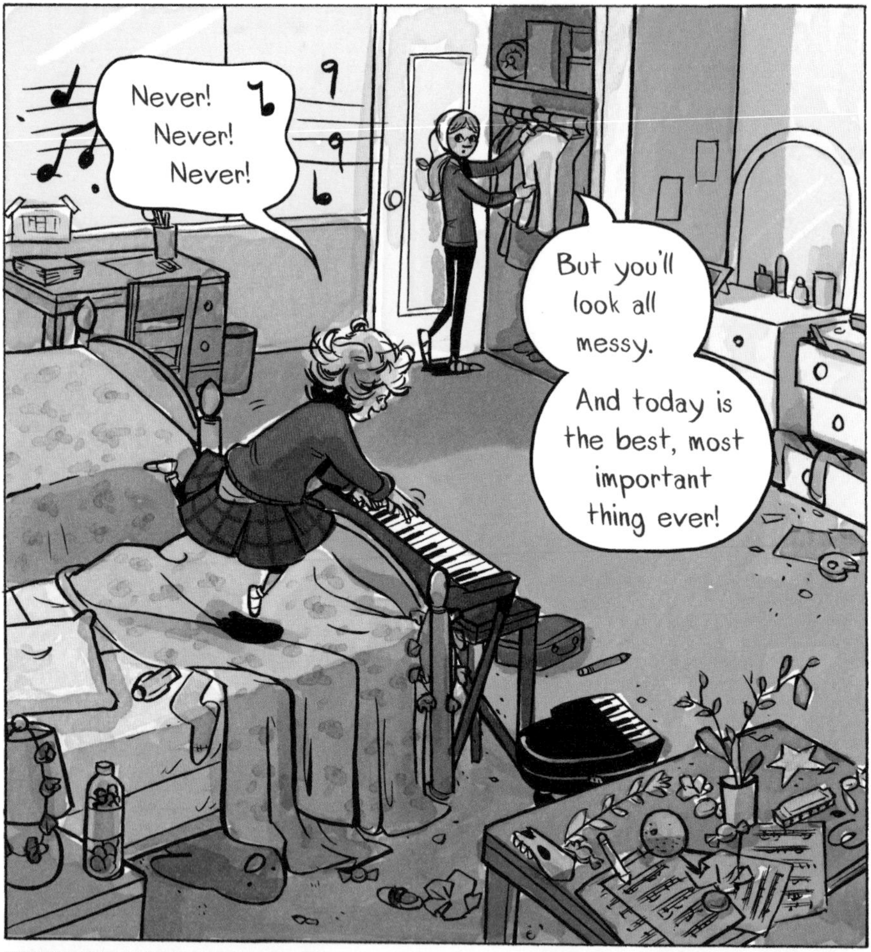
Never!
Never!
Never!
But you'll look all messy.
And today is the best, most important thing ever!

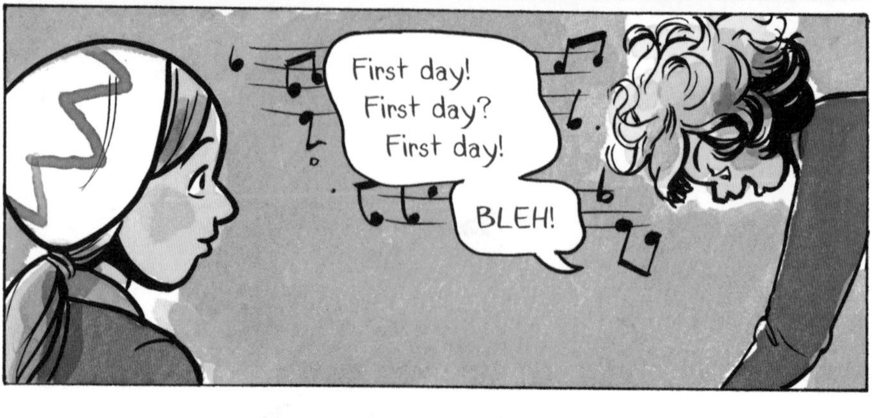
First day!
First day?
First day!
BLEH!

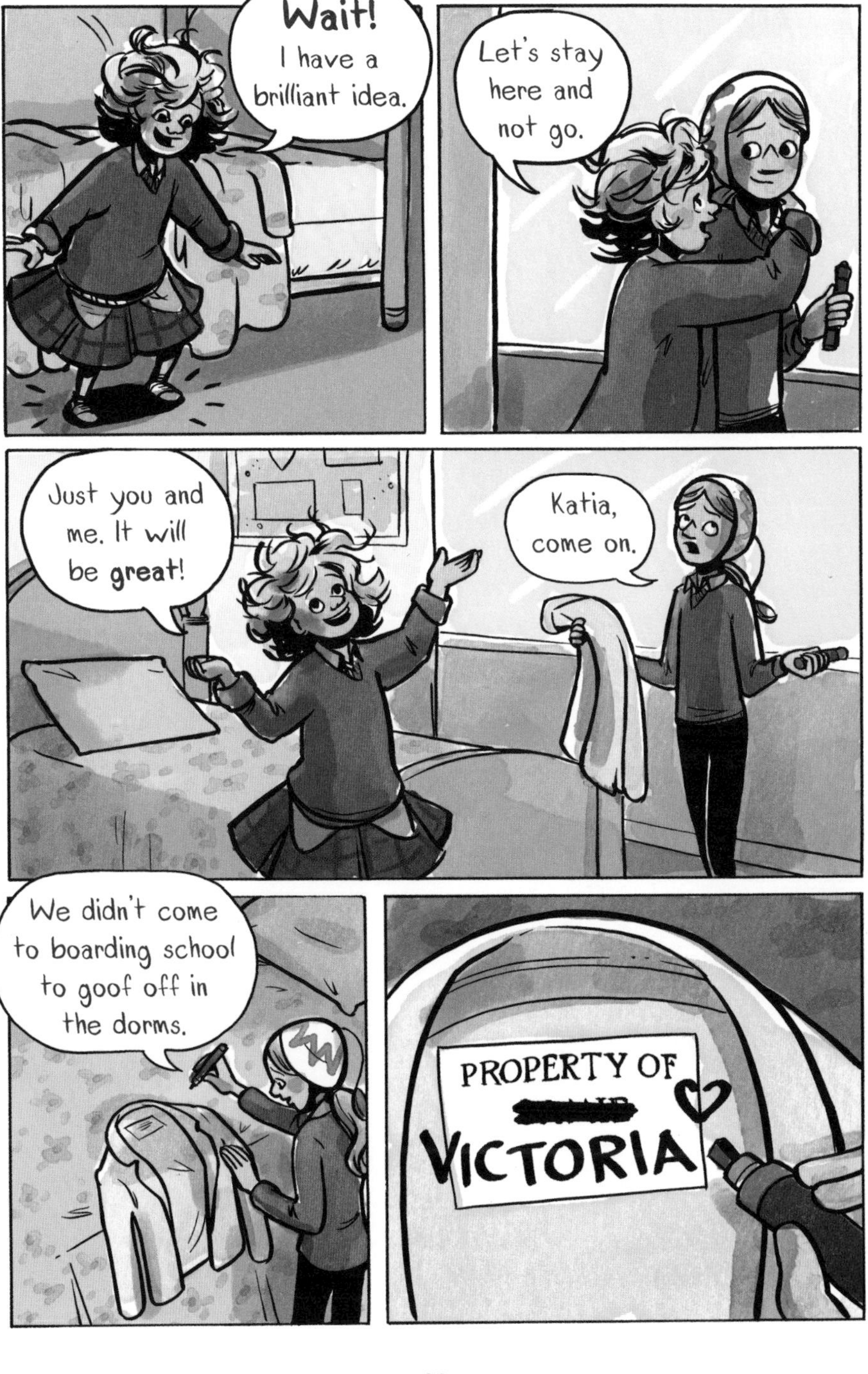

Wait! I have a brilliant idea.
Let's stay here and not go.
Just you and me. It will be **great**!
Katia, come on.
We didn't come to boarding school to goof off in the dorms.
PROPERTY OF
[redacted]
VICTORIA

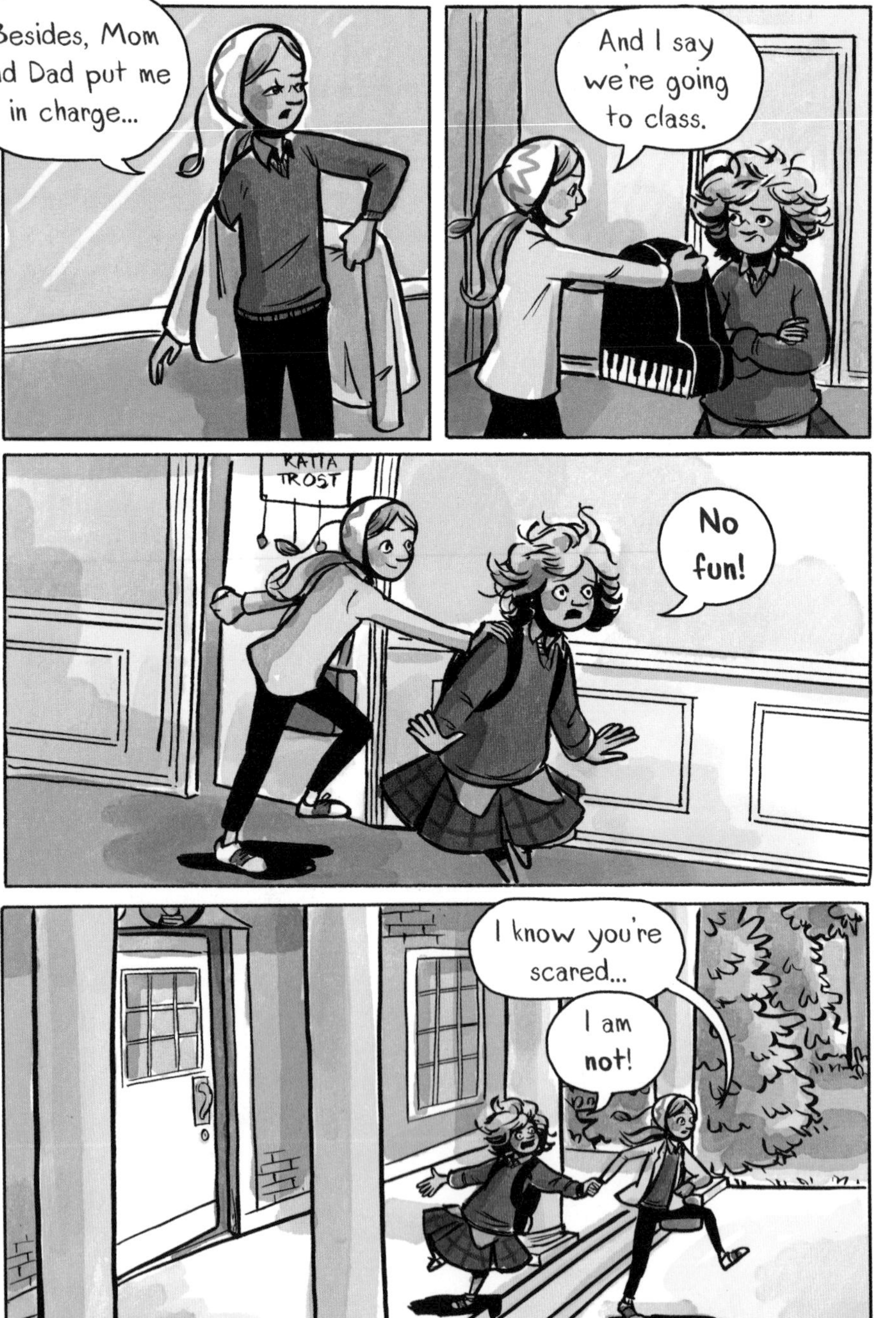
Besides, Mom and Dad put me in charge...
And I say we're going to class.
KATIA TROST
No fun!
I know you're scared...
I am **not**!

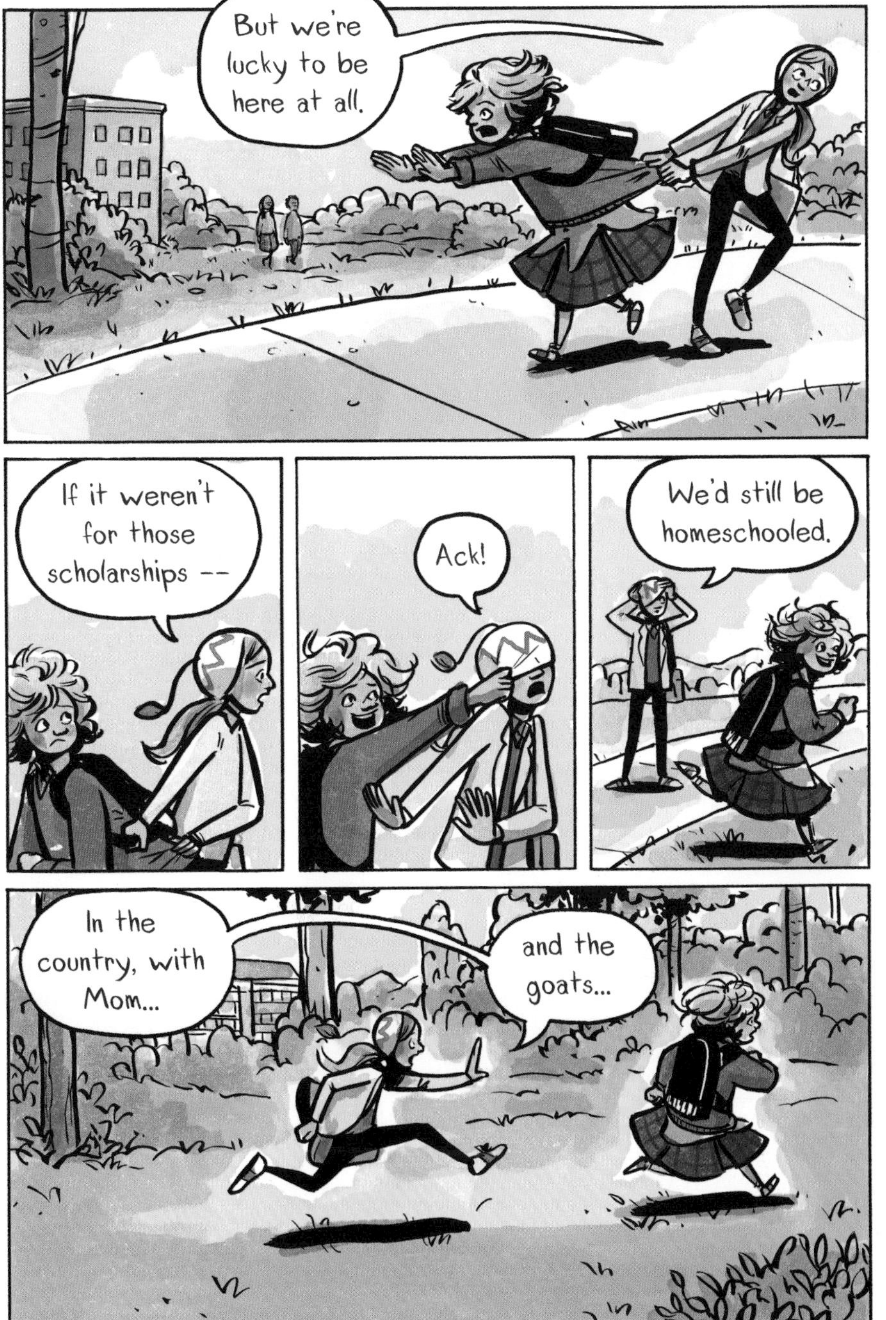
But we're lucky to be here at all.
If it weren't for those scholarships --
Ack!
We'd still be homeschooled.
In the country, with Mom...
and the goats...

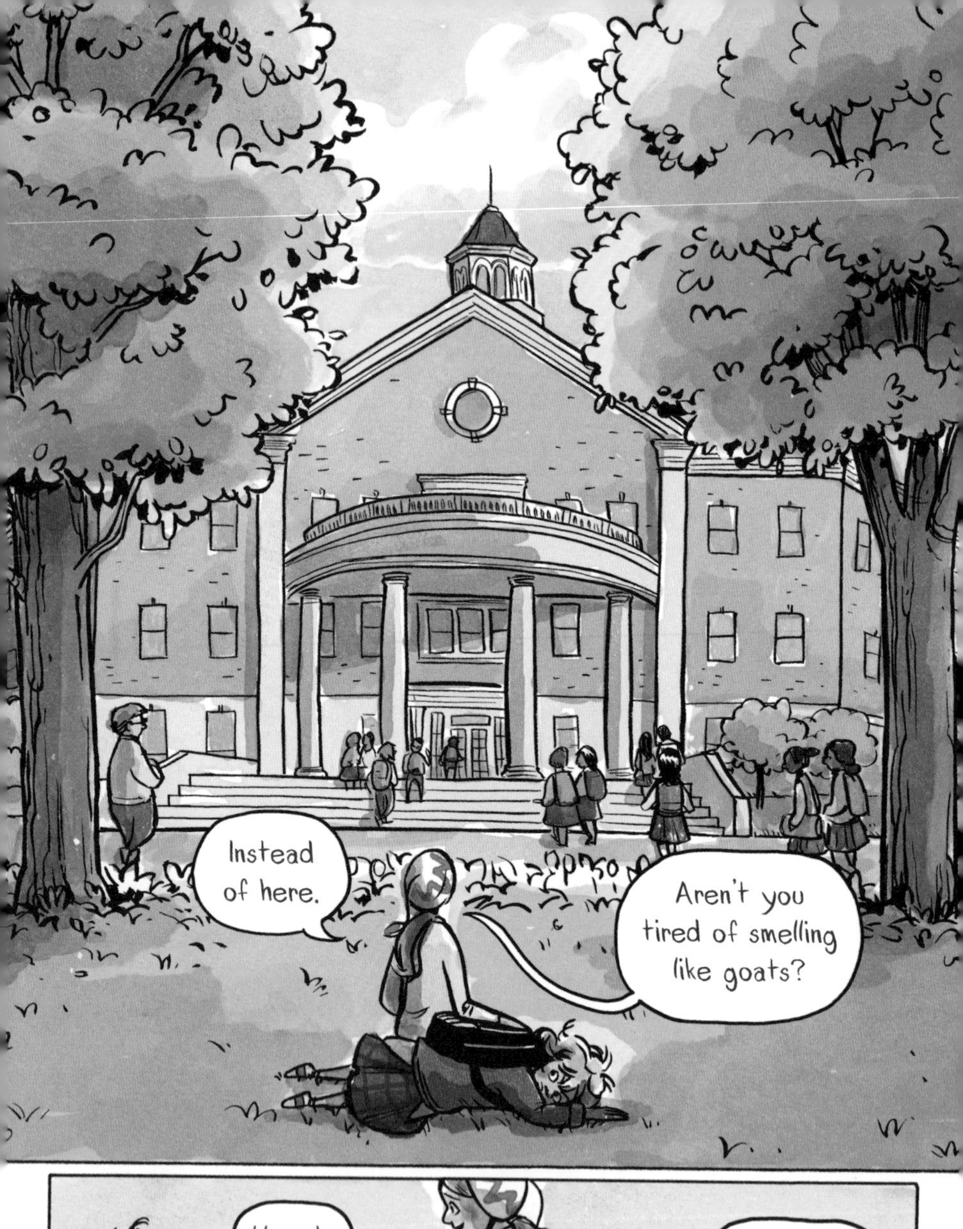
Instead of here.
Aren't you tired of smelling like goats?

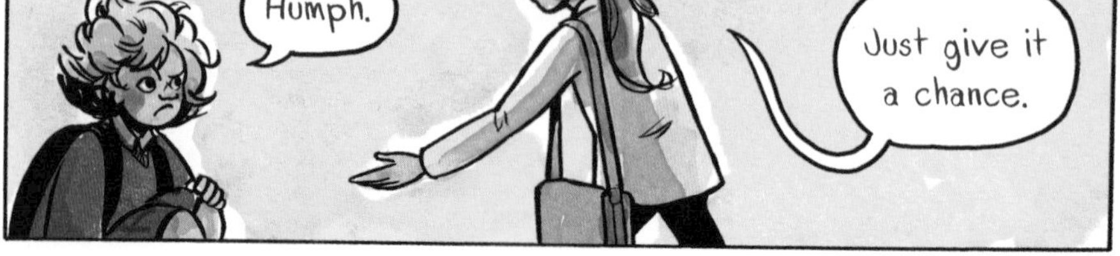
Humph.
Just give it a chance.

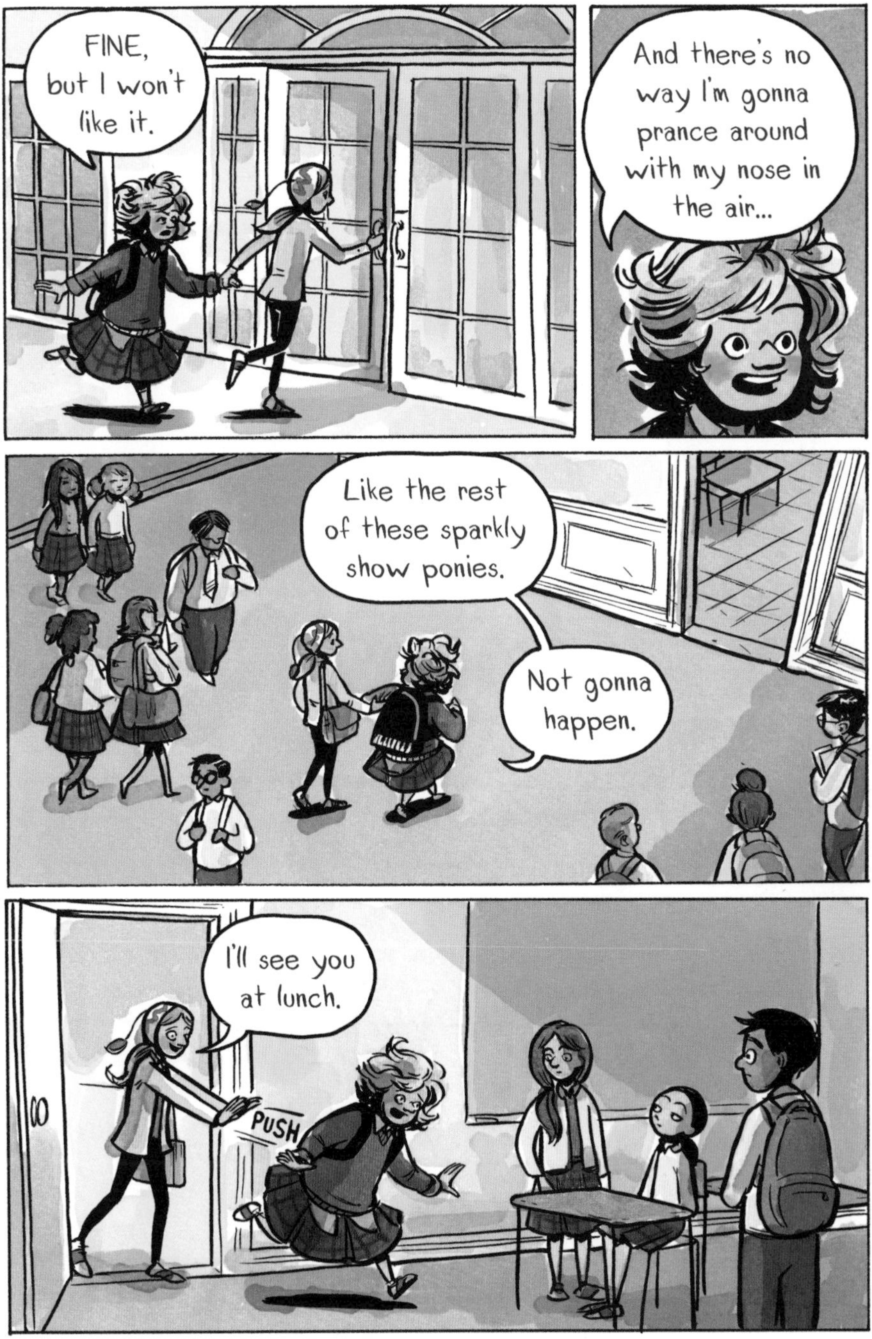
FINE, but I won't like it.
And there's no way I'm gonna prance around with my nose in the air...
Like the rest of these sparkly show ponies.
Not gonna happen.
I'll see you at lunch.
PUSH

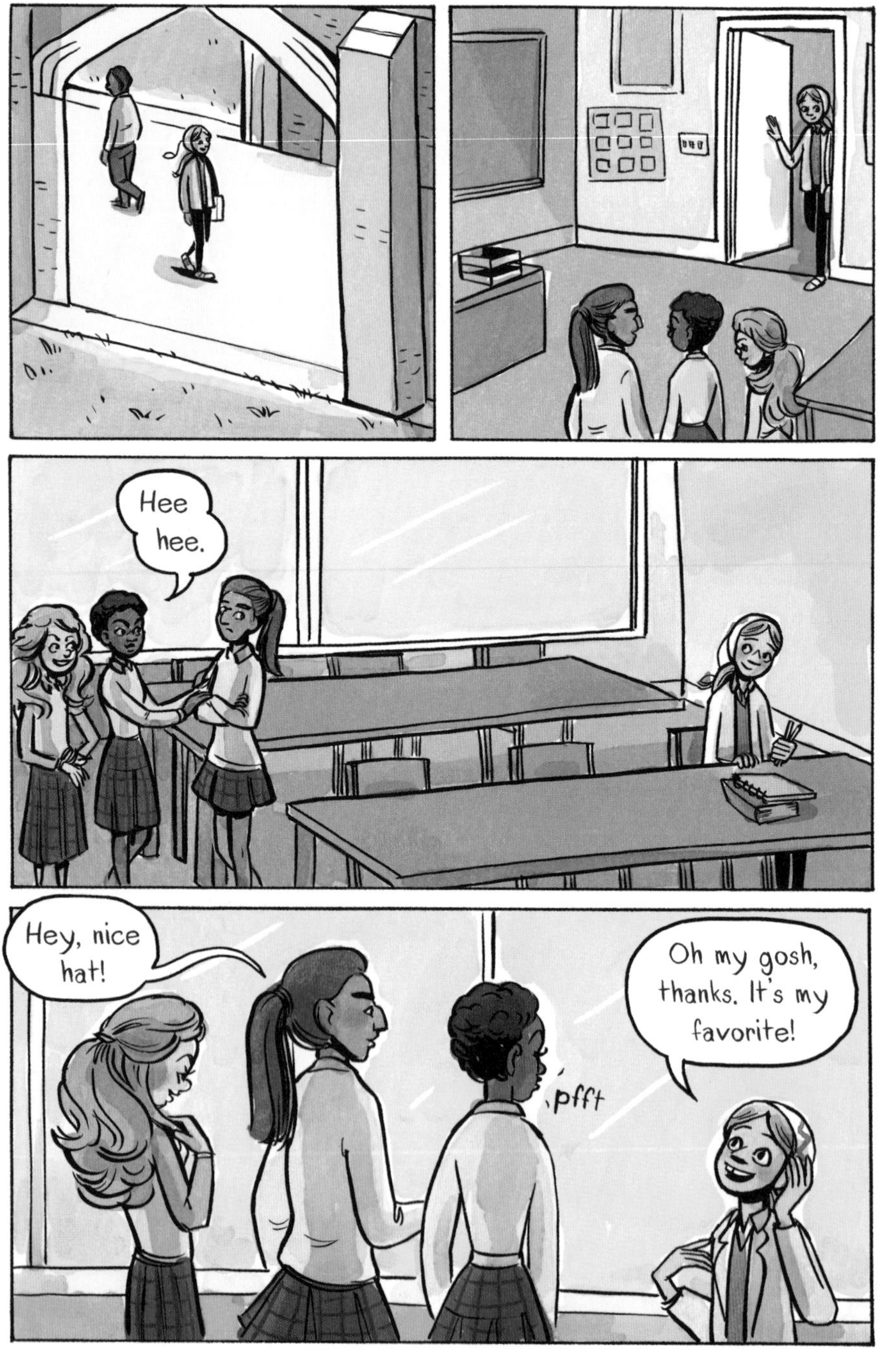
Hee hee.
Hey, nice hat!
pfft
Oh my gosh, thanks. It's my favorite!

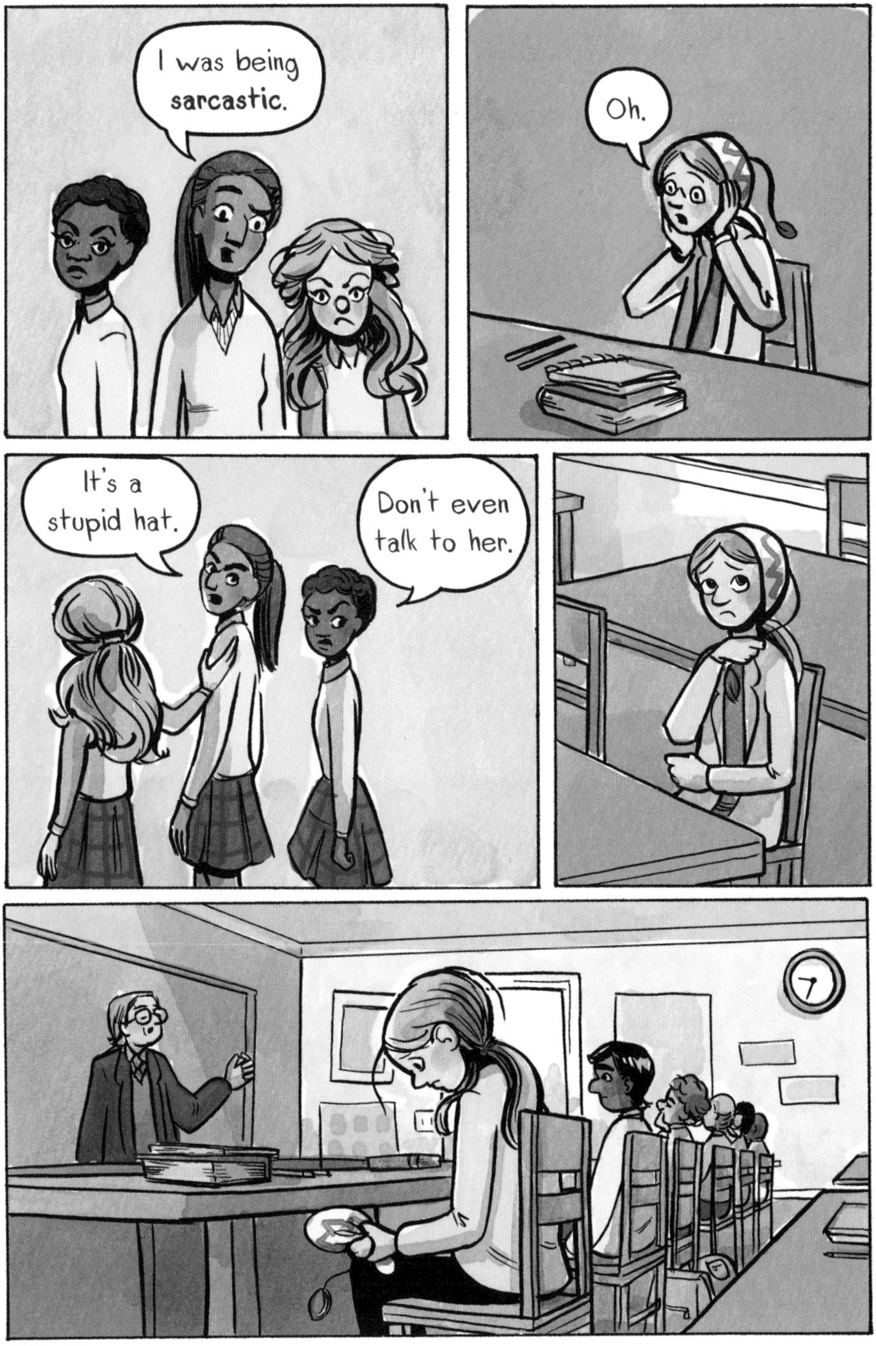
I was being **sarcastic.**
Oh.
It's a stupid hat.
Don't even talk to her.

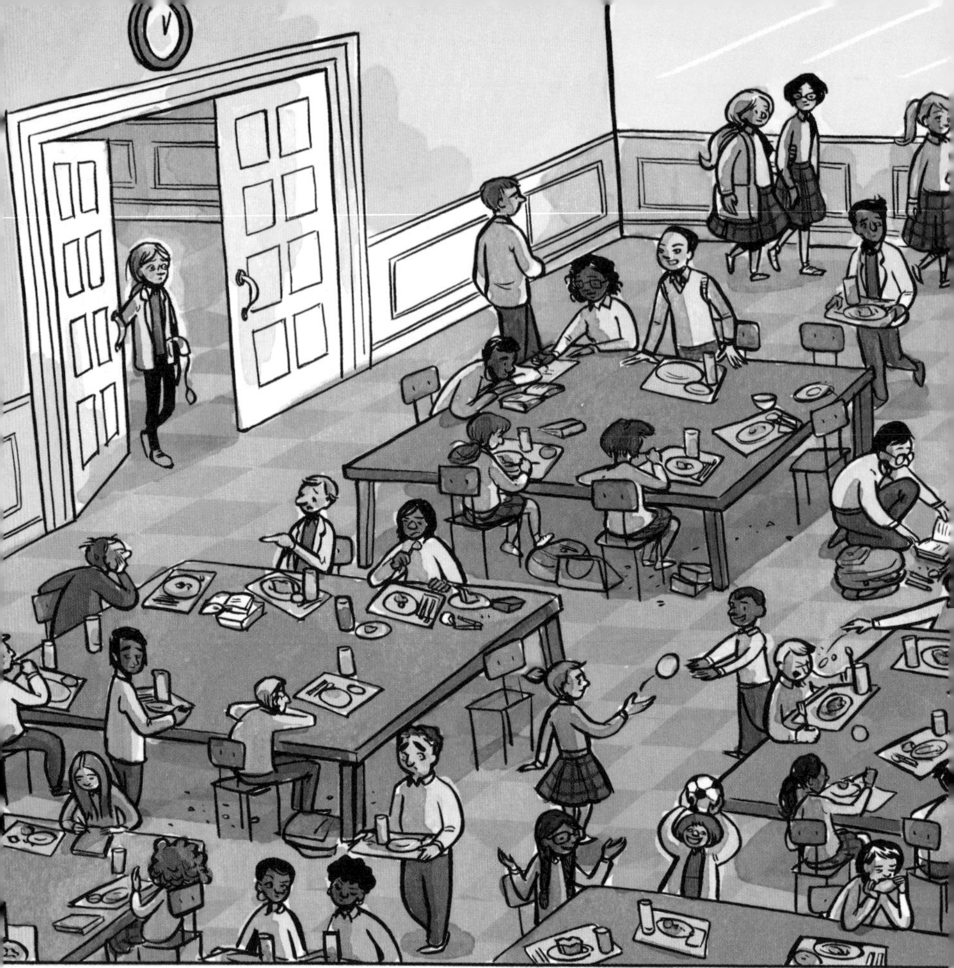

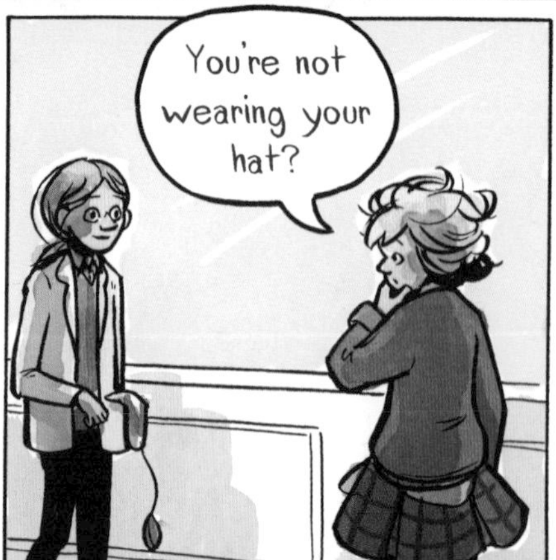
You're not wearing your hat?

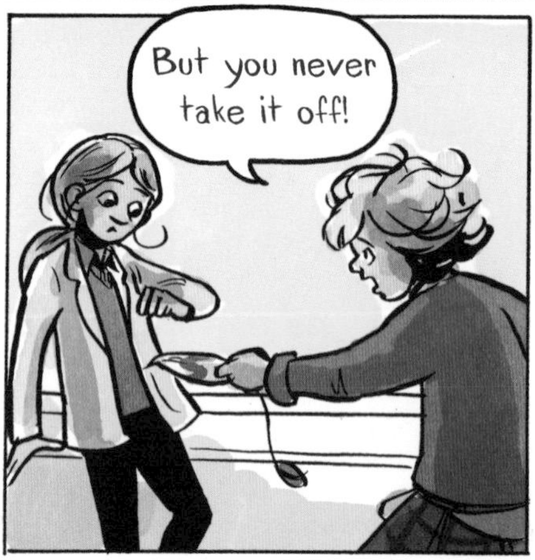
But you never take it off!

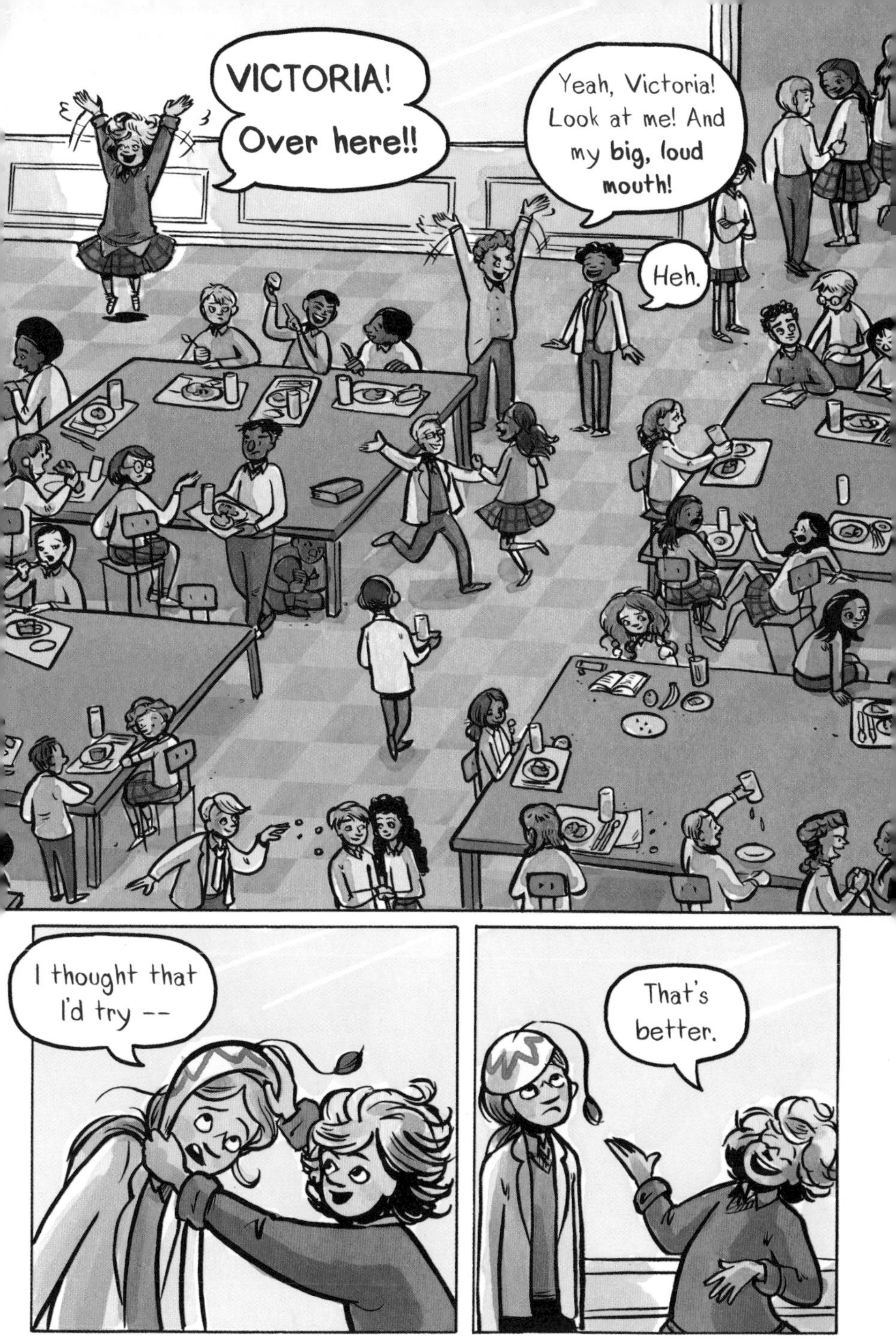
VICTORIA! Over here!!
Yeah, Victoria! Look at me! And my **big, loud mouth!**
Heh.
I thought that I'd try --
That's better.

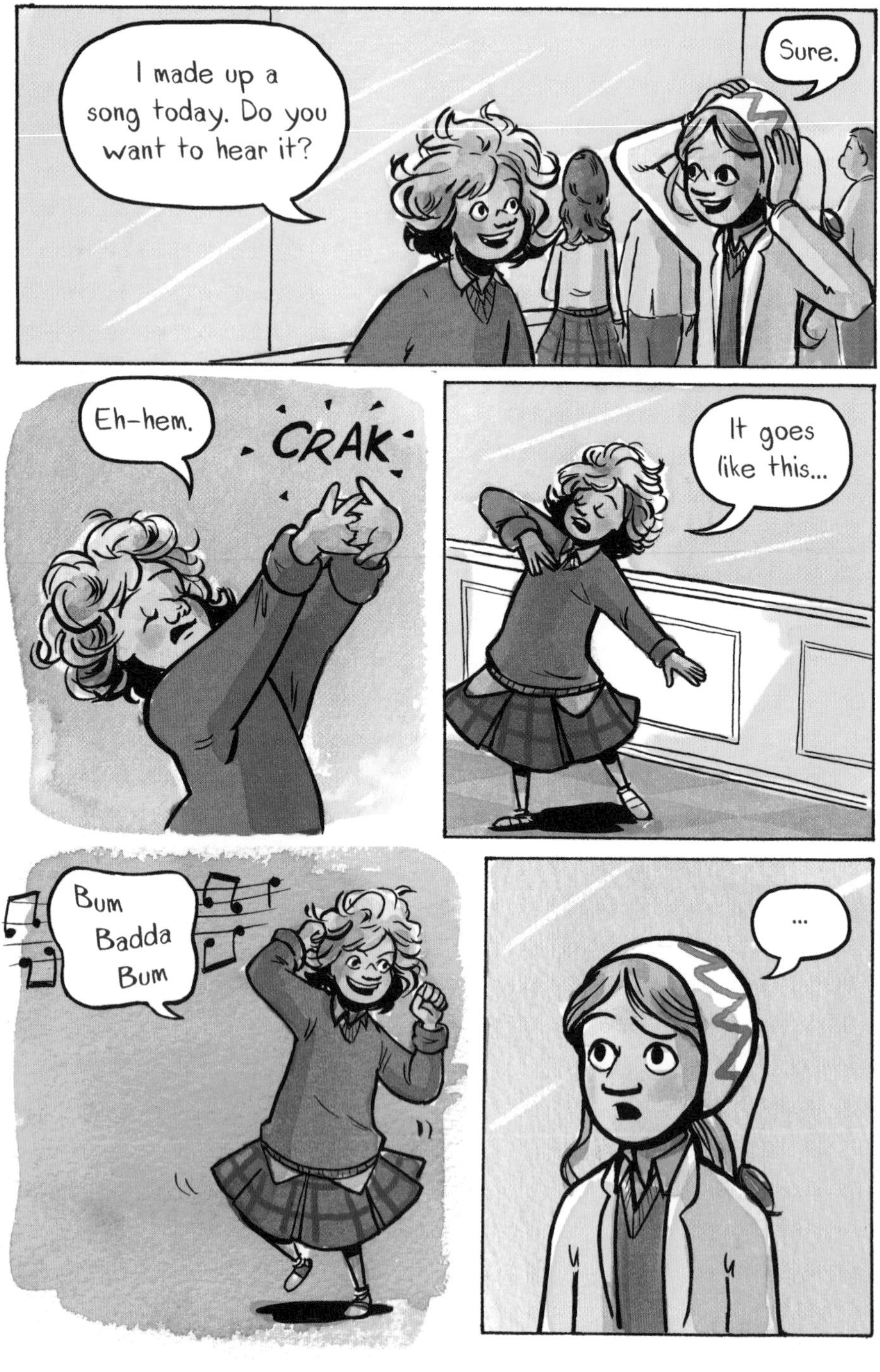
I made up a song today. Do you want to hear it?
Sure.
Eh-hem.
CRAK
It goes like this...
Bum Badda Bum
...

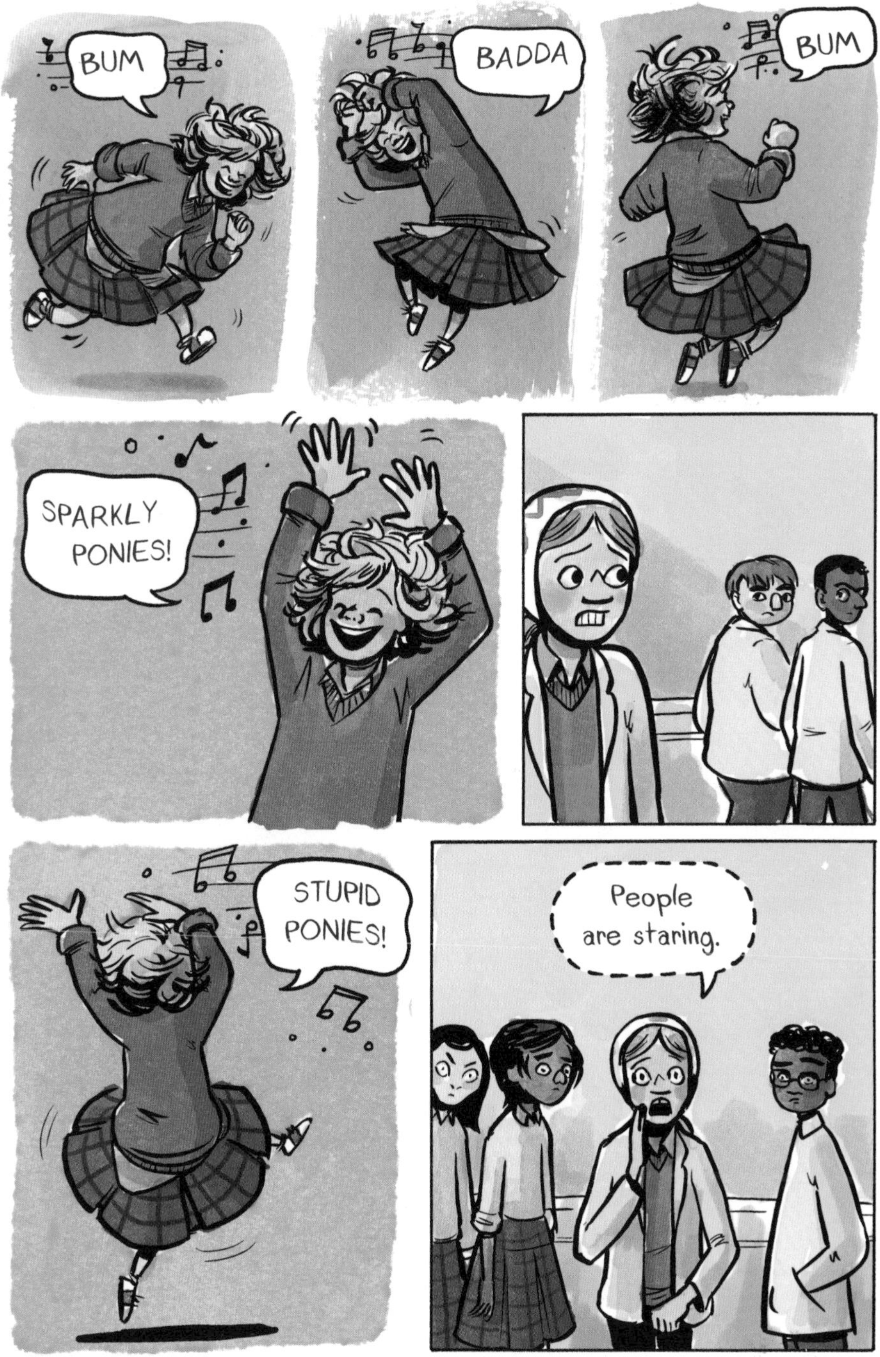
BUM
BADDA
BUM
SPARKLY PONIES!
STUPID PONIES!
People are staring.

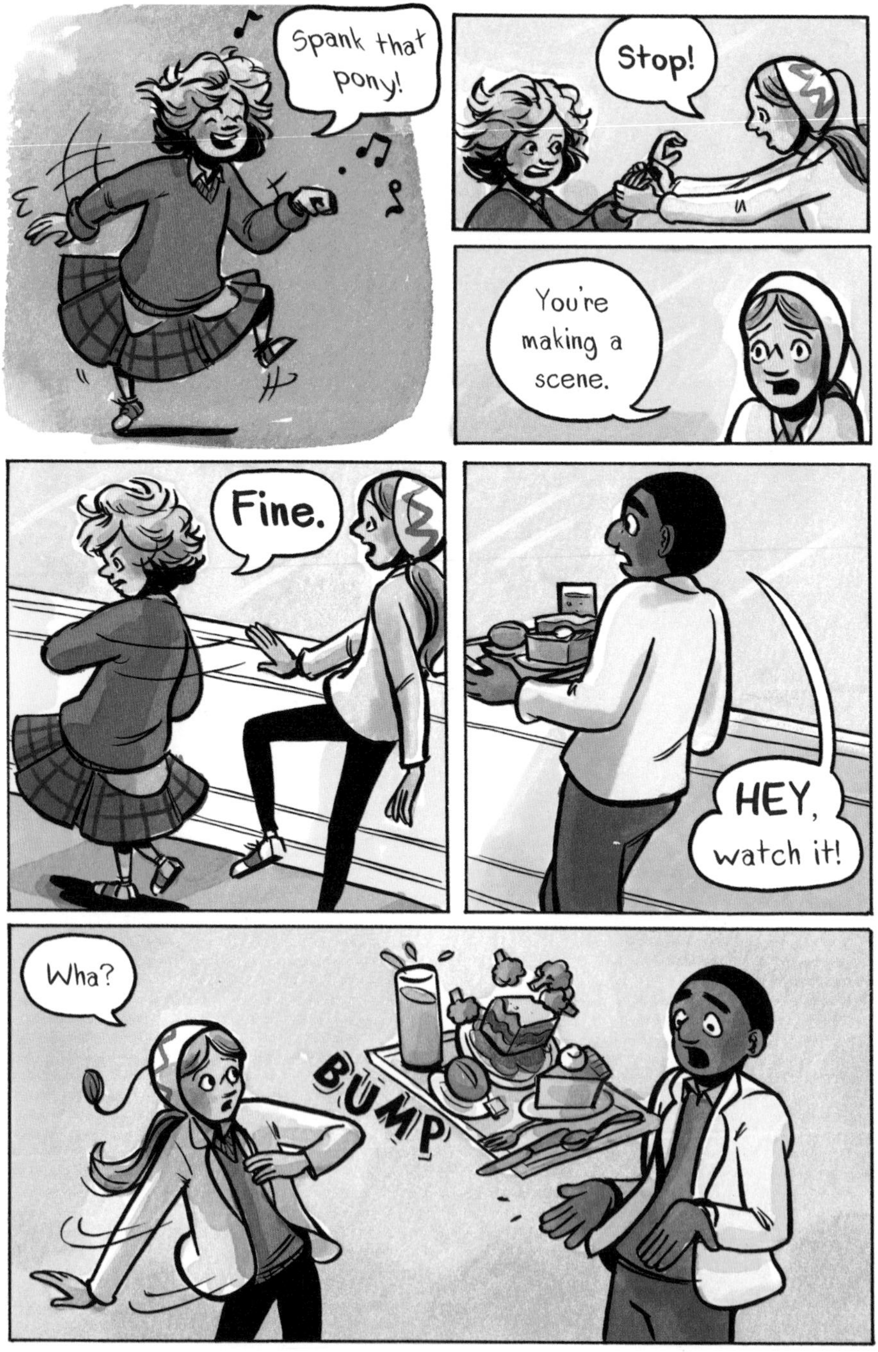
Spank that pony!
Stop!
You're making a scene.
Fine.
HEY, watch it!
Wha?
BUMP

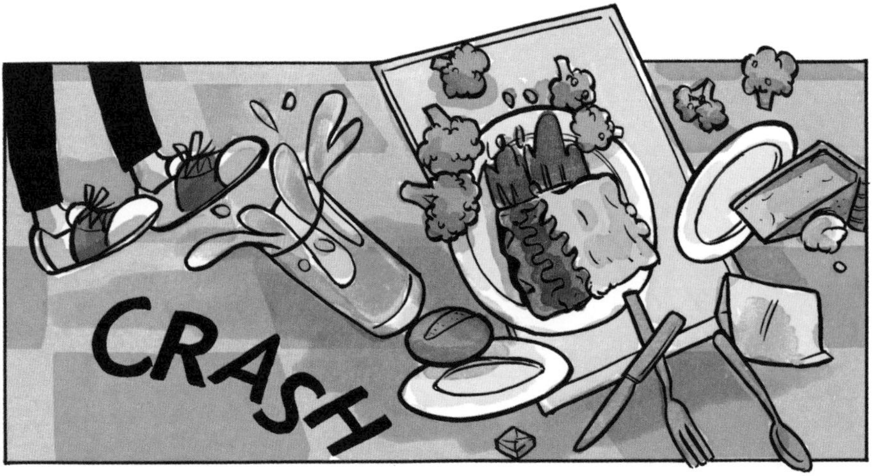
CRASH

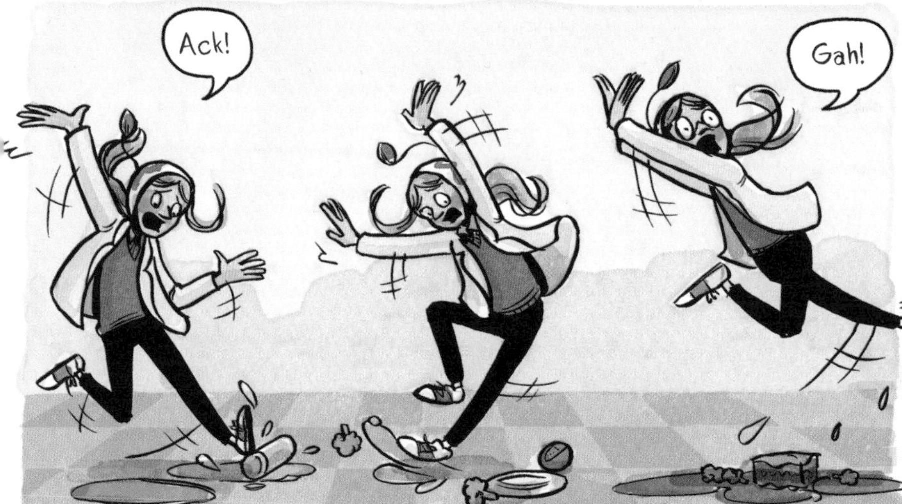
Ack!
Gah!

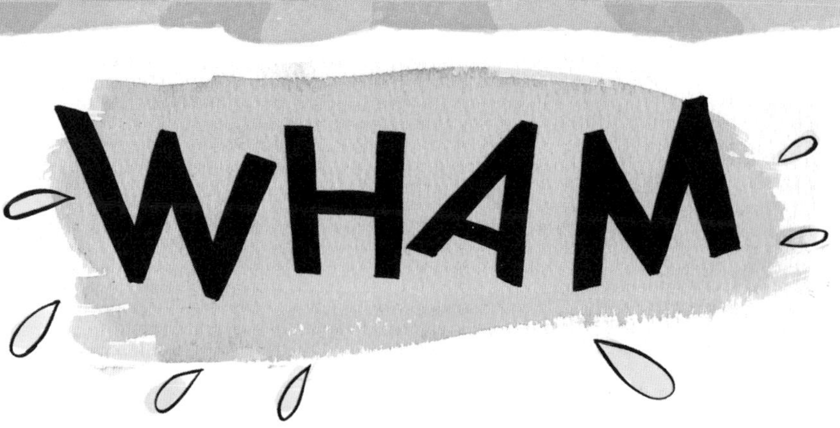
WHAM

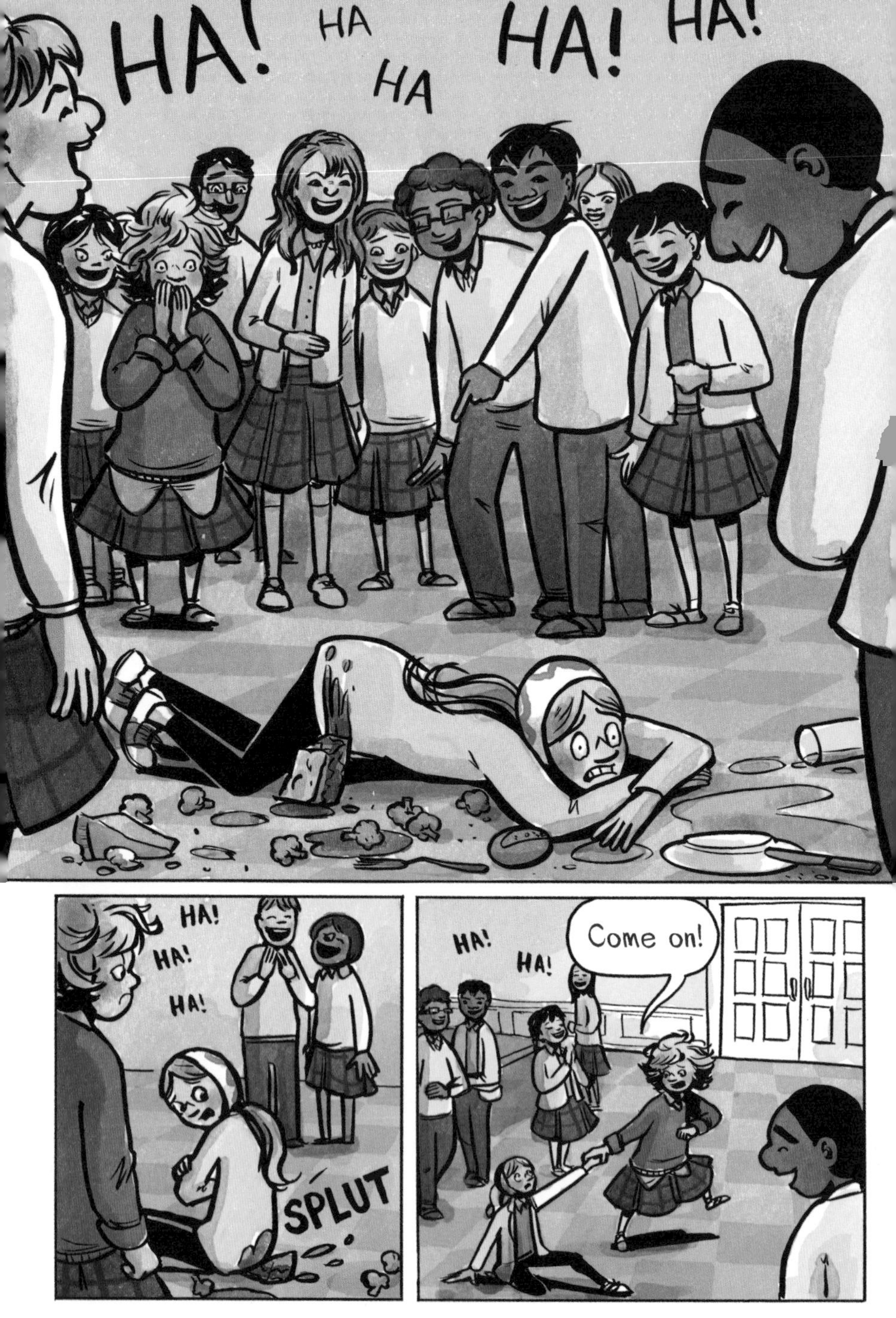
HA! HA HA HA! HA!
HA!
HA!
HA!
SPLUT
HA!
HA!
Come on!

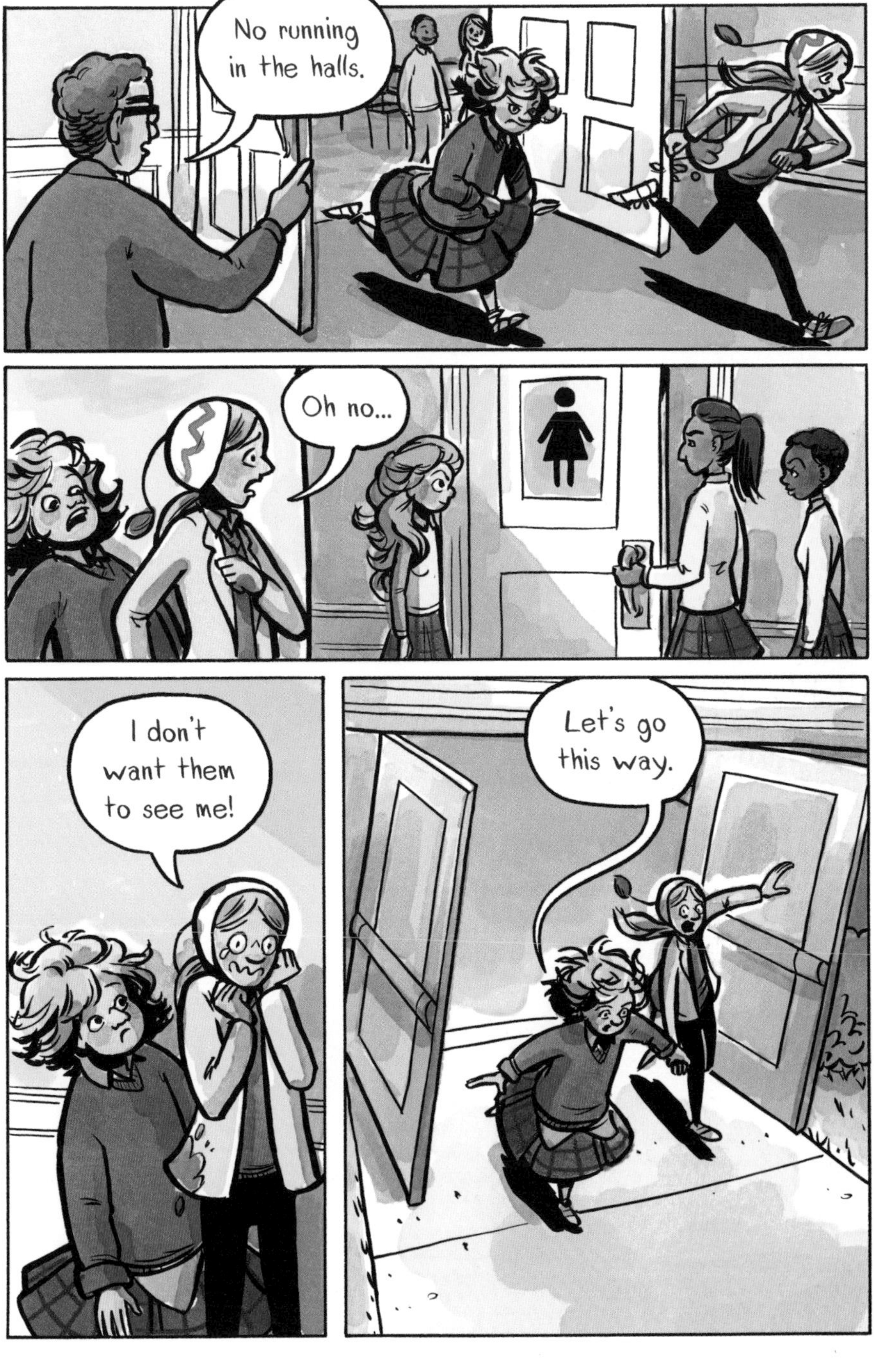
No running in the halls.
Oh no...
I don't want them to see me!
Let's go this way.

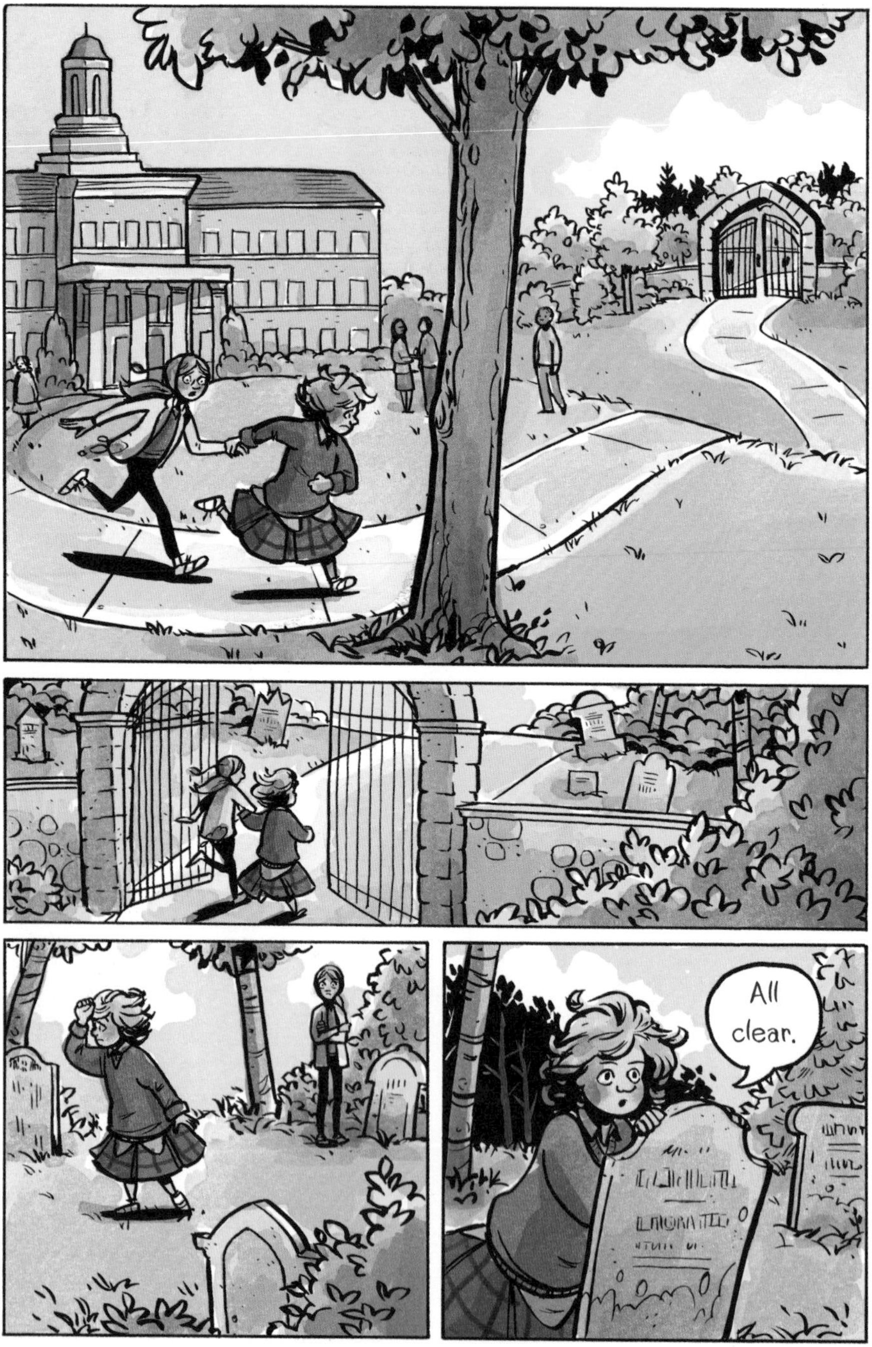
All clear.

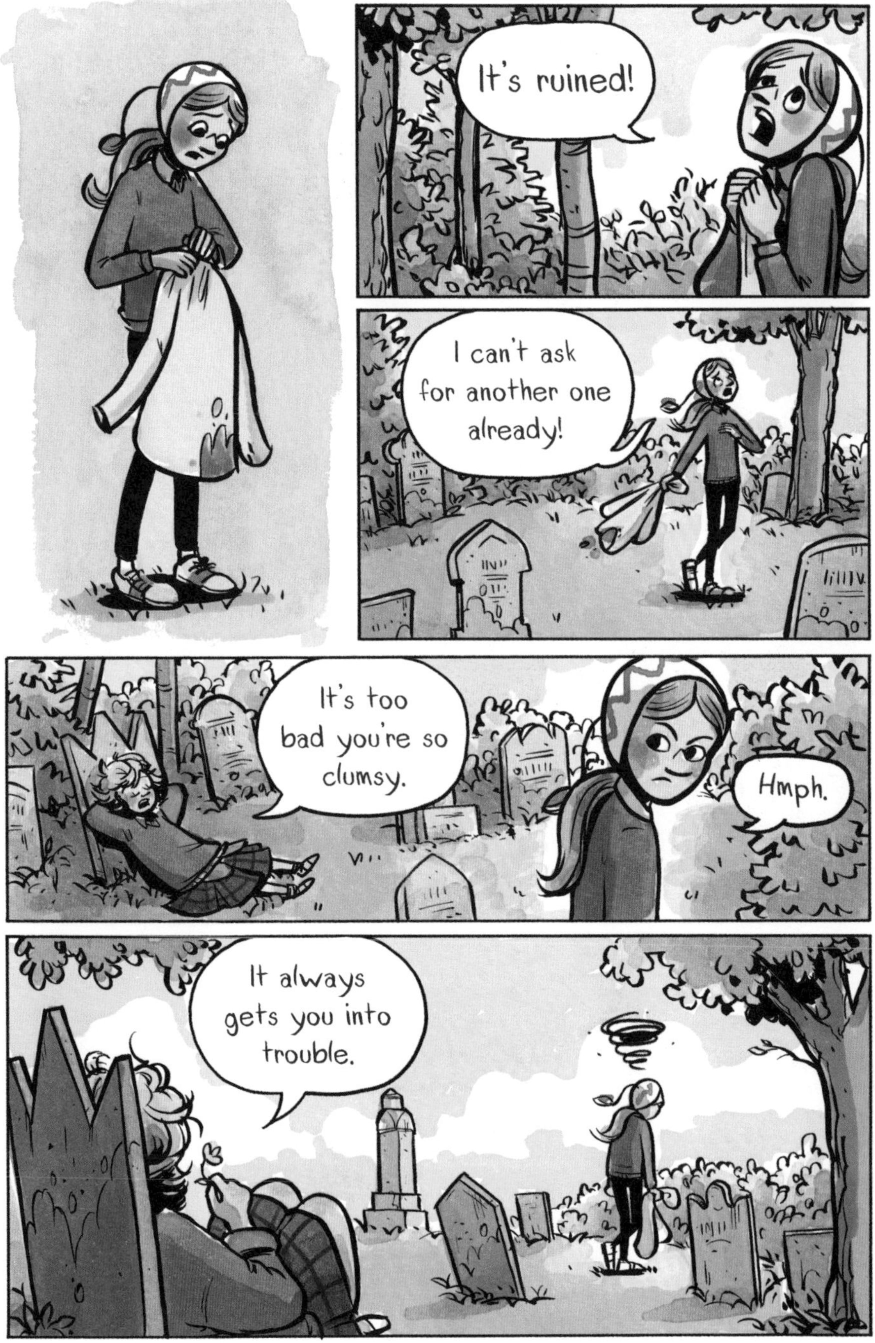
It's ruined!
I can't ask for another one already!
It's too bad you're so clumsy.
Hmph.
It always gets you into trouble.

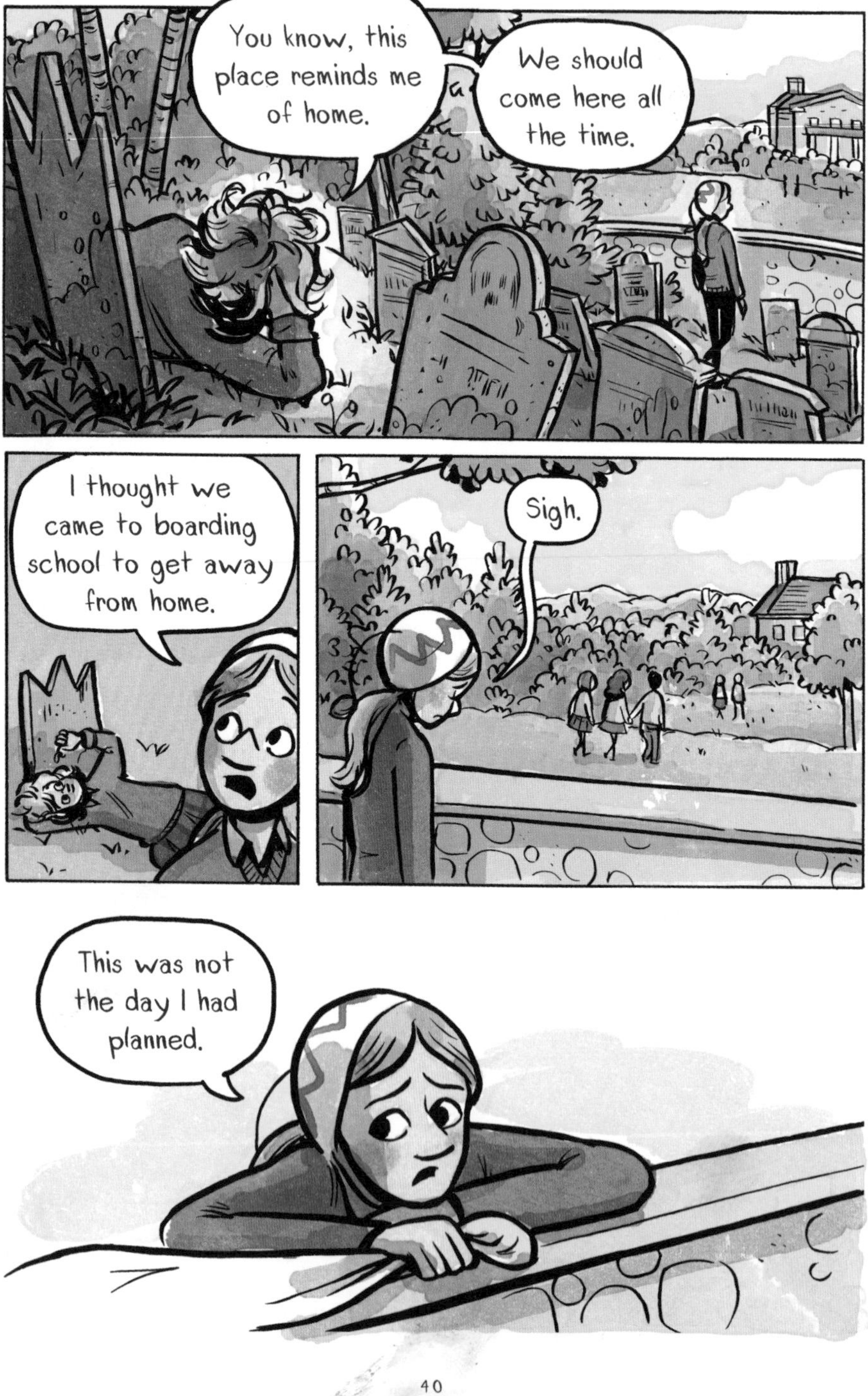
You know, this place reminds me of home.
We should come here all the time.
I thought we came to boarding school to get away from home.
Sigh.
This was not the day I had planned.

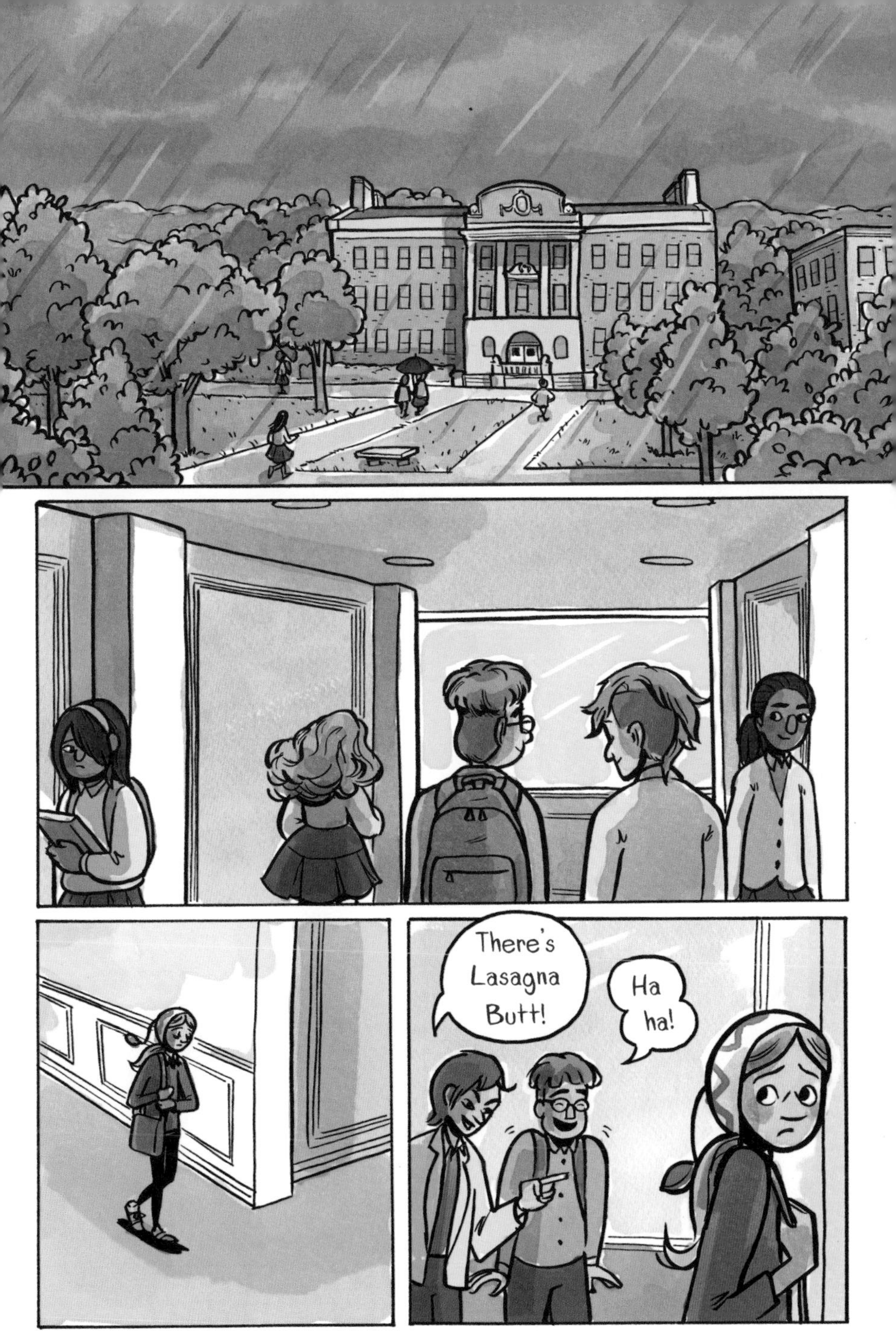
There's Lasagna Butt!
Ha ha!

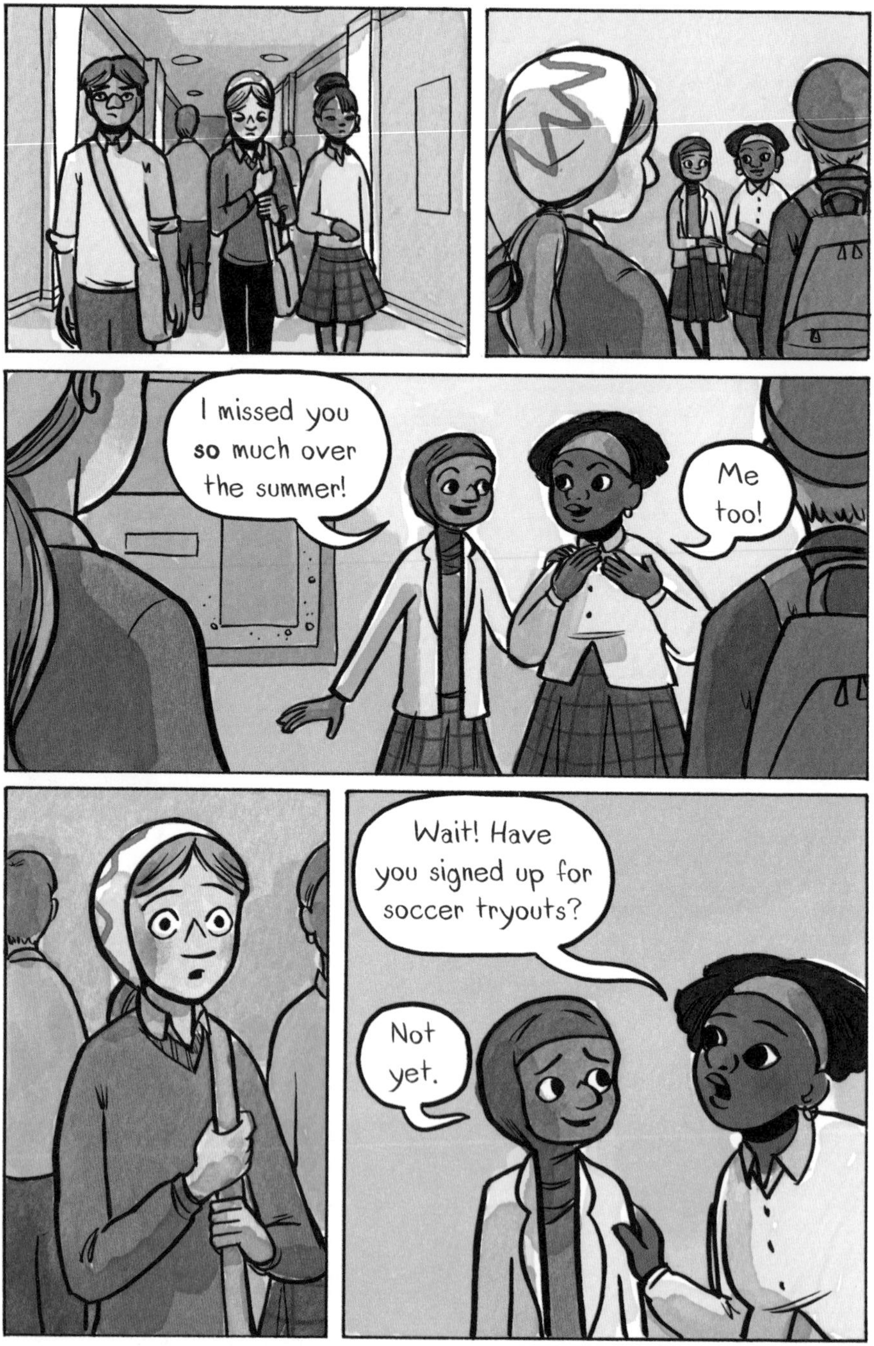
I missed you **so** much over the summer!
Me too!
Wait! Have you signed up for soccer tryouts?
Not yet.

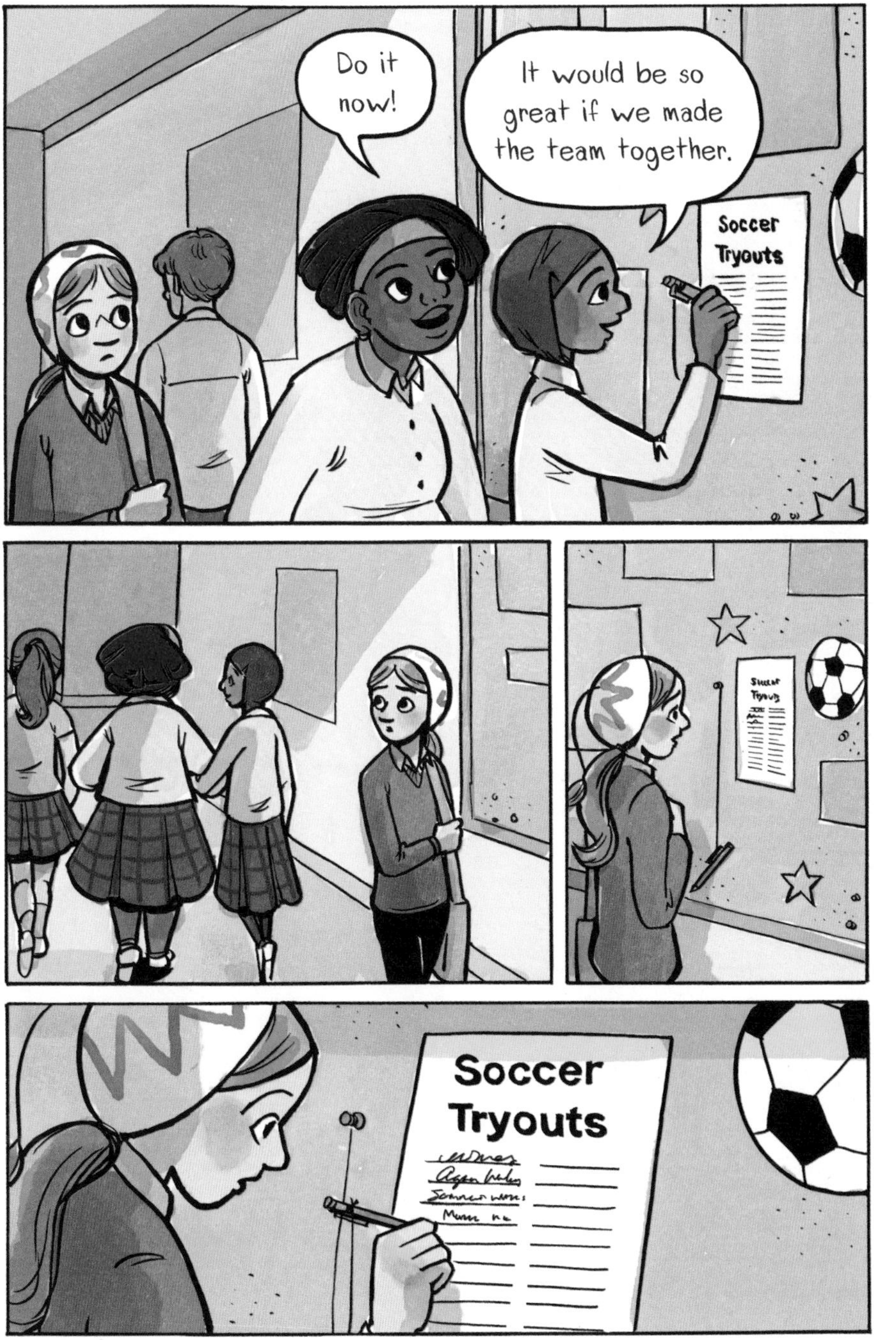
Do it now!
It would be so great if we made the team together.
Soccer Tryouts
Soccer Tryouts

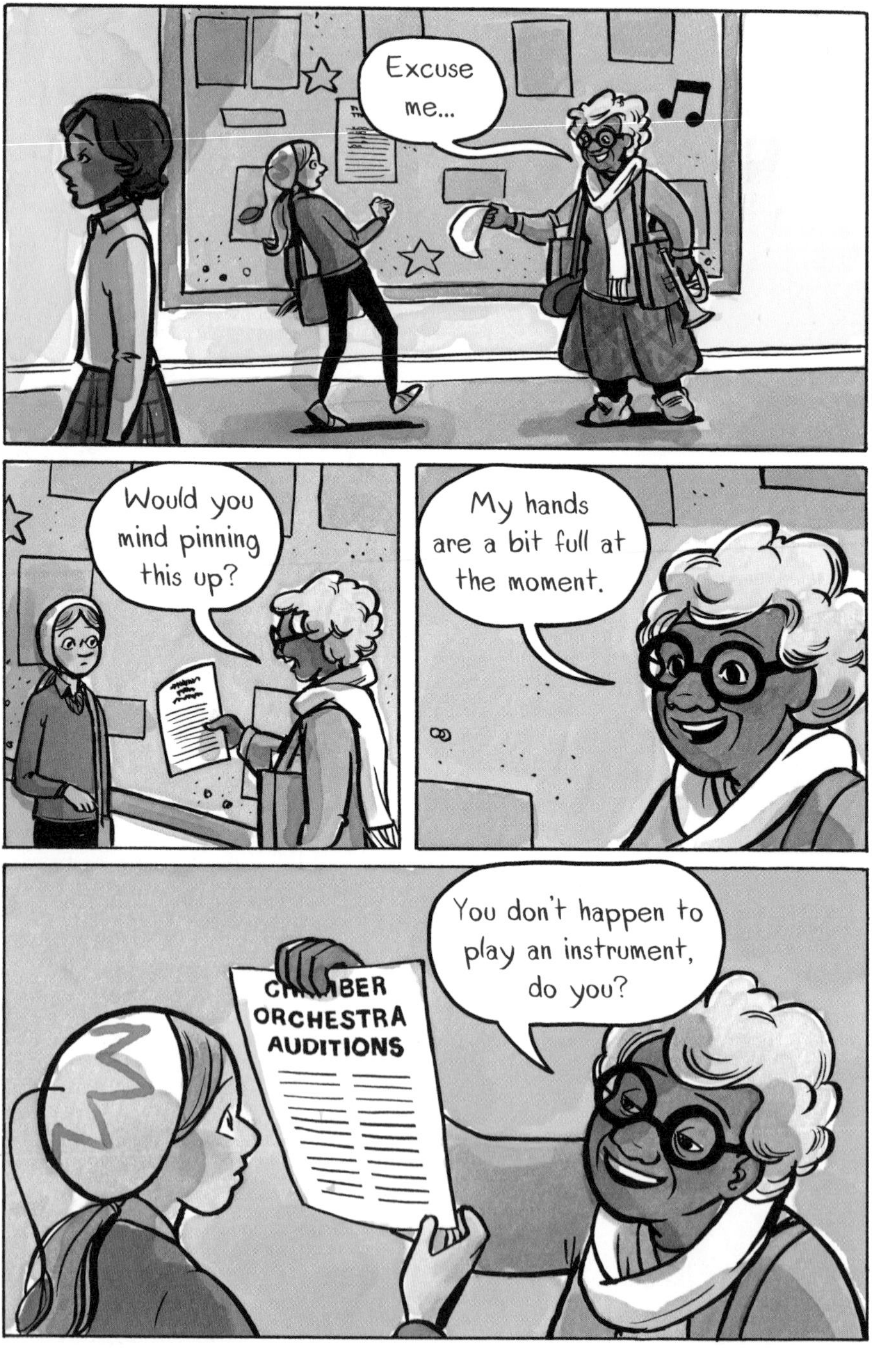
Excuse me...
Would you mind pinning this up?
My hands are a bit full at the moment.
CHAMBER ORCHESTRA AUDITIONS
You don't happen to play an instrument, do you?

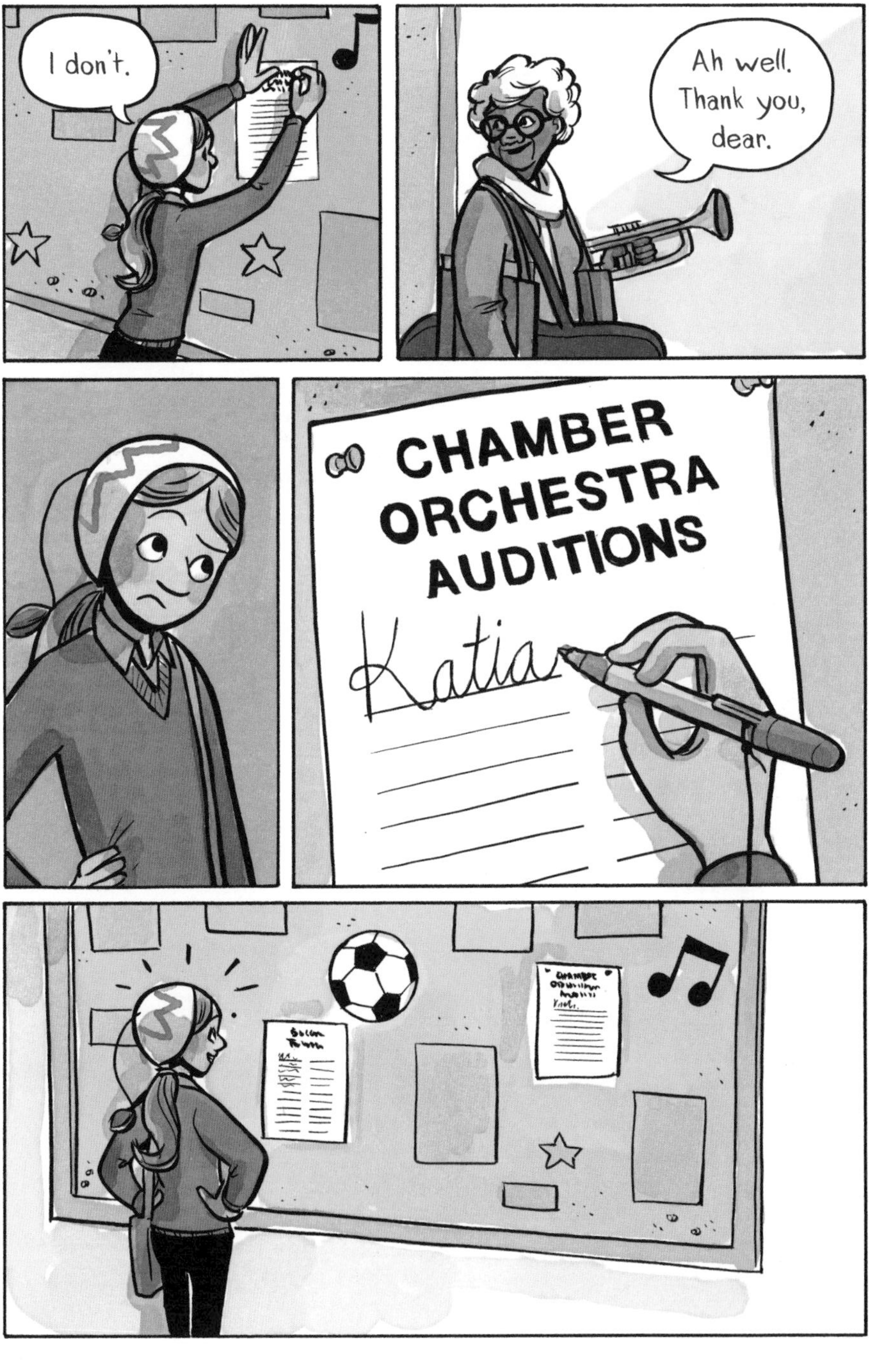
I don't.
Ah well. Thank you, dear.
CHAMBER ORCHESTRA AUDITIONS
Katia

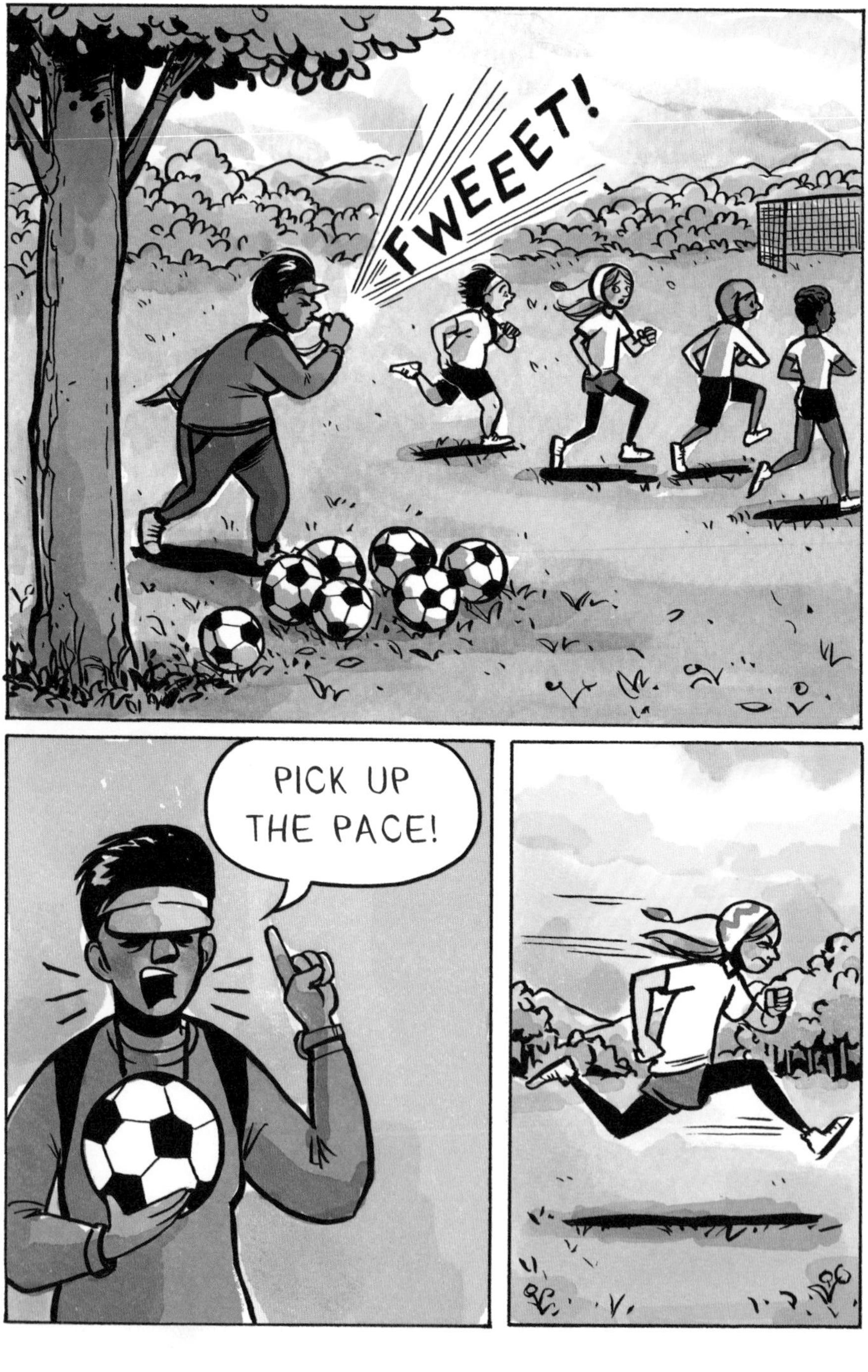
FWEEET!
PICK UP THE PACE!

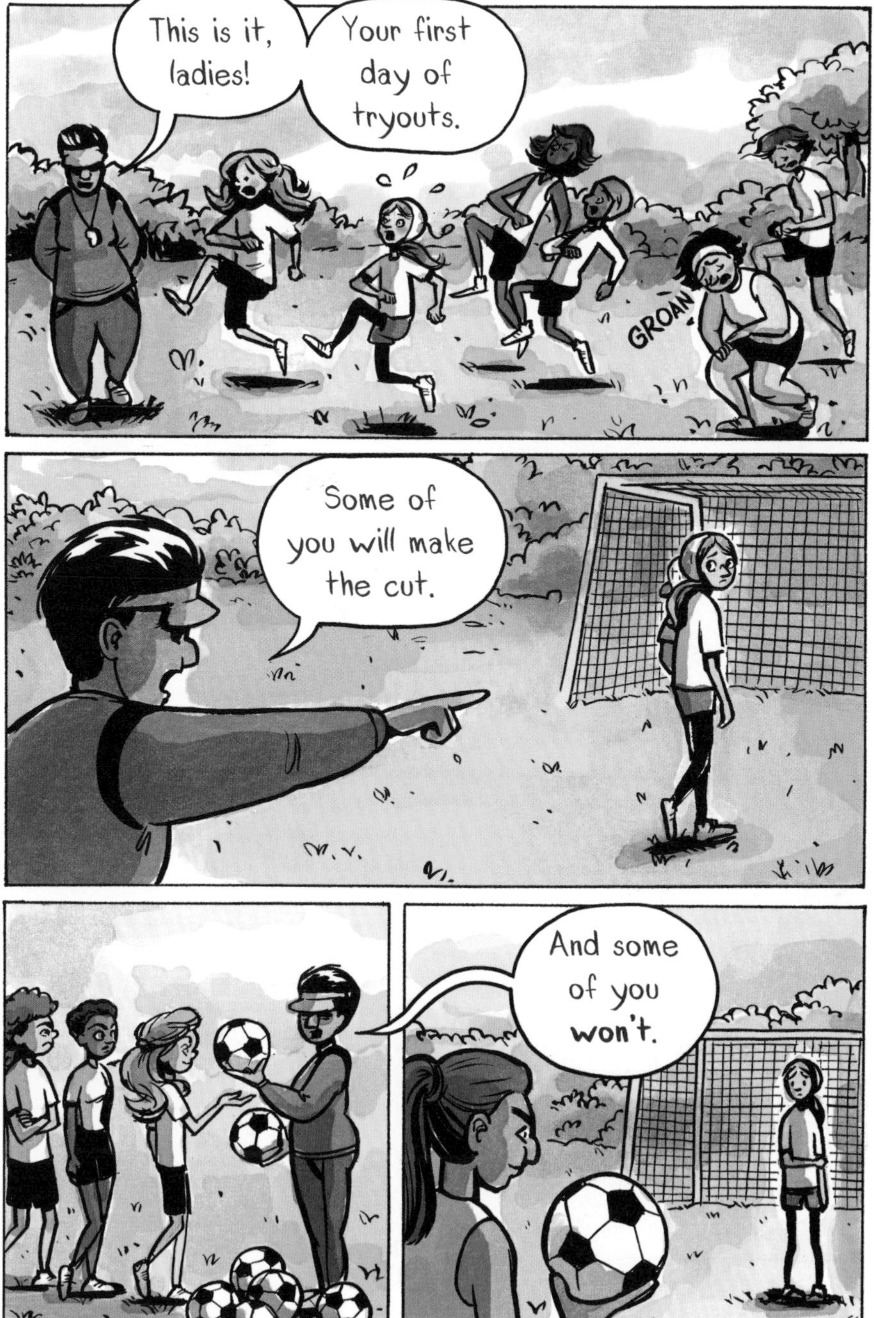
This is it, ladies!
Your first day of tryouts.
GROAN
Some of you will make the cut.
And some of you **won't**.

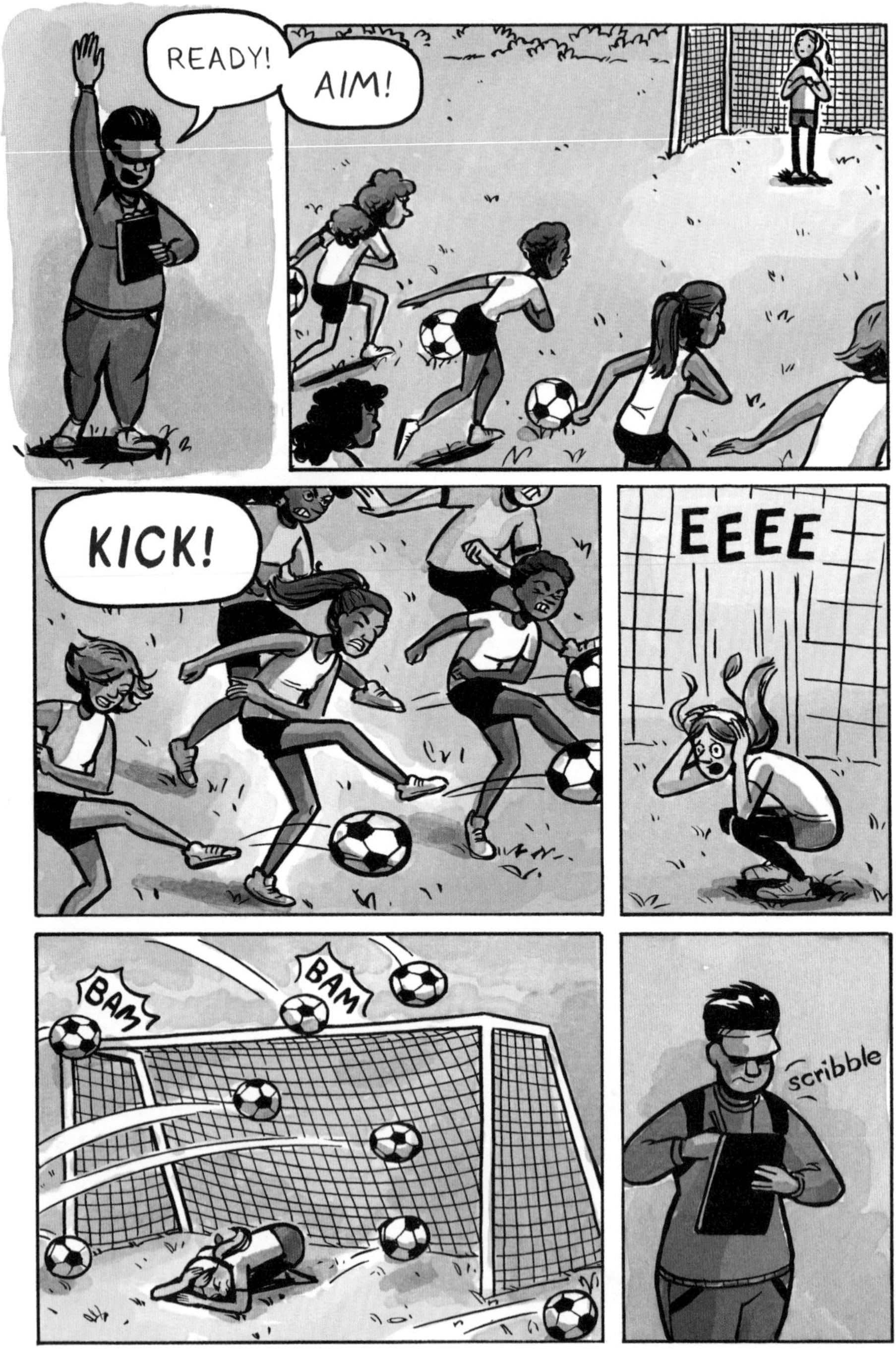
READY!
AIM!
KICK!
EEEE
BAM
BAM
scribble

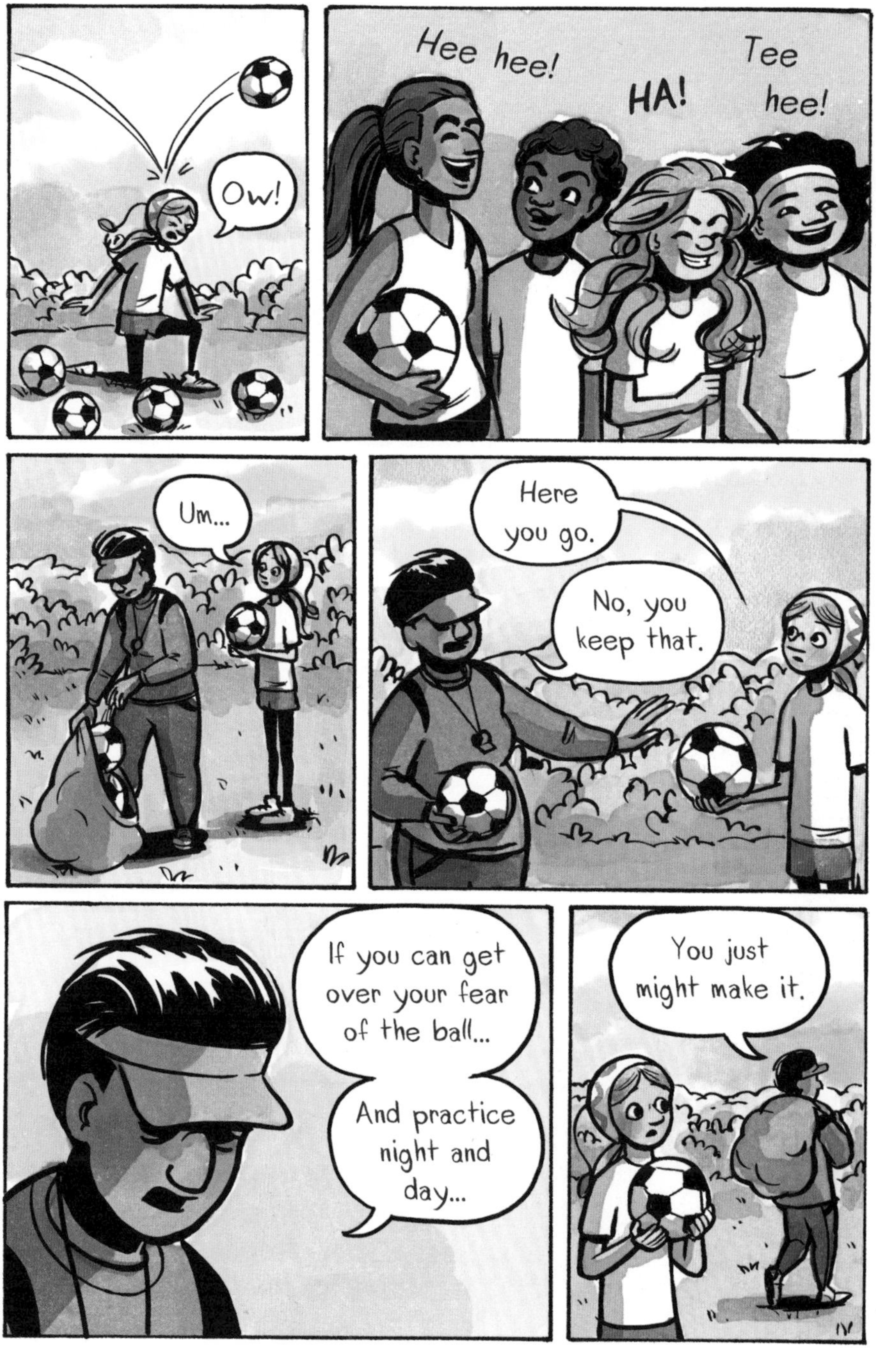
Ow!
Hee hee!
HA!
Tee hee!
Um...
Here you go.
No, you keep that.
If you can get over your fear of the ball...
And practice night and day...
You just might make it.

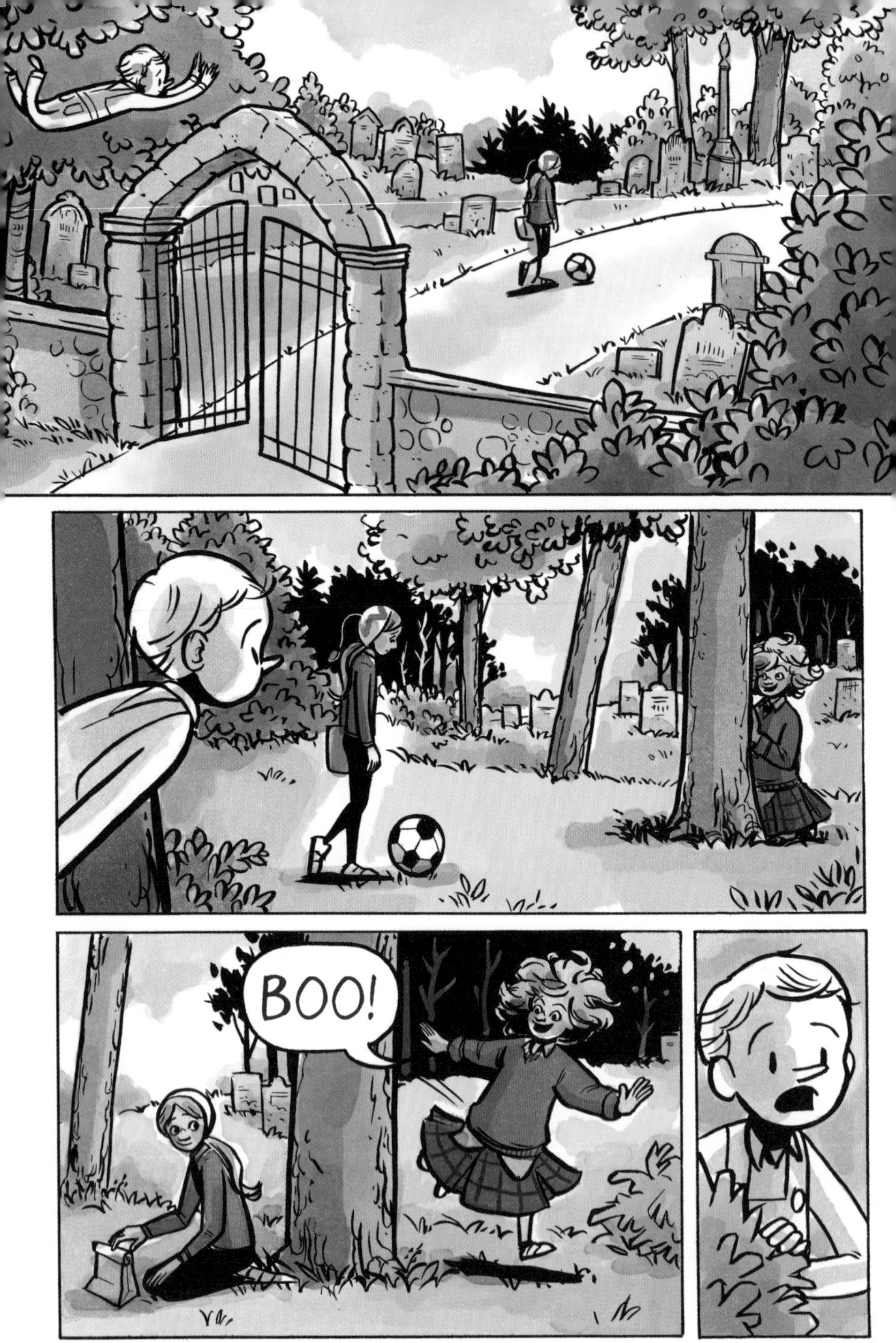
BOO!

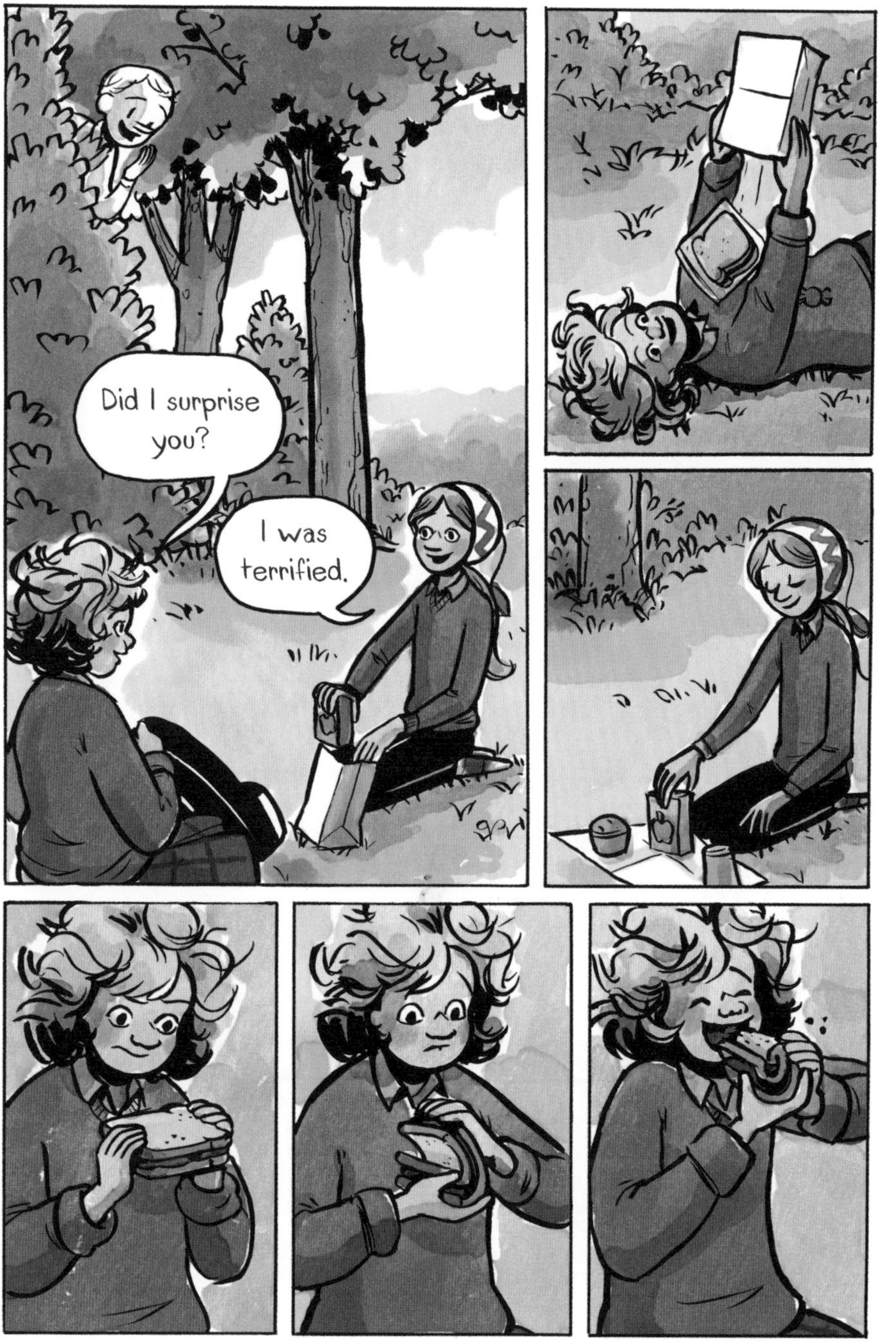
Did I surprise you?
I was terrified.

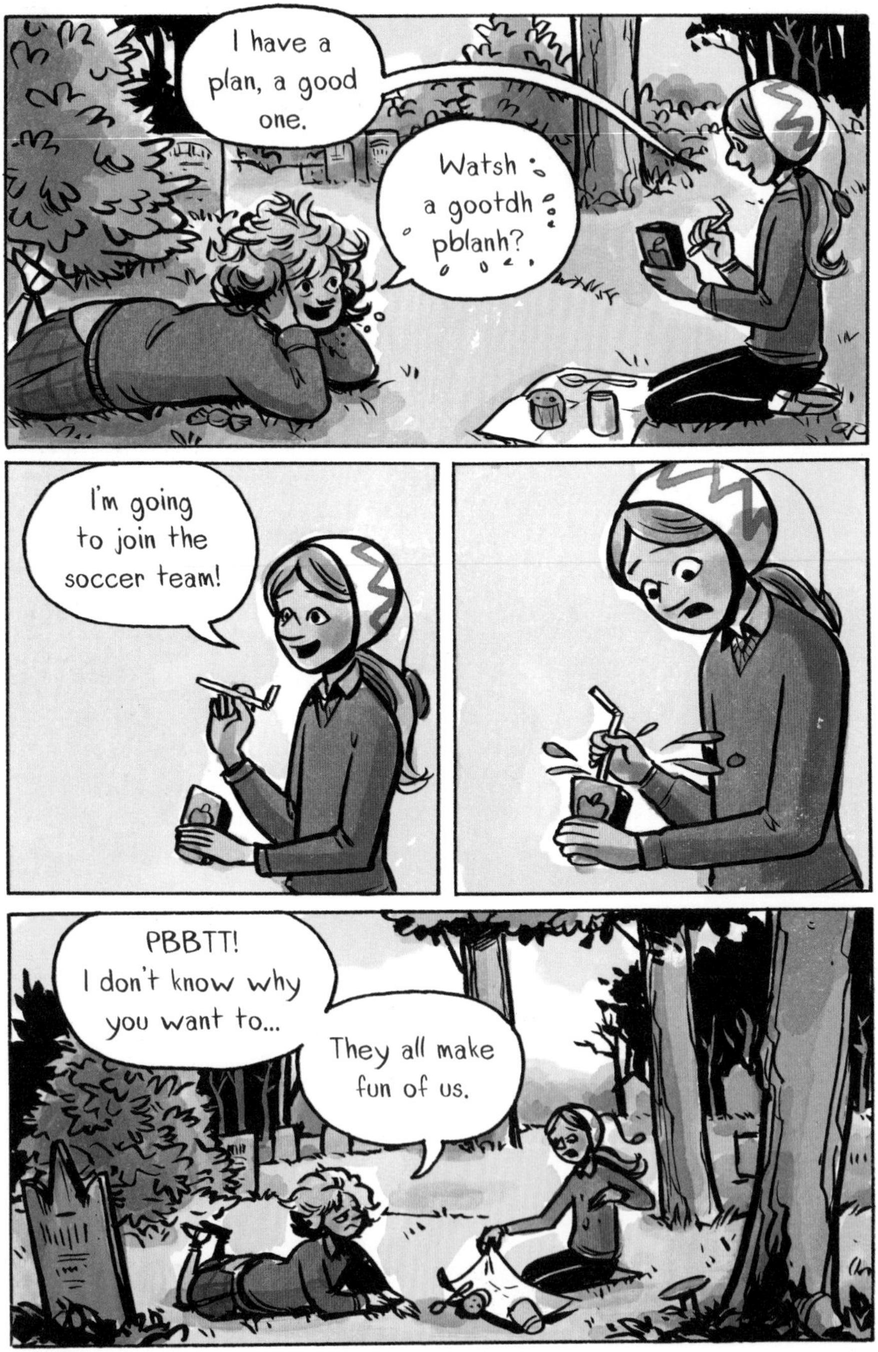
I have a plan, a good one.
Watsh a gootdh pblanh?
I'm going to join the soccer team!
PBBTT!
I don't know why you want to...
They all make fun of us.

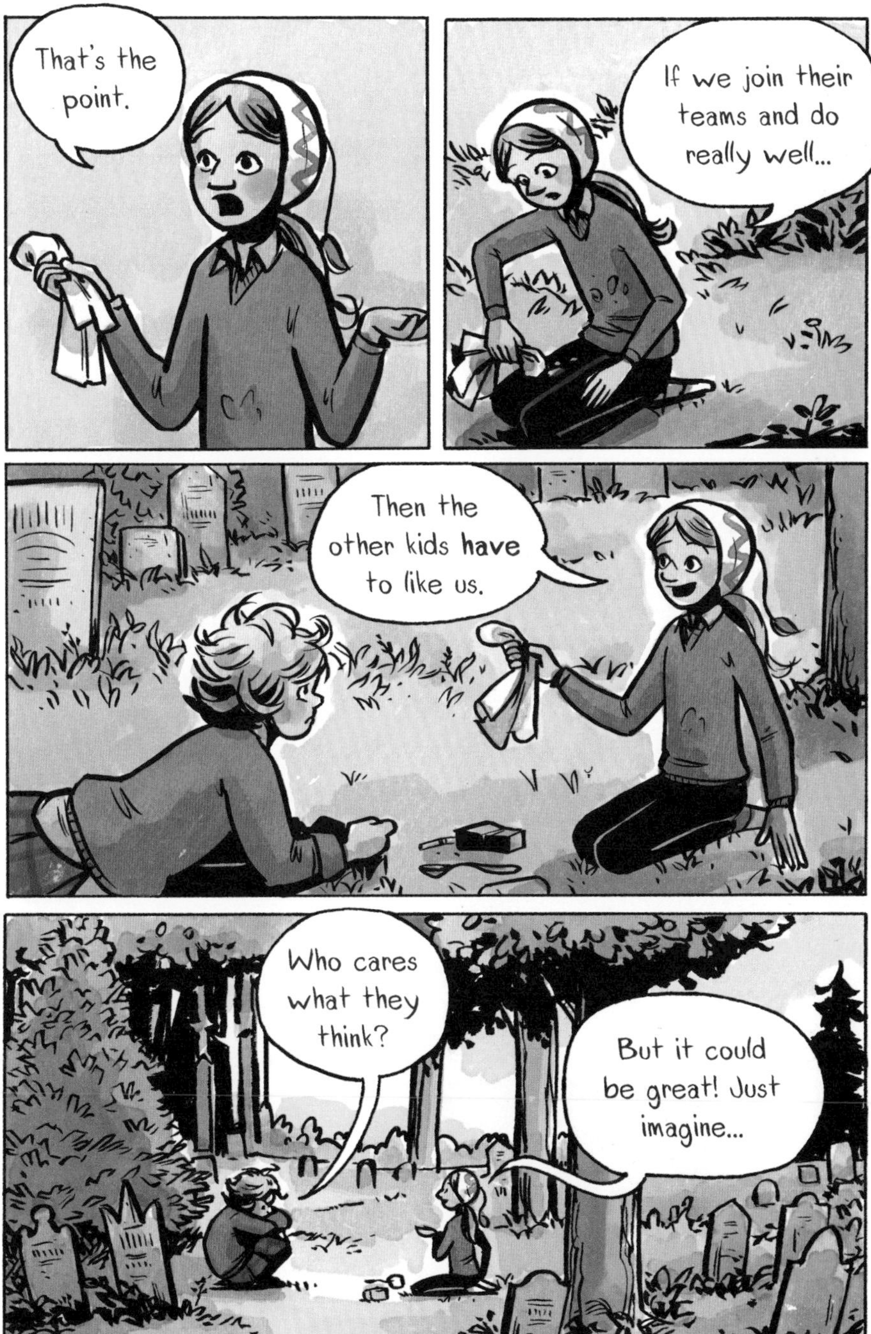
That's the point.
If we join their teams and do really well...
Then the other kids **have** to like us.
Who cares what they think?
But it could be great! Just imagine...

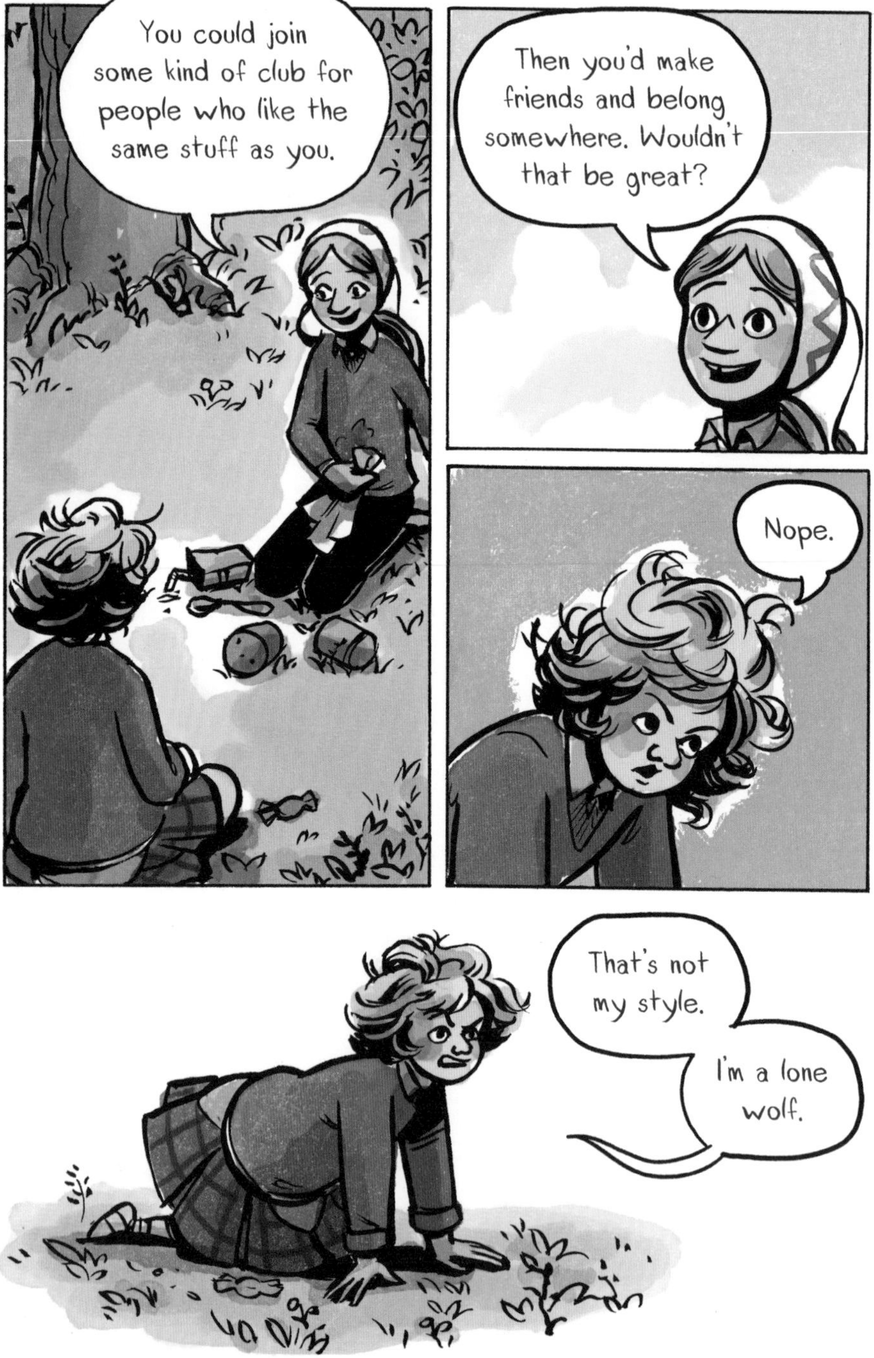
You could join some kind of club for people who like the same stuff as you.
Then you'd make friends and belong somewhere. Wouldn't that be great?
Nope.
That's not my style.
I'm a lone wolf.

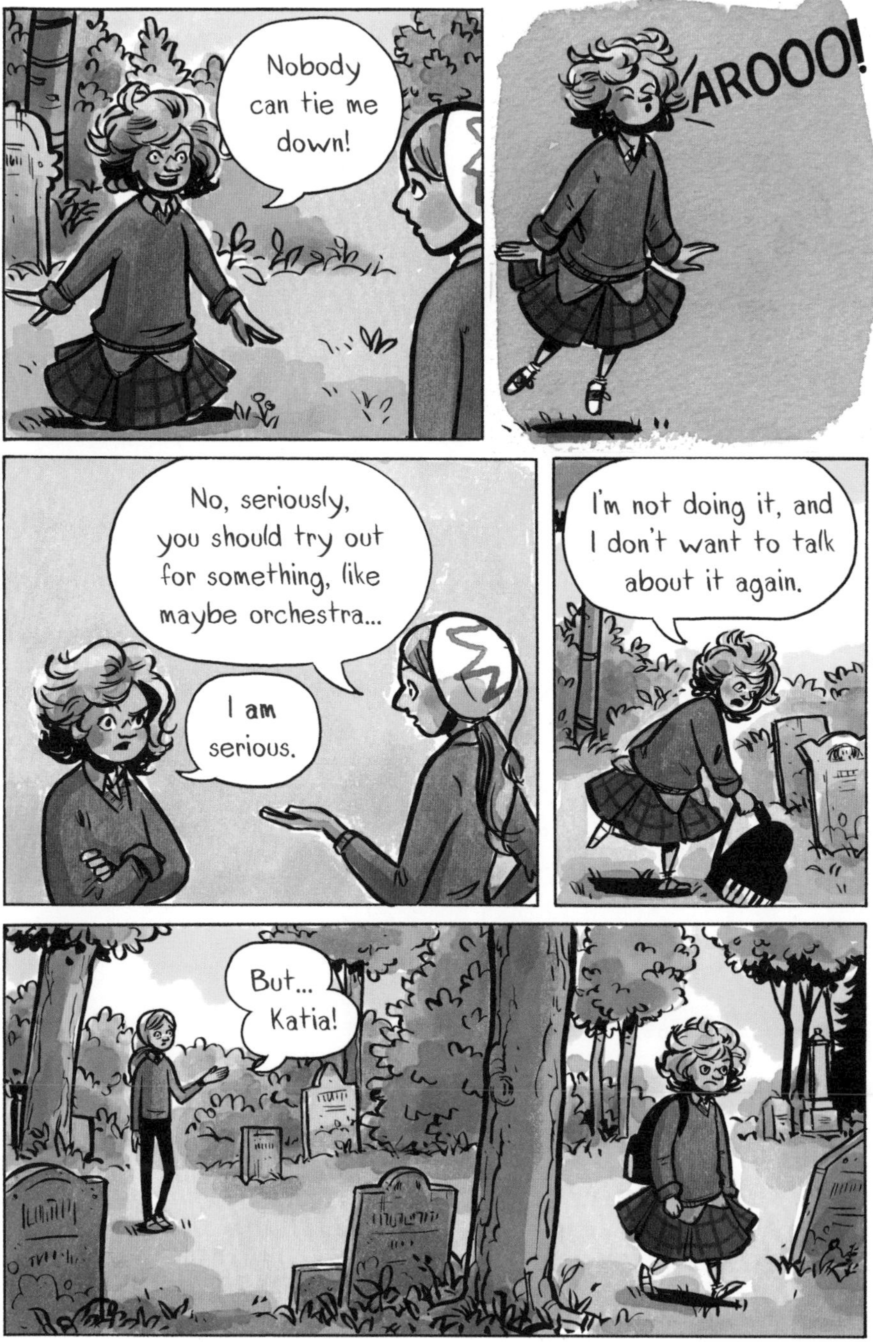
Nobody can tie me down!
AROOO!
No, seriously, you should try out for something, like maybe orchestra...
I am serious.
I'm not doing it, and I don't want to talk about it again.
But... Katia!

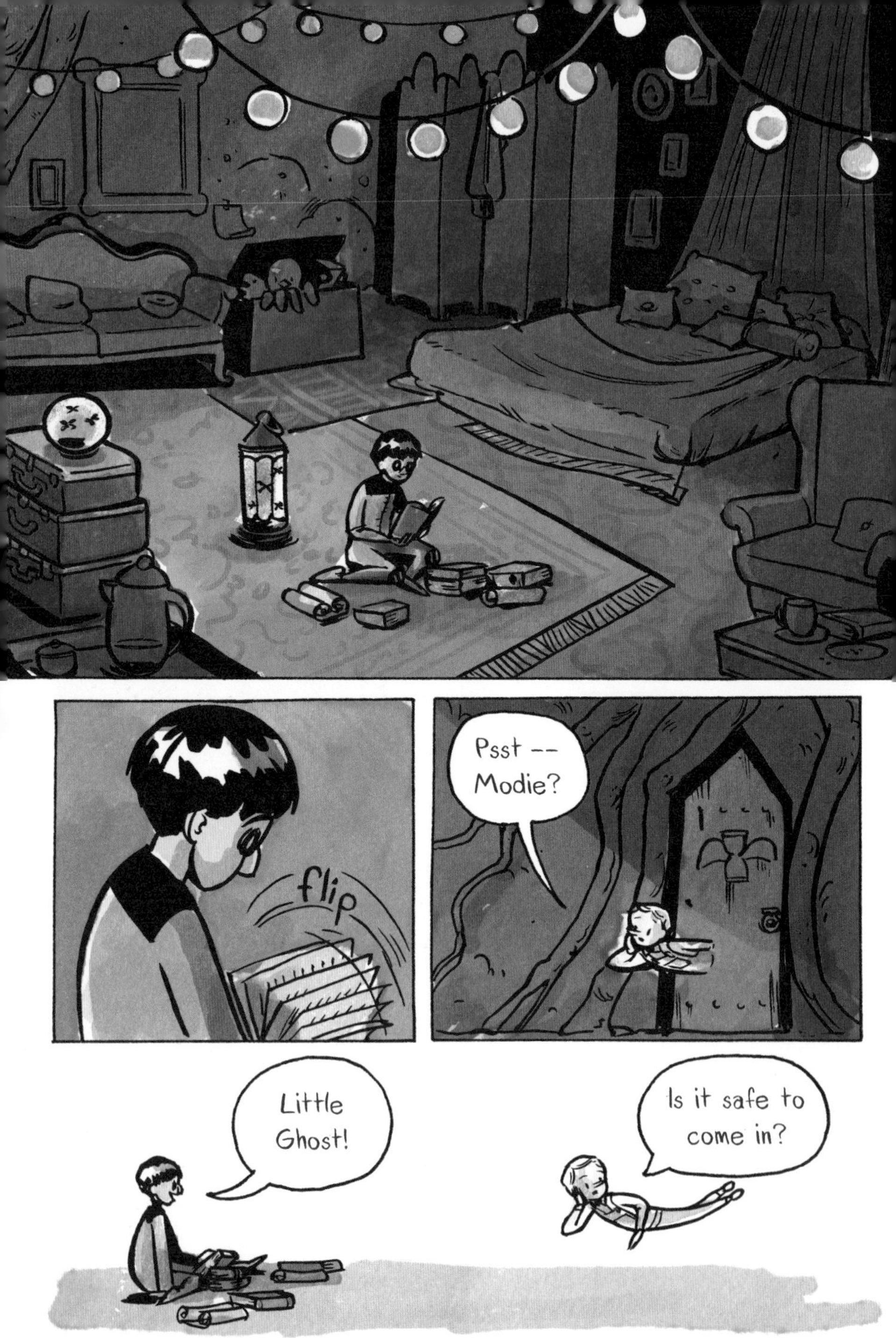
flip
Psst -- Modie?
Little Ghost!
Is it safe to come in?

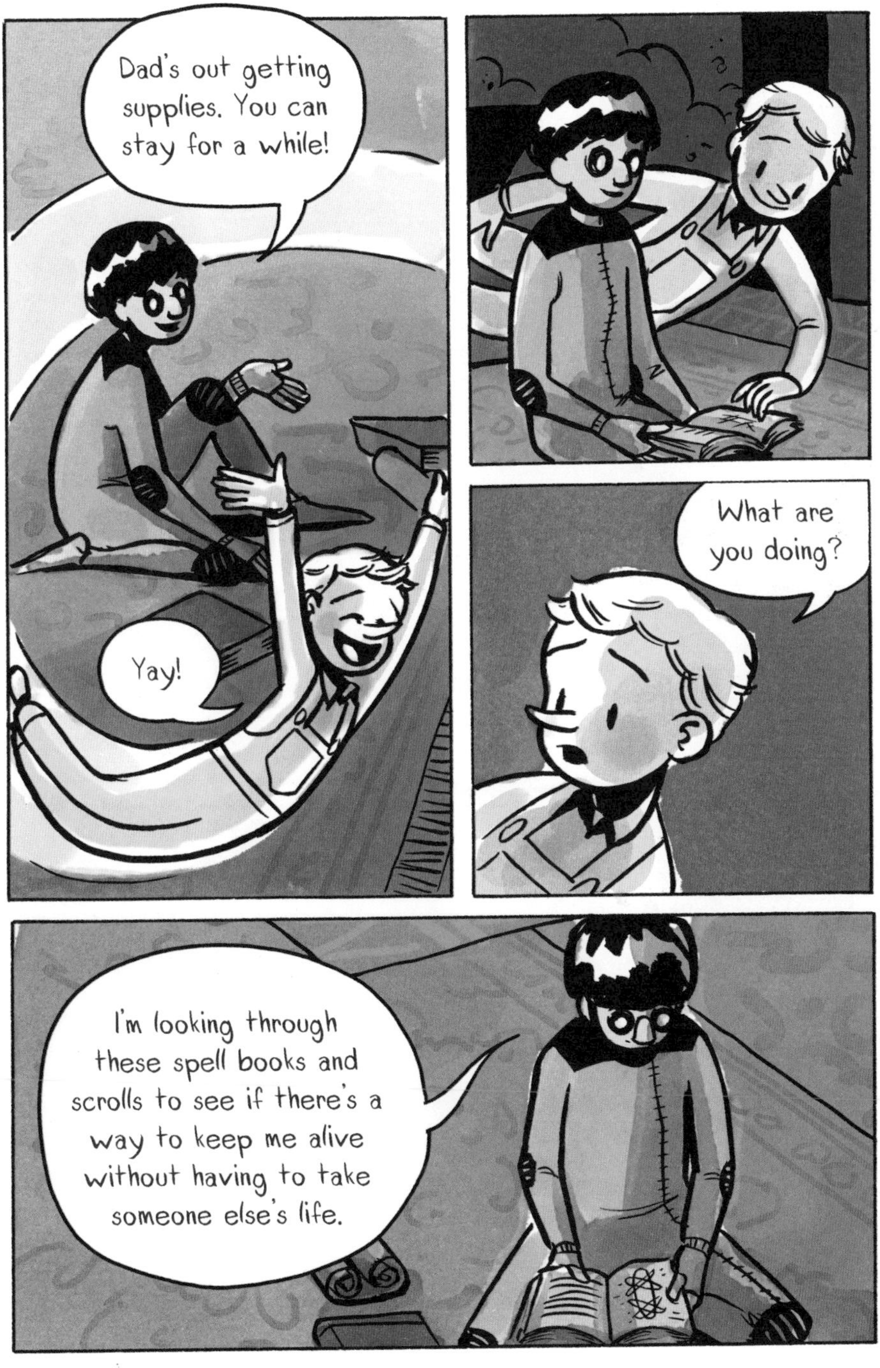

Dad's out getting supplies. You can stay for a while!
Yay!
What are you doing?
I'm looking through these spell books and scrolls to see if there's a way to keep me alive without having to take someone else's life.

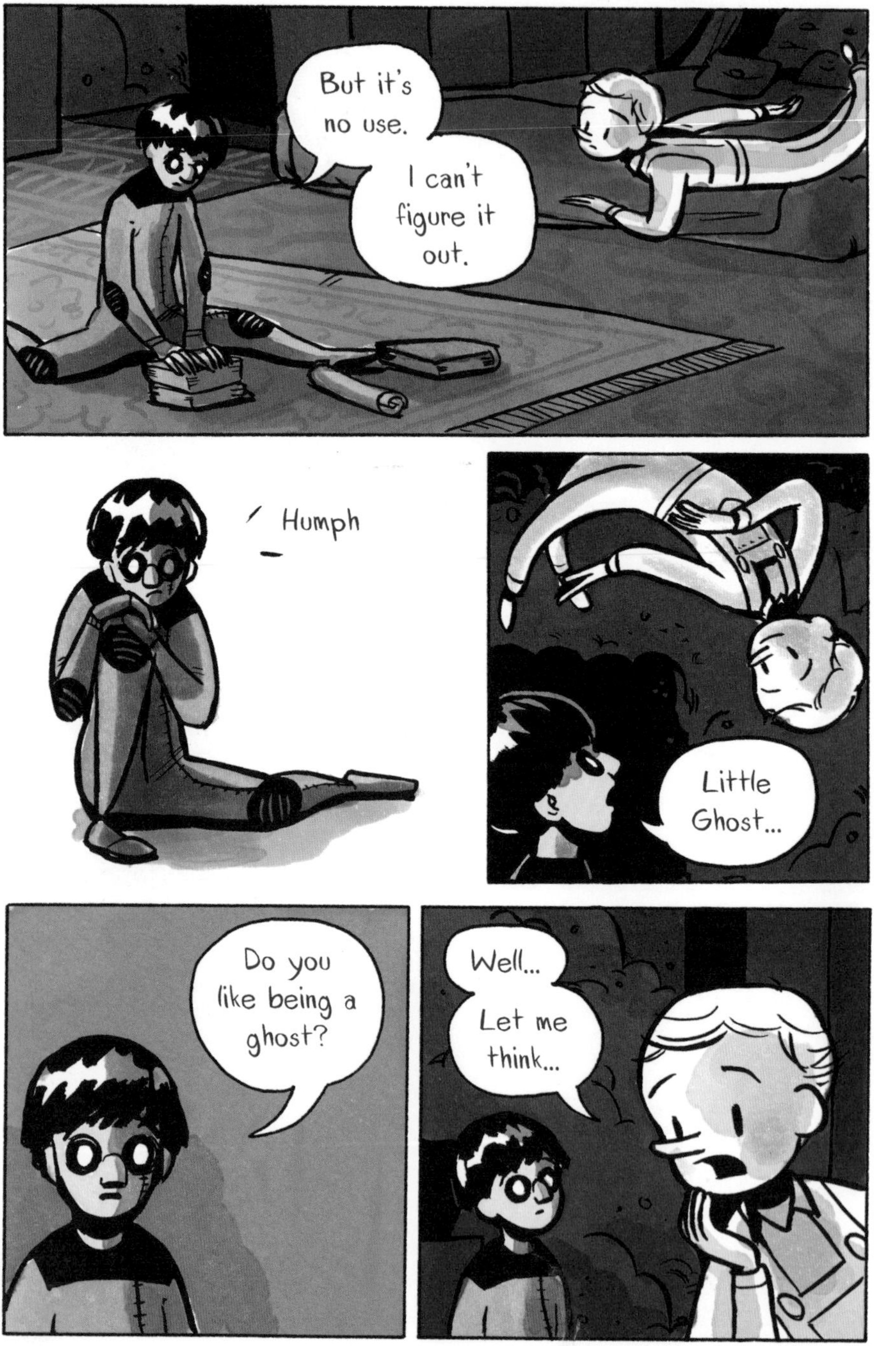
But it's no use.
I can't figure it out.
Humph
Little Ghost...
Do you like being a ghost?
Well...
Let me think...

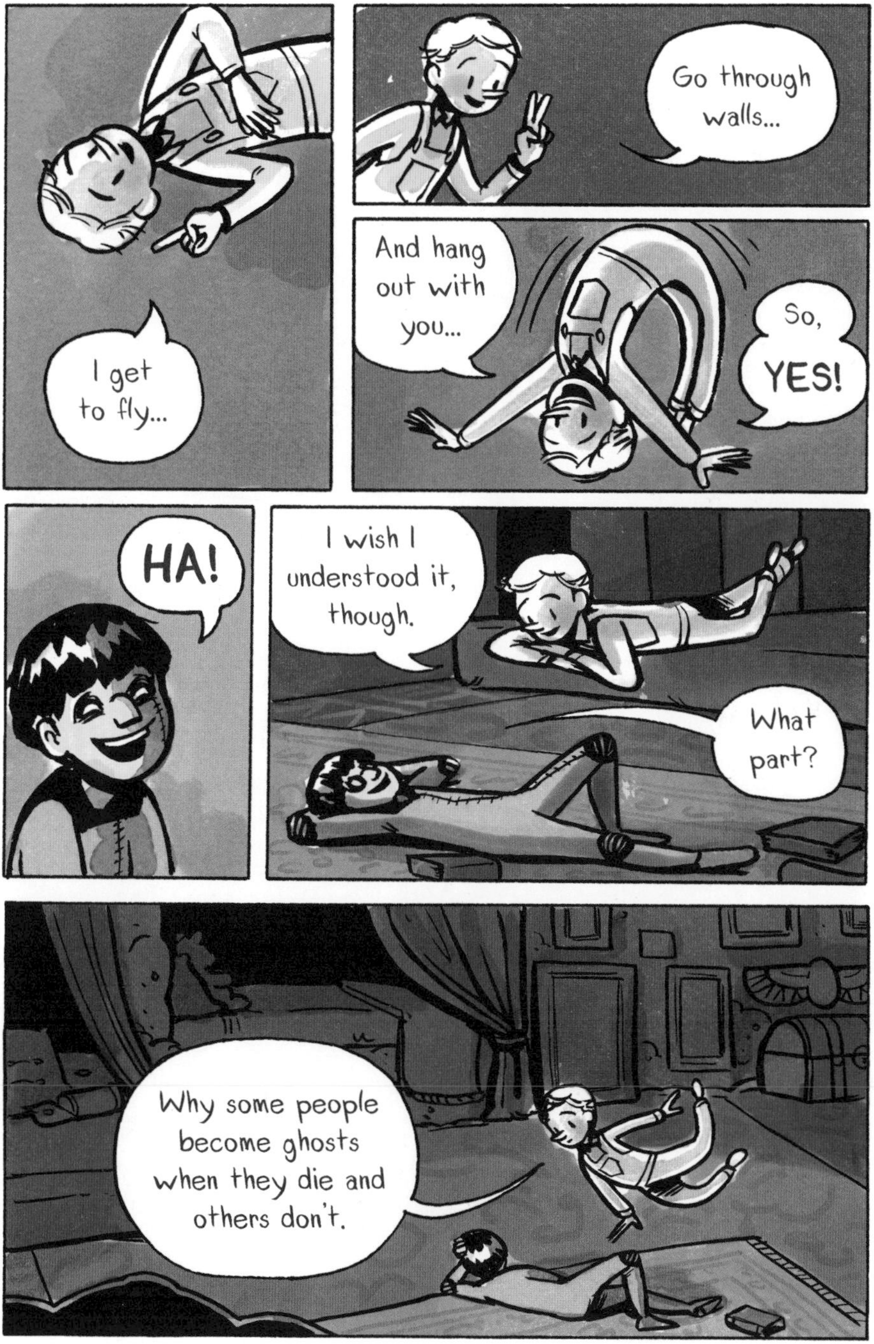
I get to fly...
Go through walls...
And hang out with you...
So, YES!
HA!
I wish I understood it, though.
What part?
Why some people become ghosts when they die and others don't.

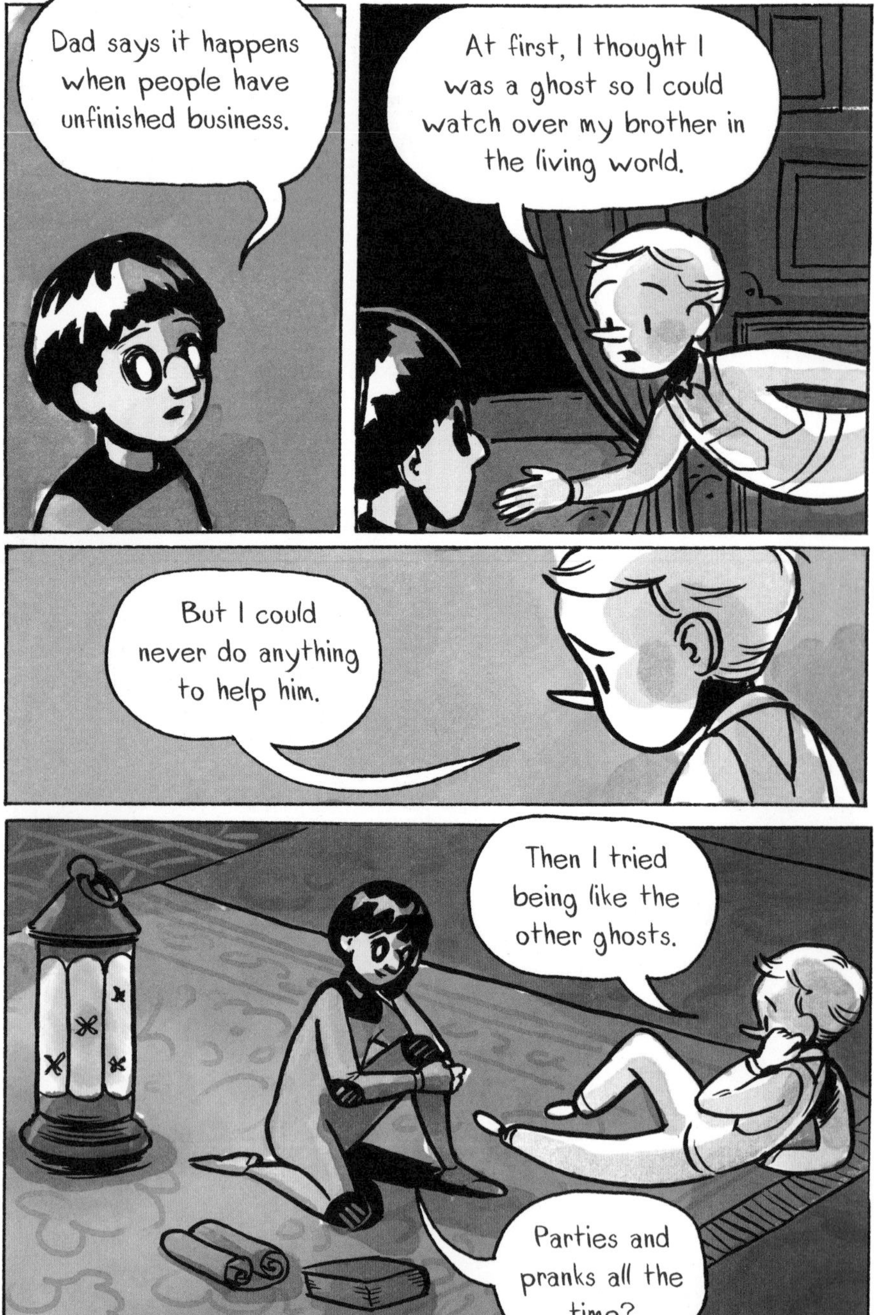
Dad says it happens when people have unfinished business.
At first, I thought I was a ghost so I could watch over my brother in the living world.
But I could never do anything to help him.
Then I tried being like the other ghosts.
Parties and pranks all the time?

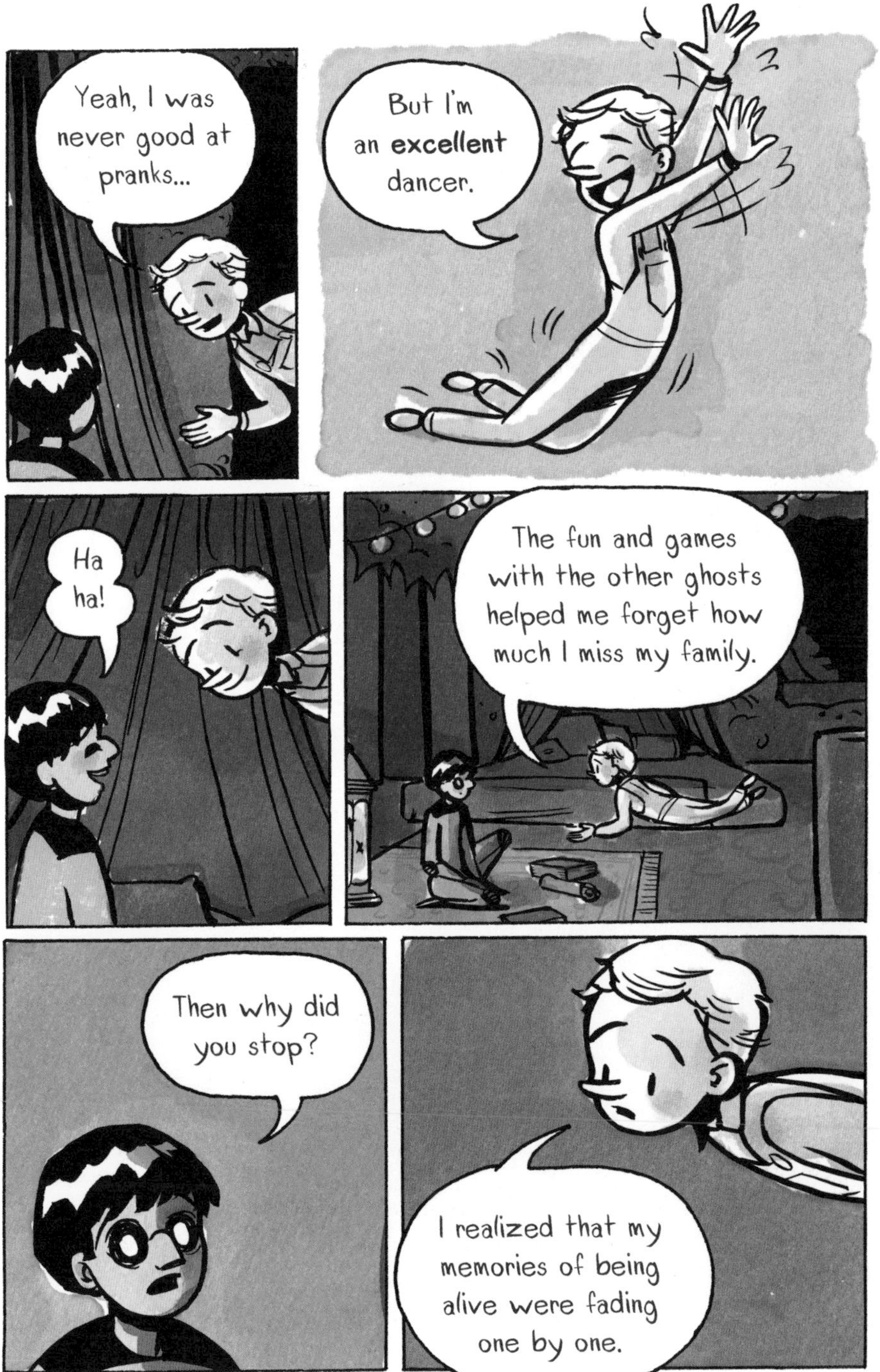
Yeah, I was never good at pranks...
But I'm an **excellent** dancer.
Ha ha!
The fun and games with the other ghosts helped me forget how much I miss my family.
Then why did you stop?
I realized that my memories of being alive were fading one by one.

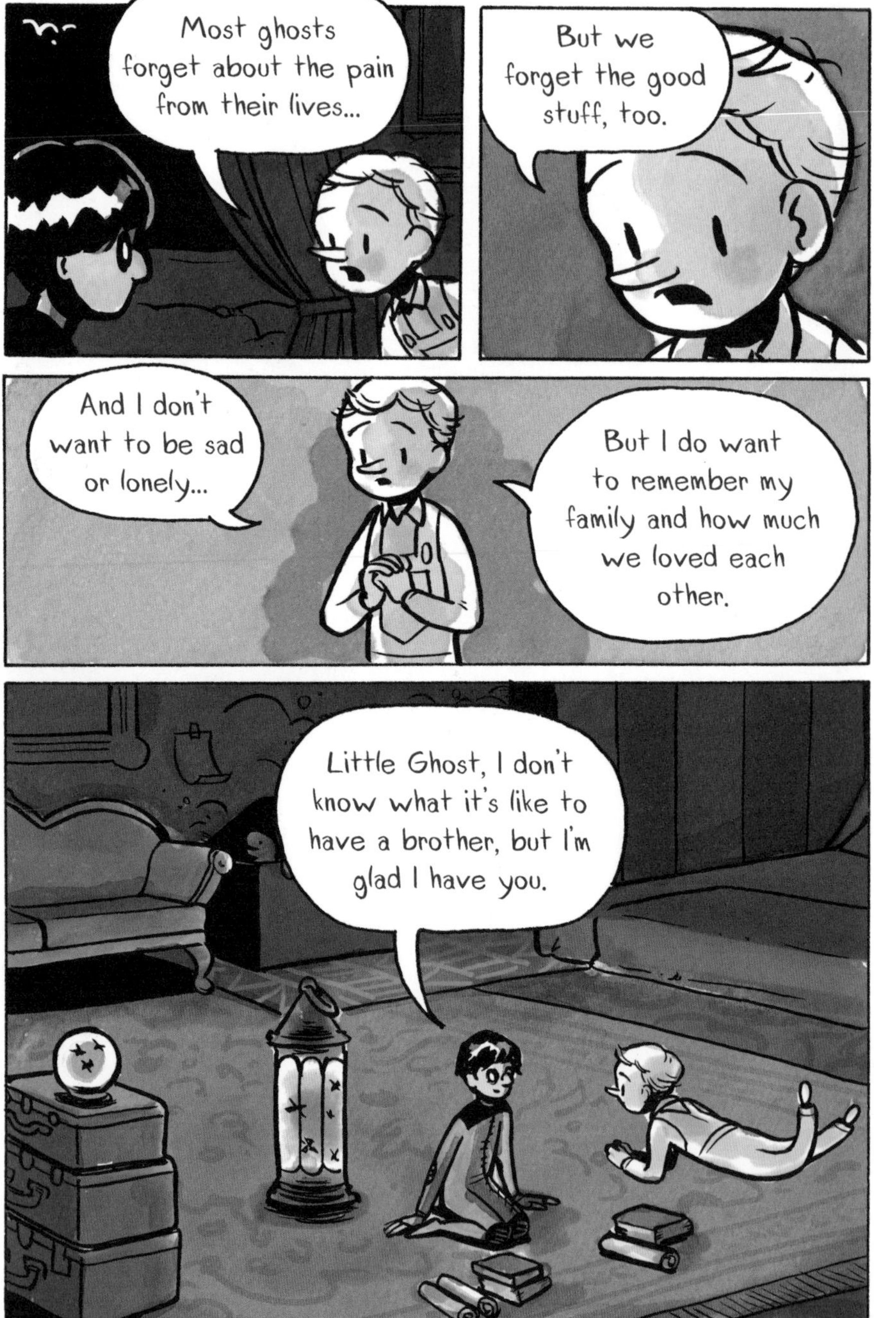
Most ghosts forget about the pain from their lives...
But we forget the good stuff, too.
And I don't want to be sad or lonely...
But I do want to remember my family and how much we loved each other.
Little Ghost, I don't know what it's like to have a brother, but I'm glad I have you.

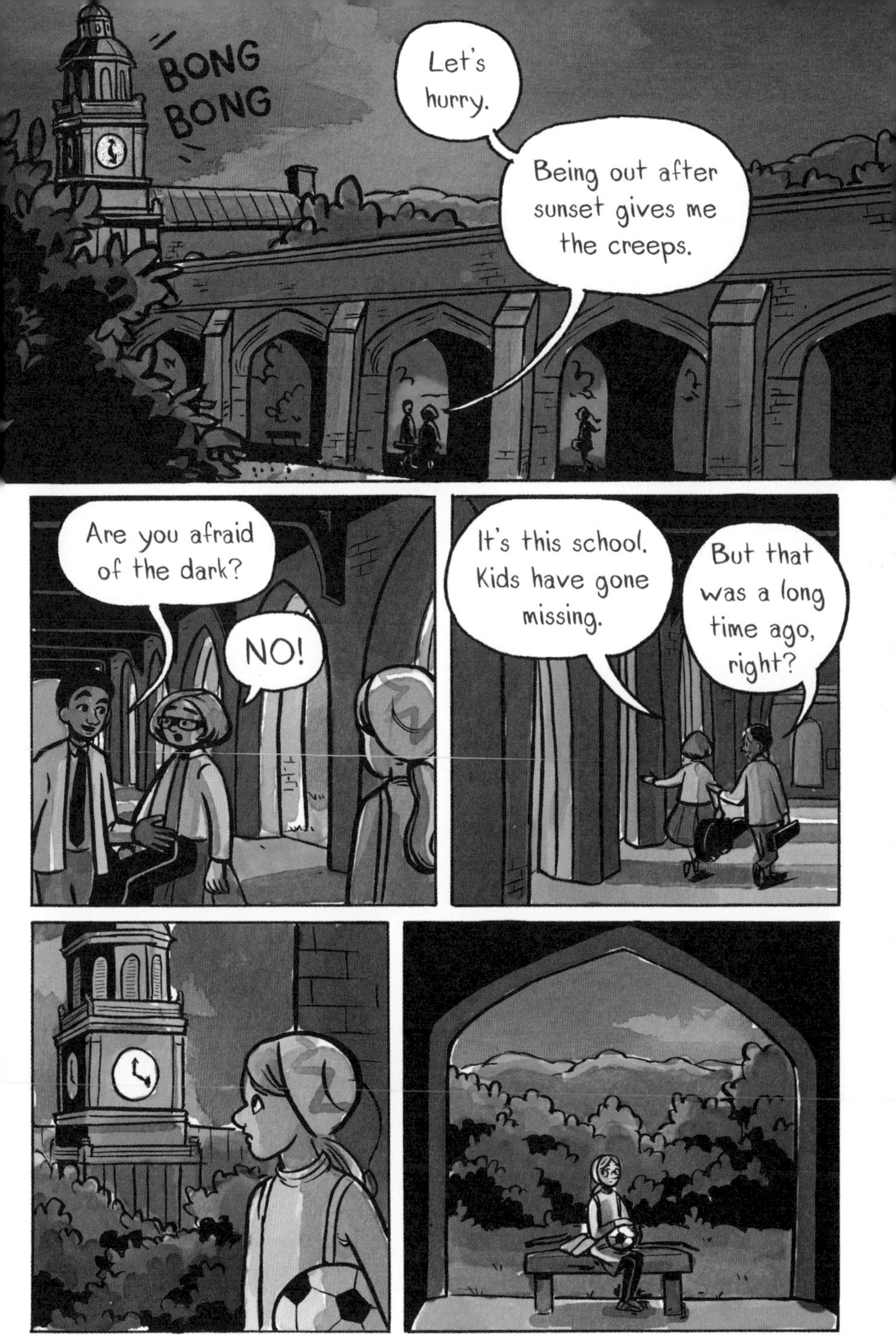
BONG BONG
Let's hurry.
Being out after sunset gives me the creeps.
Are you afraid of the dark?
NO!
It's this school. Kids have gone missing.
But that was a long time ago, right?

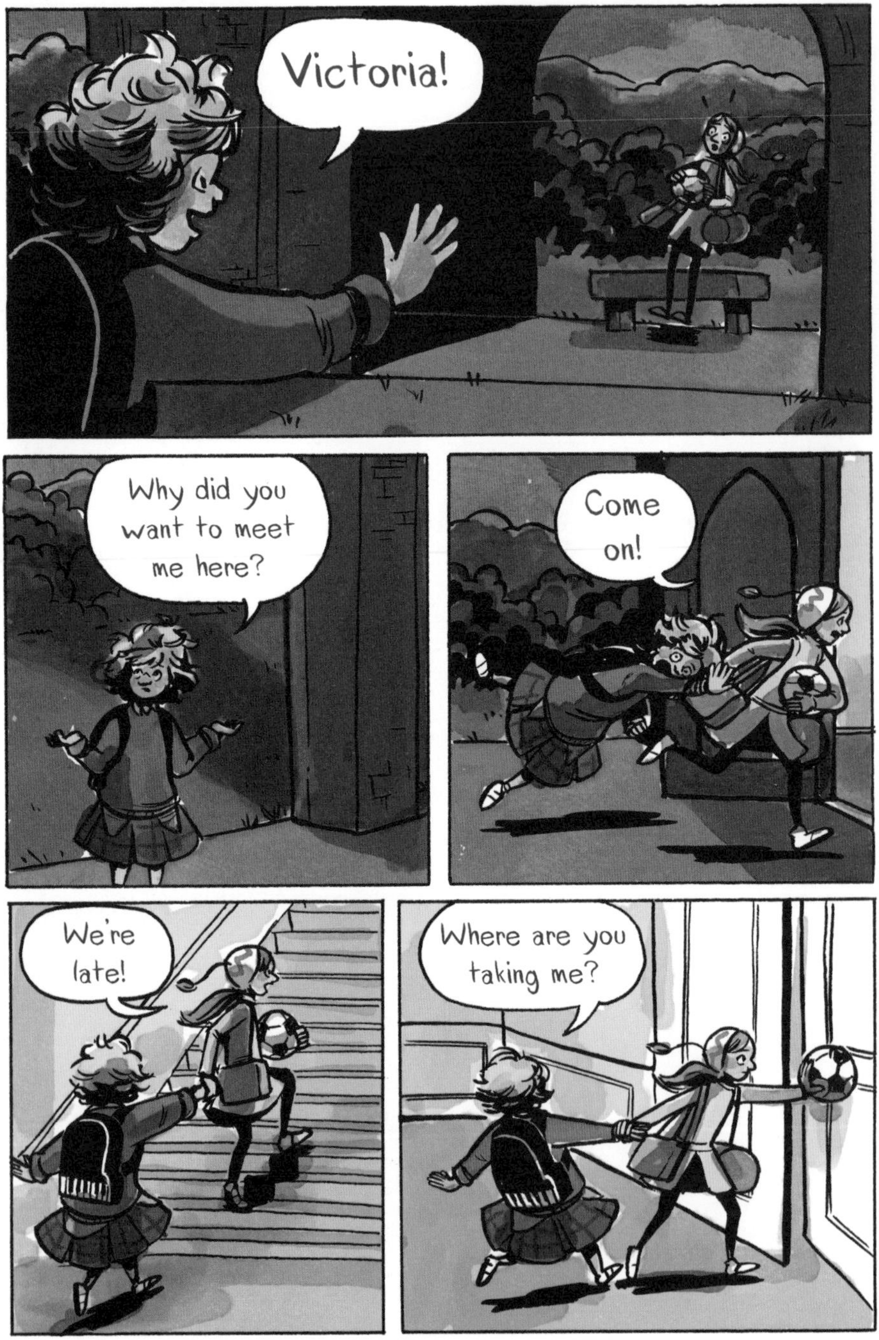
Victoria!
Why did you want to meet me here?
Come on!
We're late!
Where are you taking me?

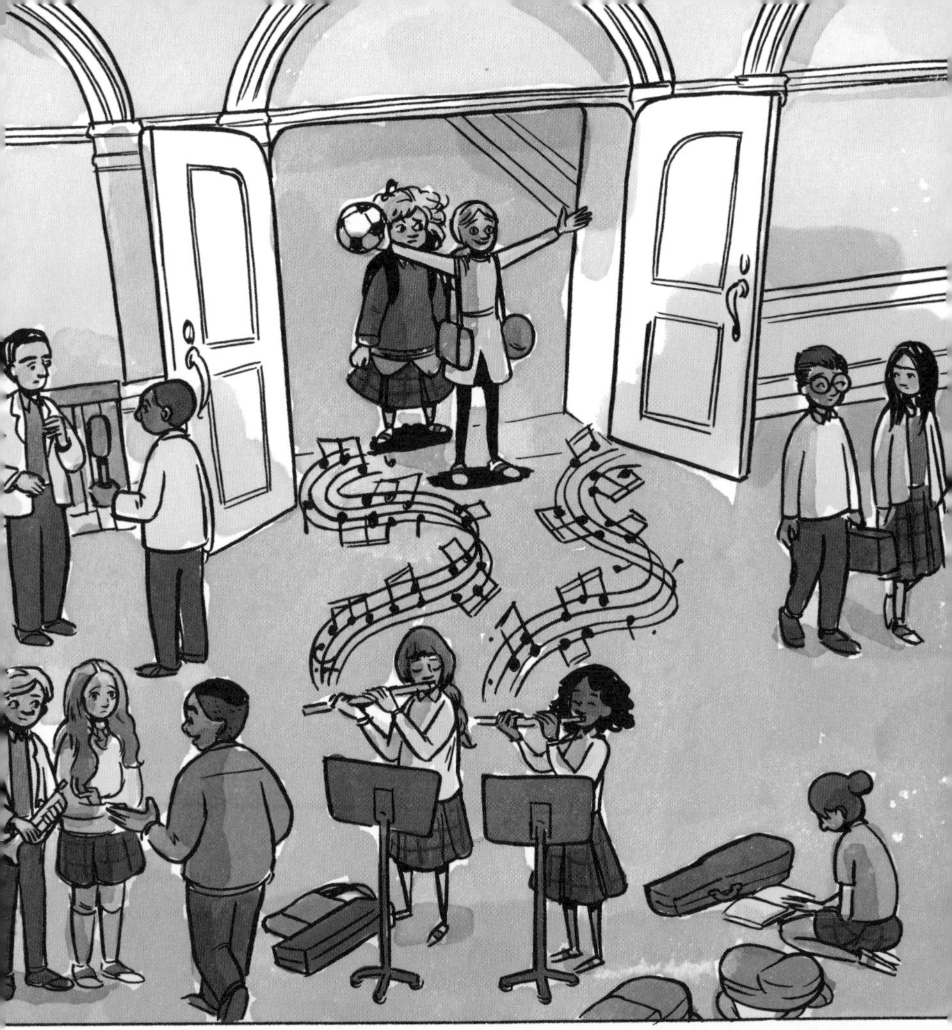

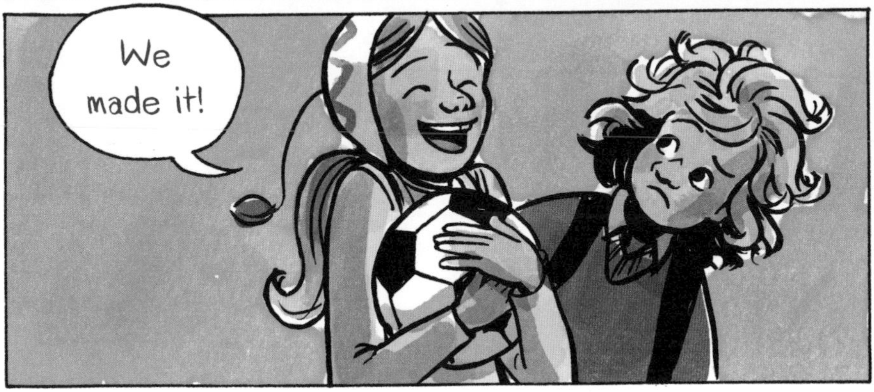
We made it!

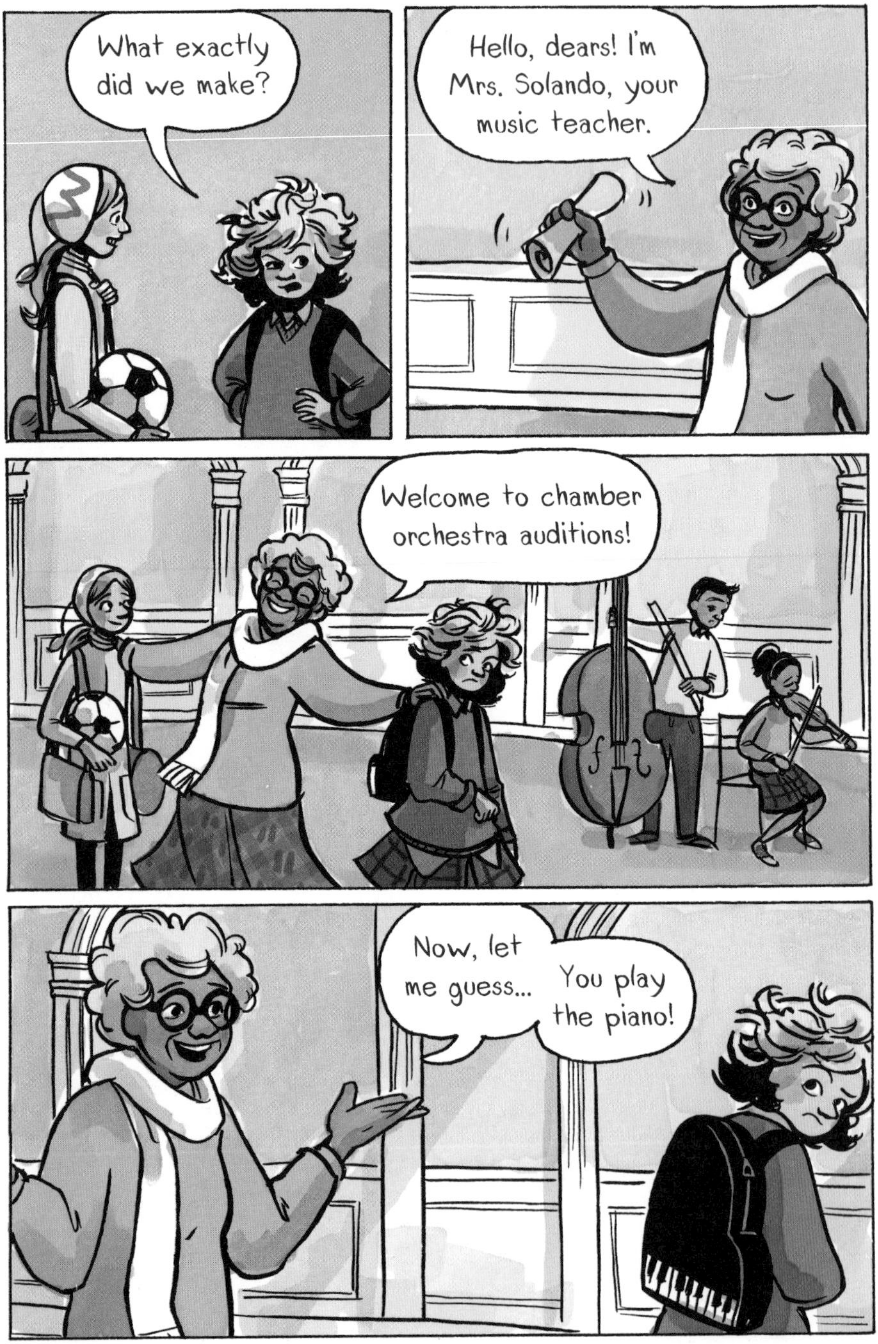
What exactly did we make?
Hello, dears! I'm Mrs. Solando, your music teacher.
Welcome to chamber orchestra auditions!
Now, let me guess...
You play the piano!

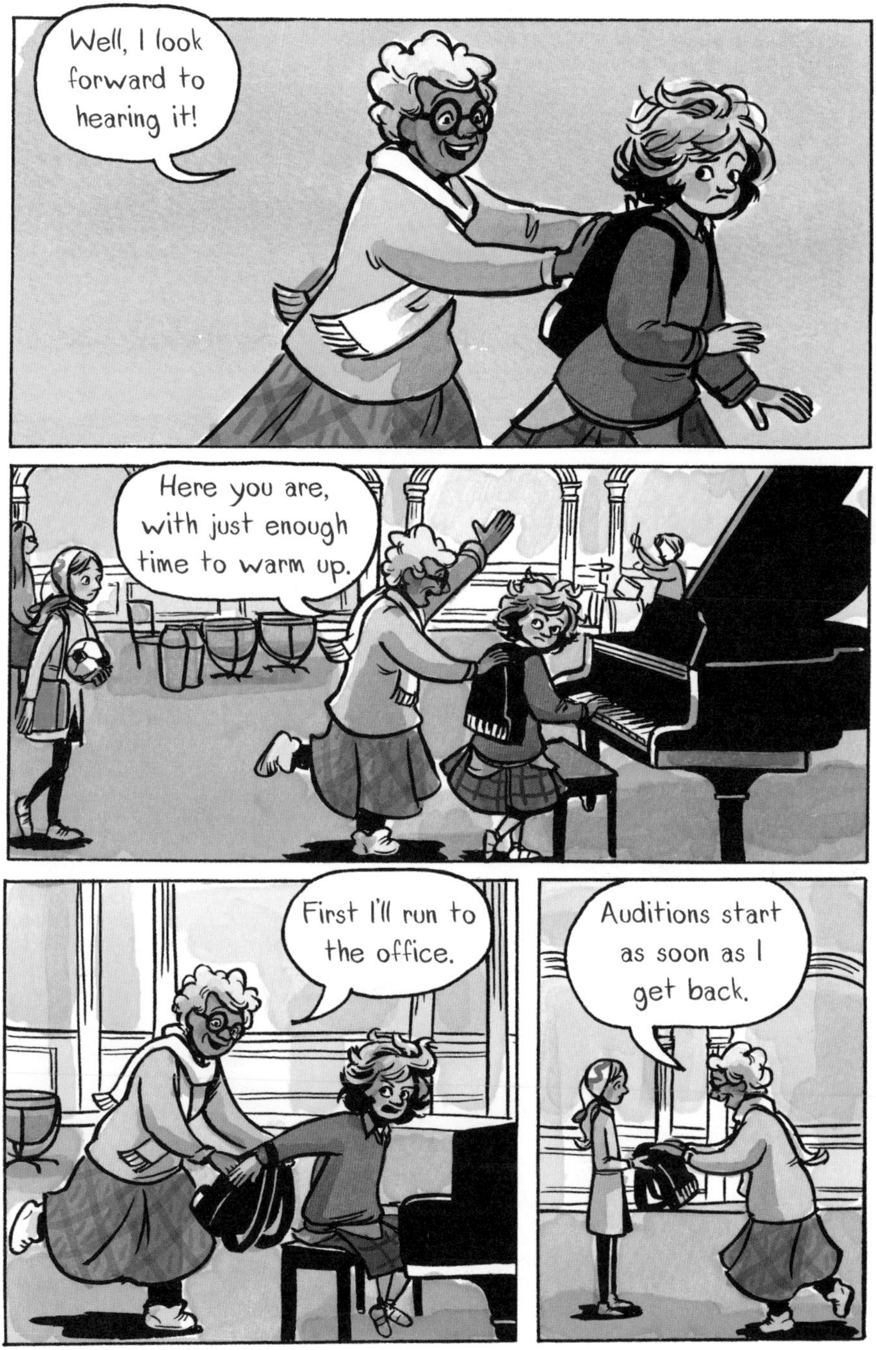
Well, I look forward to hearing it!
Here you are, with just enough time to warm up.
First I'll run to the office.
Auditions start as soon as I get back.

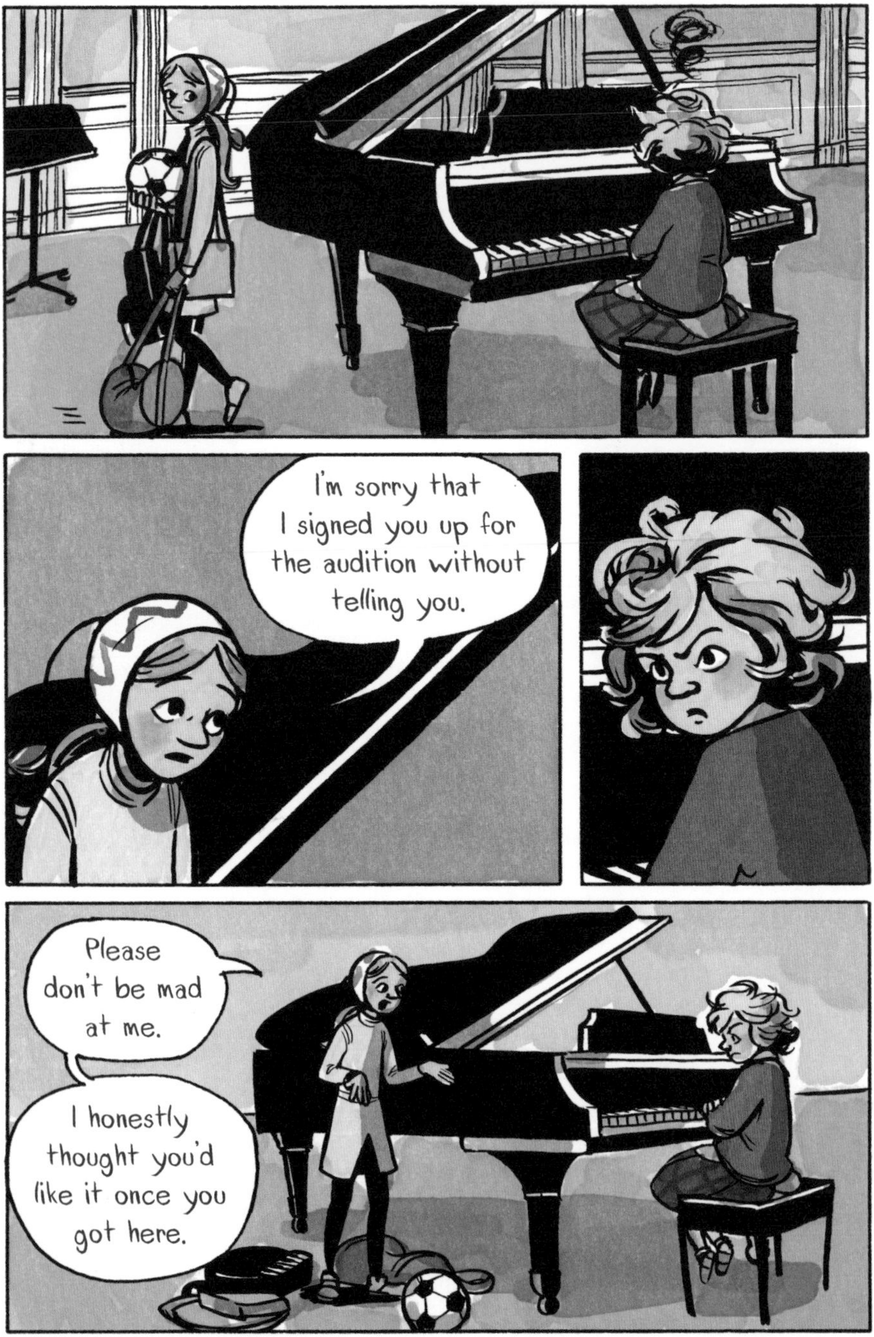
I'm sorry that I signed you up for the audition without telling you.
Please don't be mad at me.
I honestly thought you'd like it once you got here.

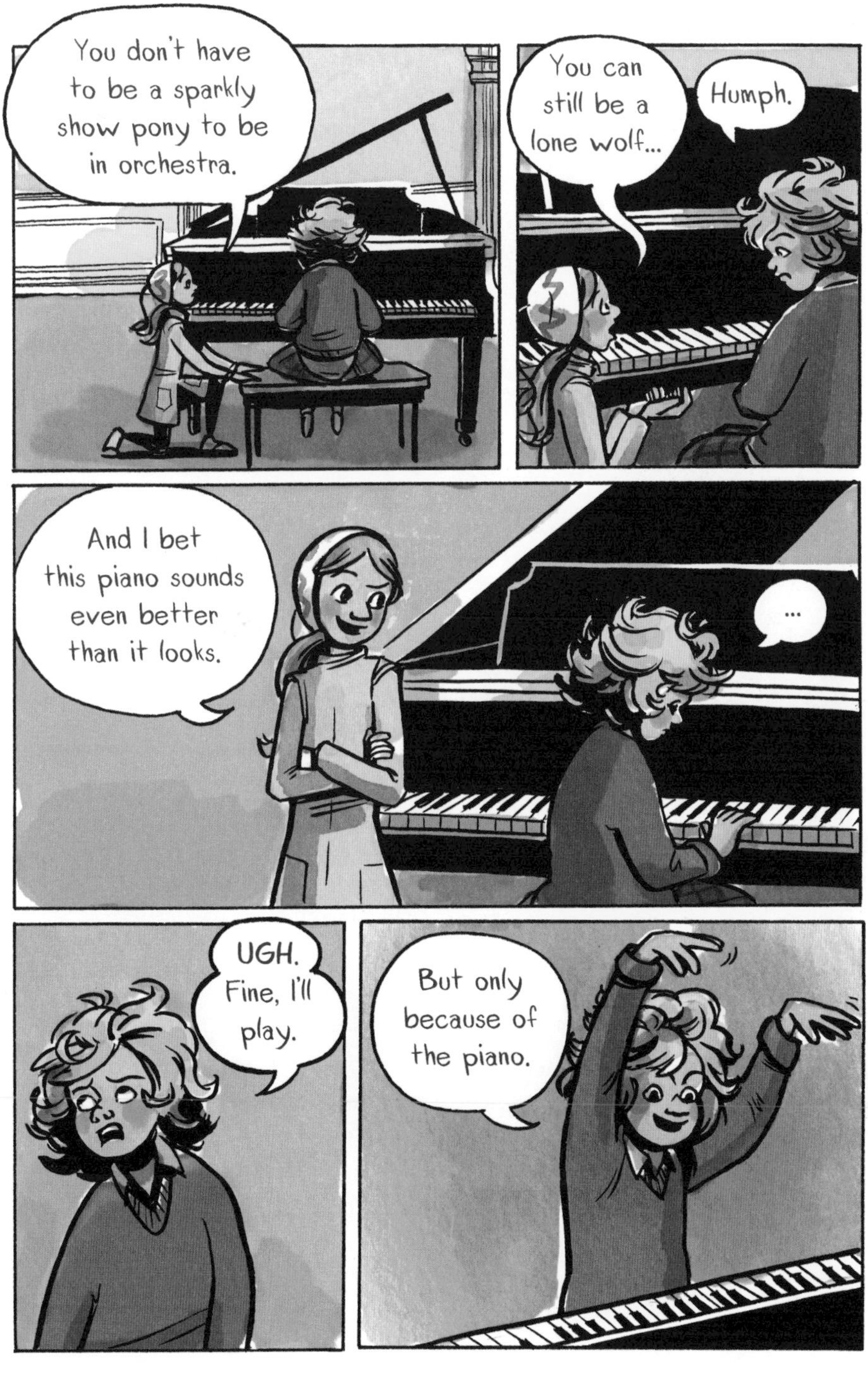
You don't have to be a sparkly show pony to be in orchestra.
You can still be a lone wolf...
Humph.
And I bet this piano sounds even better than it looks.
...
UGH. Fine, I'll play.
But only because of the piano.

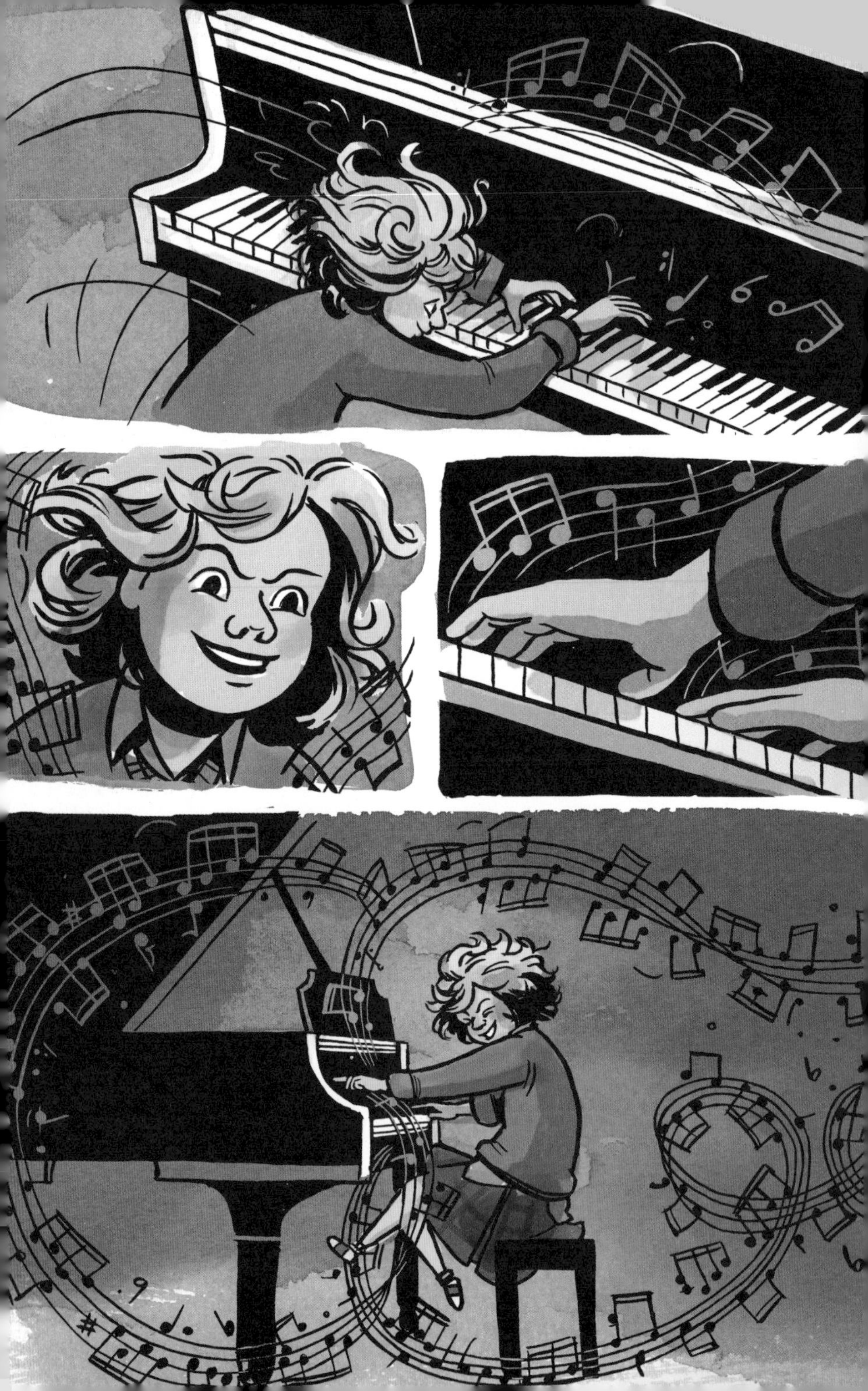

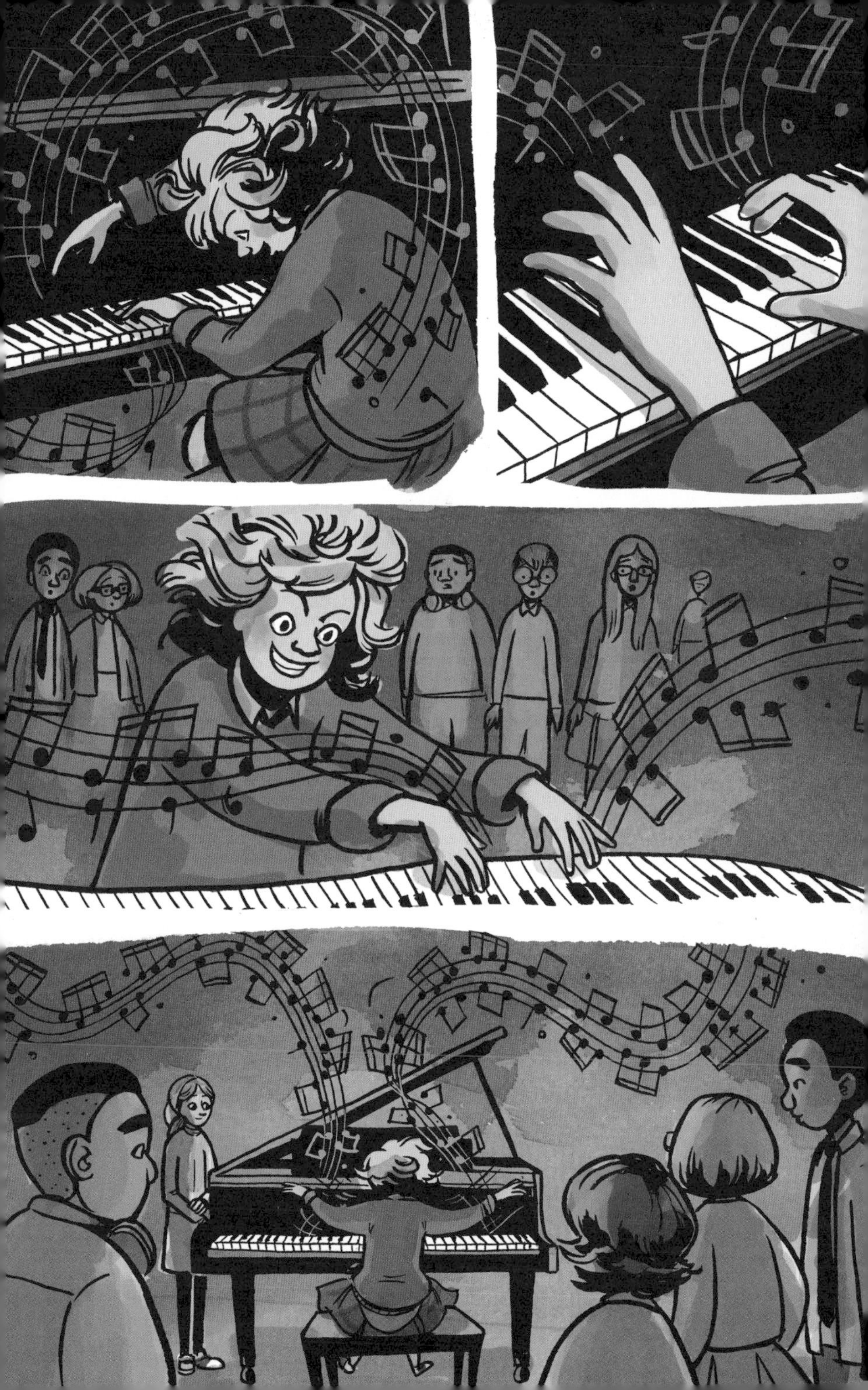

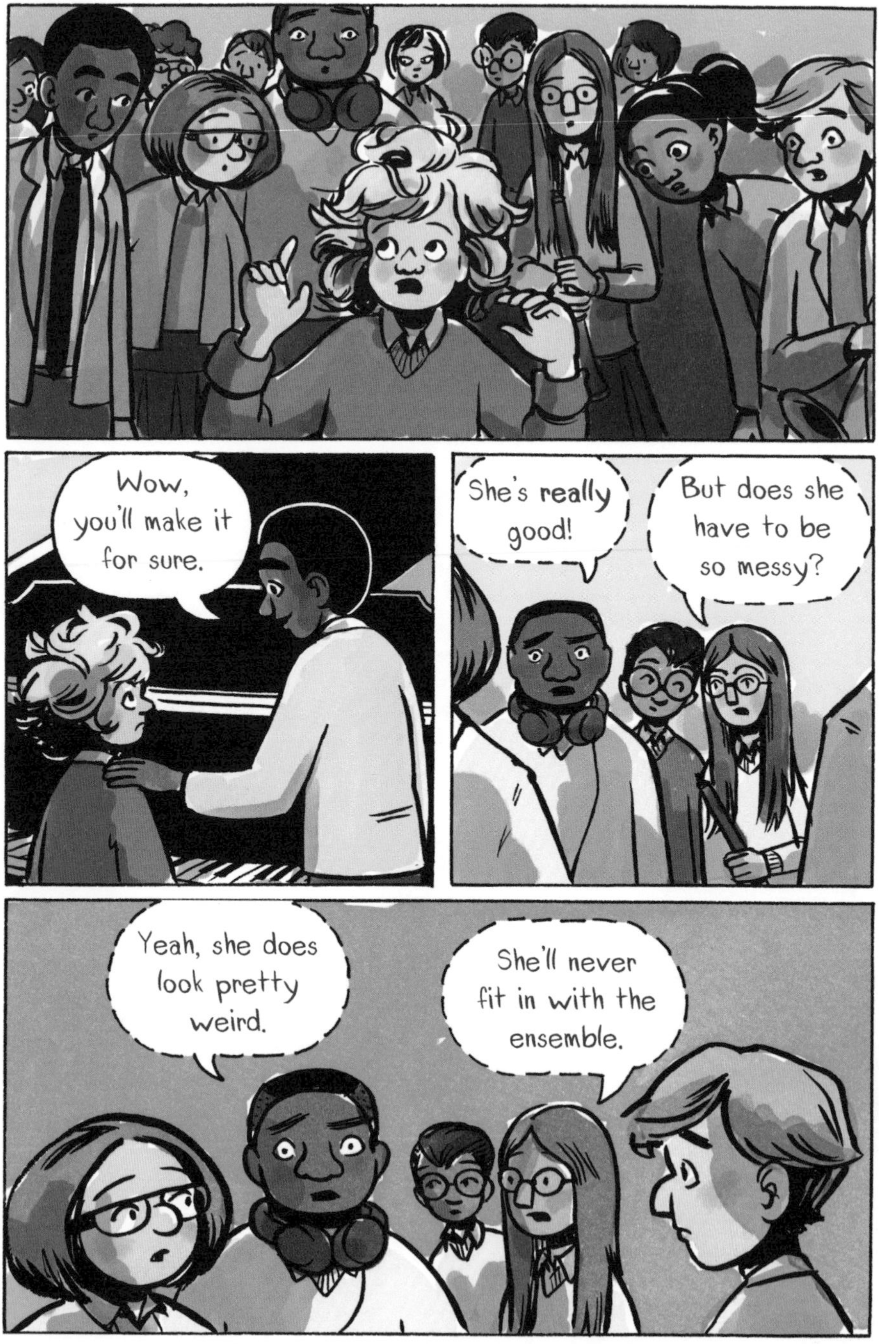
Wow, you'll make it for sure.
She's really good!
But does she have to be so messy?
Yeah, she does look pretty weird.
She'll never fit in with the ensemble.

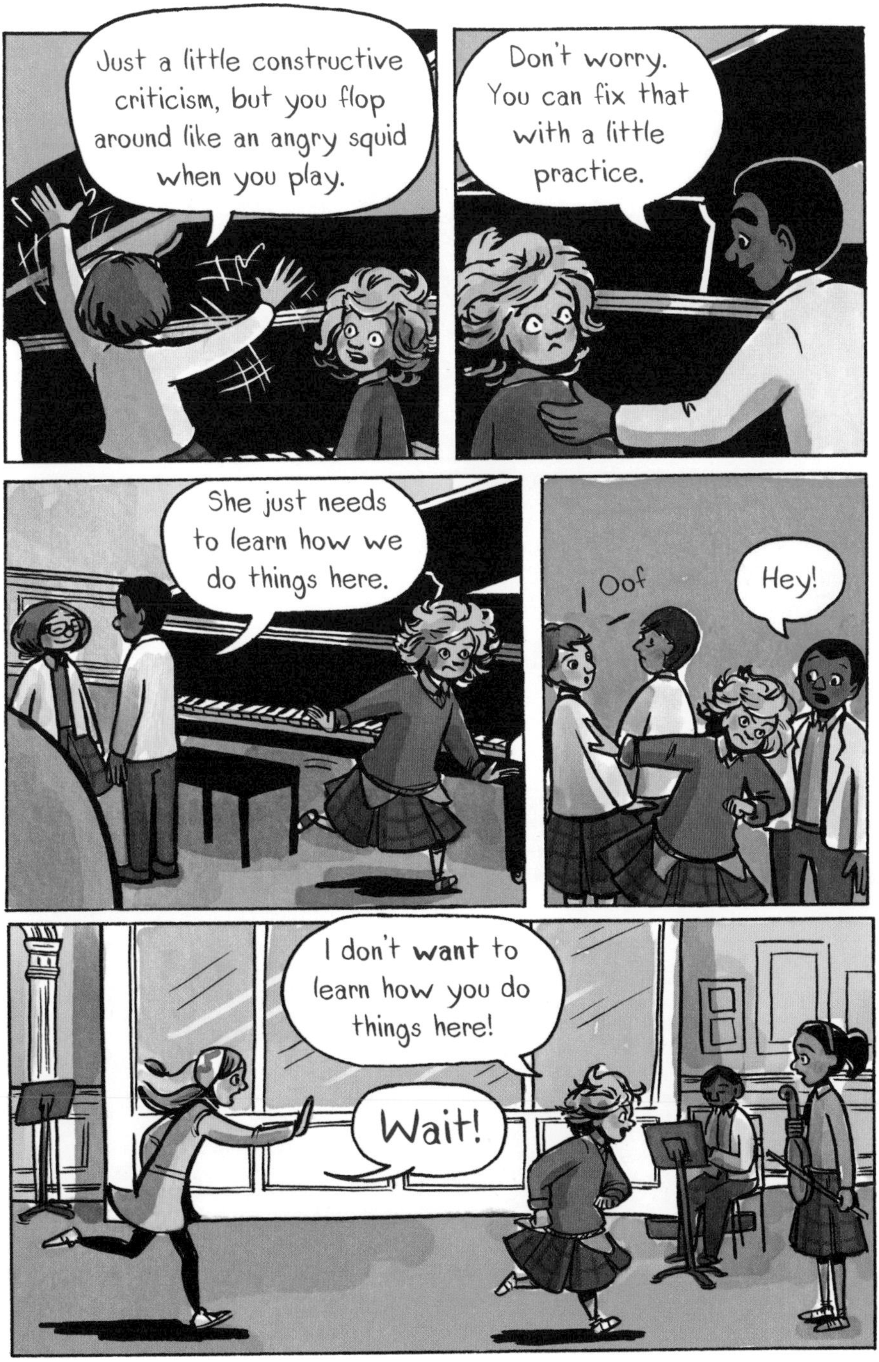
Just a little constructive criticism, but you flop around like an angry squid when you play.
Don't worry. You can fix that with a little practice.
She just needs to learn how we do things here.
Oof
Hey!
I don't **want** to learn how you do things here!
Wait!

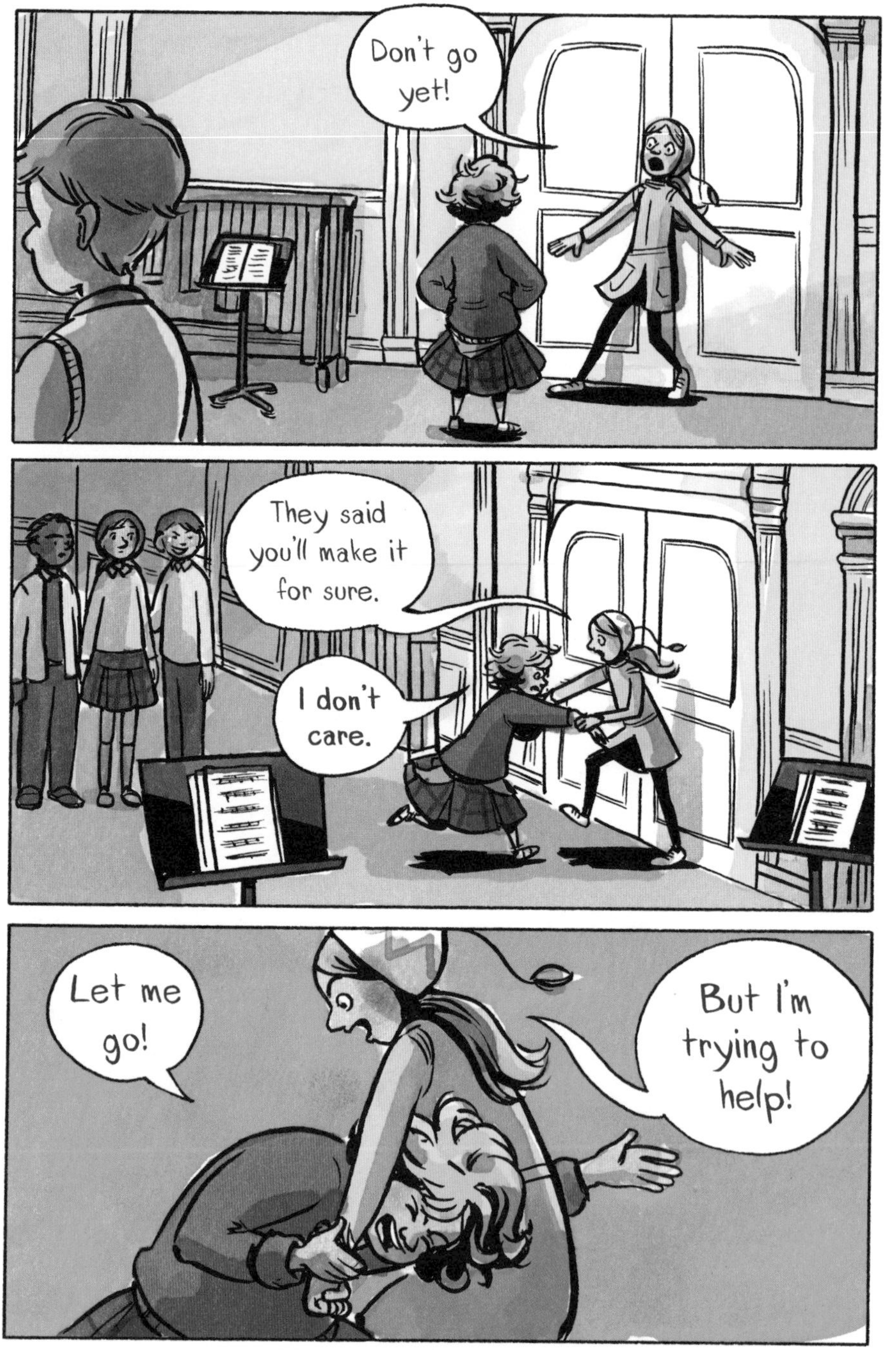
Don't go yet!
They said you'll make it for sure.
I don't care.
Let me go!
But I'm trying to help!

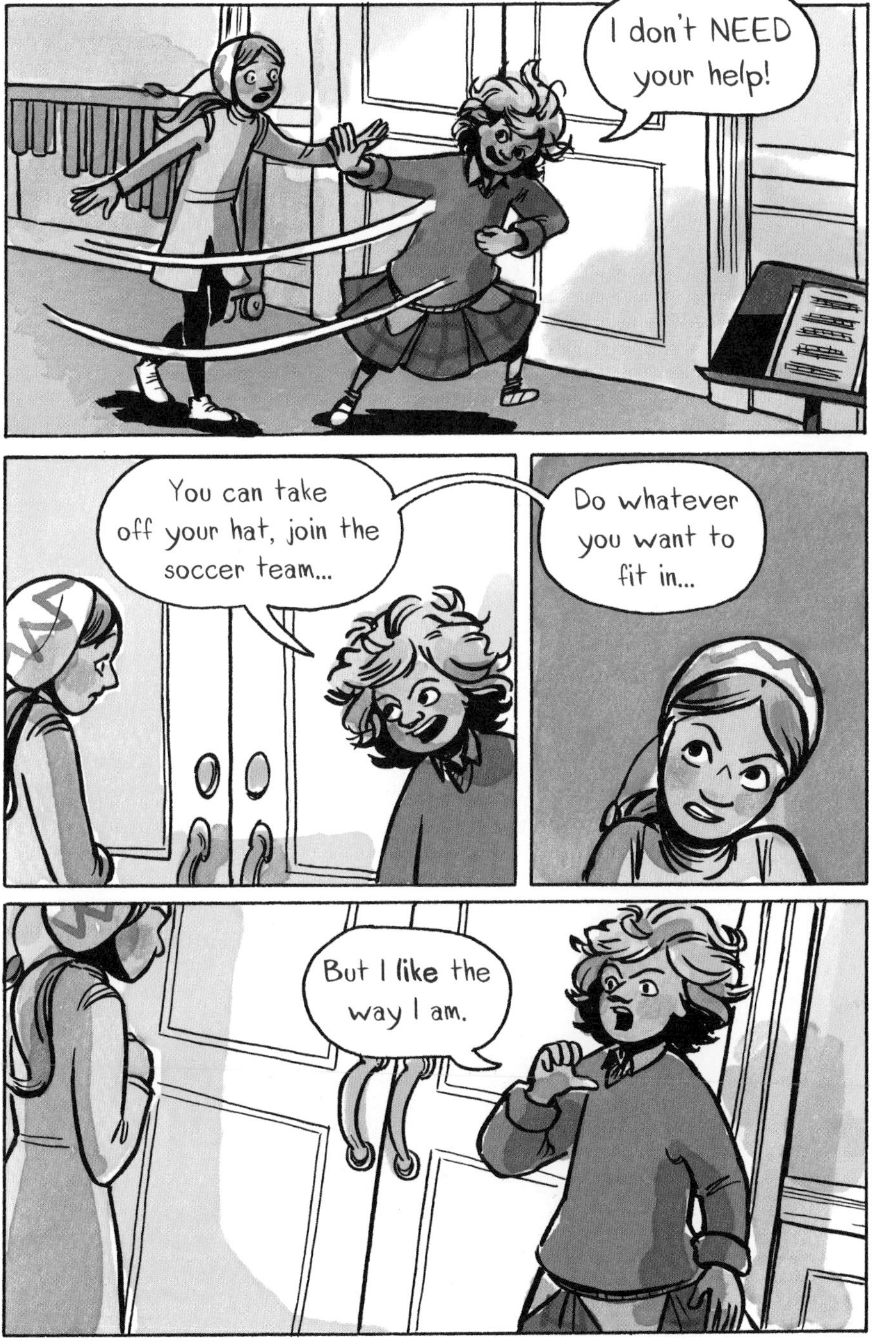
I don't NEED your help!
You can take off your hat, join the soccer team...
Do whatever you want to fit in...
But I **like** the way I am.

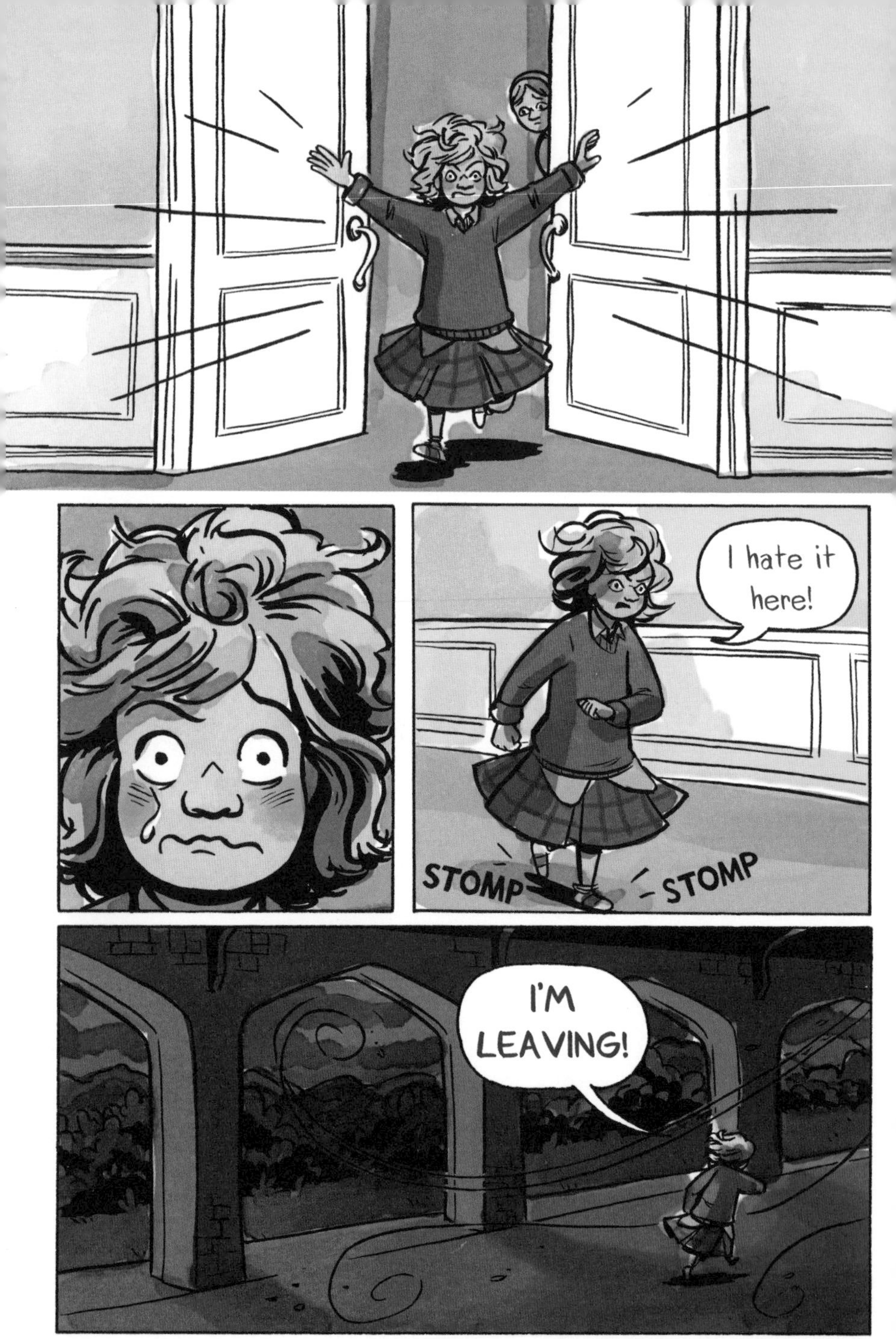
I hate it here!
STOMP
STOMP
I'M LEAVING!

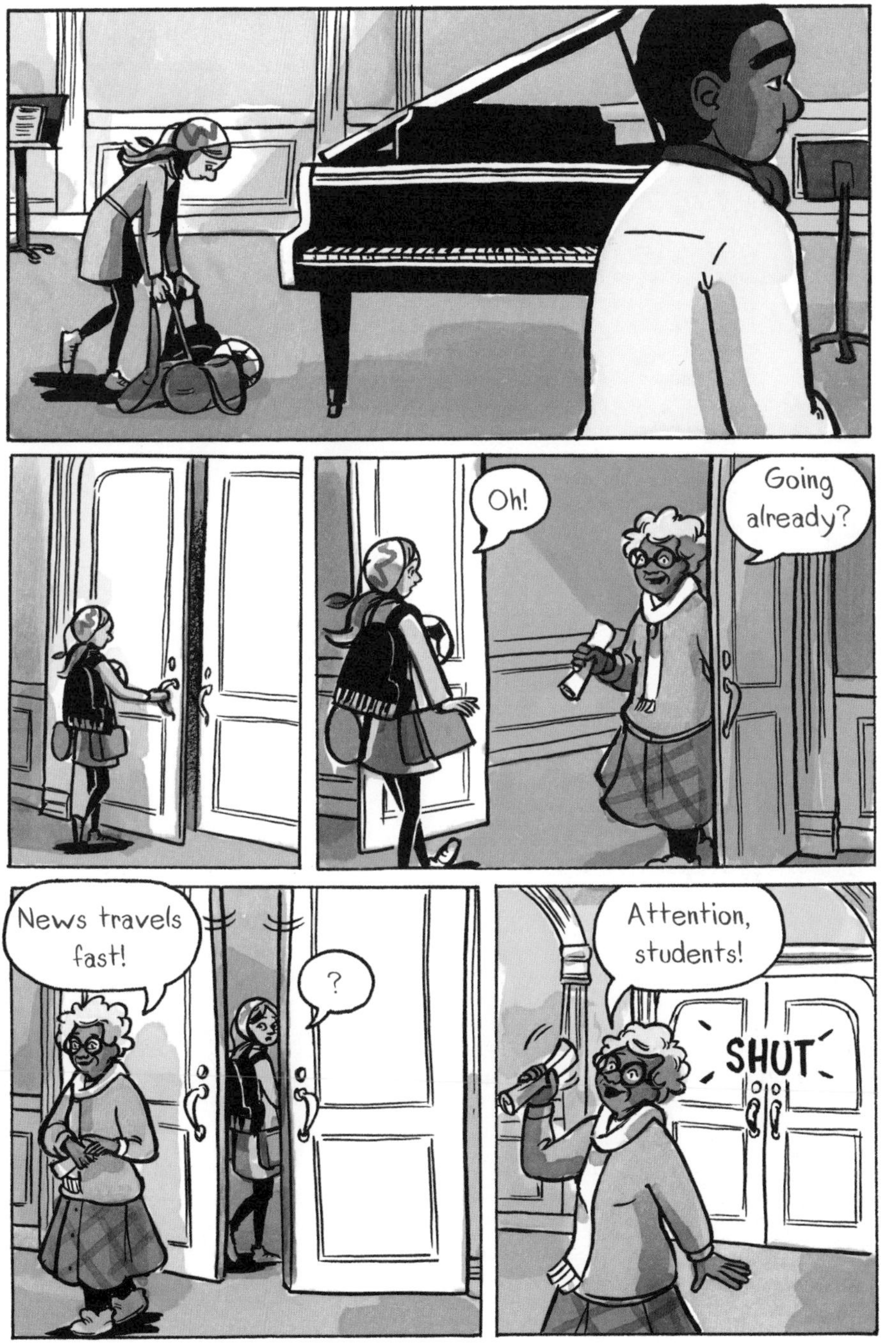
Oh!
Going already?
News travels fast!
?
Attention, students!
SHUT

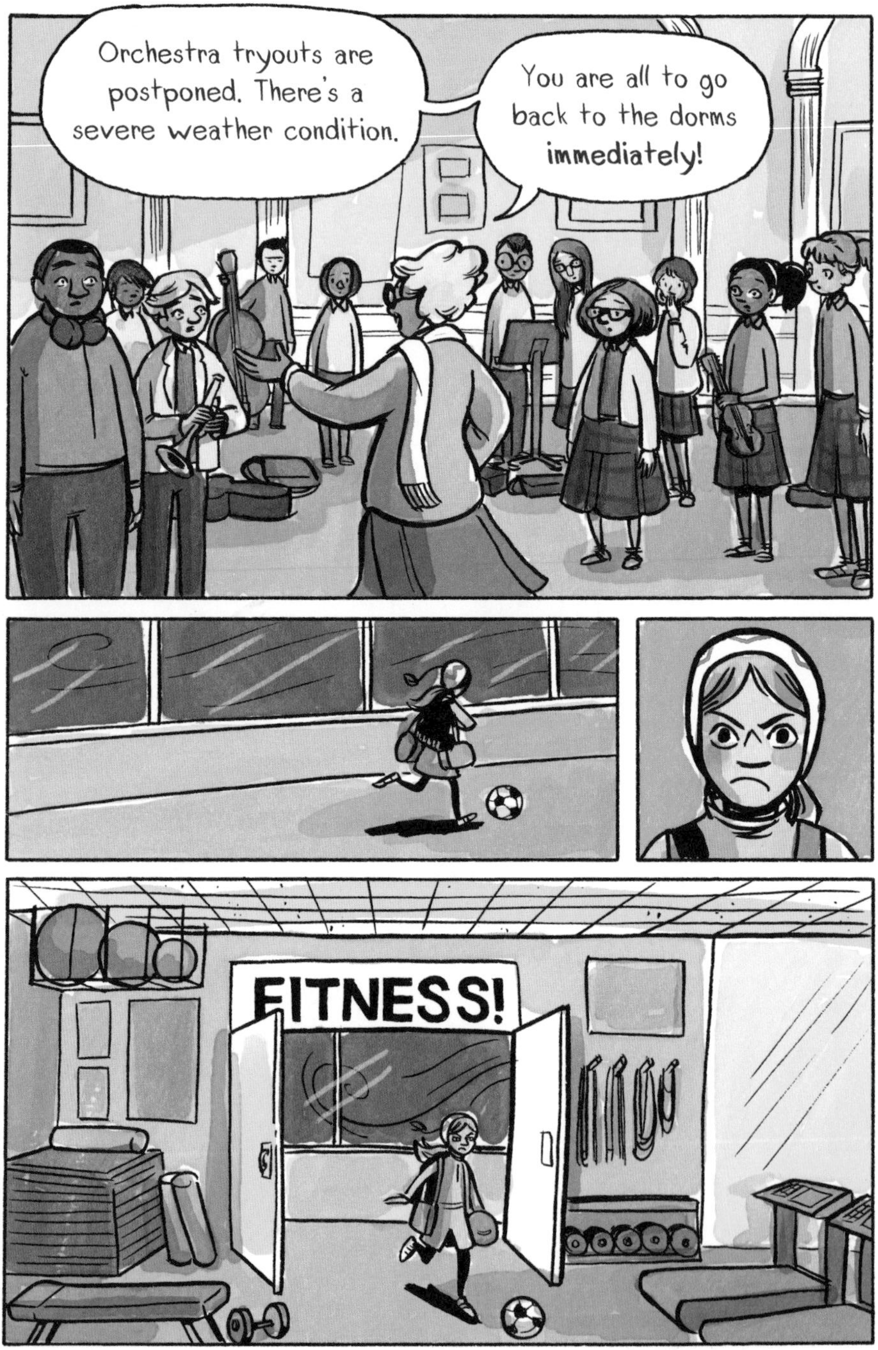

Orchestra tryouts are postponed. There's a severe weather condition.
You are all to go back to the dorms **immediately**!
FITNESS!

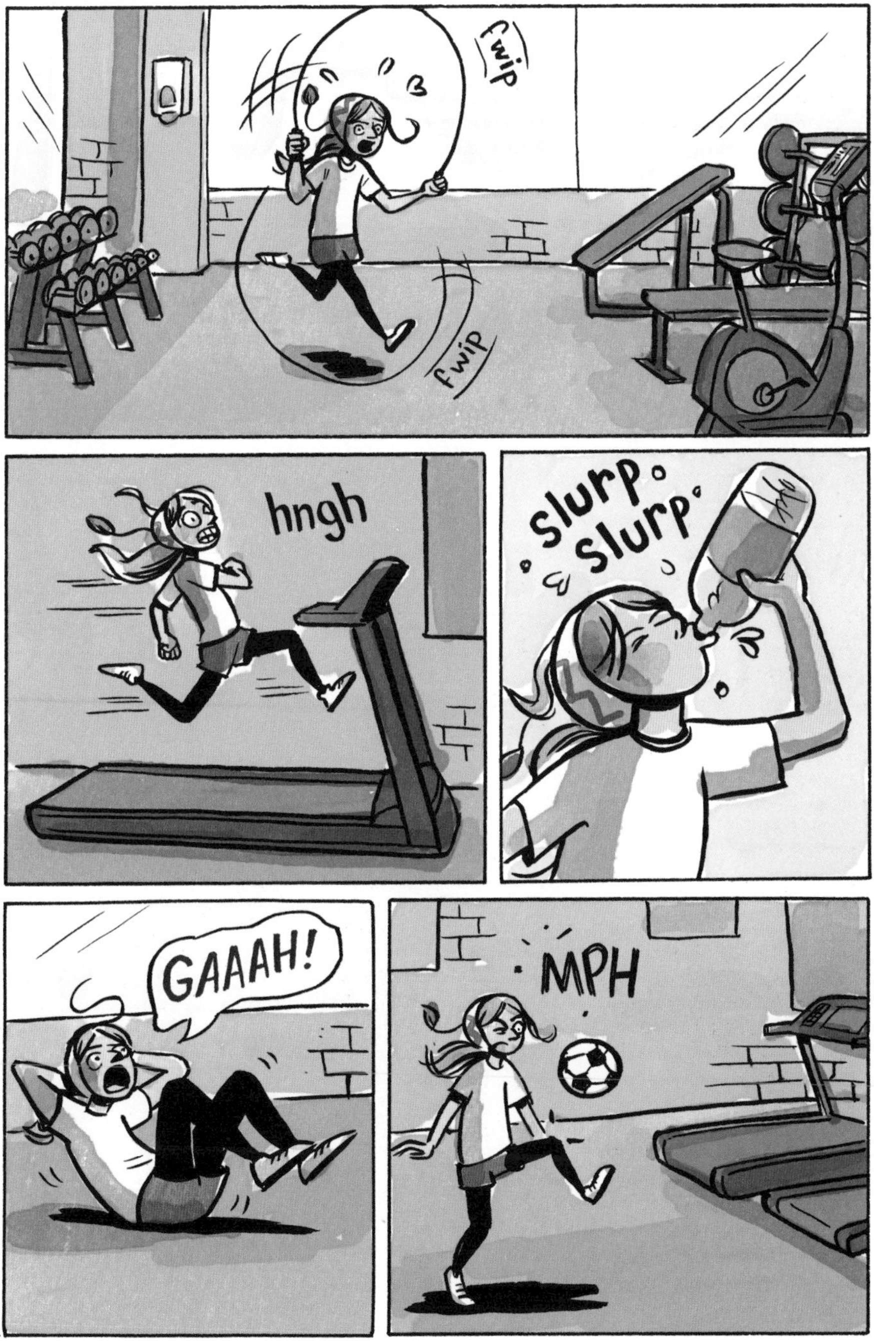
fwip
fwip
hngh
slurp
slurp
GAAAH!
MPH

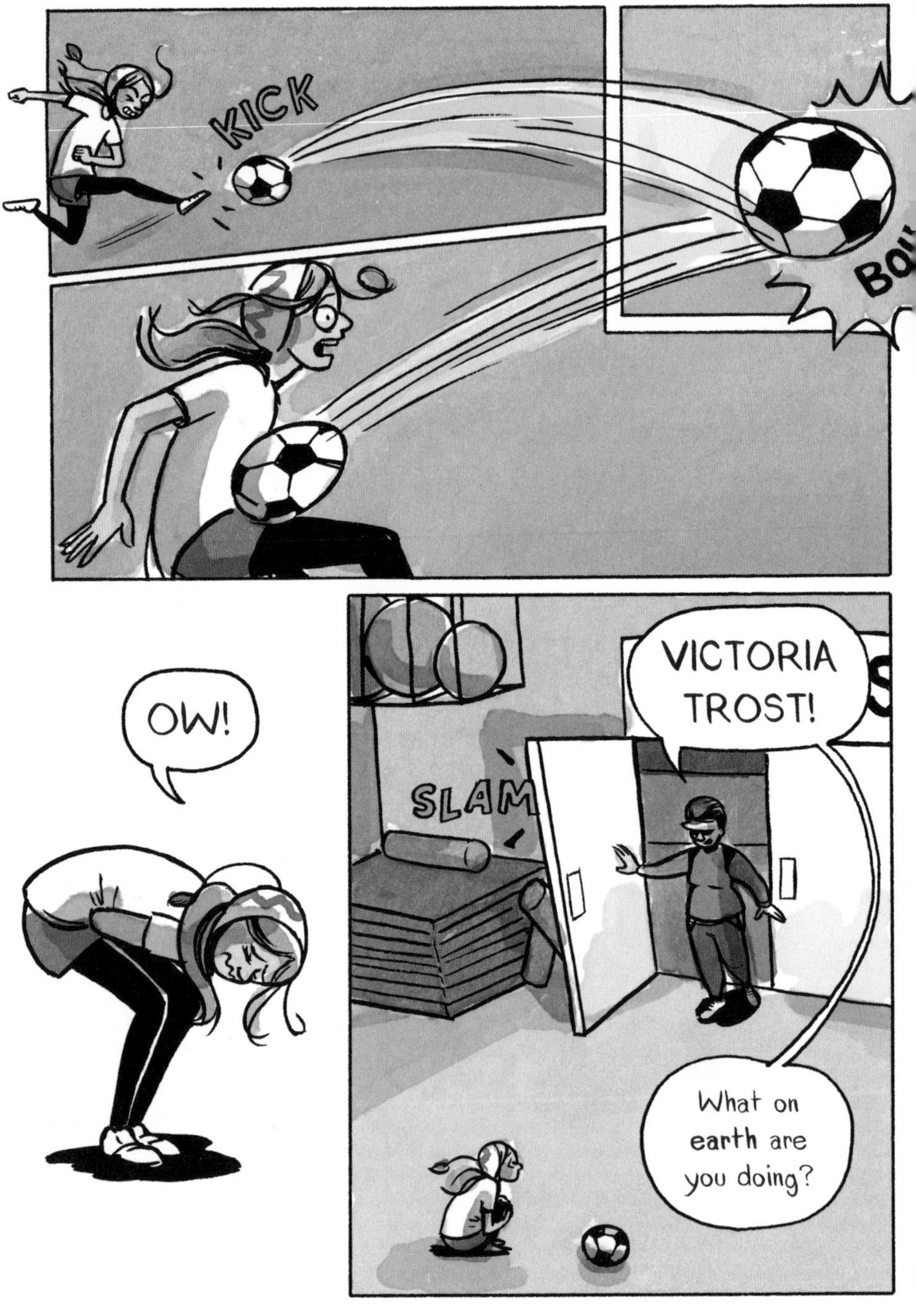
KICK
OW!
SLAM
VICTORIA TROST!
What on **earth** are you doing?

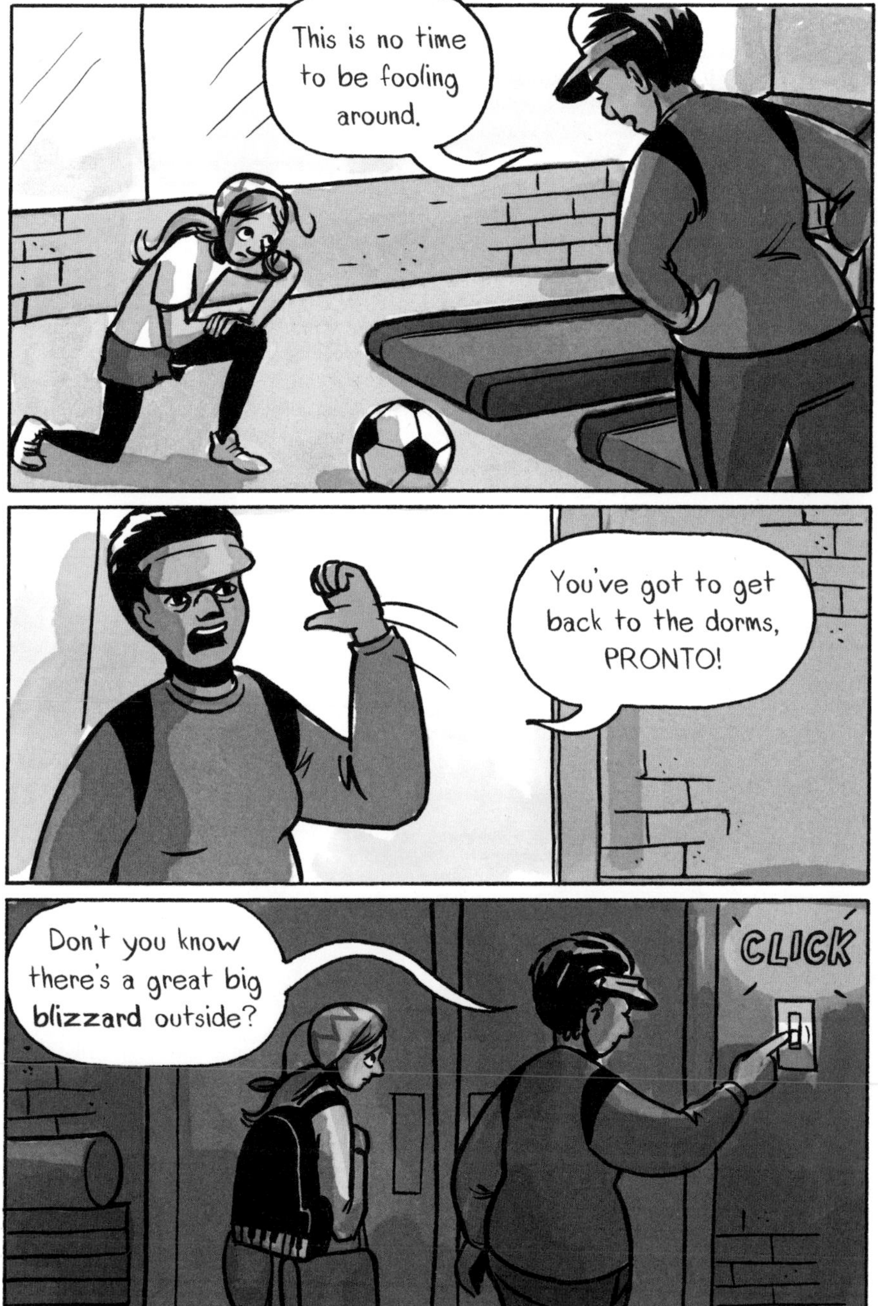
This is no time to be fooling around.
You've got to get back to the dorms, PRONTO!
Don't you know there's a great big **blizzard** outside?
CLICK

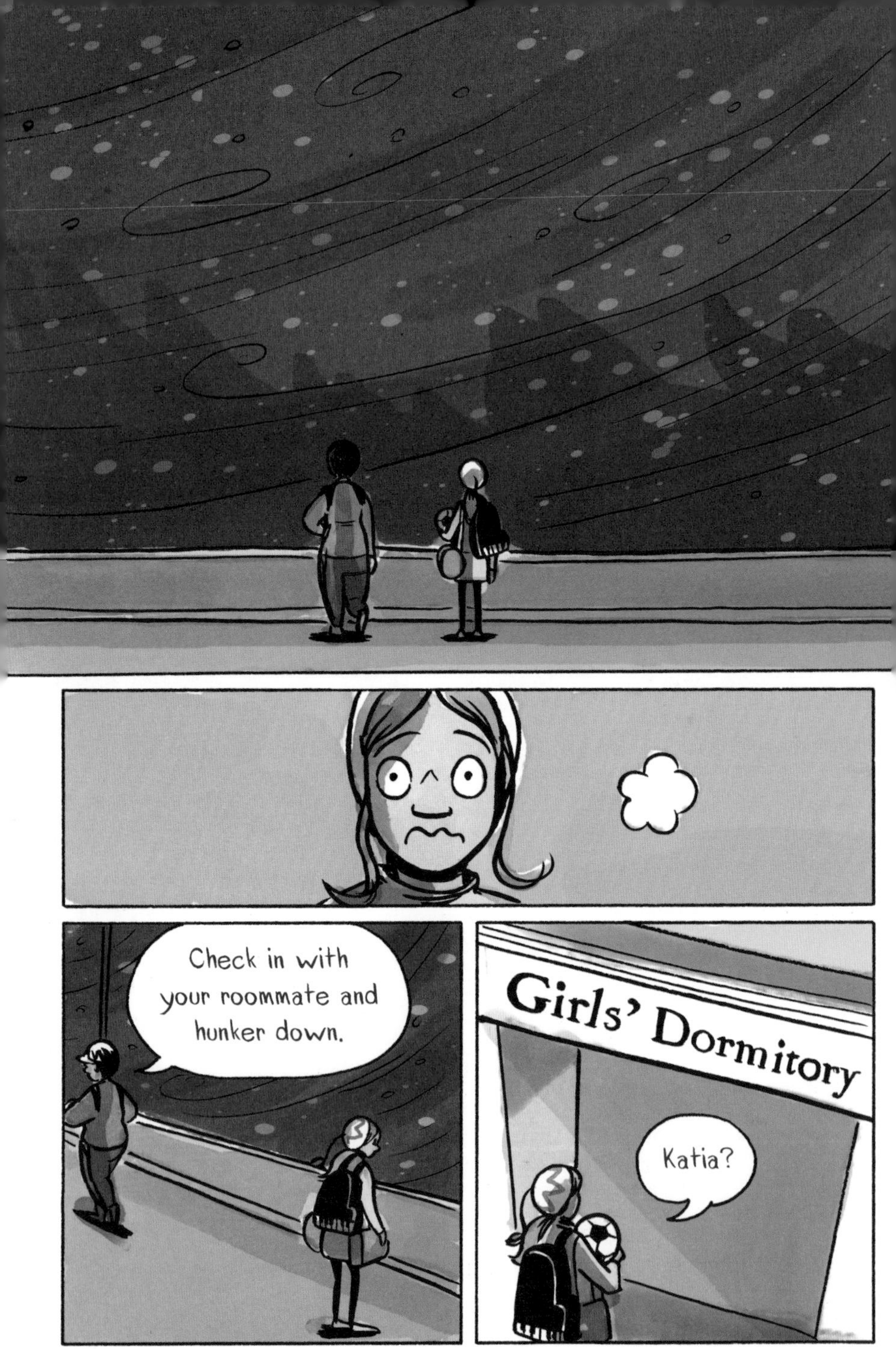
Check in with your roommate and hunker down.
Girls' Dormitory
Katia?

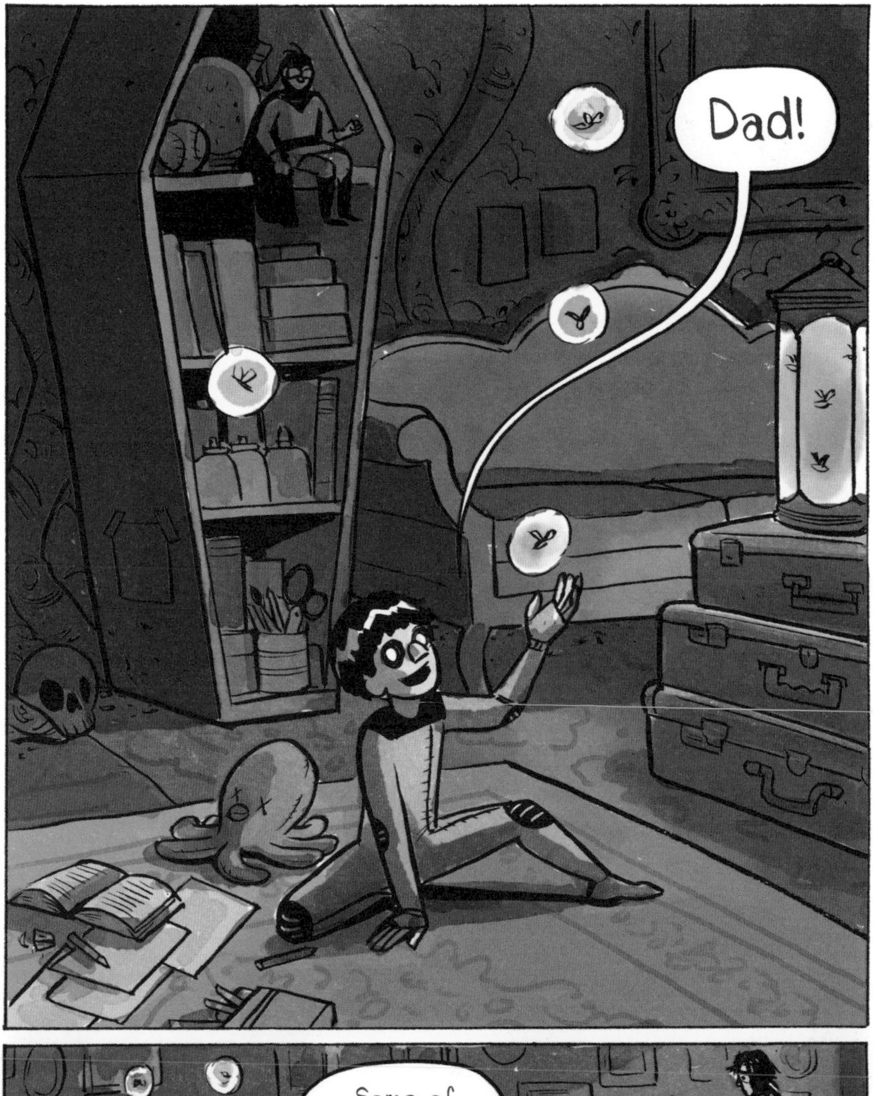
Dad!

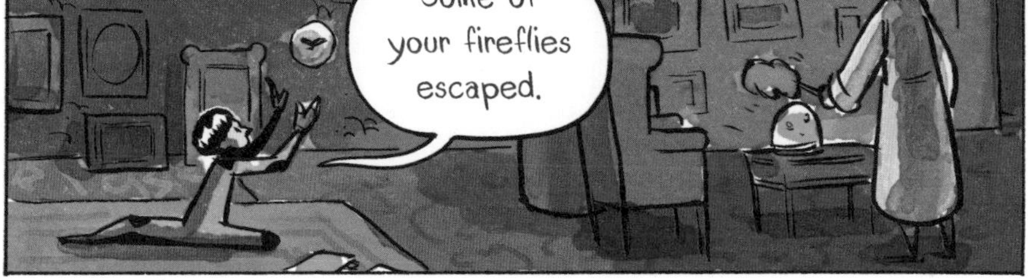
Some of your fireflies escaped.

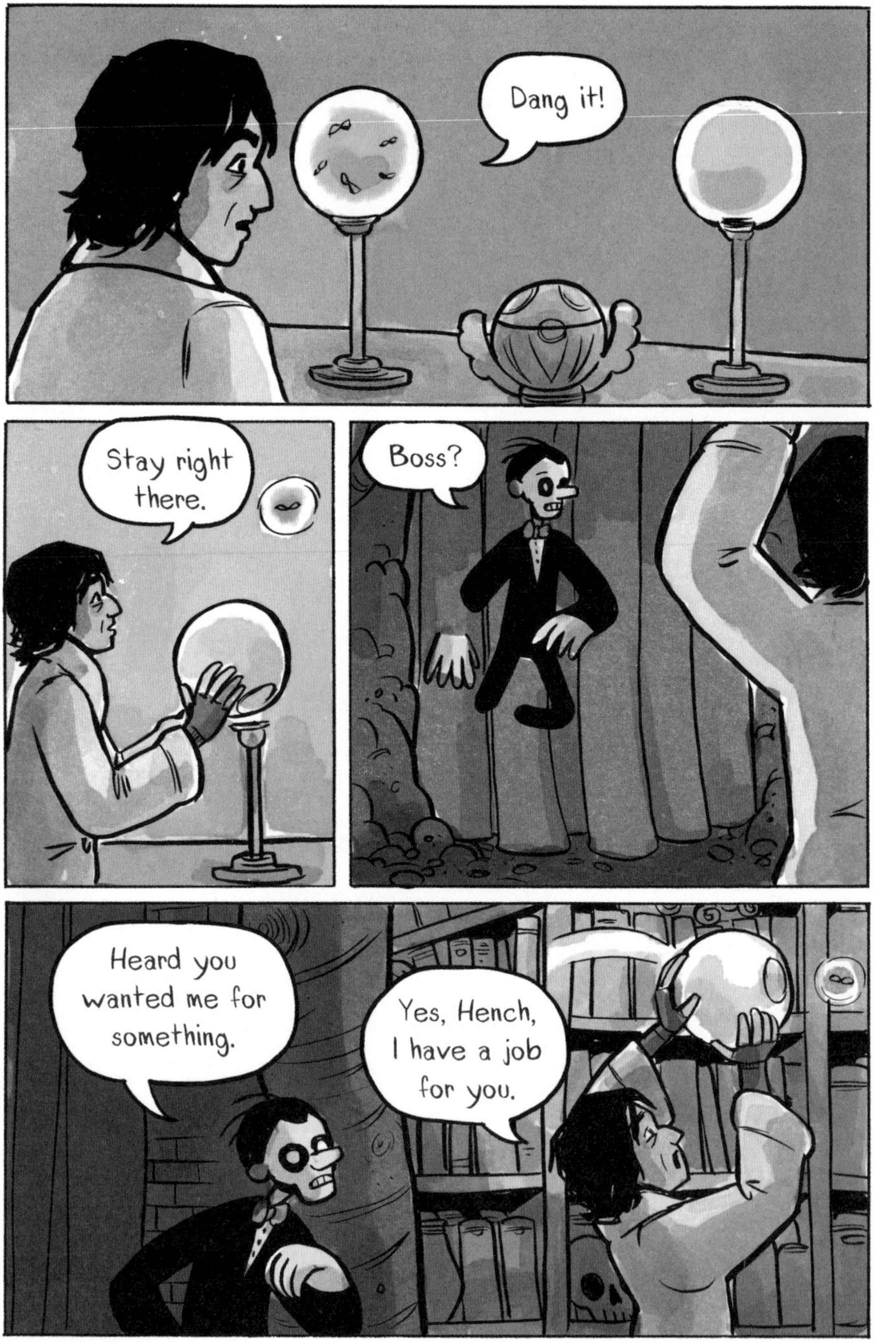
Dang it!
Stay right there.
Boss?
Heard you wanted me for something.
Yes, Hench, I have a job for you.

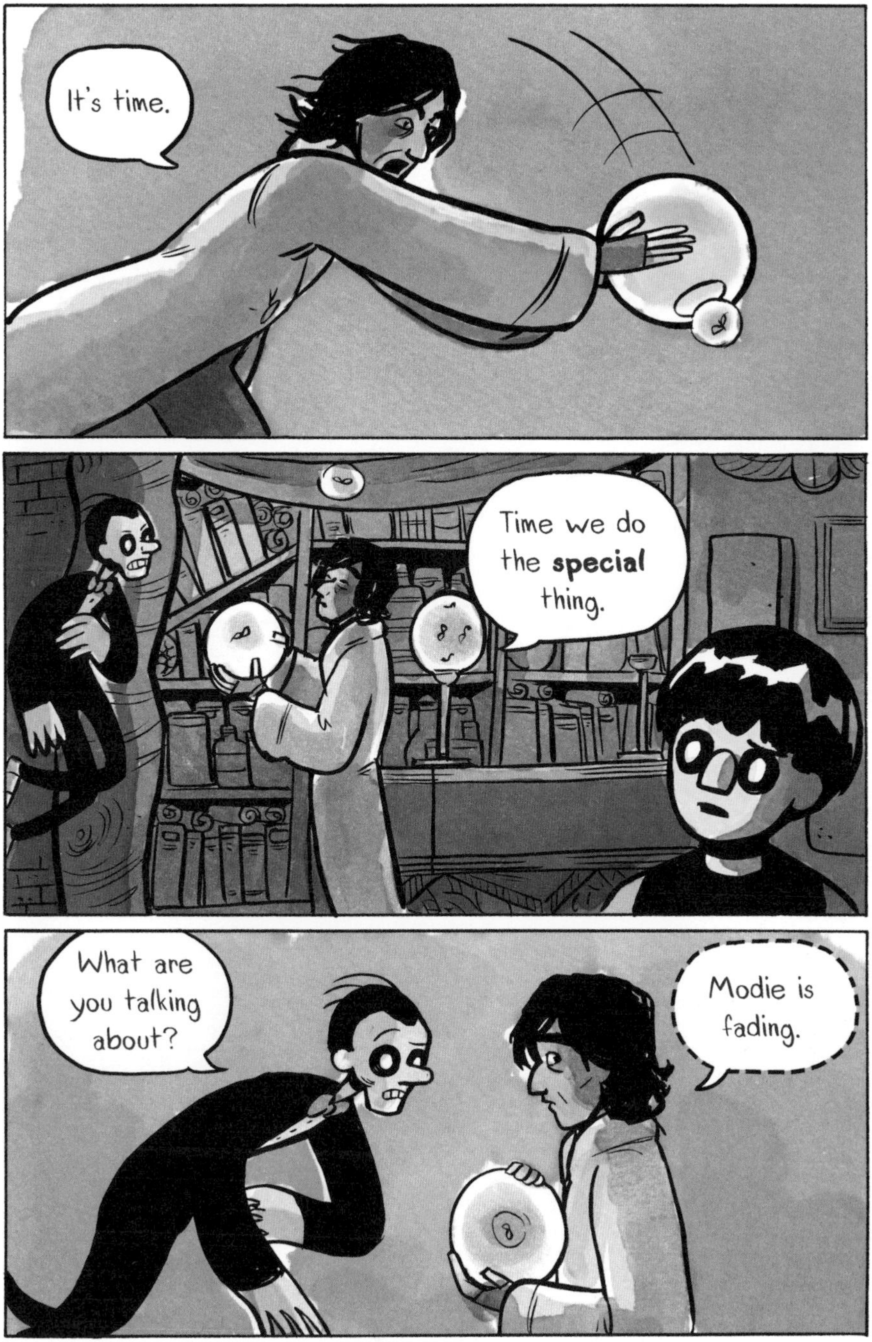
It's time.
Time we do the **special** thing.
What are you talking about?
Modie is fading.

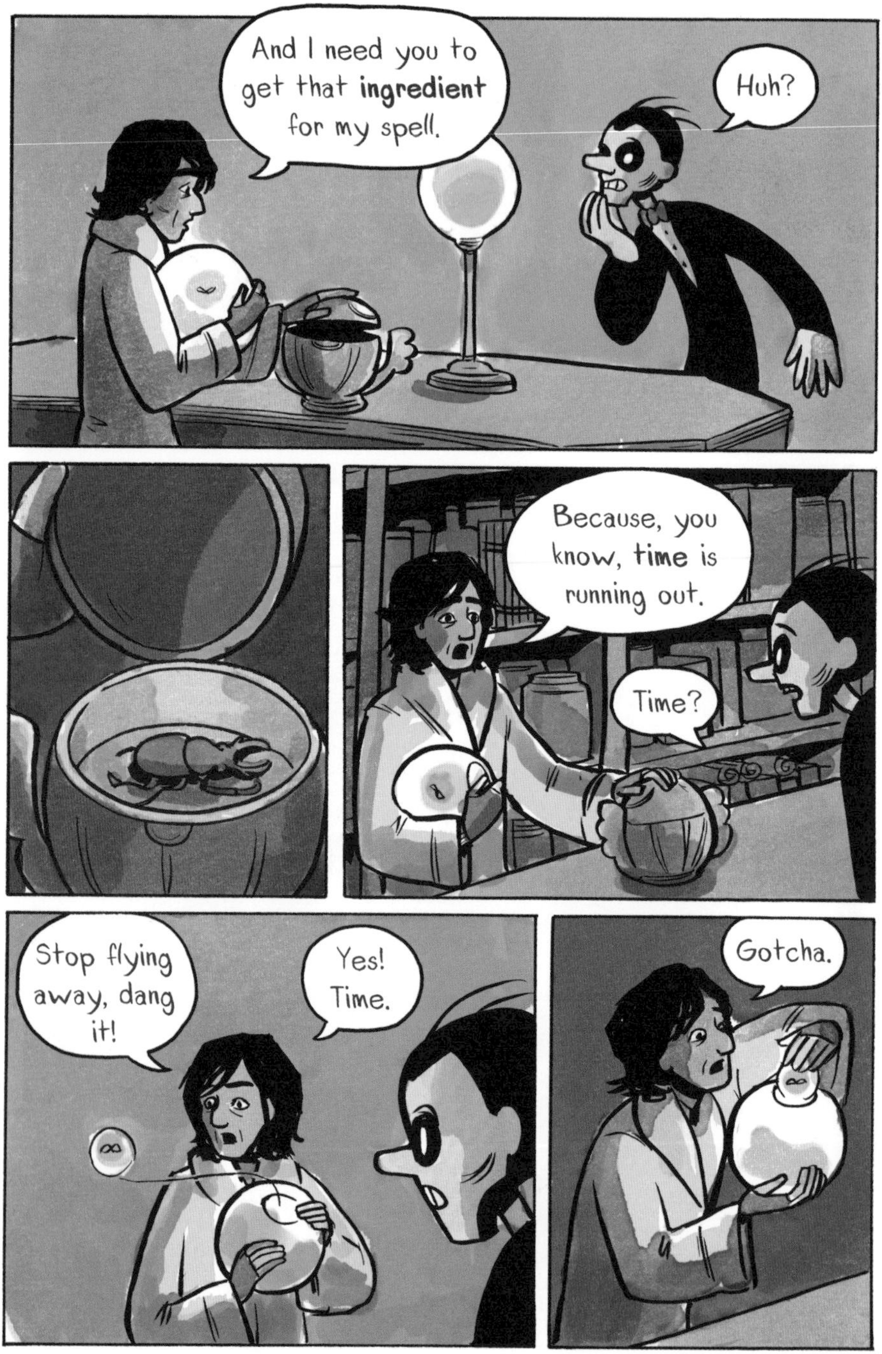
And I need you to get that **ingredient** for my spell.
Huh?
Because, you know, **time** is running out.
Time?
Stop flying away, dang it!
Yes! Time.
Gotcha.

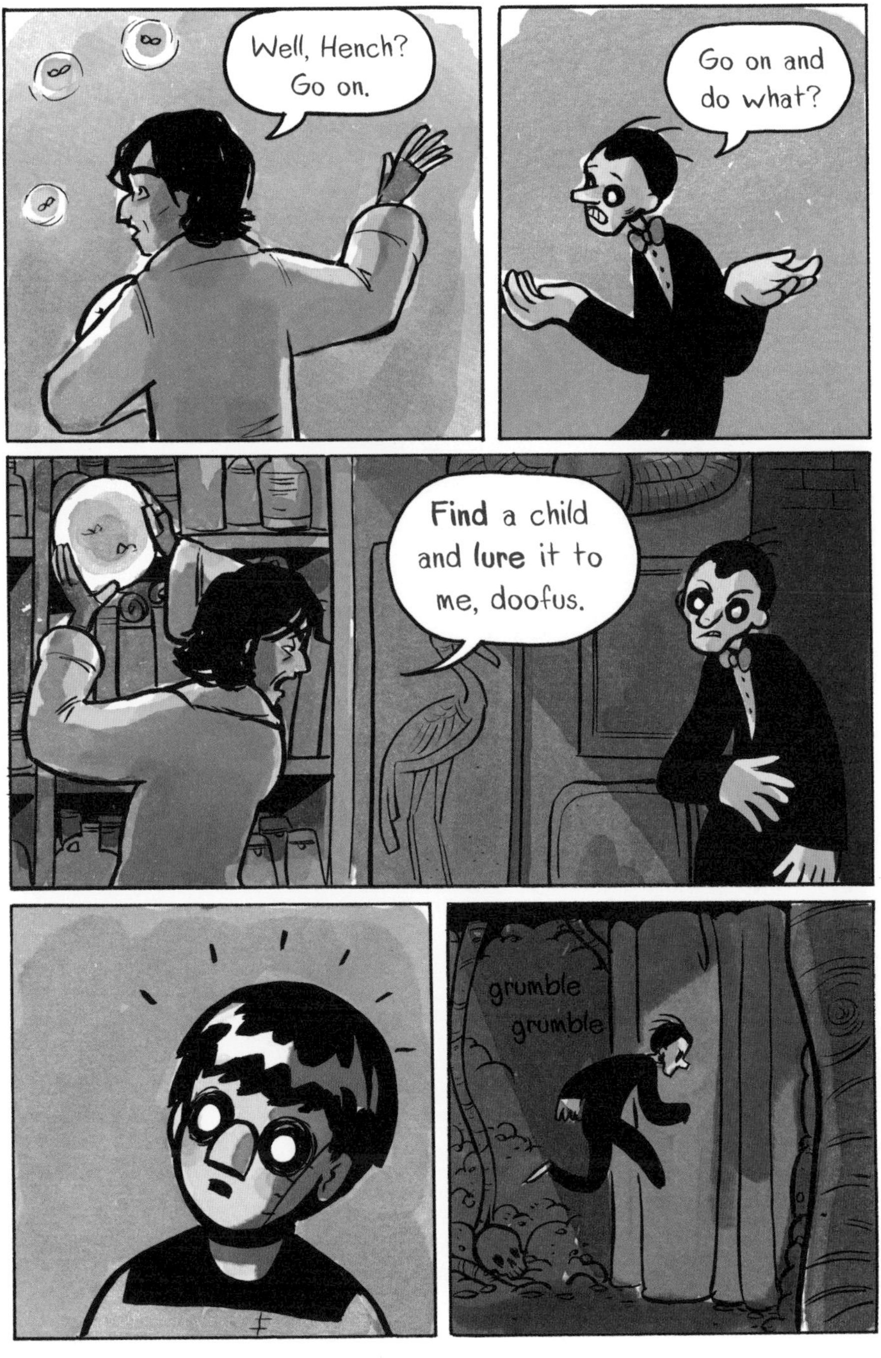
Well, Hench? Go on.
Go on and do what?
Find a child and lure it to me, doofus.
grumble
grumble

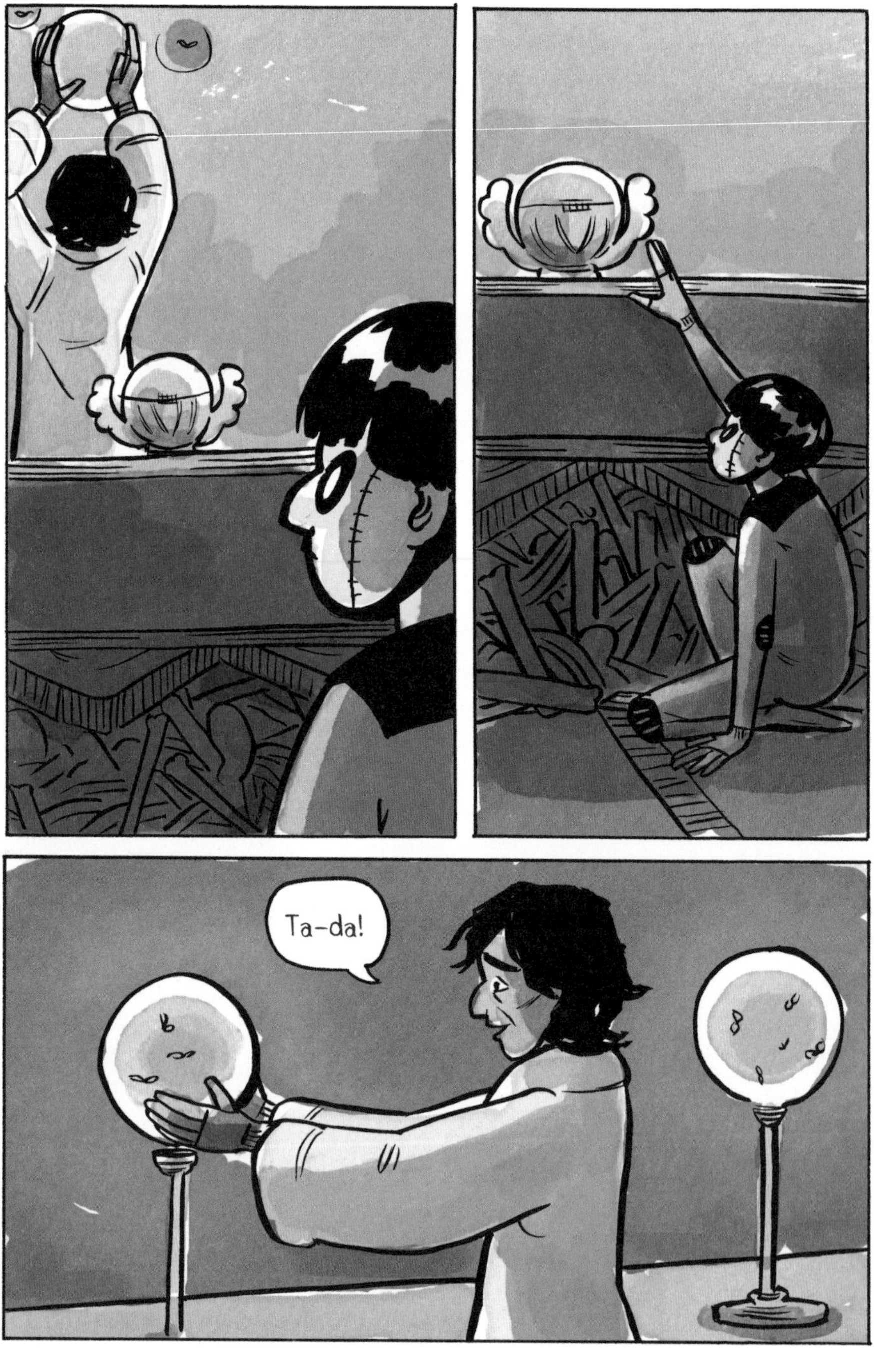
Ta-da!

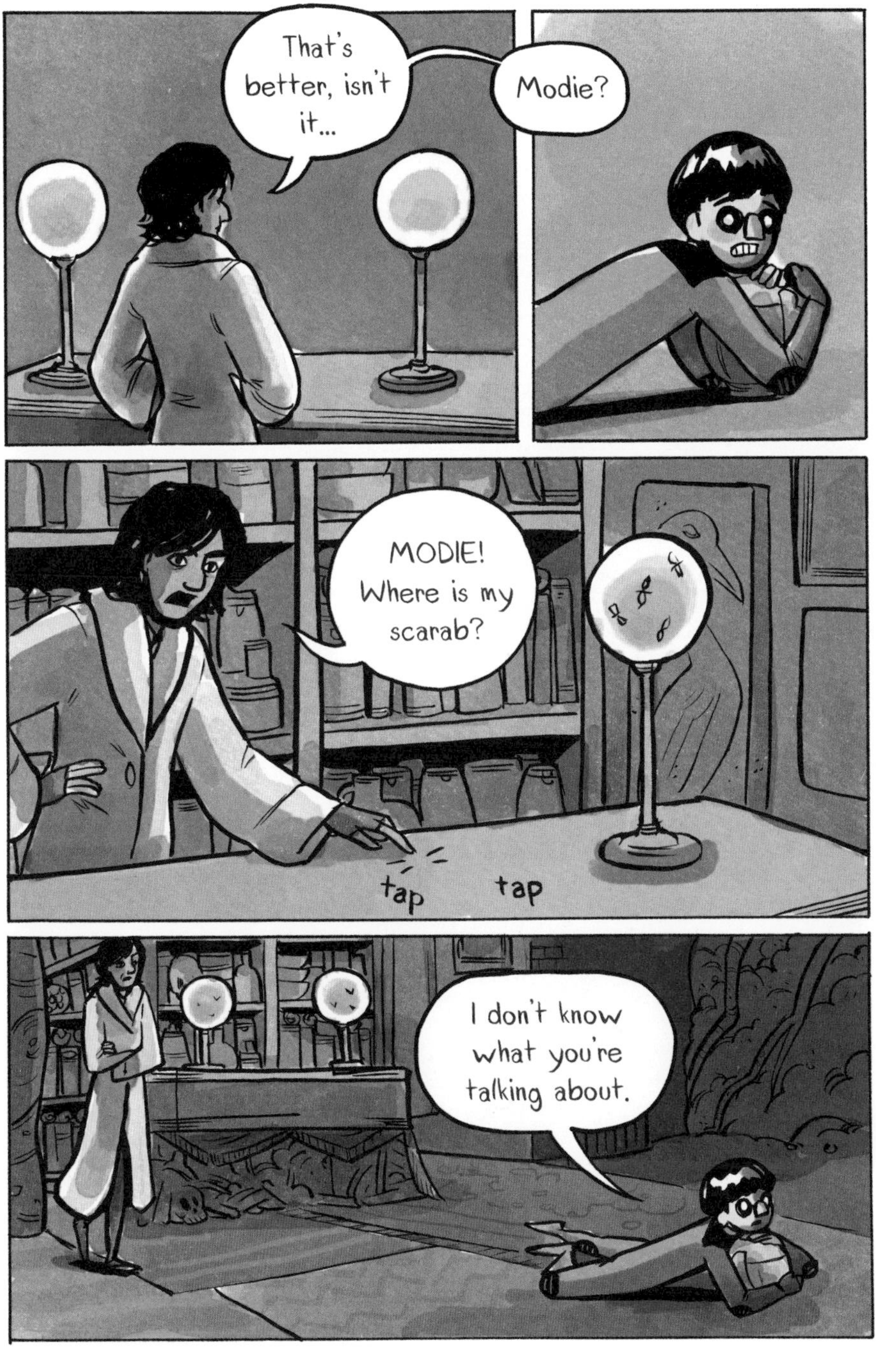
That's better, isn't it...
Modie?
MODIE! Where is my scarab?
tap tap
I don't know what you're talking about.

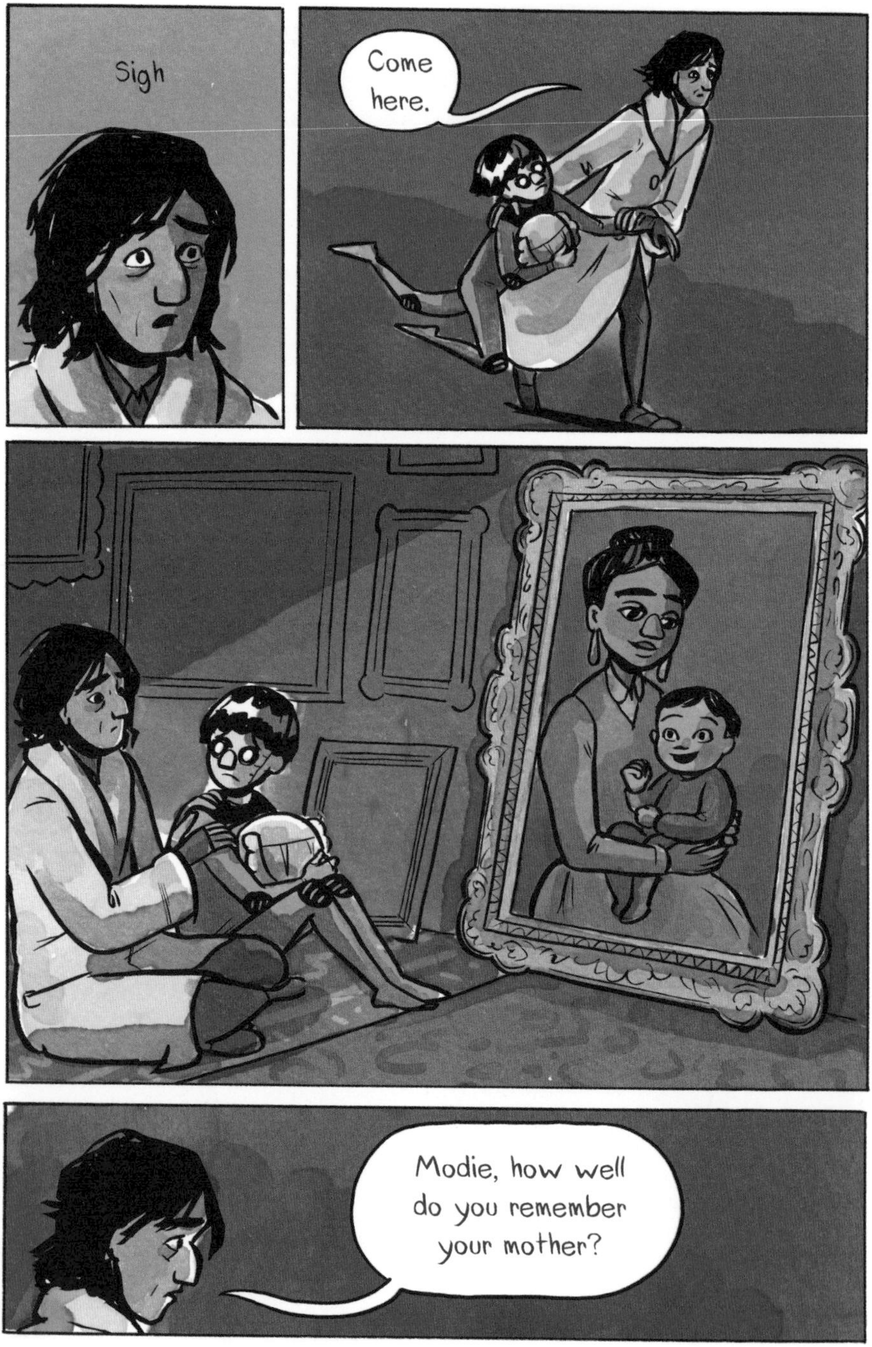
Sigh
Come here.
Modie, how well do you remember your mother?

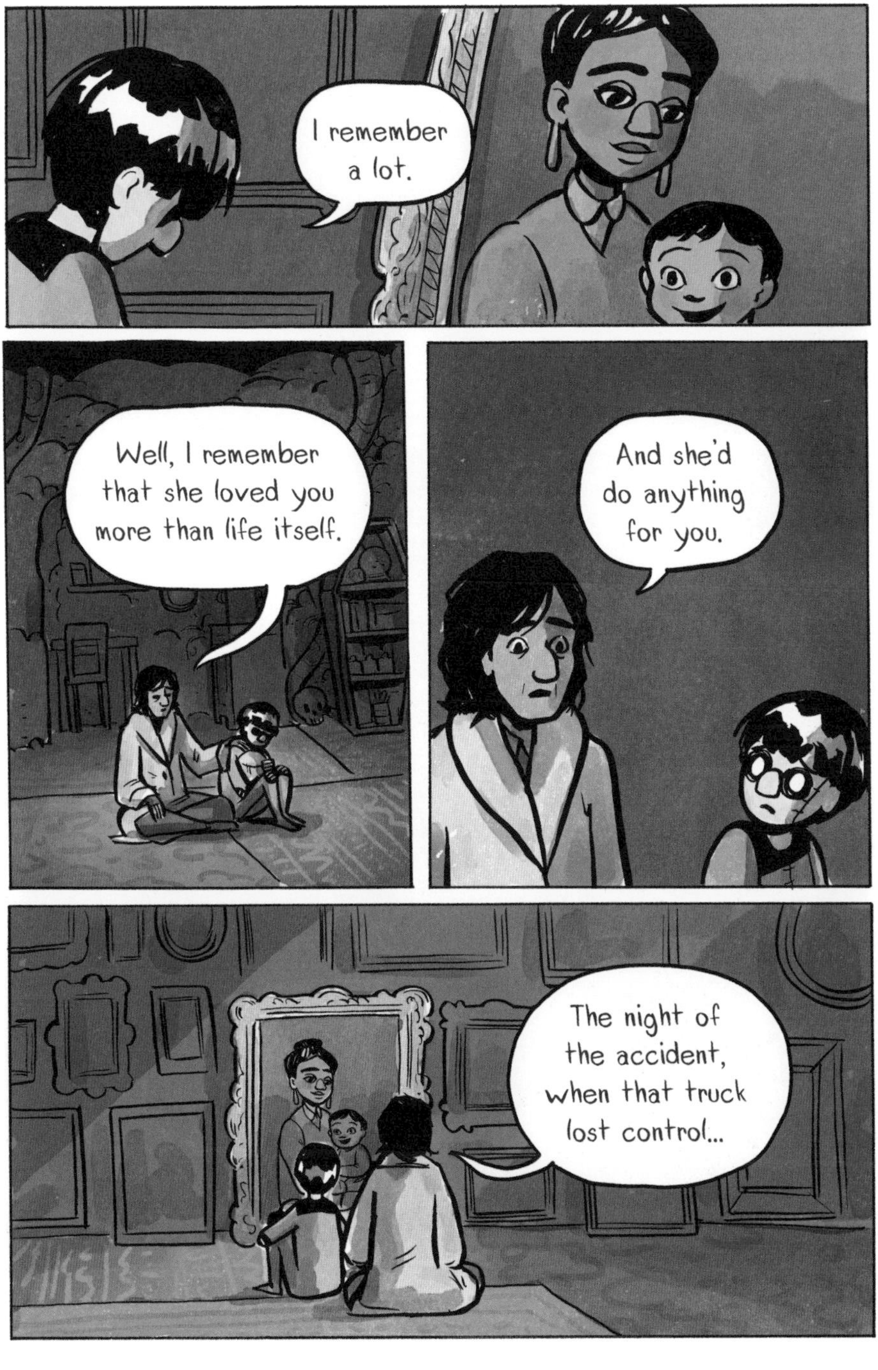
I remember a lot.
Well, I remember that she loved you more than life itself.
And she'd do anything for you.
The night of the accident, when that truck lost control...

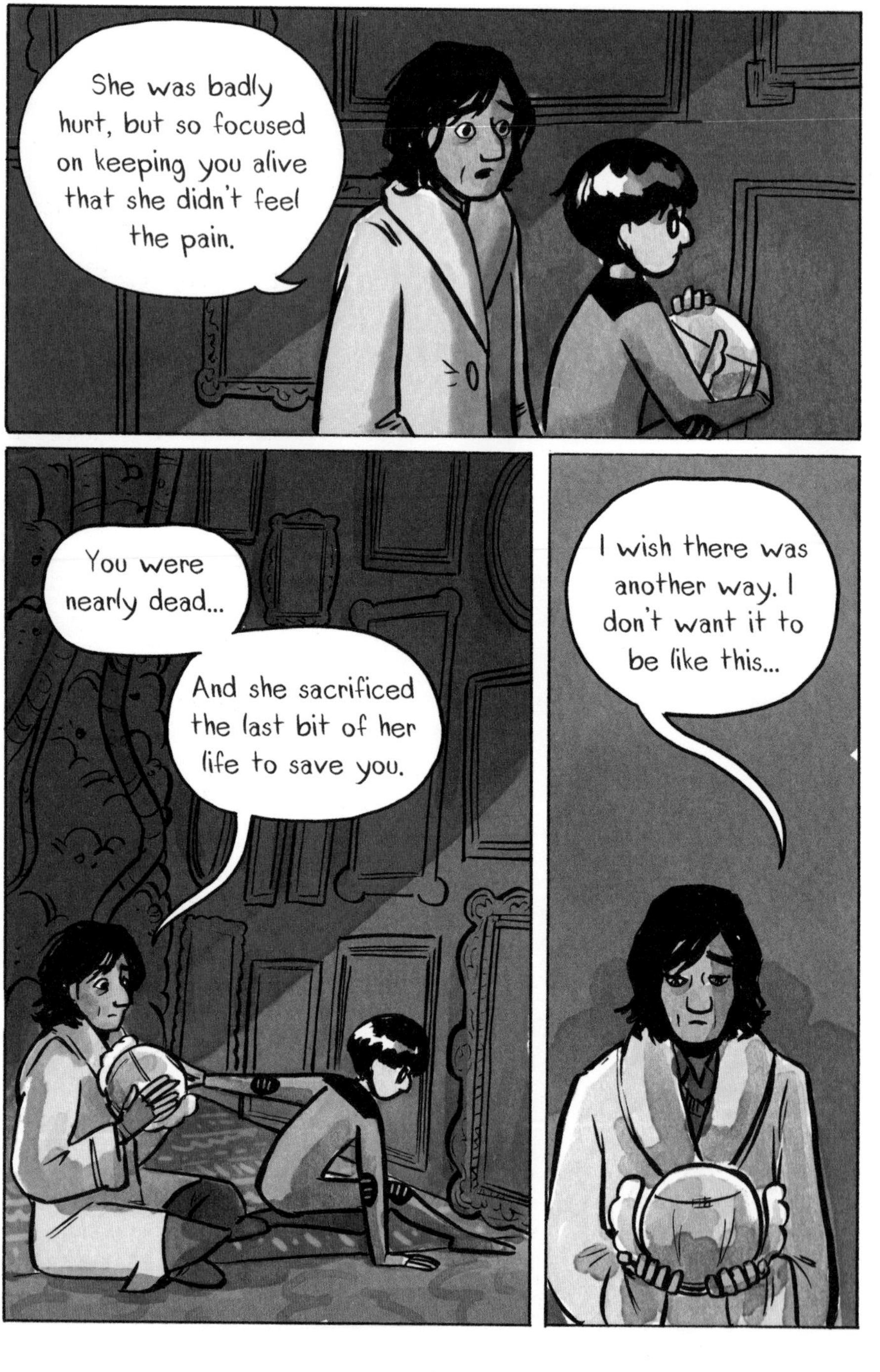
She was badly hurt, but so focused on keeping you alive that she didn't feel the pain.
You were nearly dead...
And she sacrificed the last bit of her life to save you.
I wish there was another way. I don't want it to be like this...

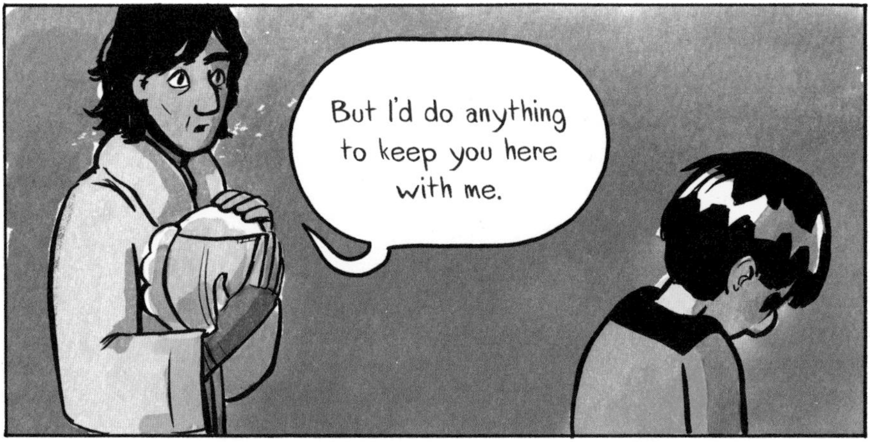
But I'd do anything to keep you here with me.

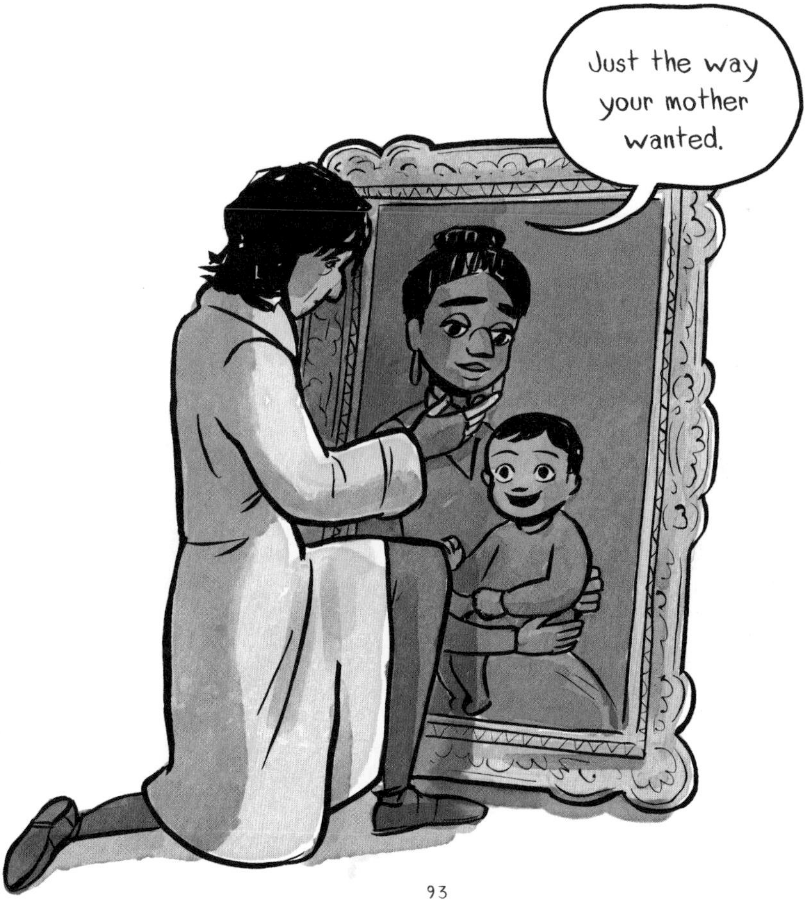
Just the way your mother wanted.

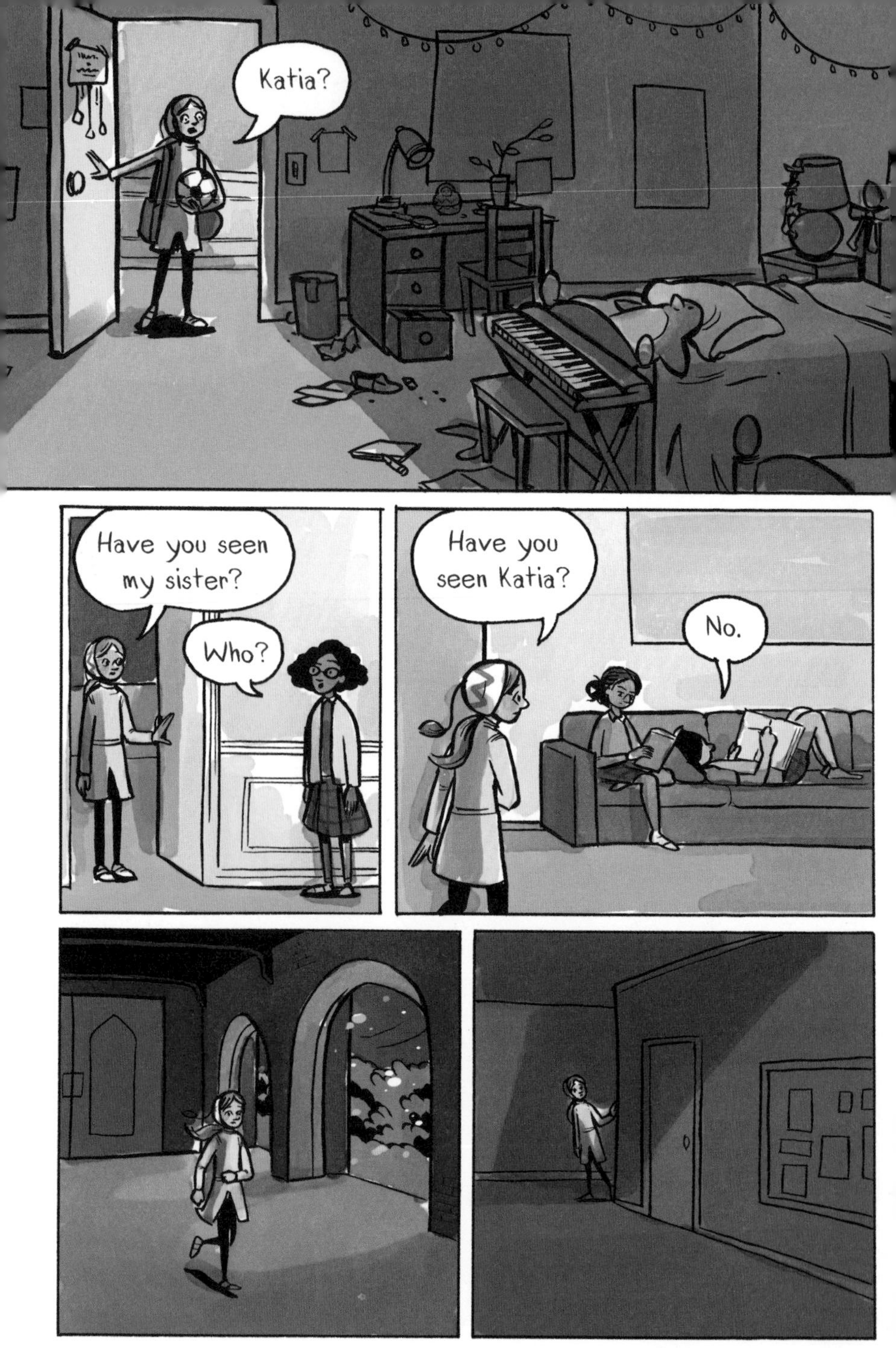
Katia?
Have you seen my sister?
Who?
Have you seen Katia?
No.

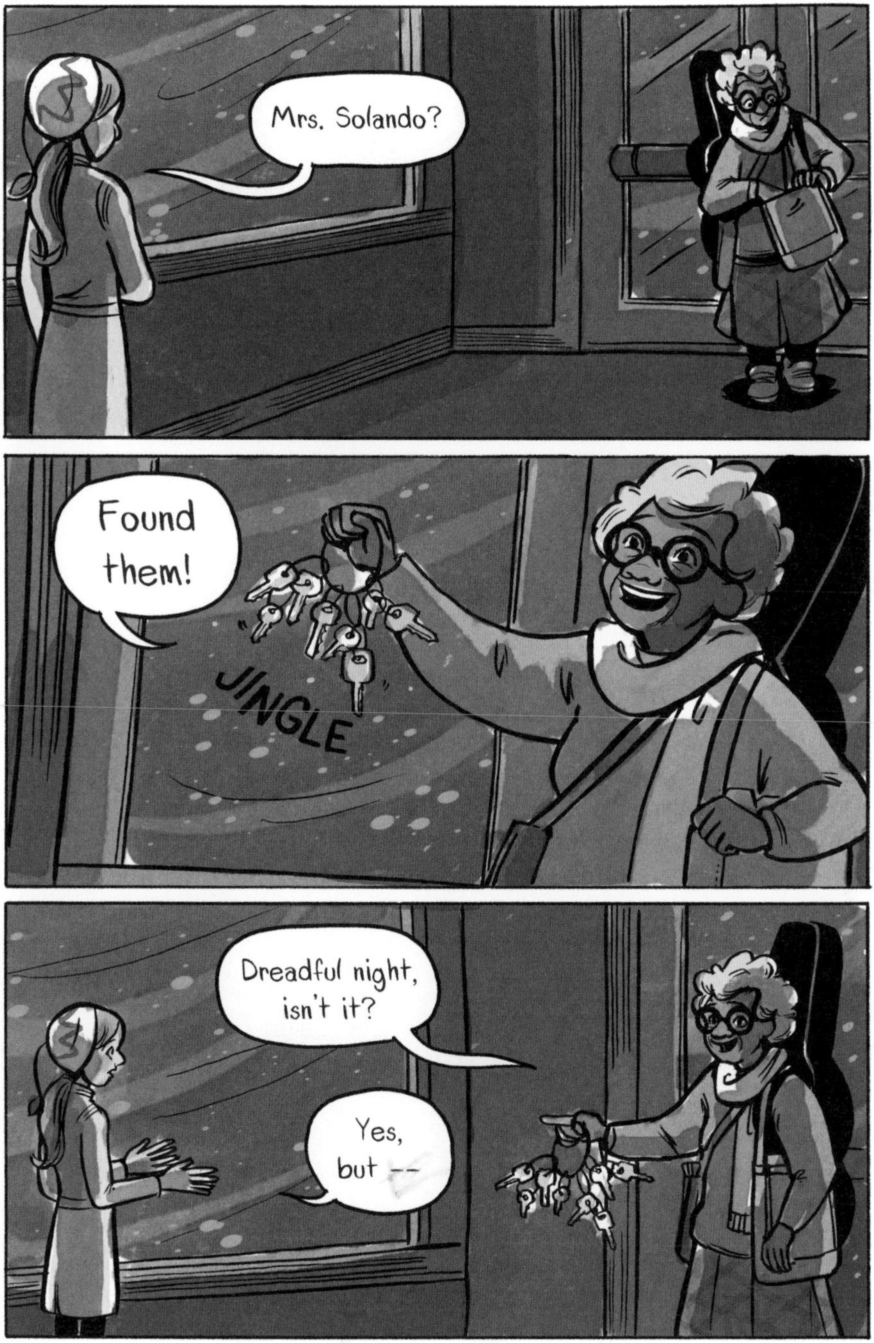
Mrs. Solando?
Found them!
JINGLE
Dreadful night, isn't it?
Yes, but --

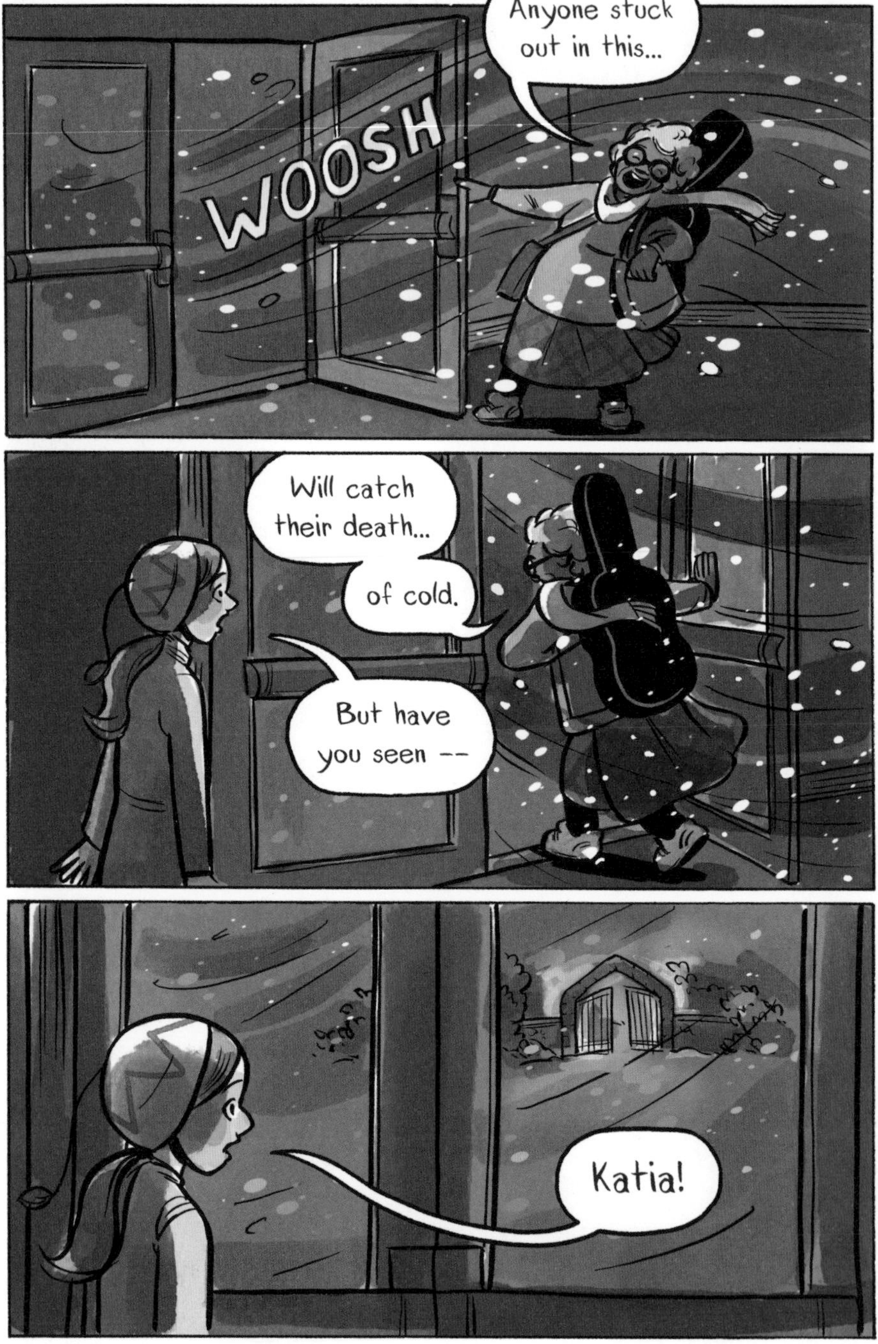
Anyone stuck out in this...
WOOSH
Will catch their death...
of cold.
But have you seen --
Katia!

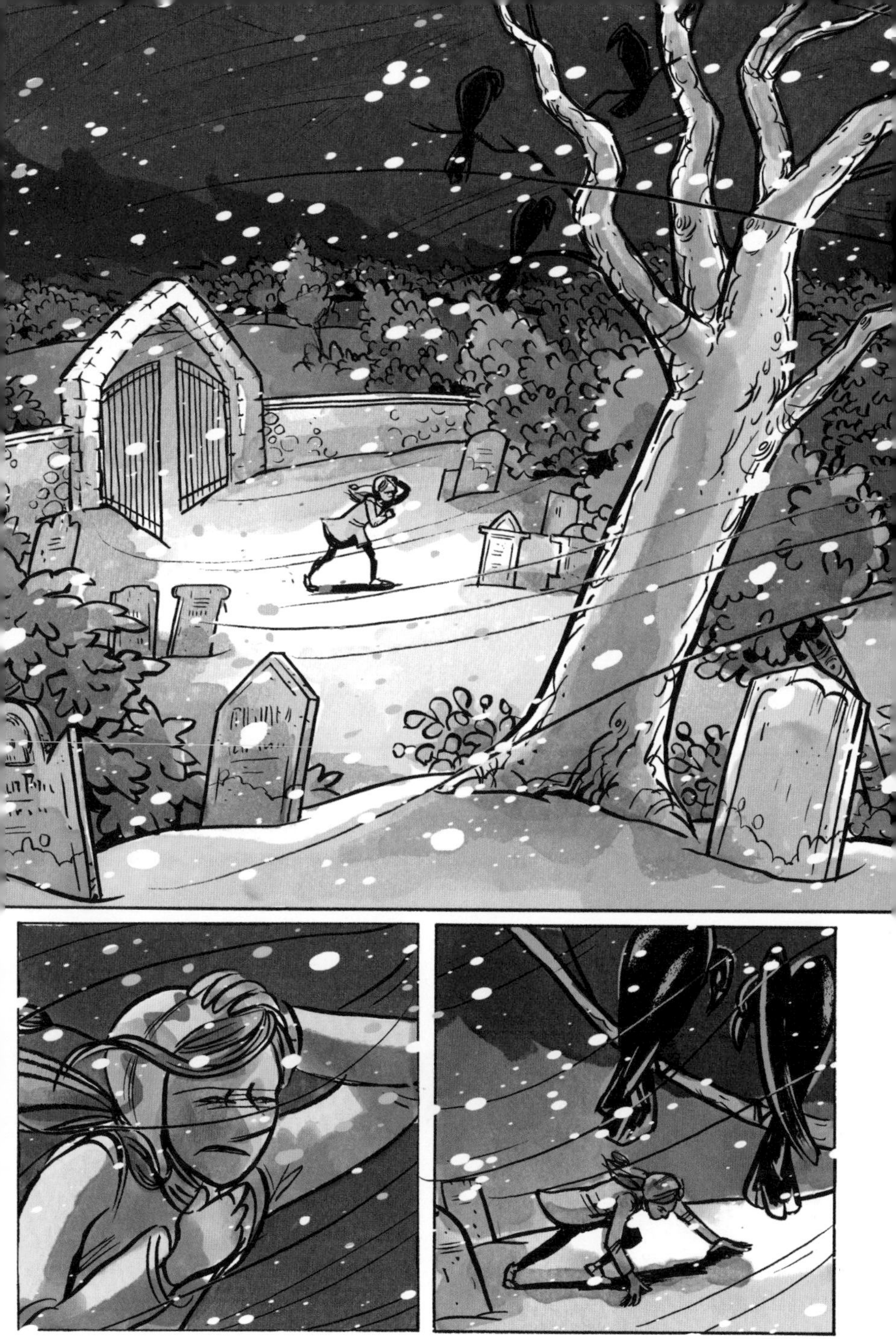

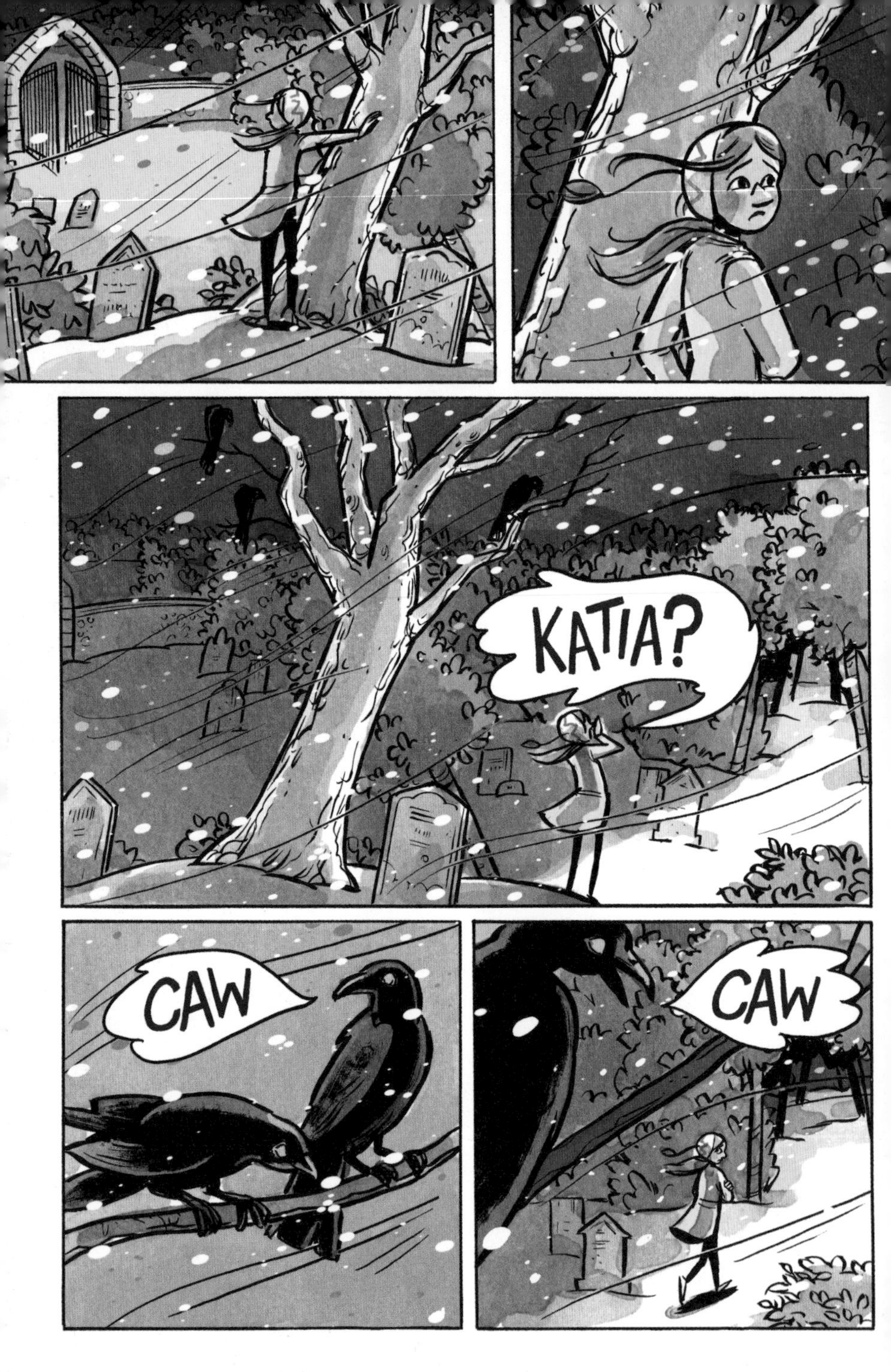
KATIA?
CAW
CAW

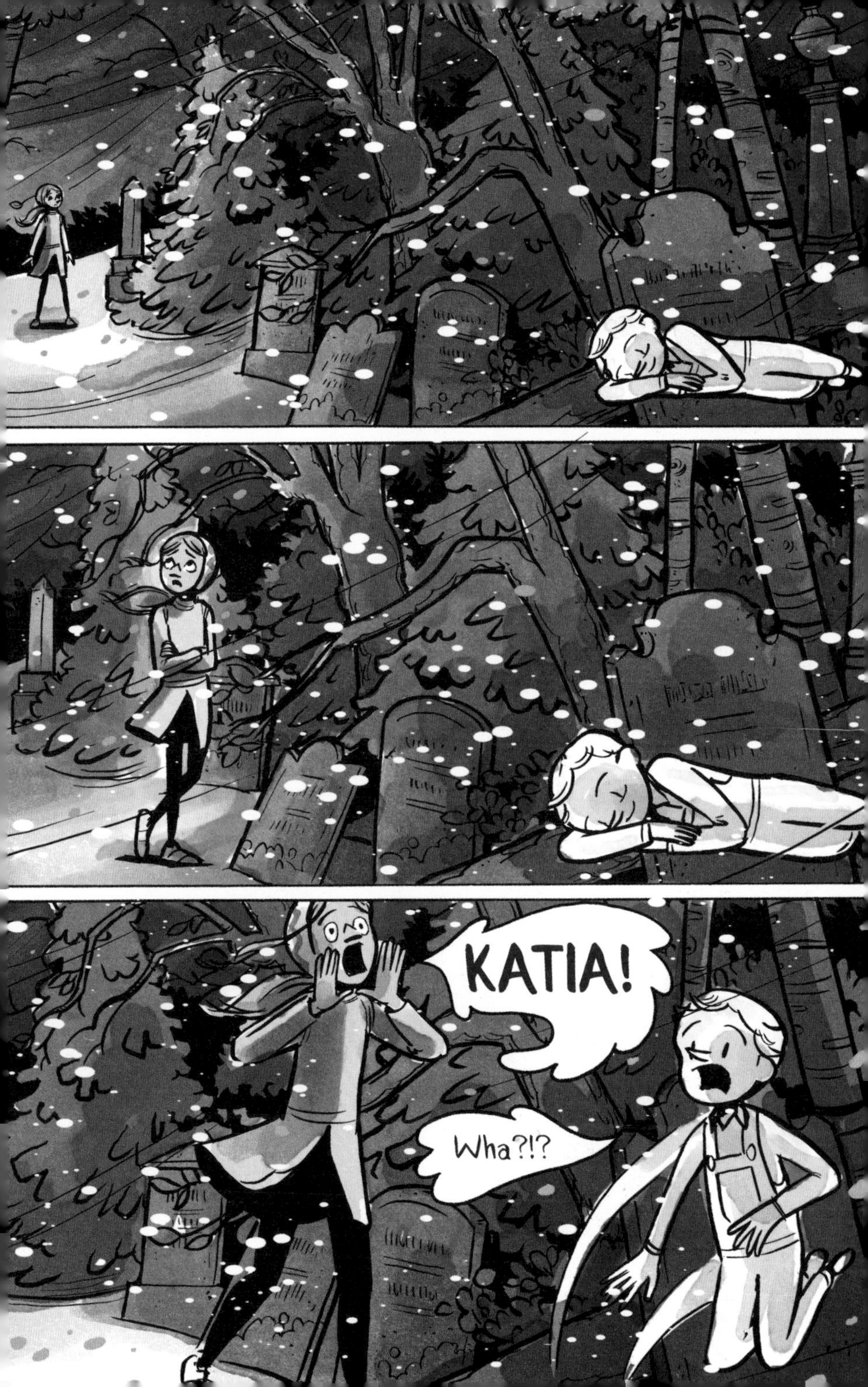
KATIA!
Wha?!?

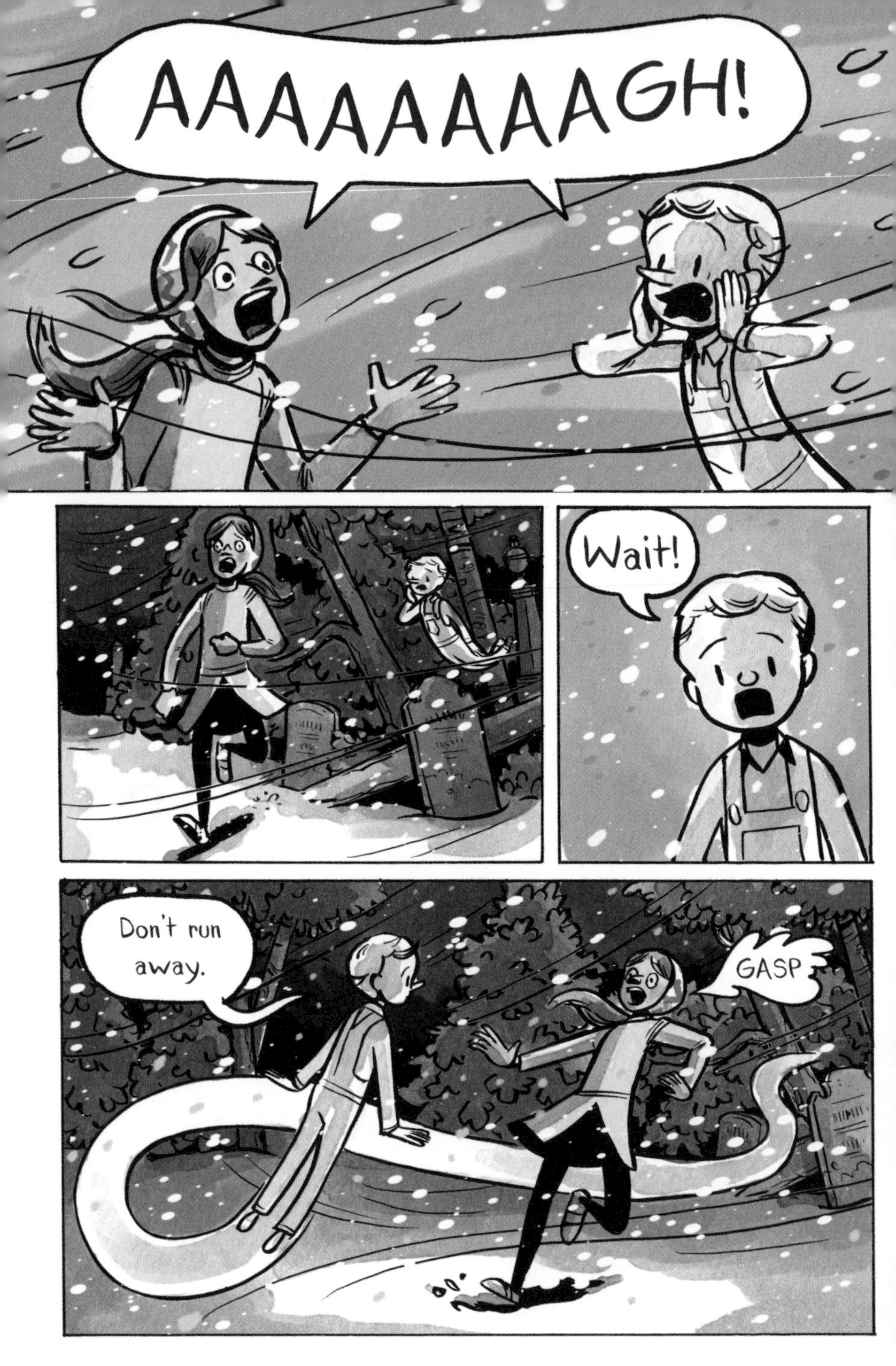
AAAAAAAAAGH!
Wait!
Don't run away.
GASP

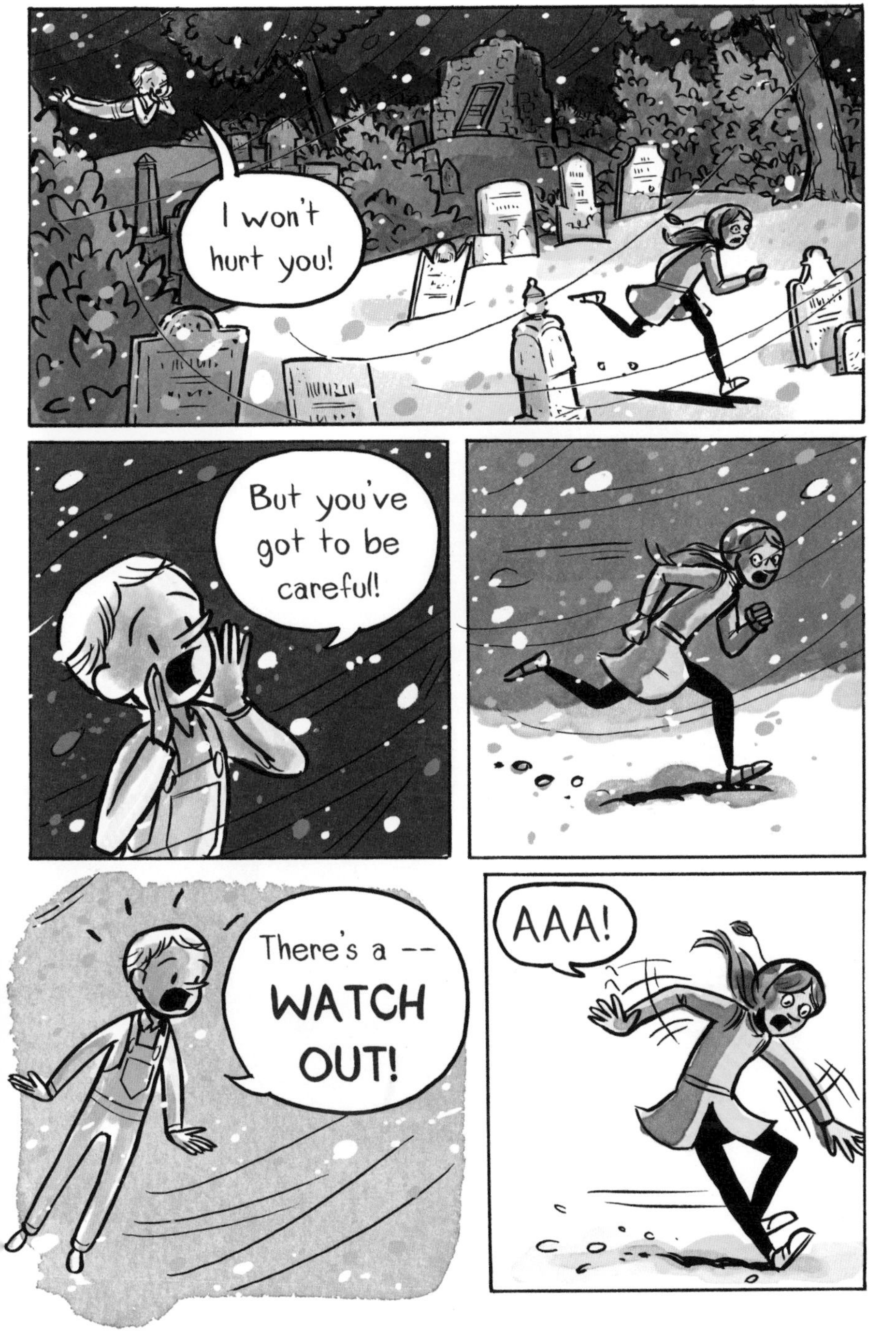
I won't hurt you!
But you've got to be careful!
There's a -- WATCH OUT!
AAA!

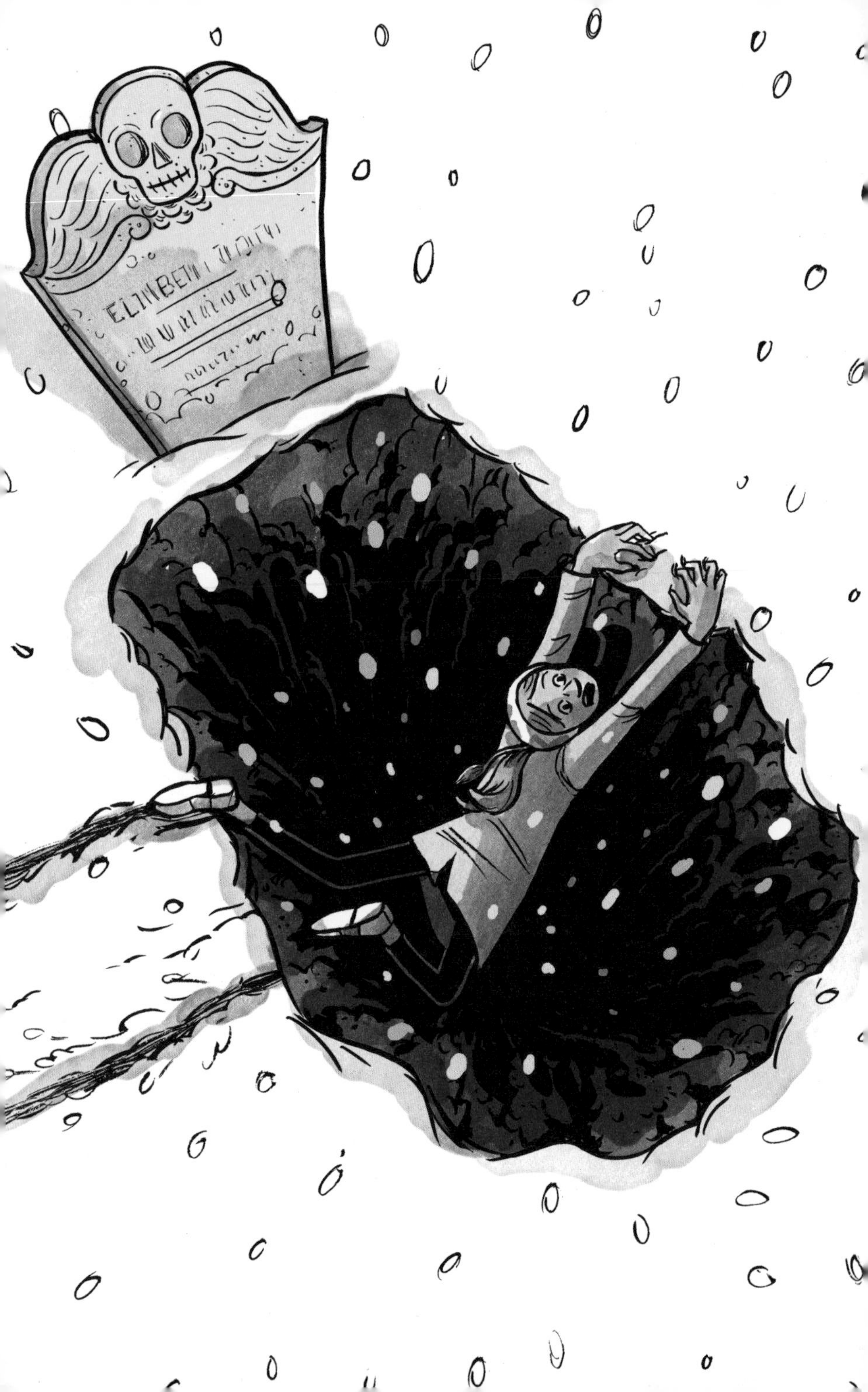

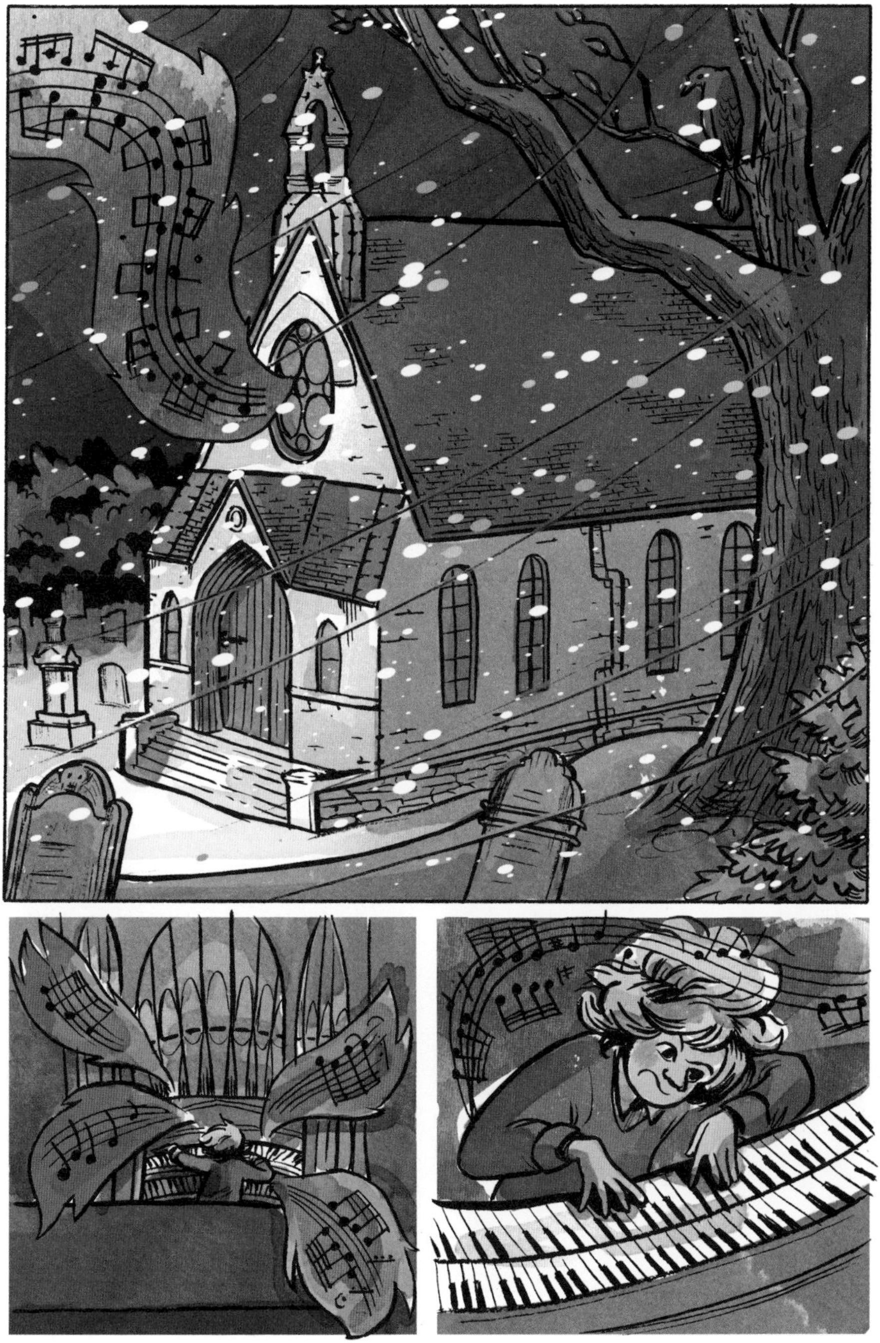

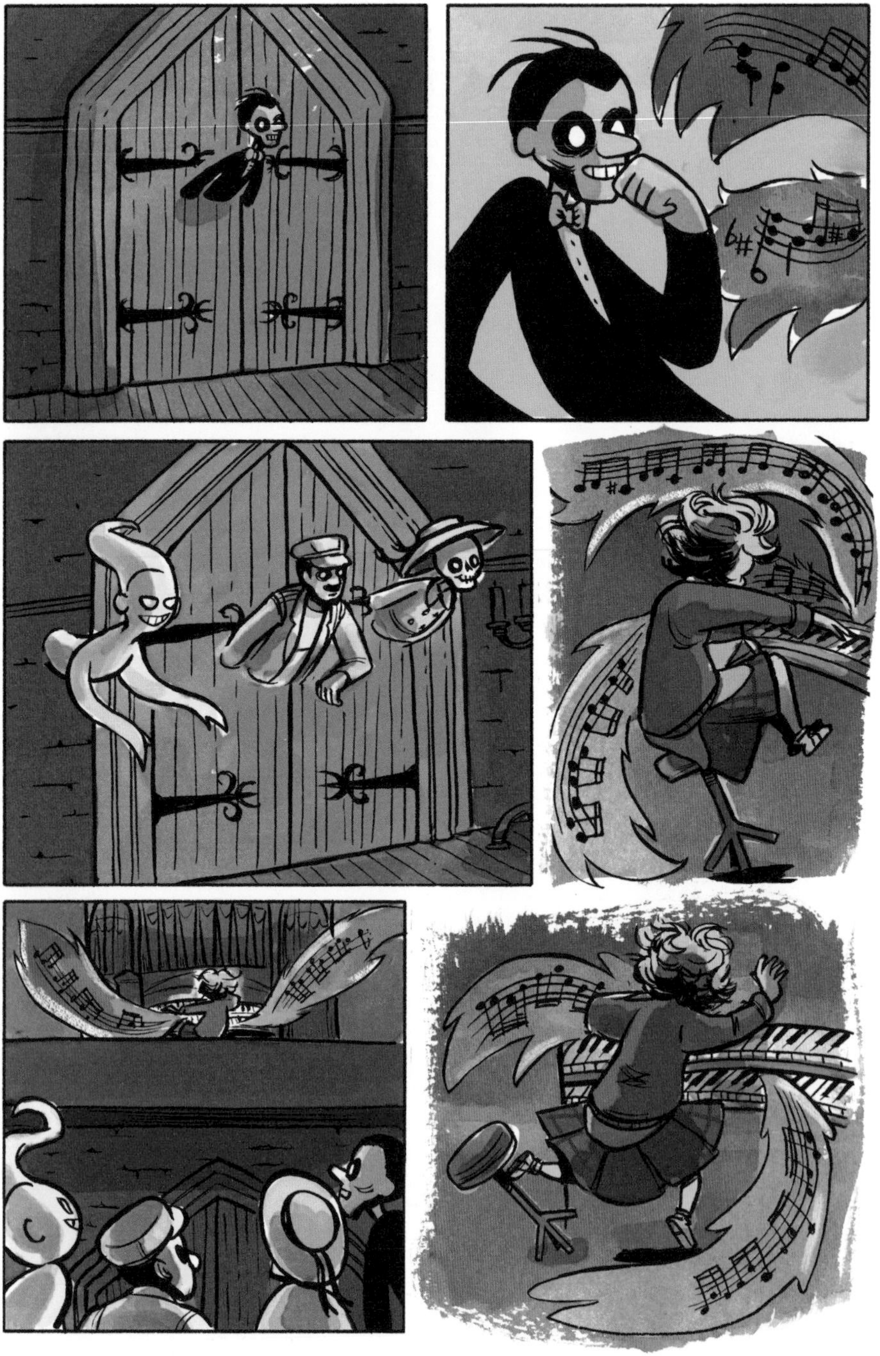

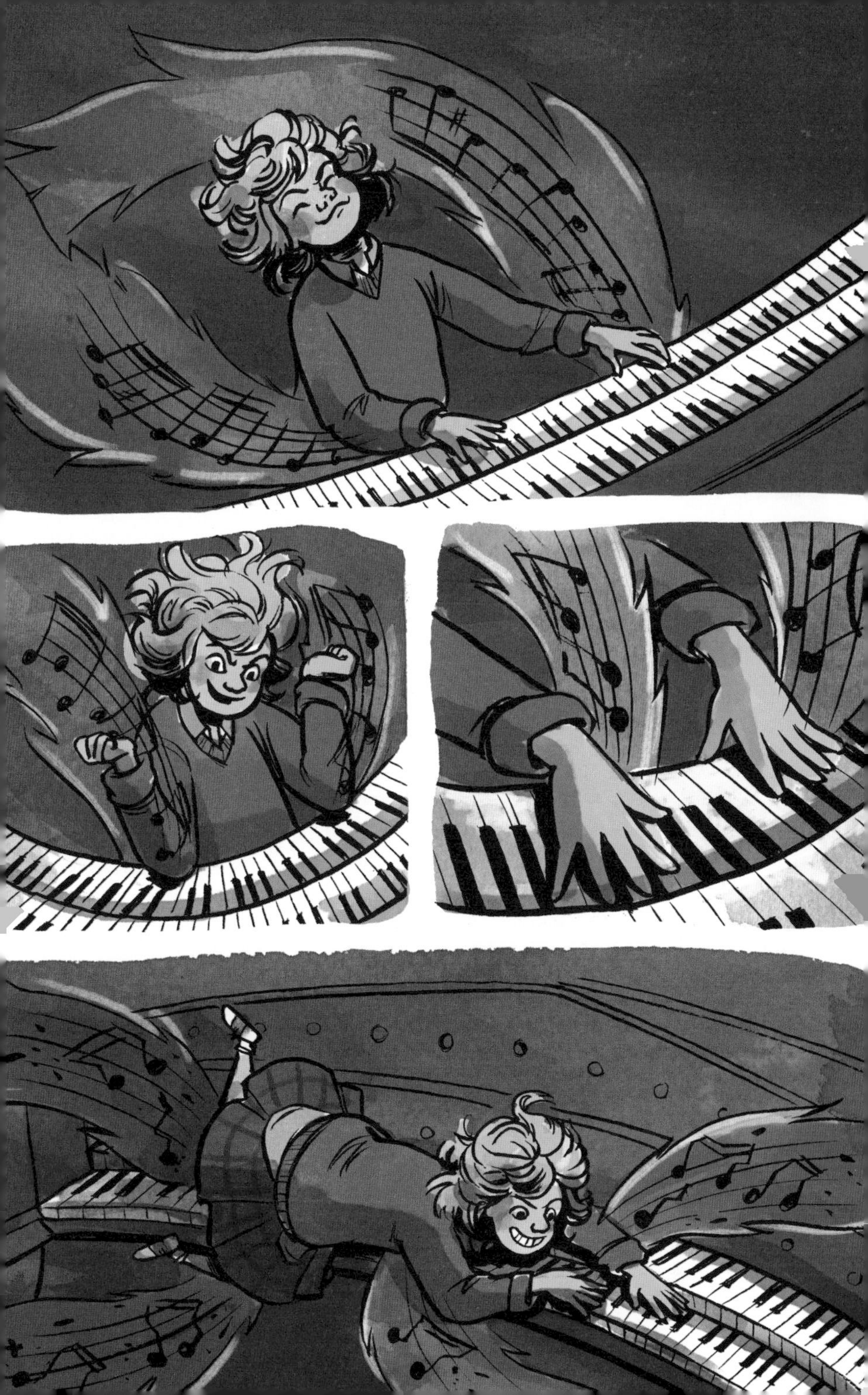

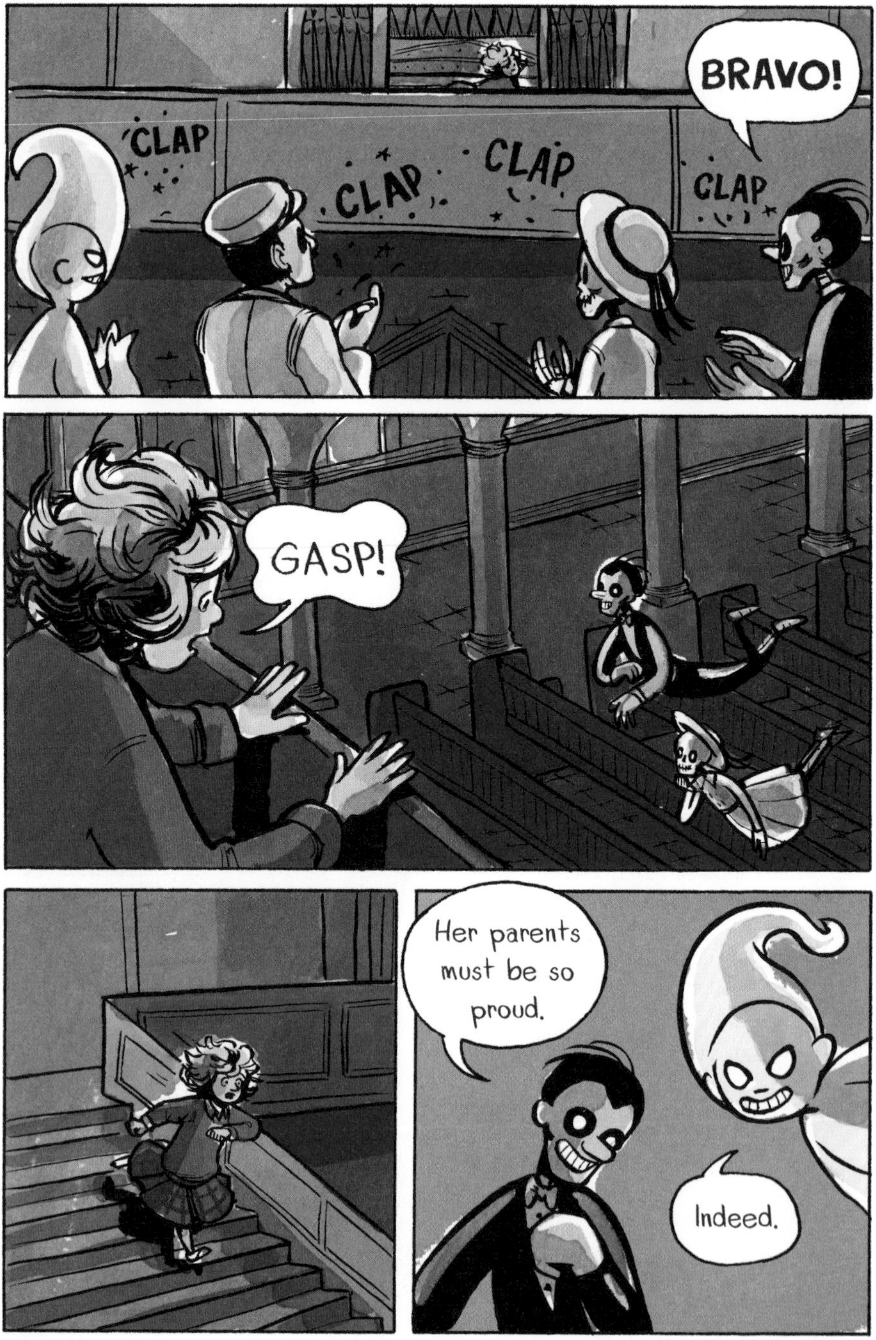
CLAP
CLAP
CLAP
CLAP
BRAVO!
GASP!
Her parents must be so proud.
Indeed.

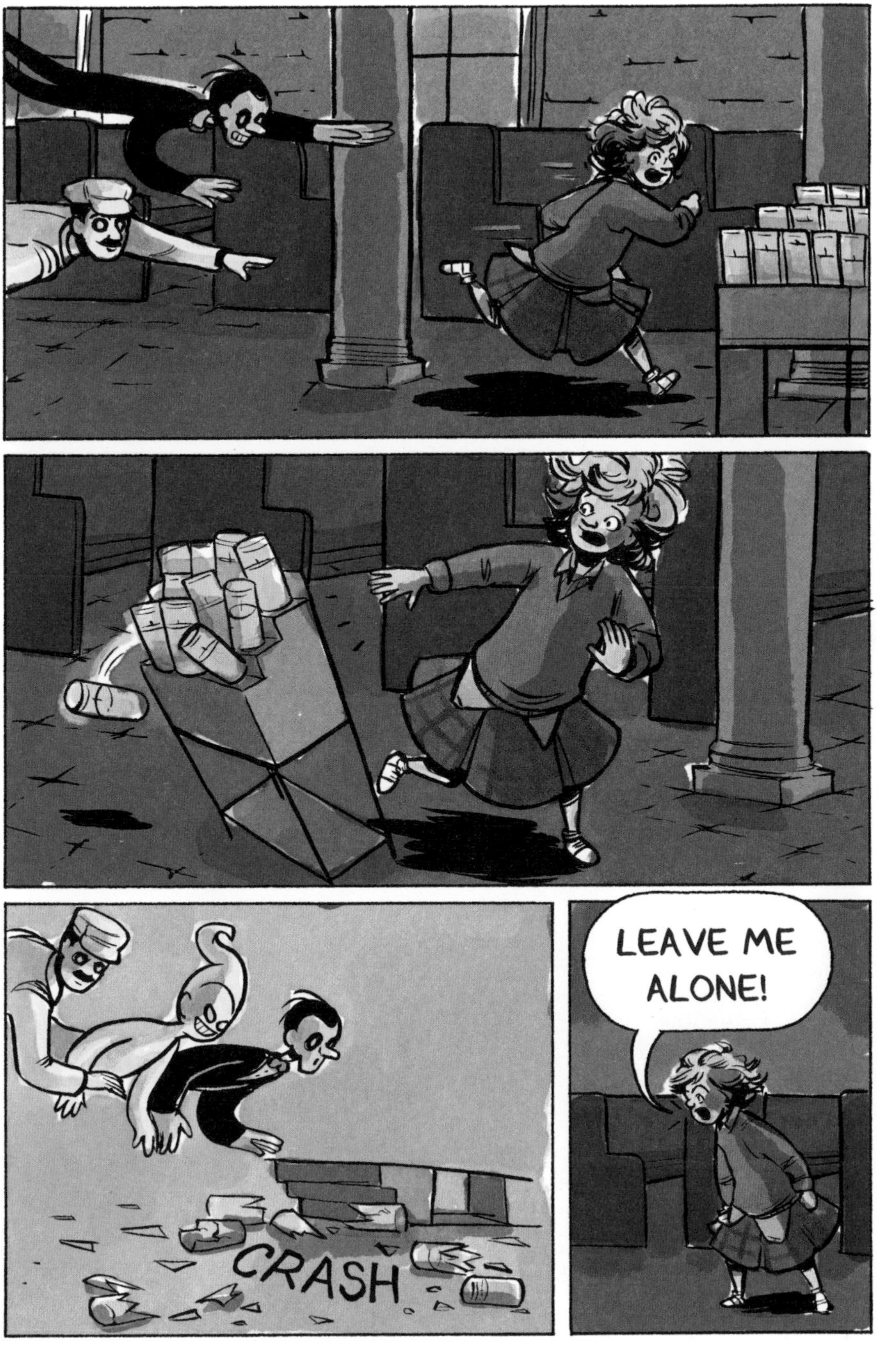
CRASH
LEAVE ME ALONE!

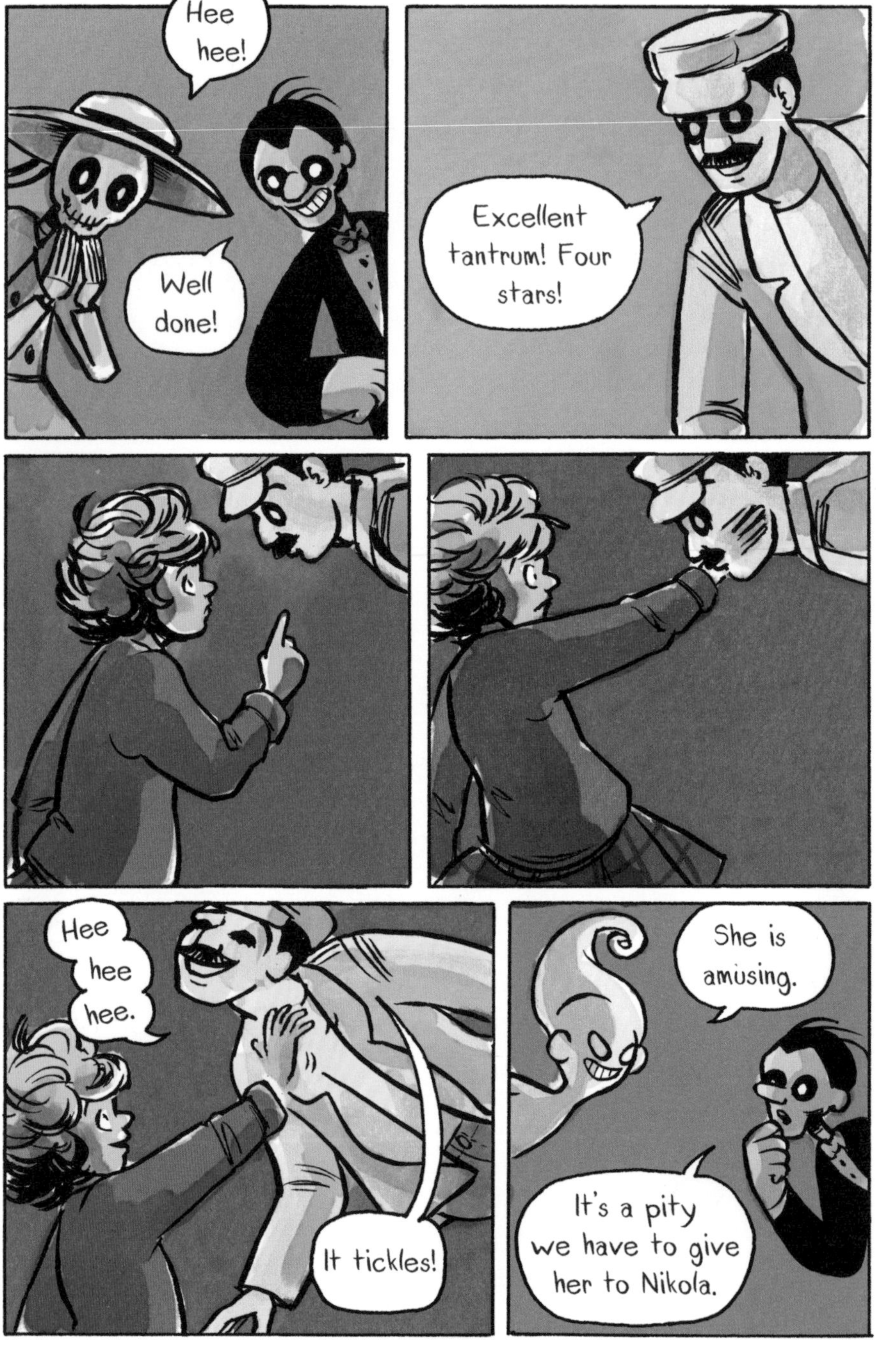
Hee hee!
Well done!
Excellent tantrum! Four stars!
Hee hee hee.
It tickles!
She is amusing.
It's a pity we have to give her to Nikola.

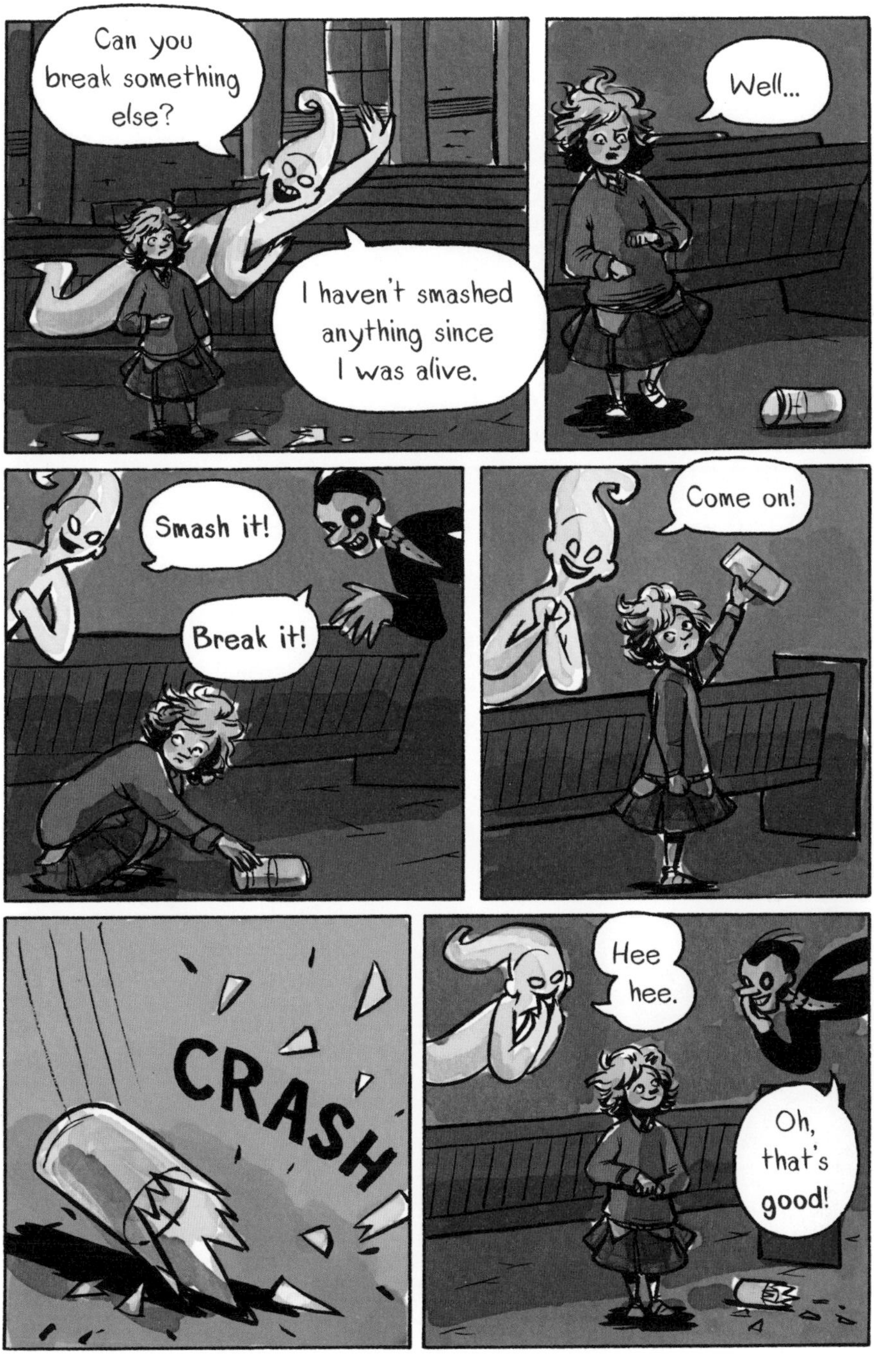
Can you break something else?
I haven't smashed anything since I was alive.
Well...
Smash it!
Break it!
Come on!
CRASH
Hee hee.
Oh, that's good!

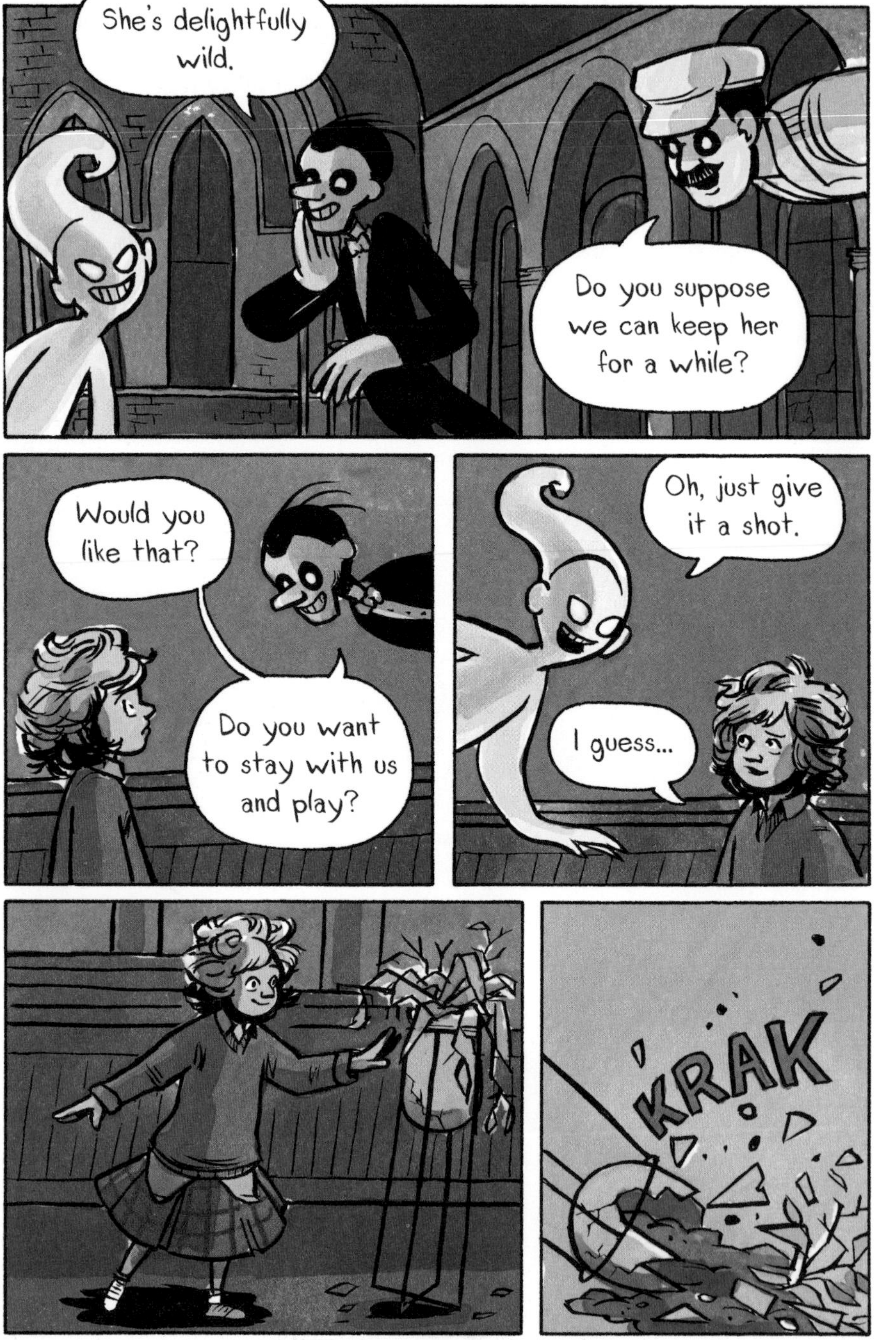
She's delightfully wild.
Do you suppose we can keep her for a while?
Would you like that?
Do you want to stay with us and play?
Oh, just give it a shot.
I guess...
KRAK

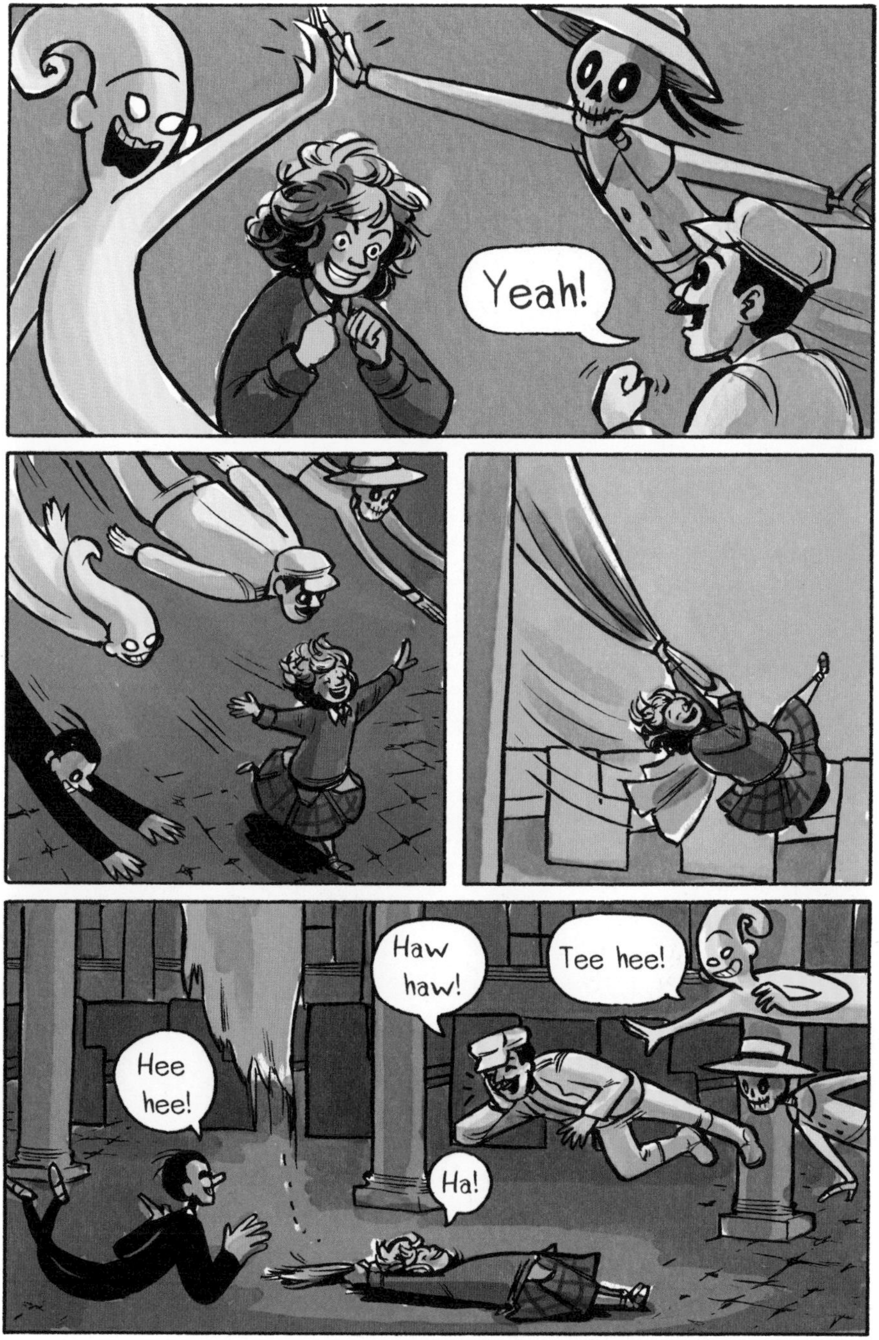
Yeah!
Haw haw!
Tee hee!
Hee hee!
Ha!

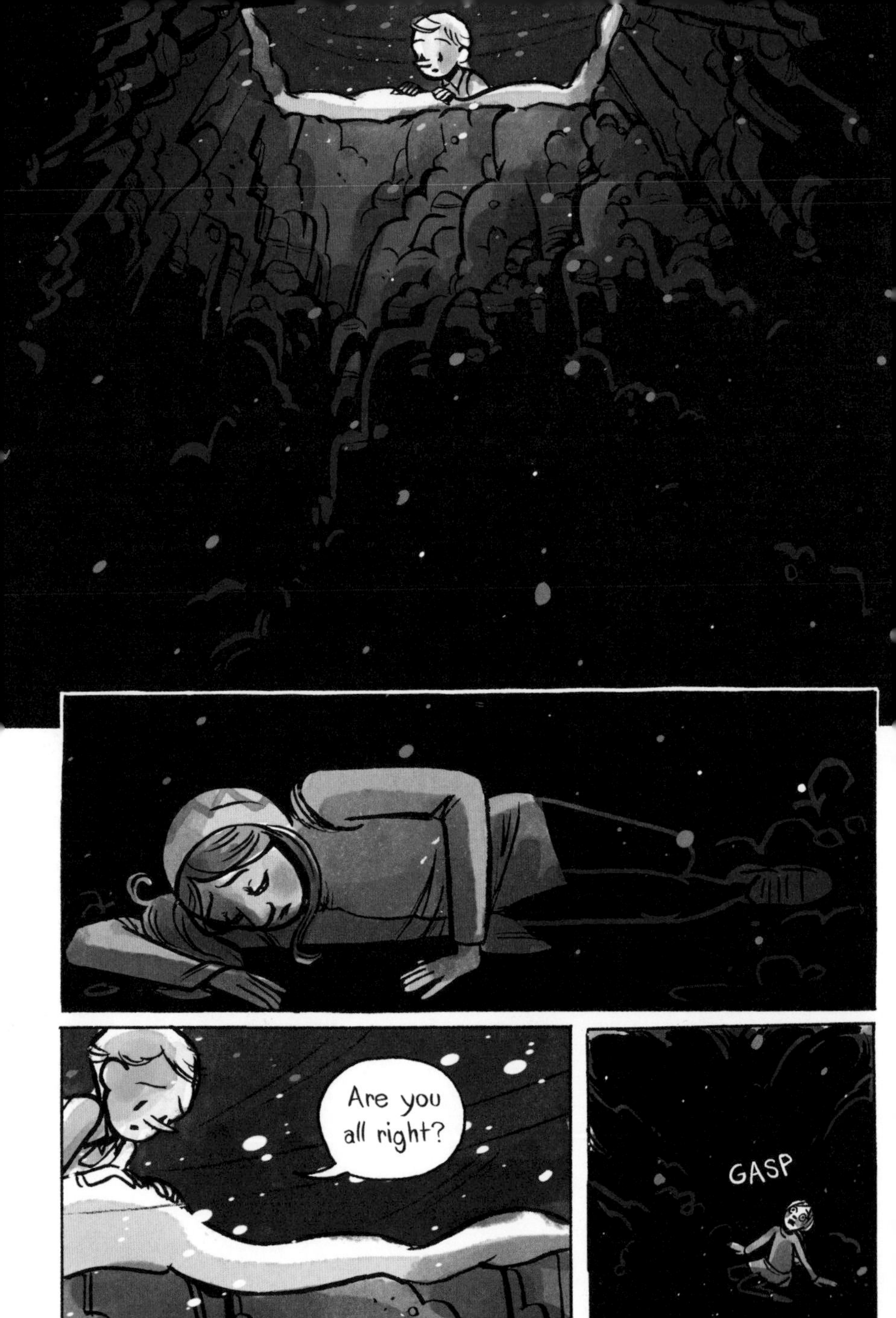
Are you all right?
GASP

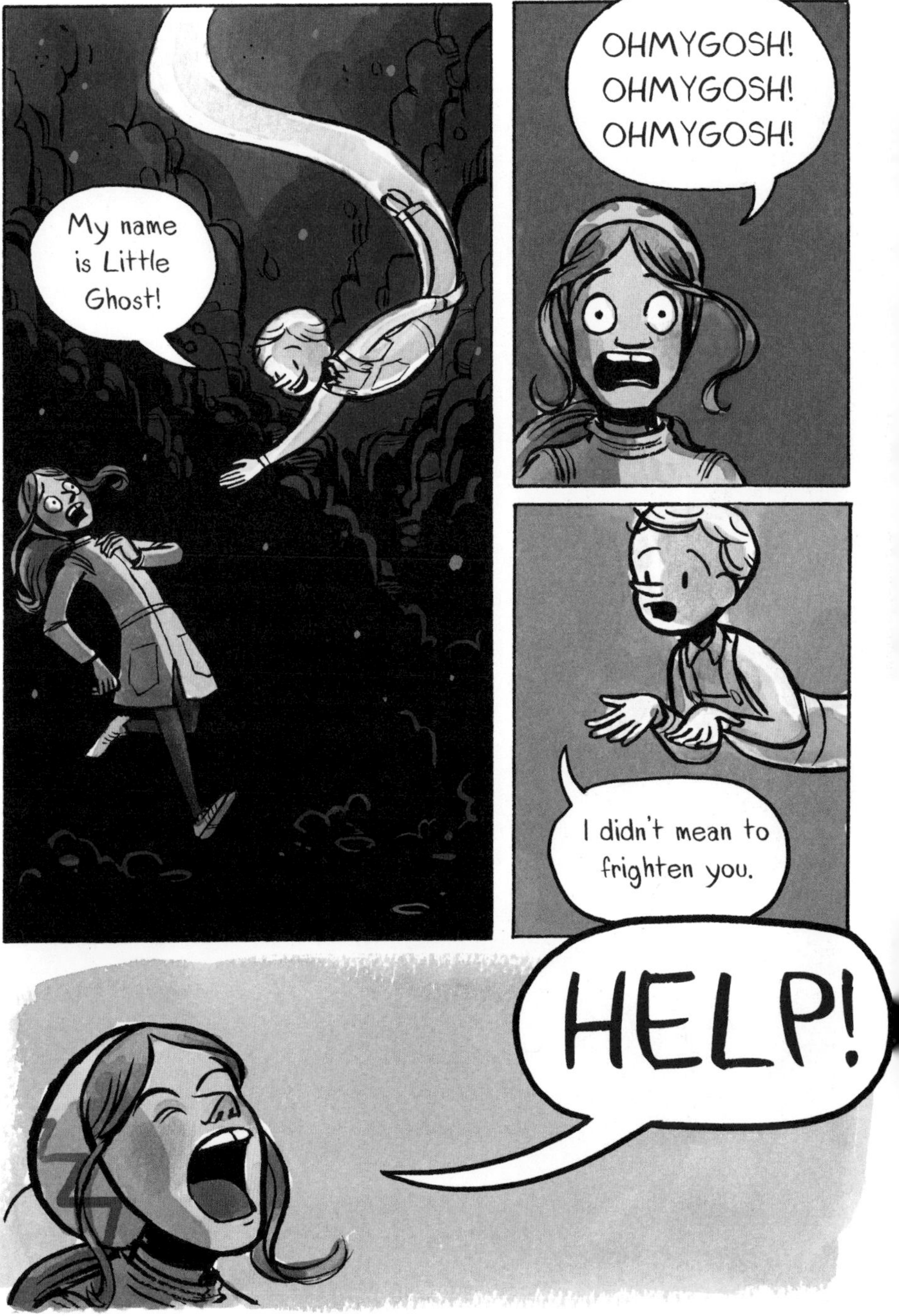
My name is Little Ghost!
OHMYGOSH! OHMYGOSH! OHMYGOSH!
I didn't mean to frighten you.
HELP!

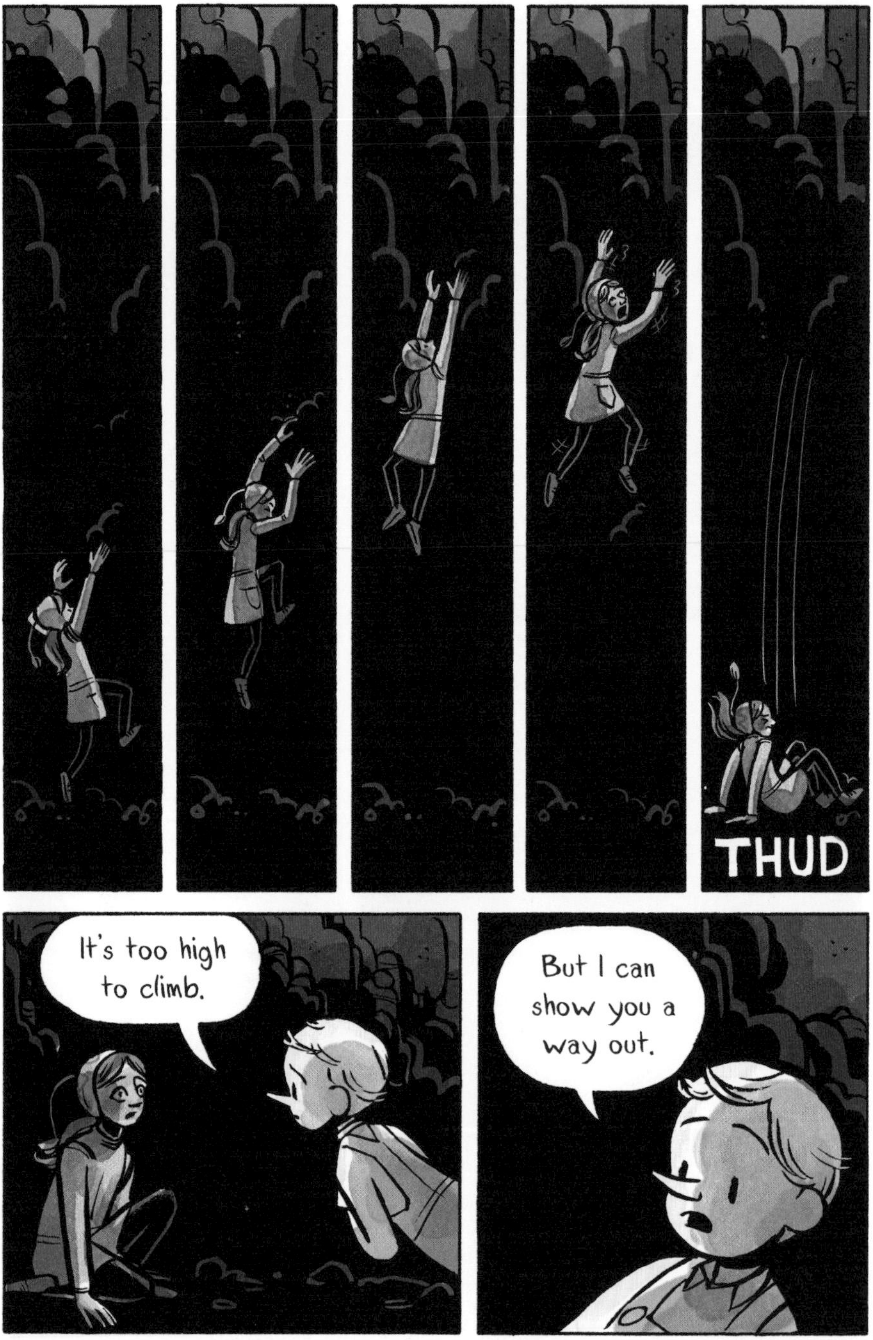
THUD
It's too high to climb.
But I can show you a way out.

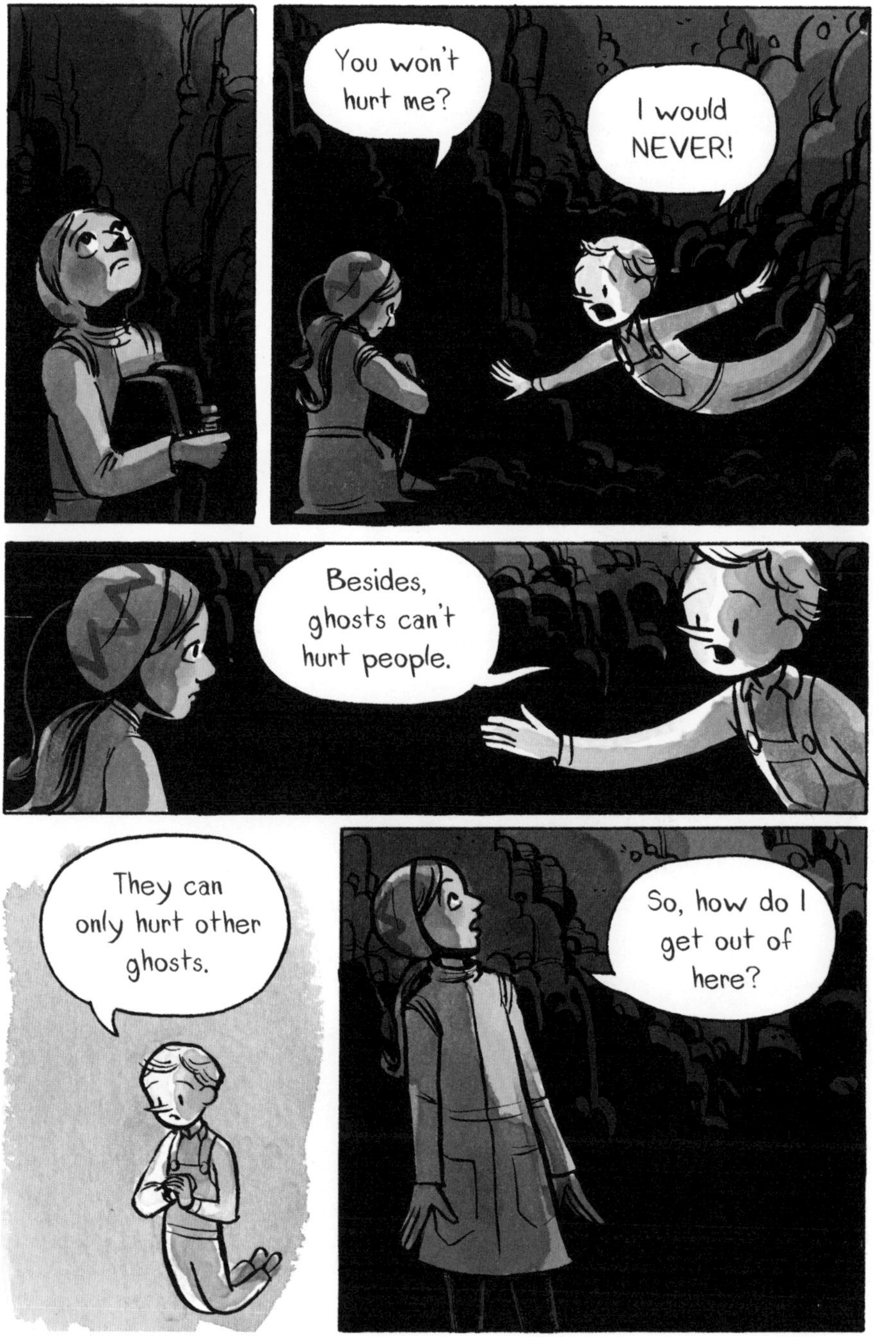
You won't hurt me?
I would NEVER!
Besides, ghosts can't hurt people.
They can only hurt other ghosts.
So, how do I get out of here?

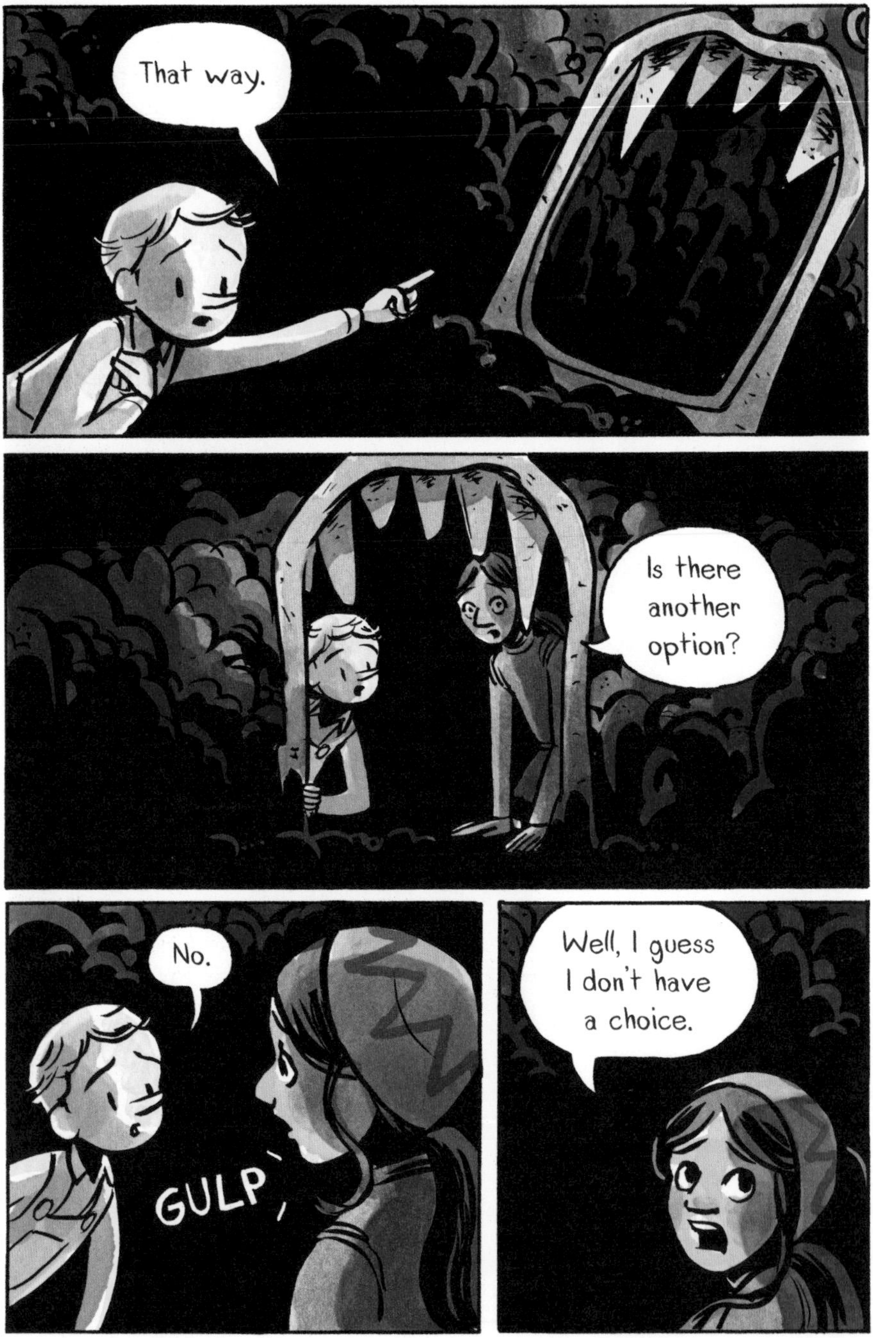
That way.
Is there another option?
No.
GULP
Well, I guess I don't have a choice.

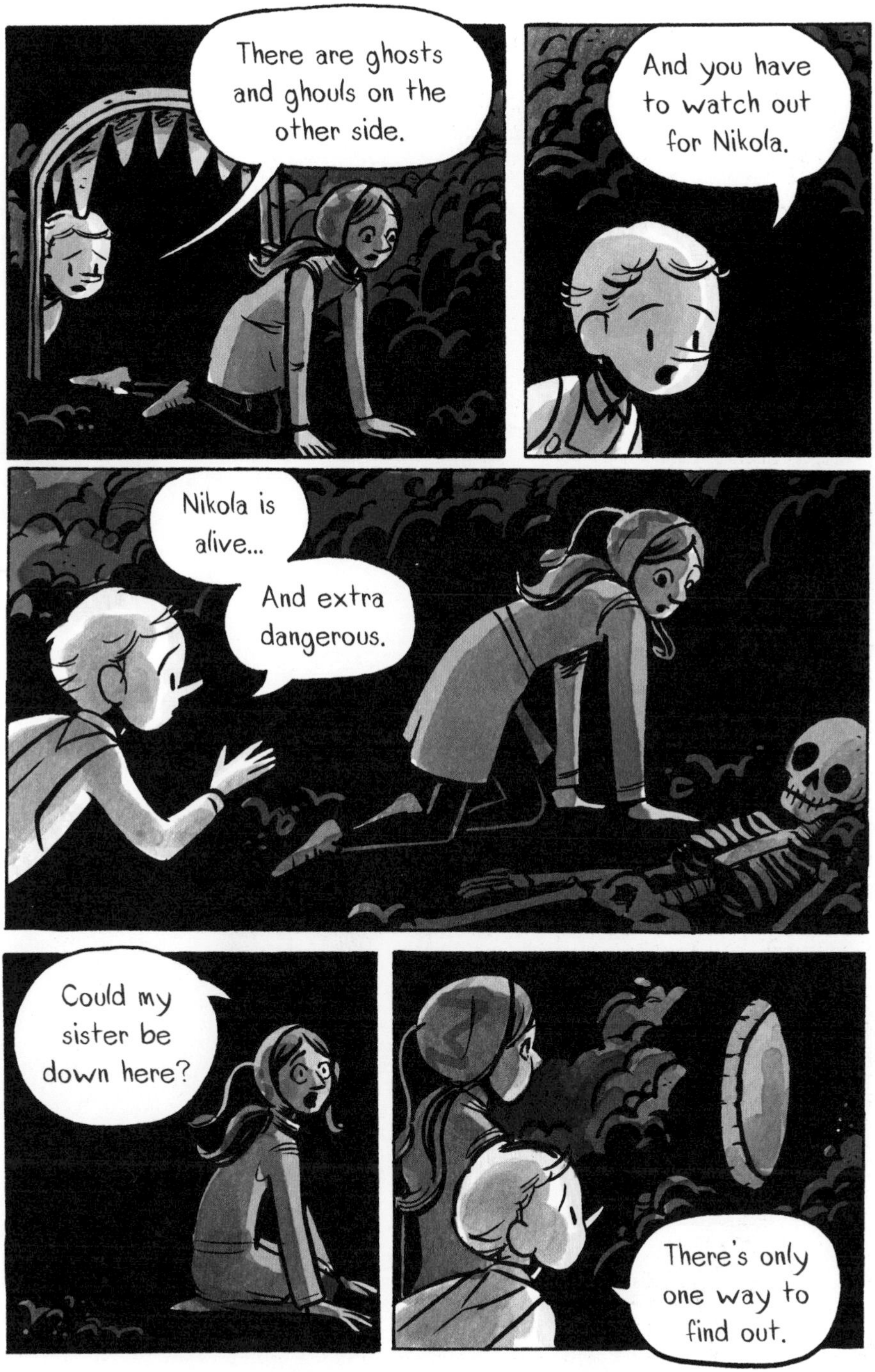
There are ghosts and ghouls on the other side.
And you have to watch out for Nikola.
Nikola is alive...
And extra dangerous.
Could my sister be down here?
There's only one way to find out.

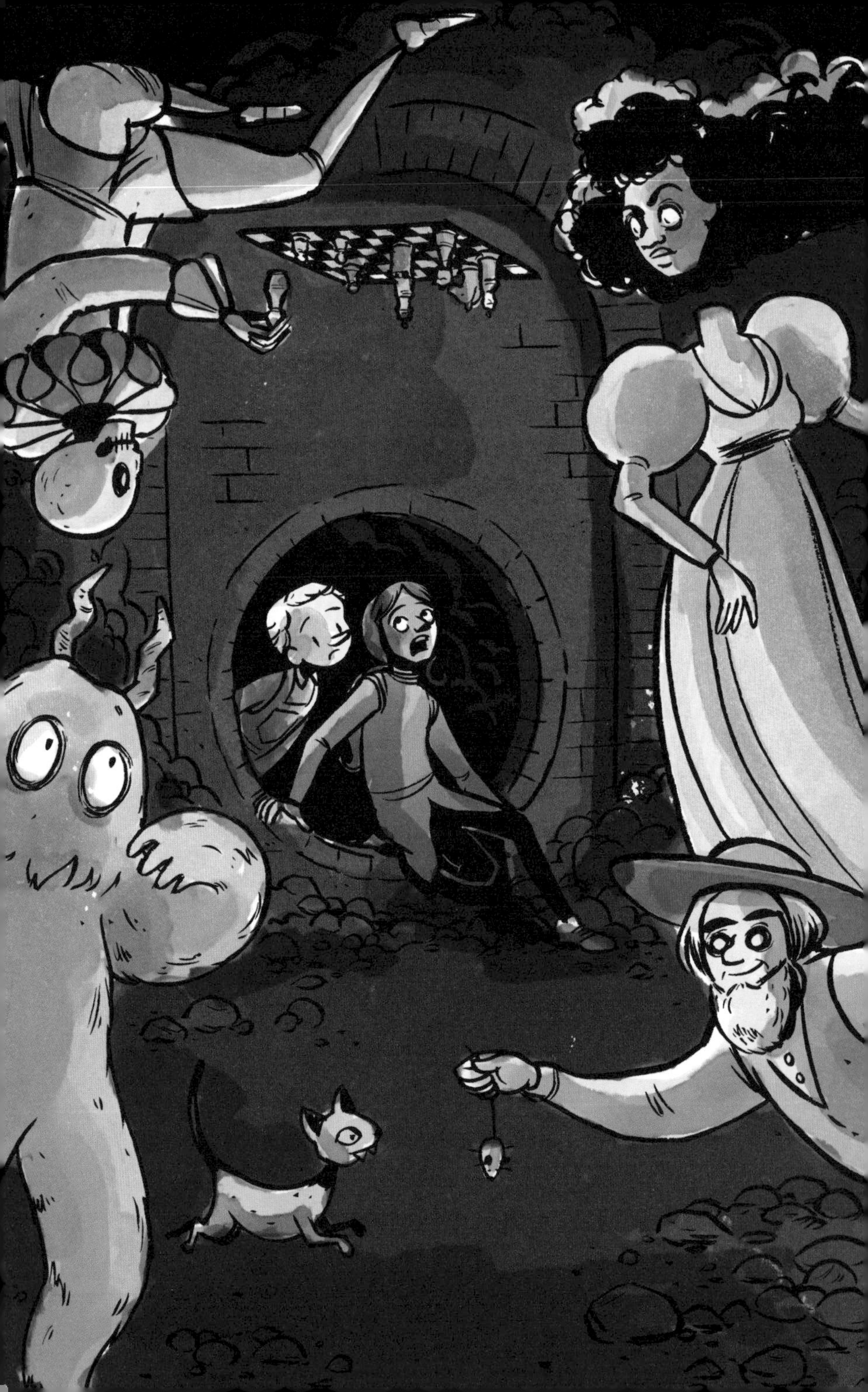

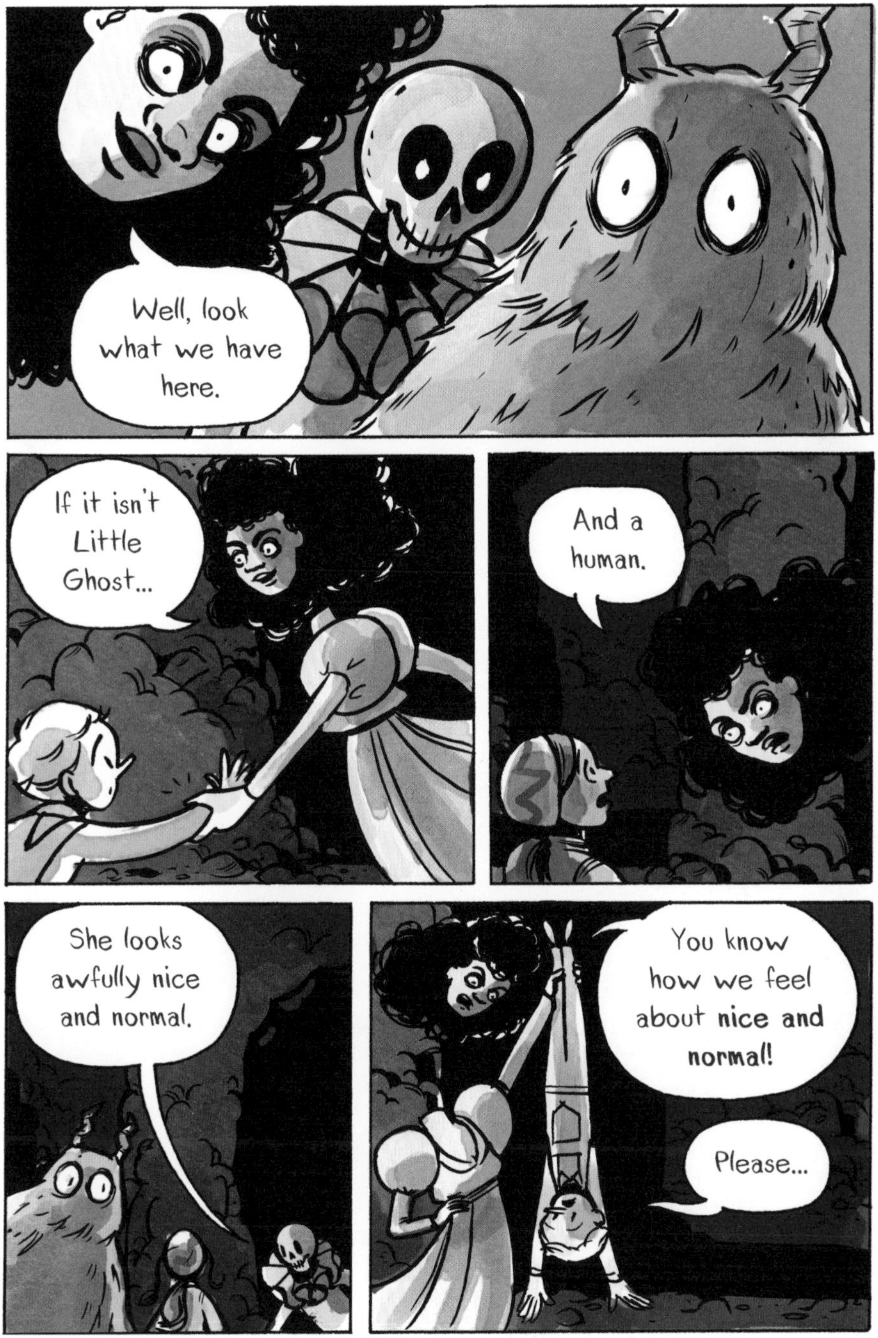
Well, look what we have here.
If it isn't Little Ghost...
And a human.
She looks awfully nice and normal.
You know how we feel about **nice and normal!**
Please...

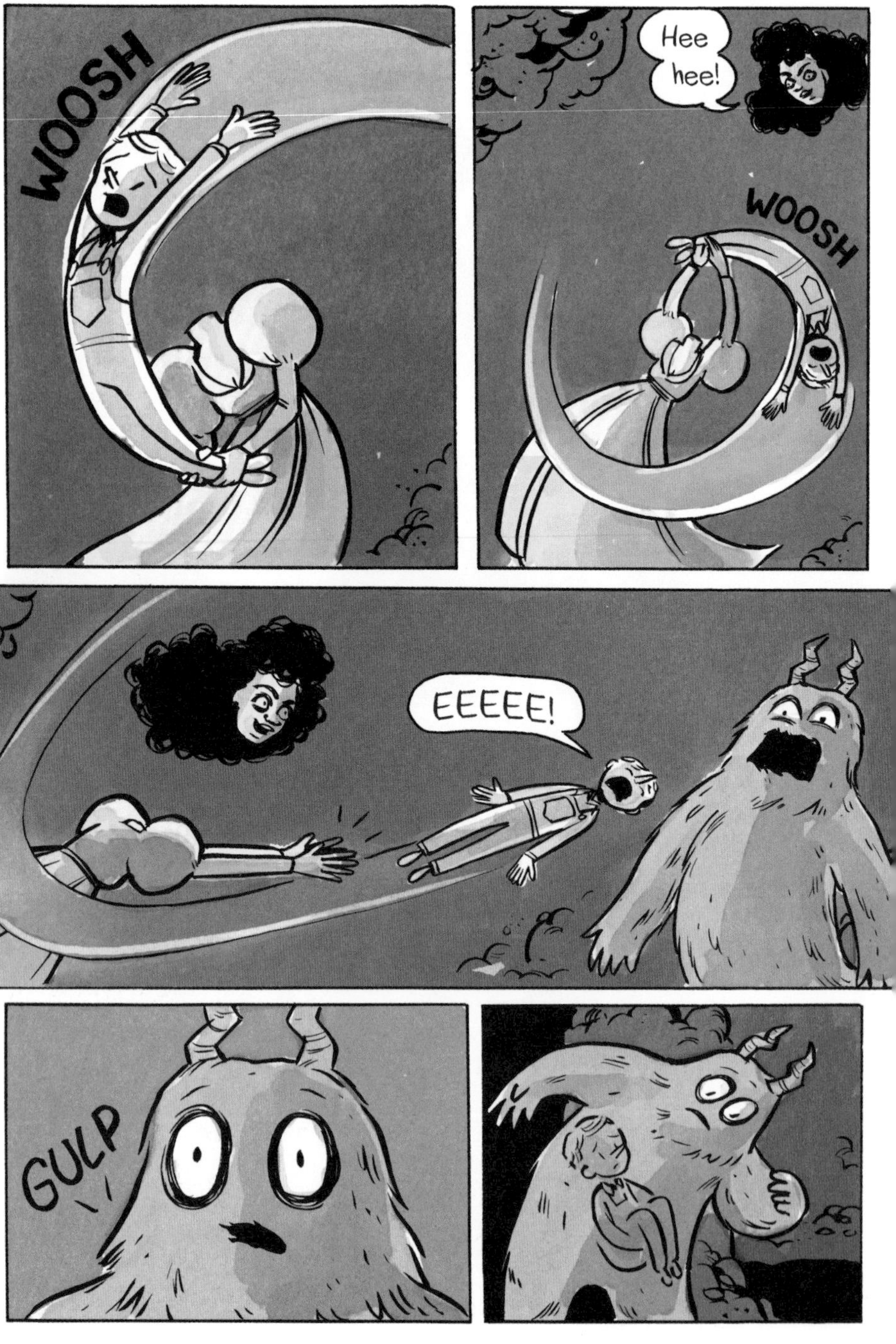
WOOSH
Hee hee!
WOOSH
EEEEE!
GULP

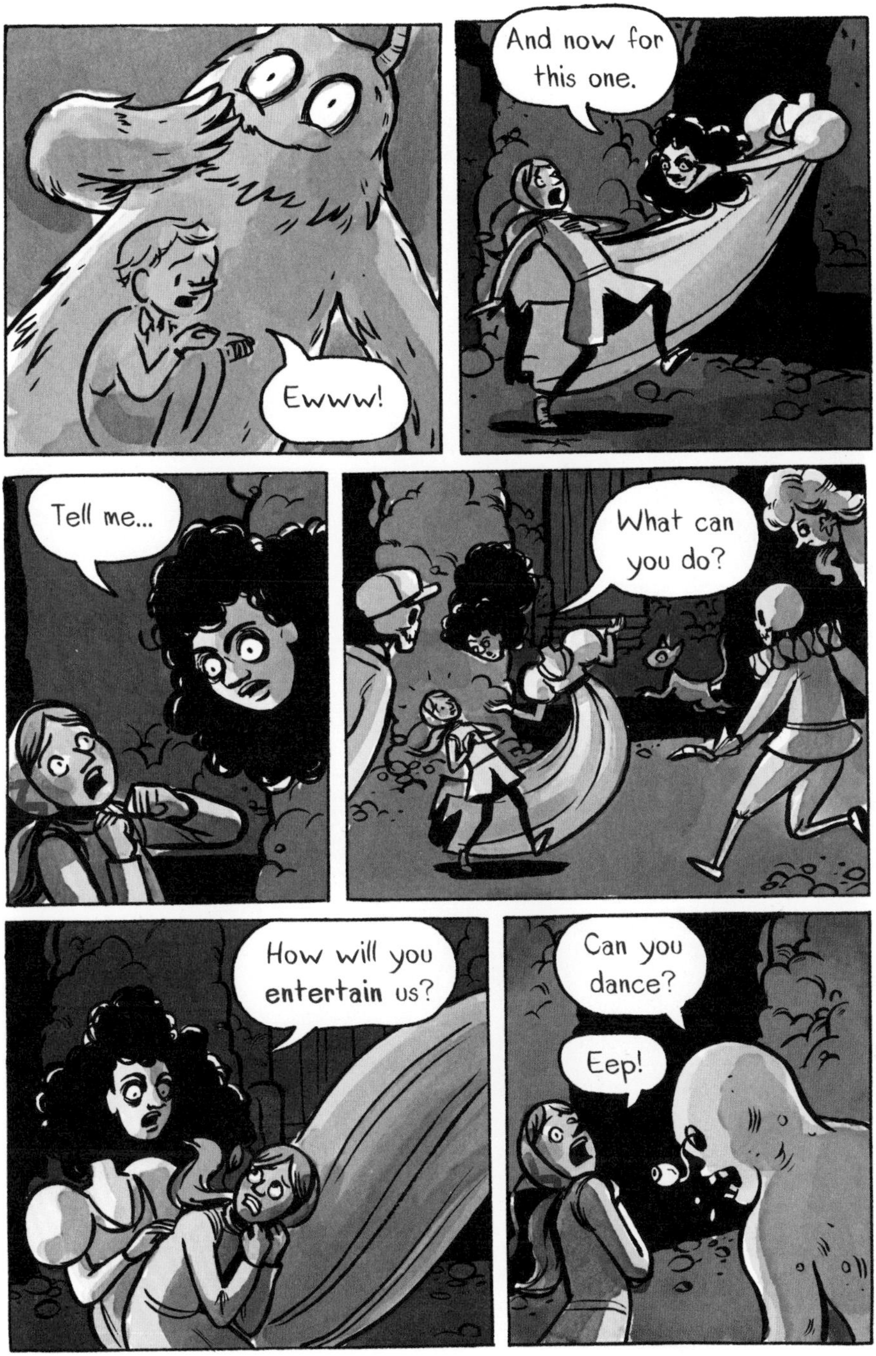
Ewww!
And now for this one.
Tell me...
What can you do?
How will you entertain us?
Can you dance?
Eep!

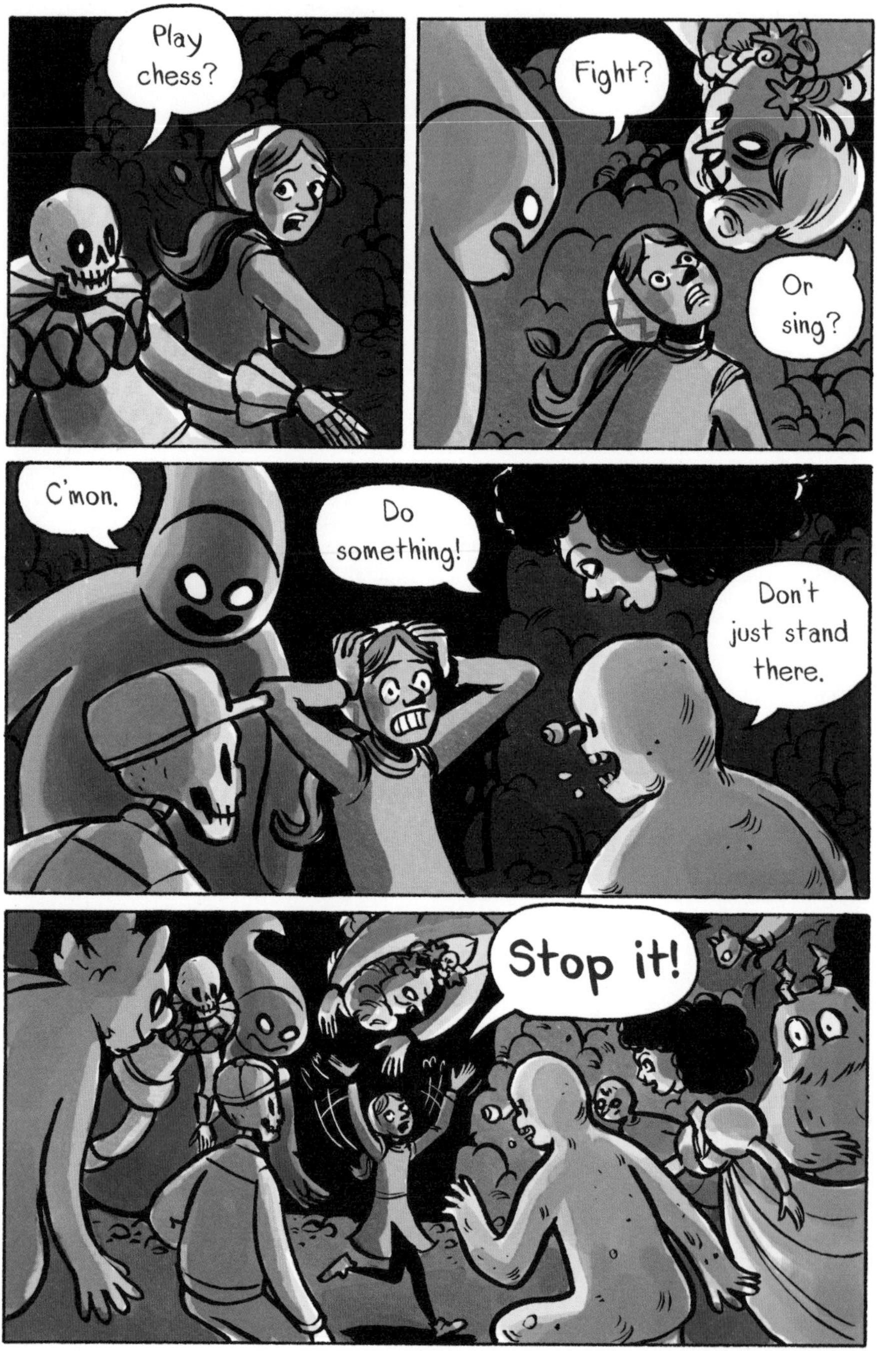
Play chess?
Fight?
Or sing?
C'mon.
Do something!
Don't just stand there.
Stop it!

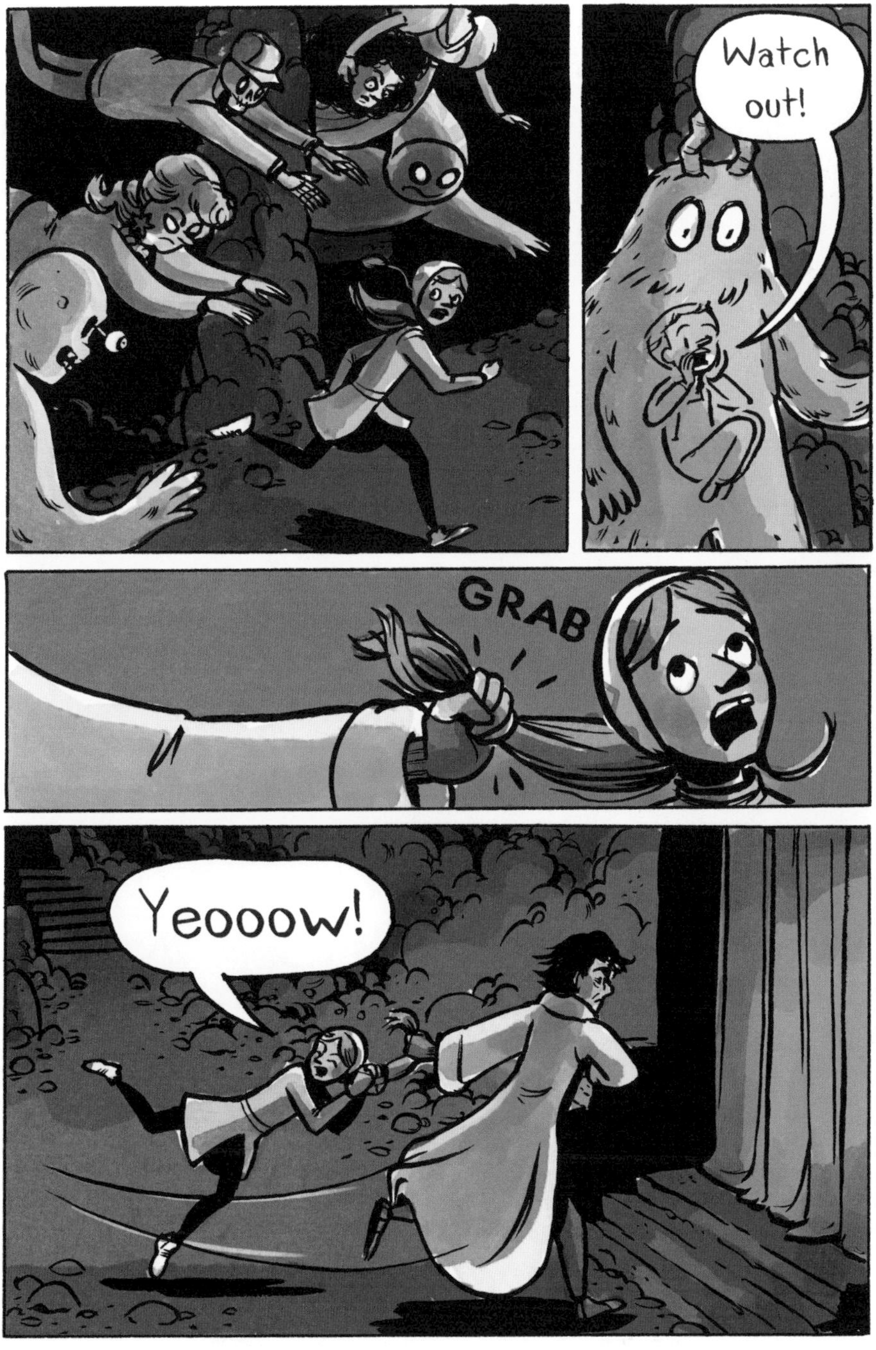
Watch out!
GRAB
Yeooow!

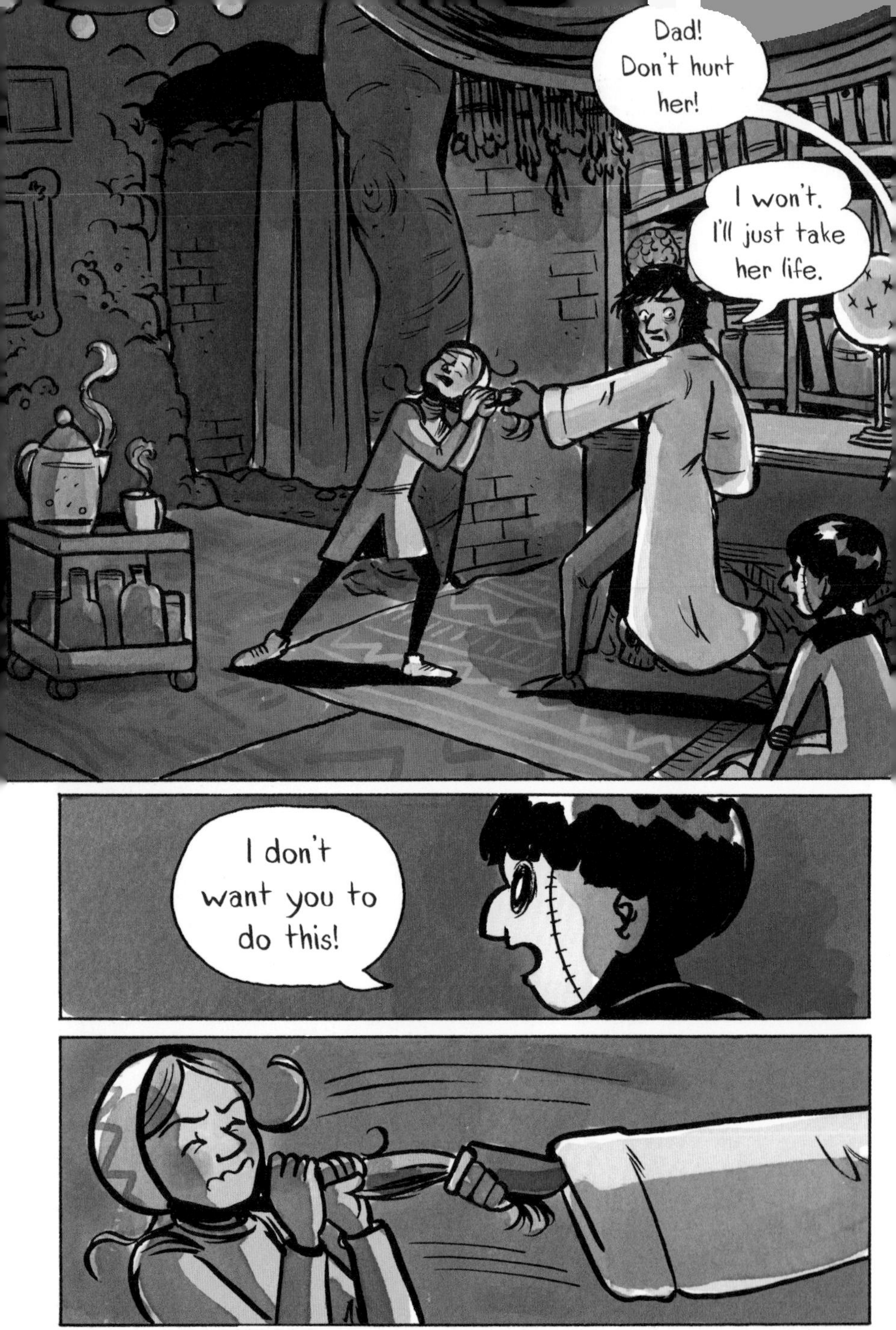
Dad! Don't hurt her!
I won't. I'll just take her life.
I don't want you to do this!

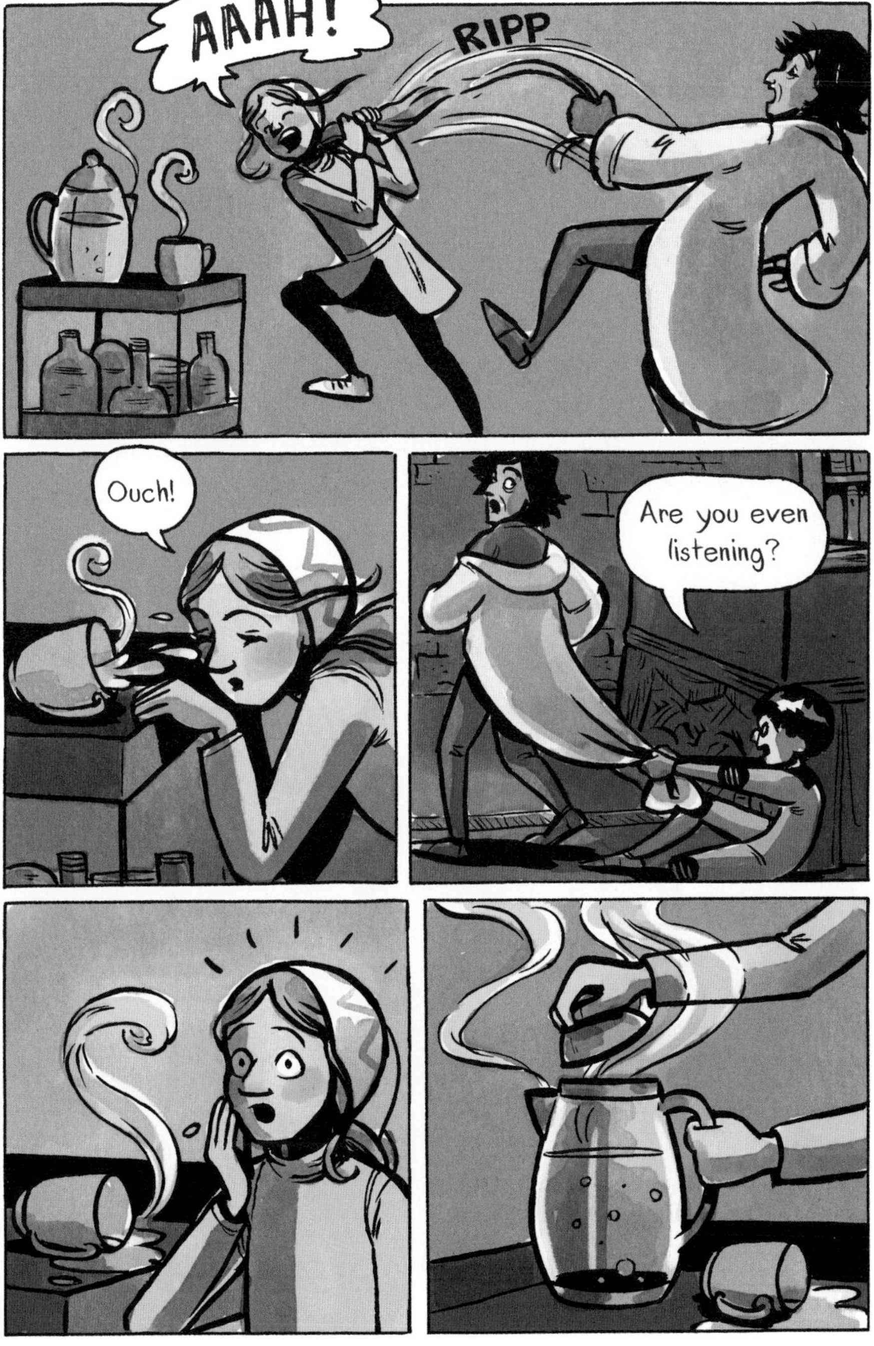
AAAH!
RIPP
Ouch!
Are you even listening?

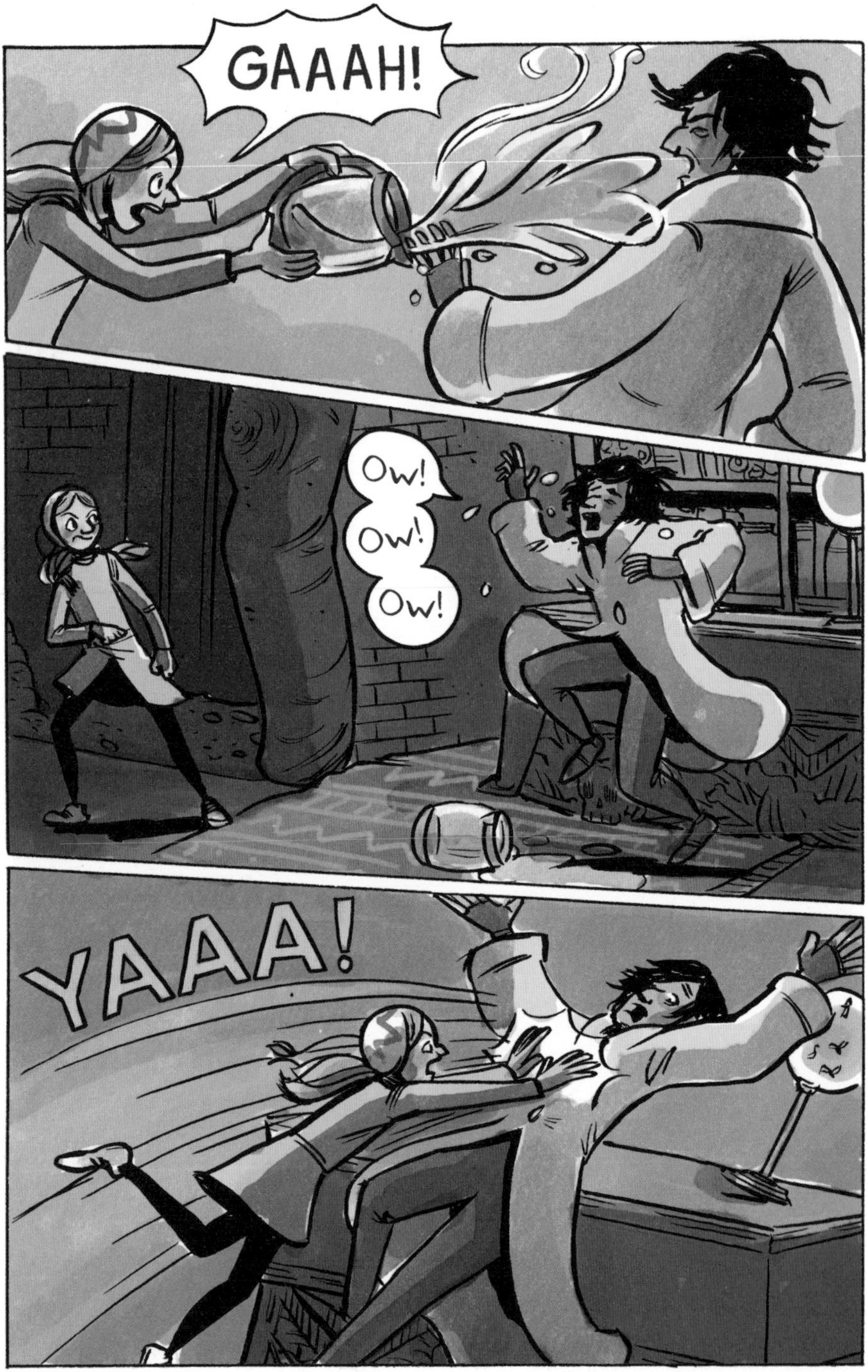
GAAAH!
Ow!
Ow!
Ow!
YAAA!

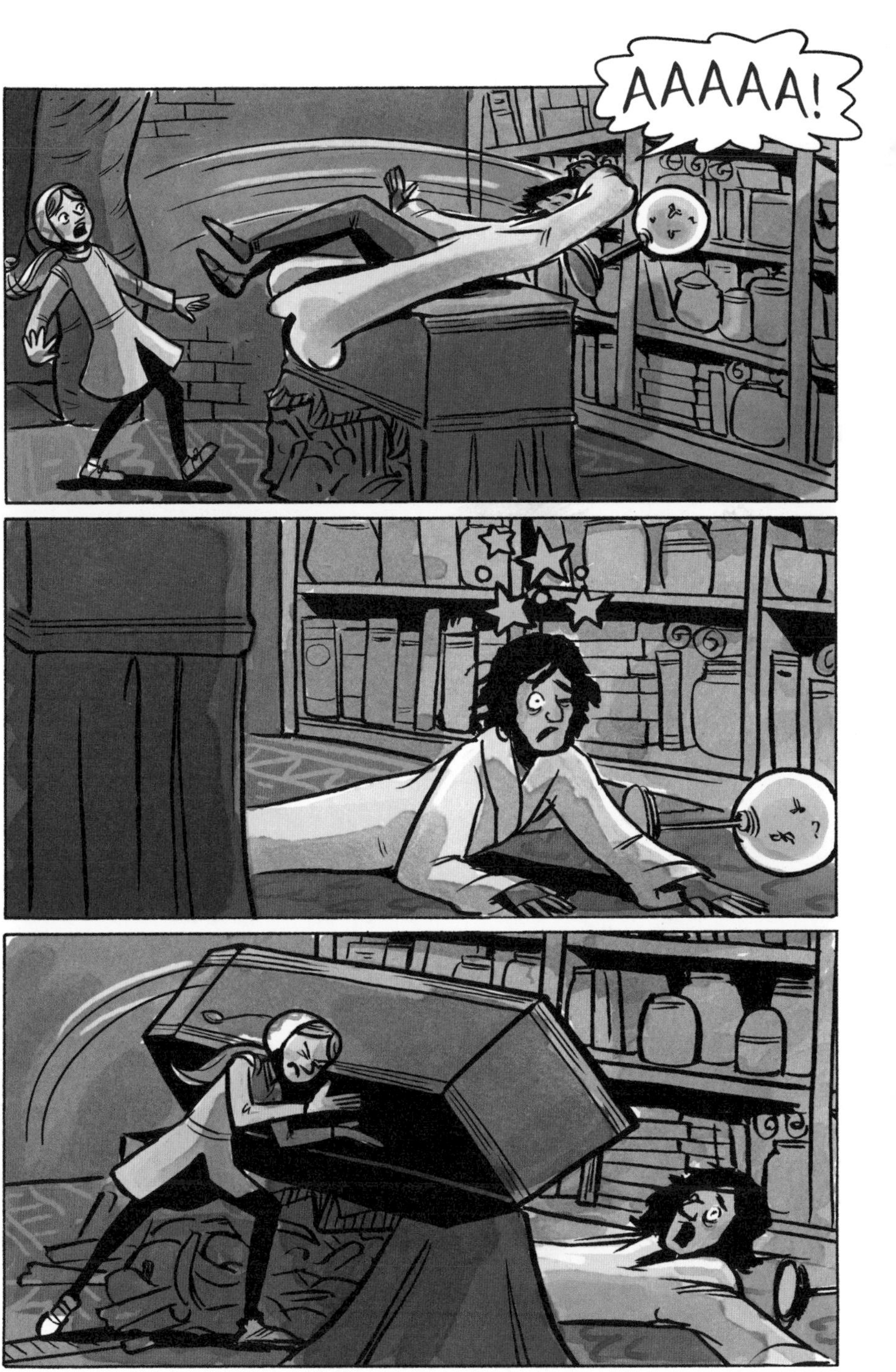
AAAAA!

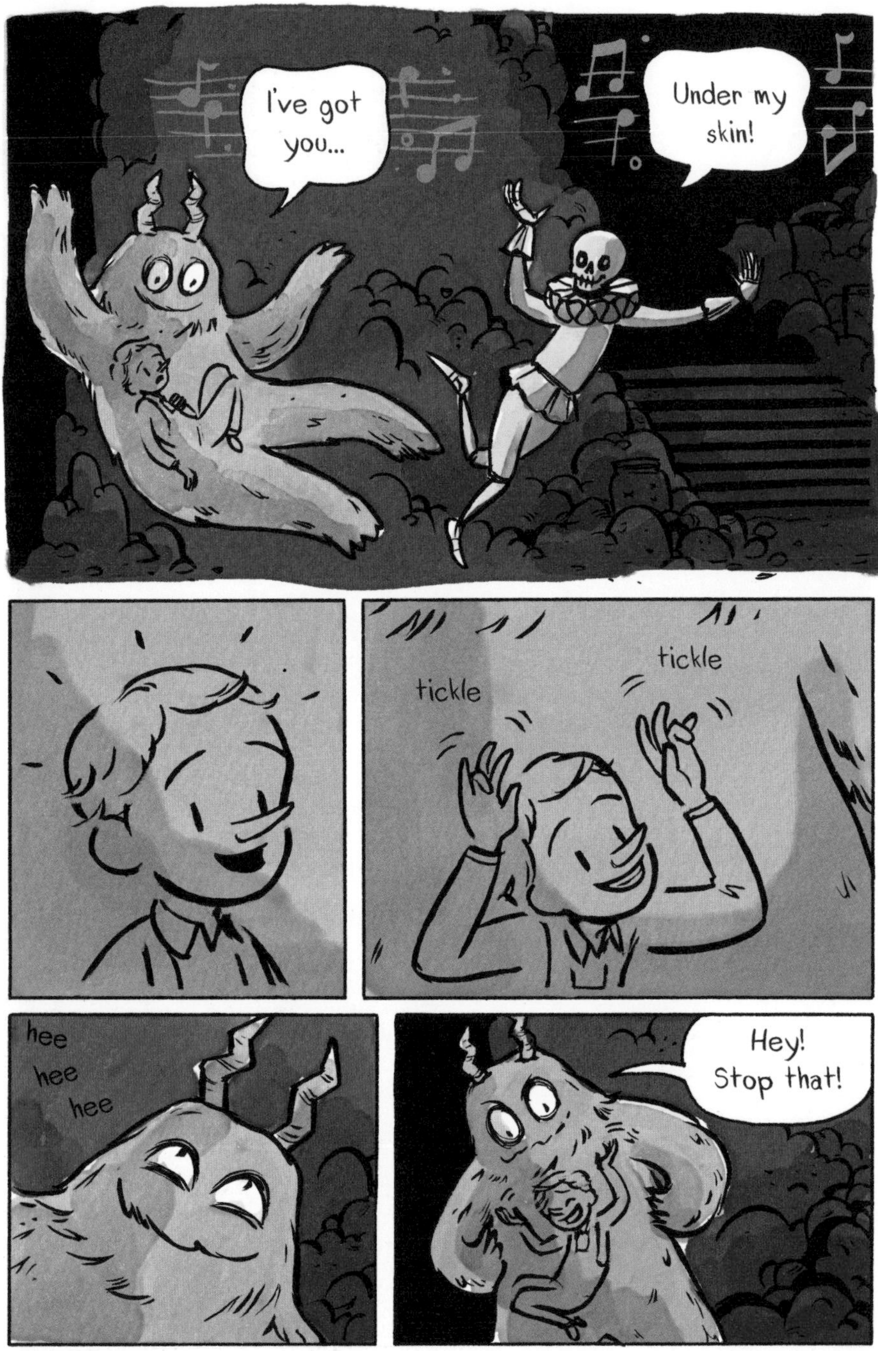
I've got you...
Under my skin!
tickle
tickle
hee
hee
hee
Hey! Stop that!

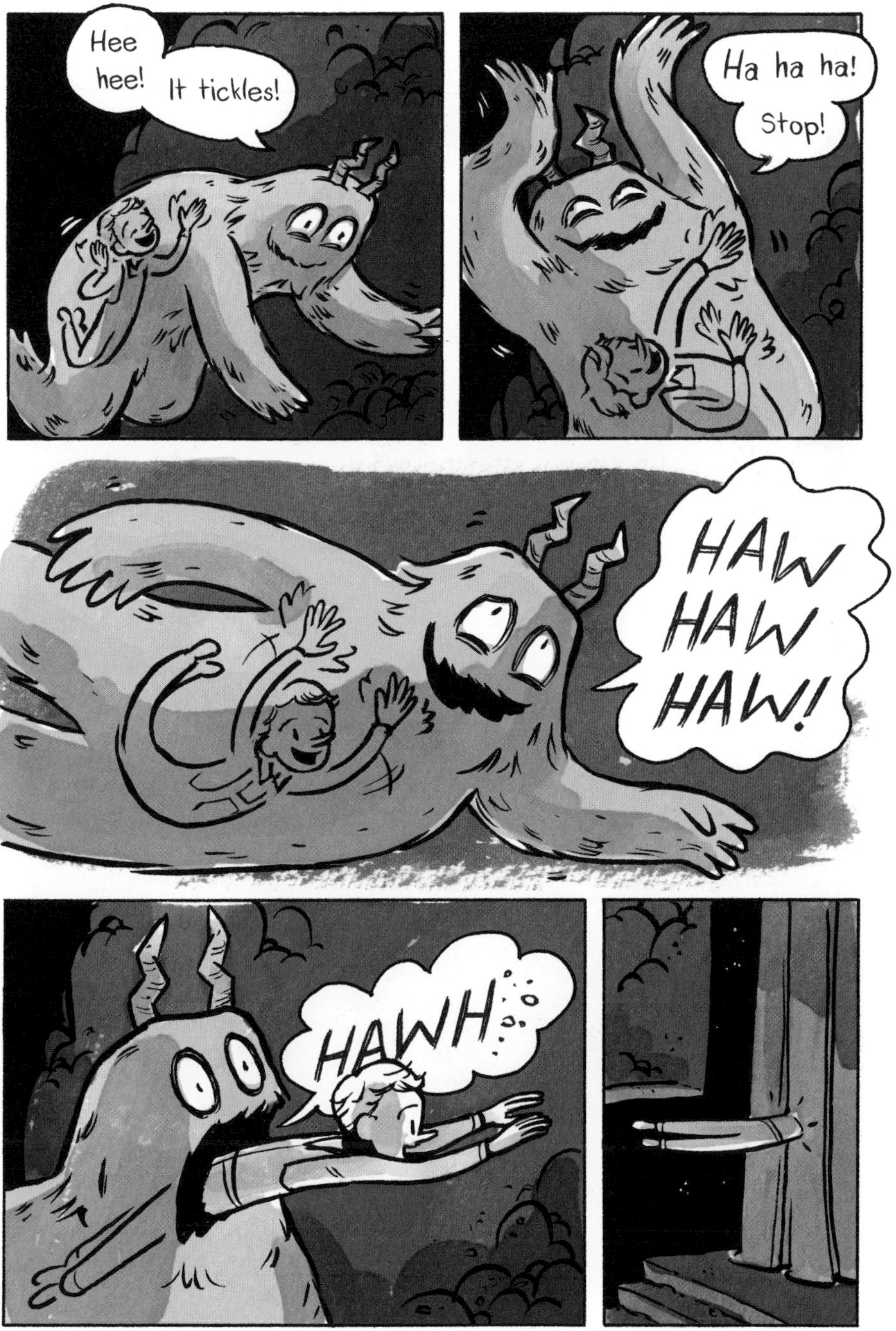
Hee hee!
It tickles!
Ha ha ha!
Stop!
HAW HAW HAW!
HAWH

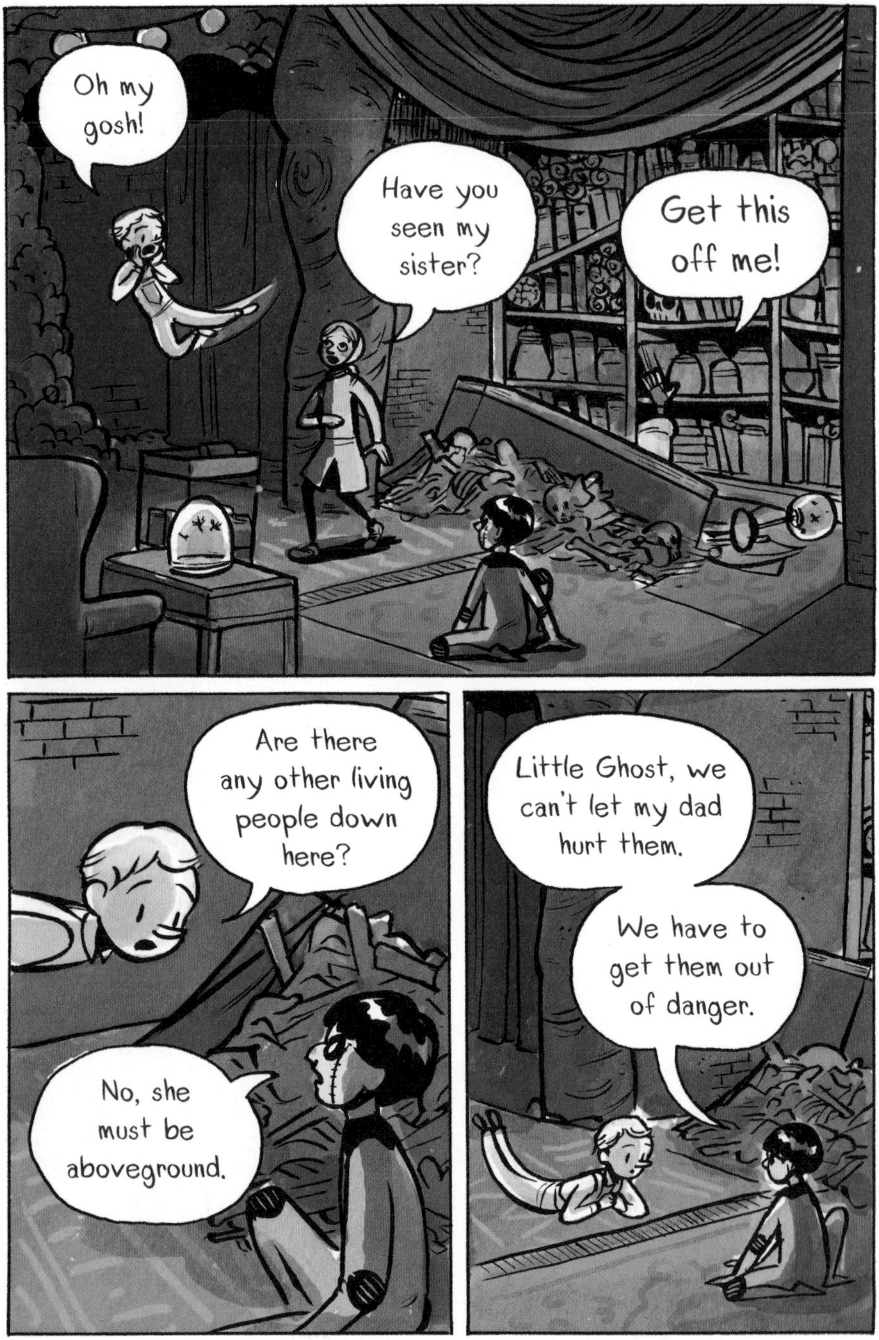
Oh my gosh!
Have you seen my sister?
Get this off me!
Are there any other living people down here?
No, she must be aboveground.
Little Ghost, we can't let my dad hurt them.
We have to get them out of danger.

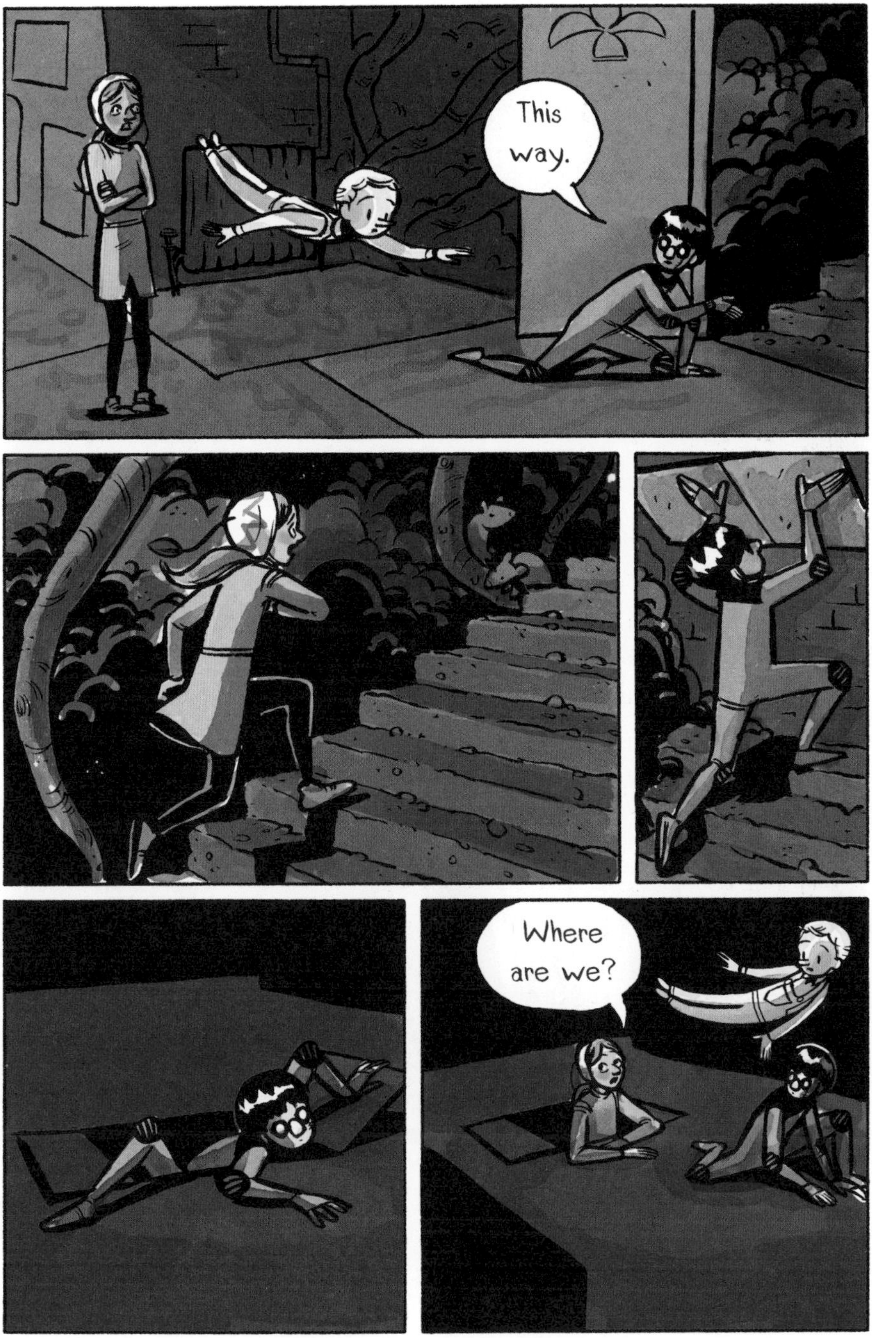
This way.
Where are we?

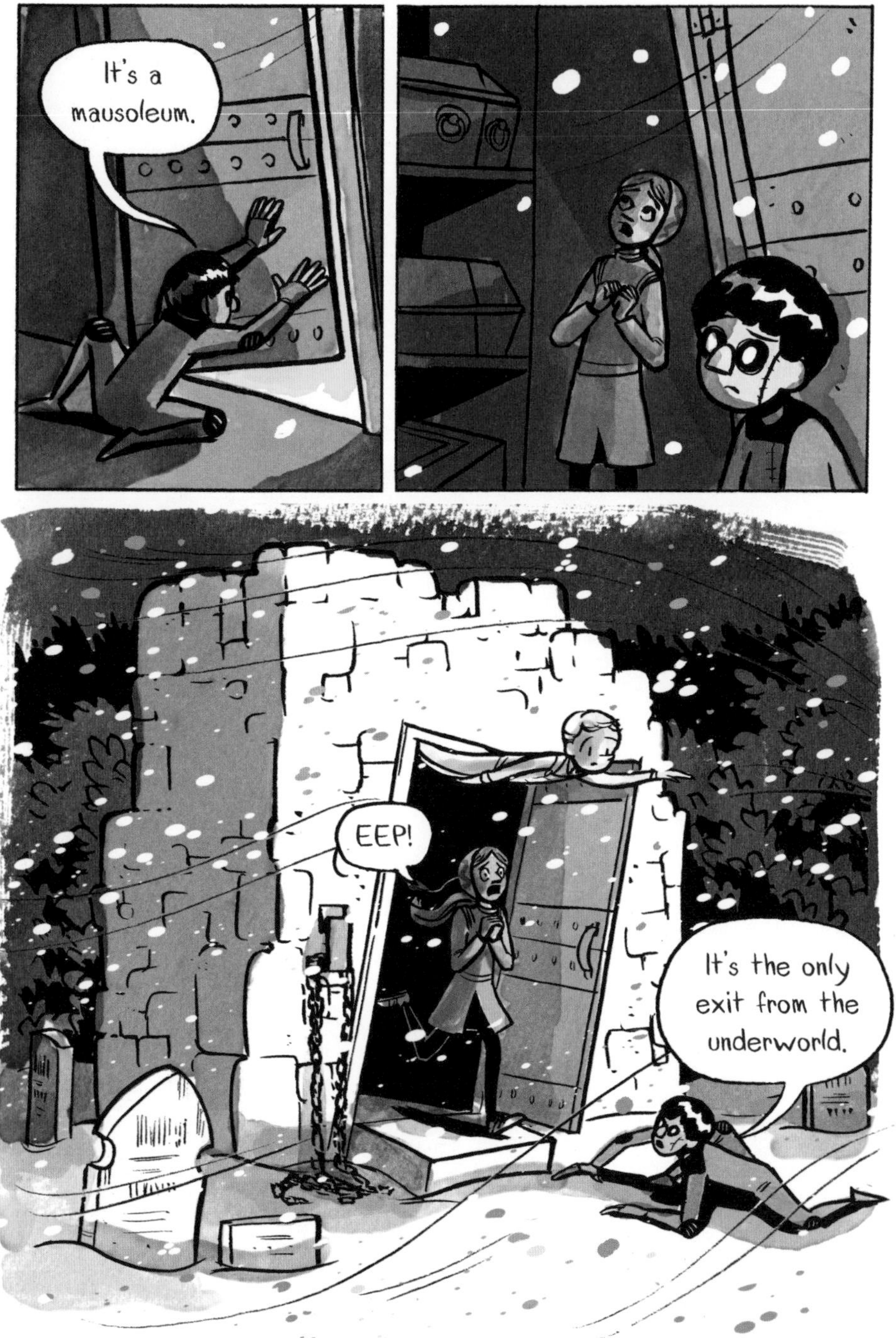
It's a mausoleum.
EEP!
It's the only exit from the underworld.

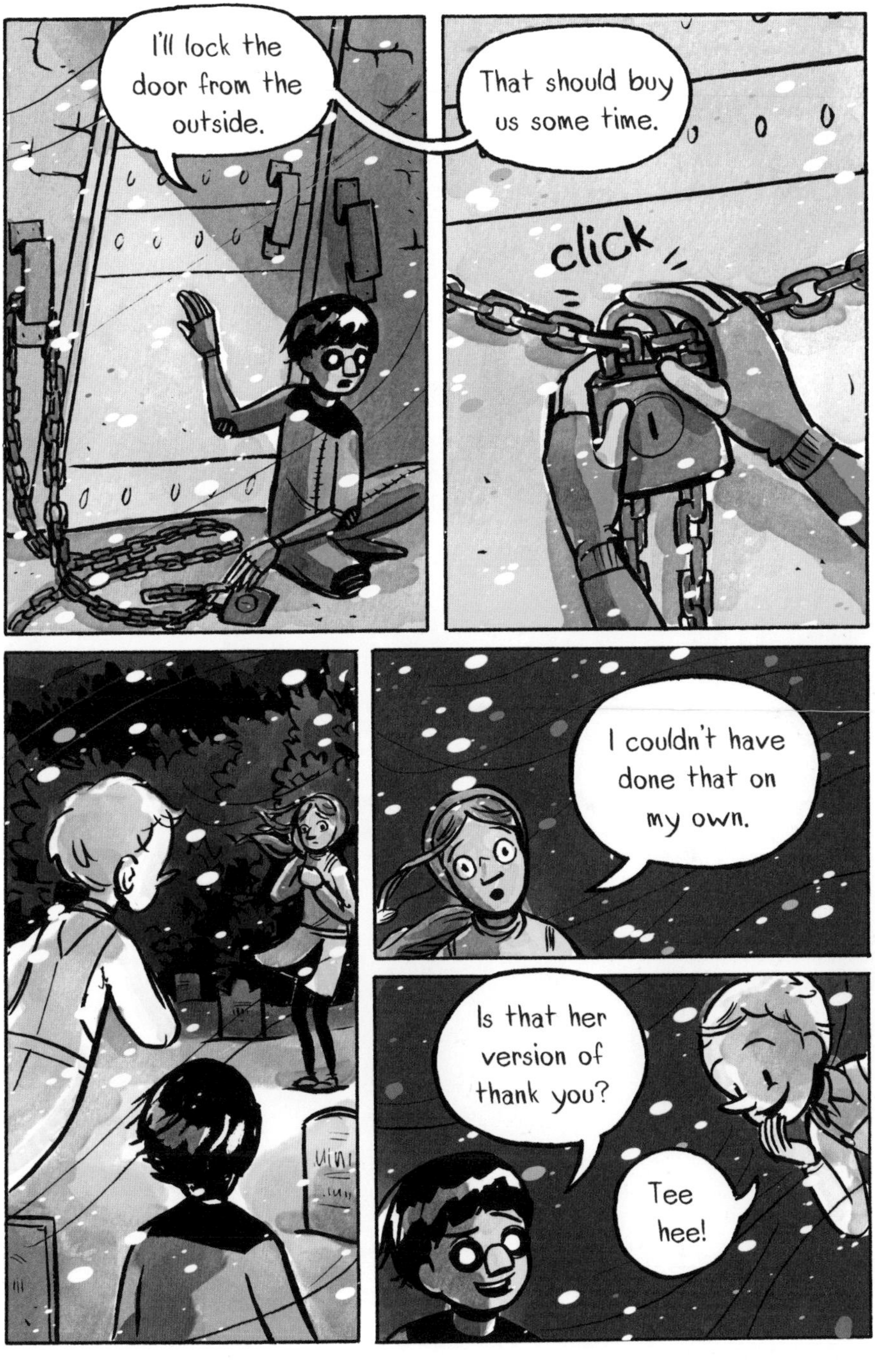
I'll lock the door from the outside.
That should buy us some time.
click
I couldn't have done that on my own.
Is that her version of thank you?
Tee hee!

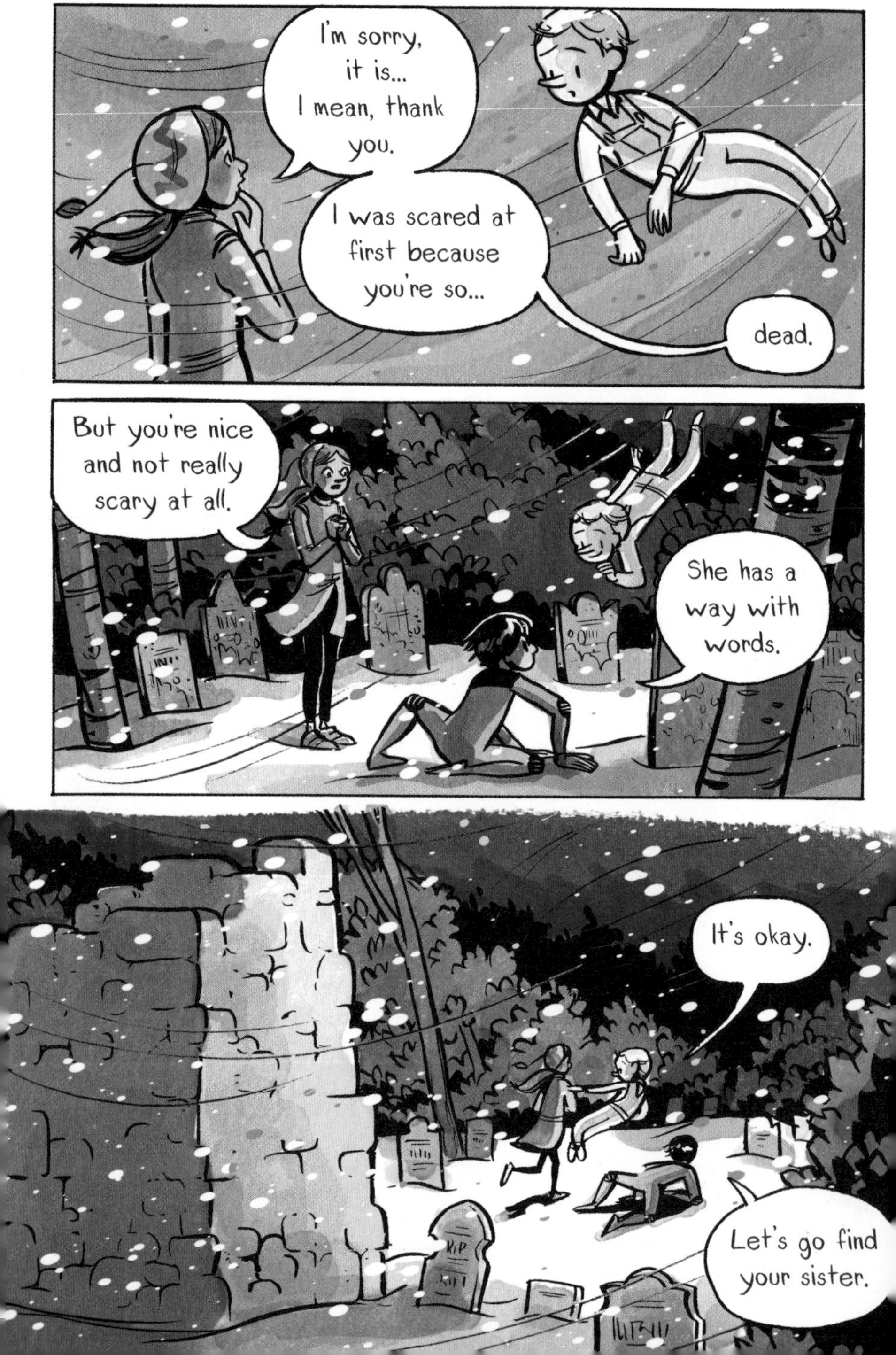
I'm sorry, it is... I mean, thank you.
I was scared at first because you're so...
dead.
But you're nice and not really scary at all.
She has a way with words.
It's okay.
Let's go find your sister.

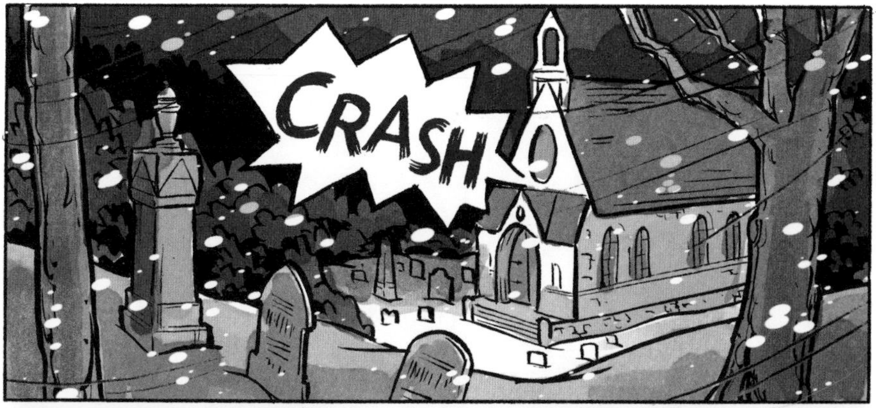
CRASH

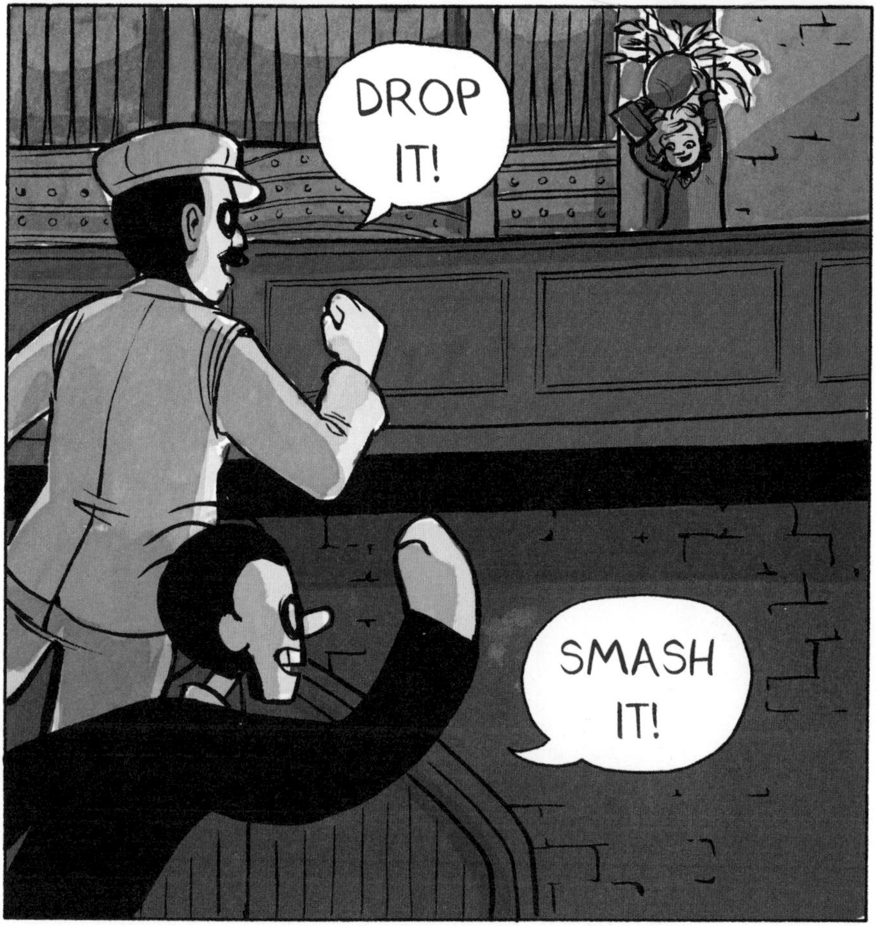
DROP IT!
SMASH IT!

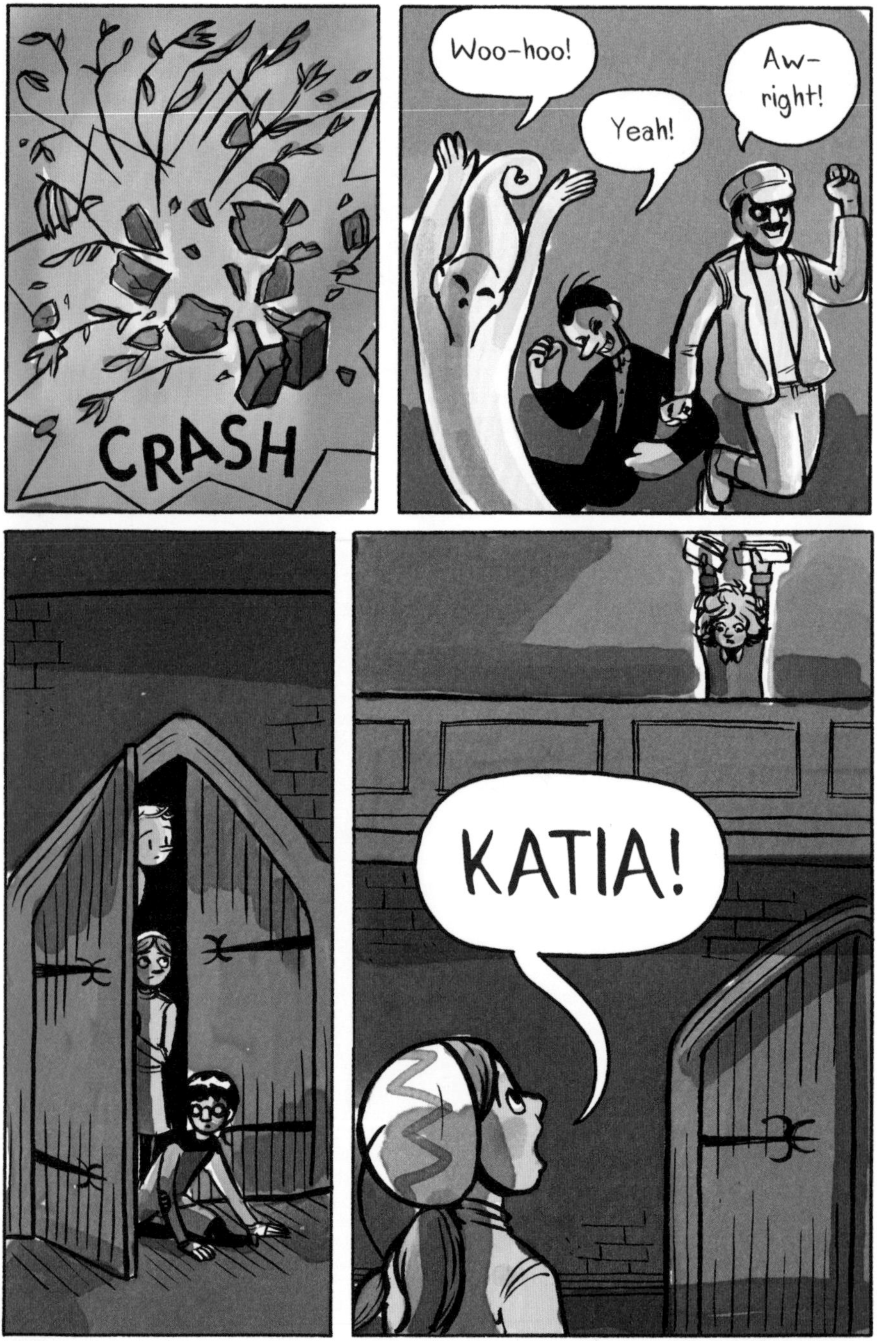
CRASH
Woo-hoo!
Yeah!
Aw-right!
KATIA!

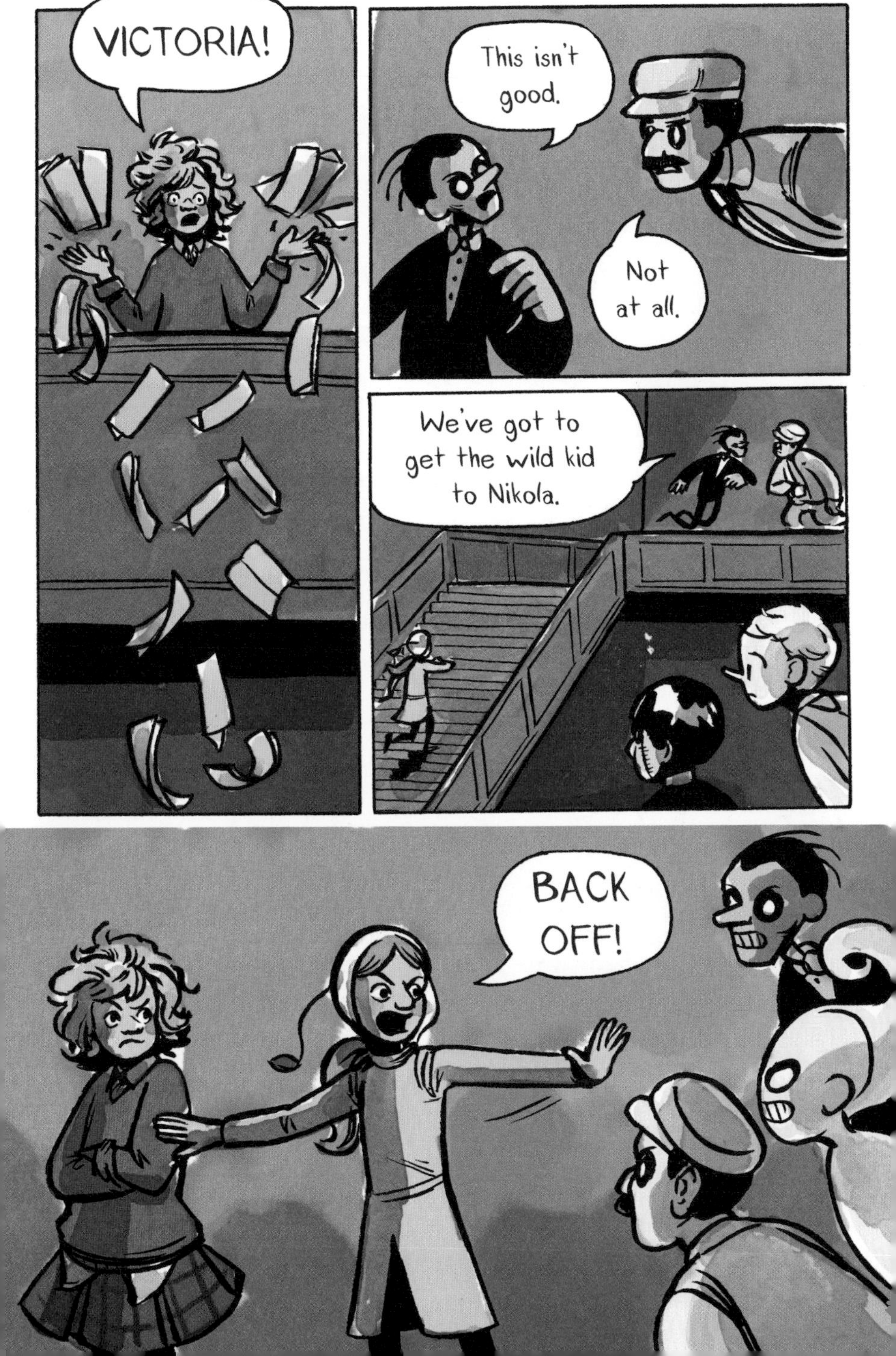
VICTORIA!
This isn't good.
Not at all.
We've got to get the wild kid to Nikola.
BACK OFF!

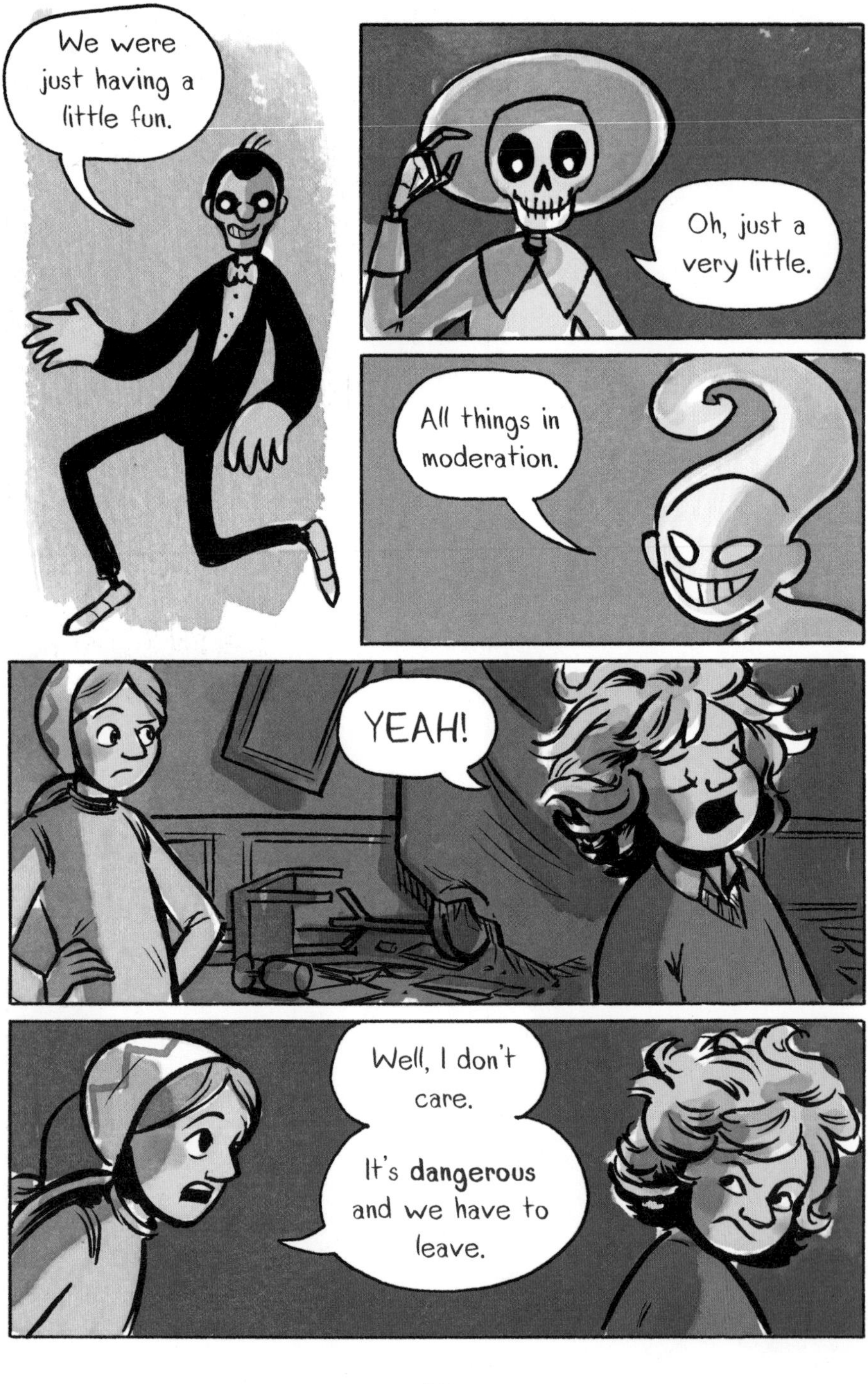
We were just having a little fun.
Oh, just a very little.
All things in moderation.
YEAH!
Well, I don't care.
It's **dangerous** and we have to leave.

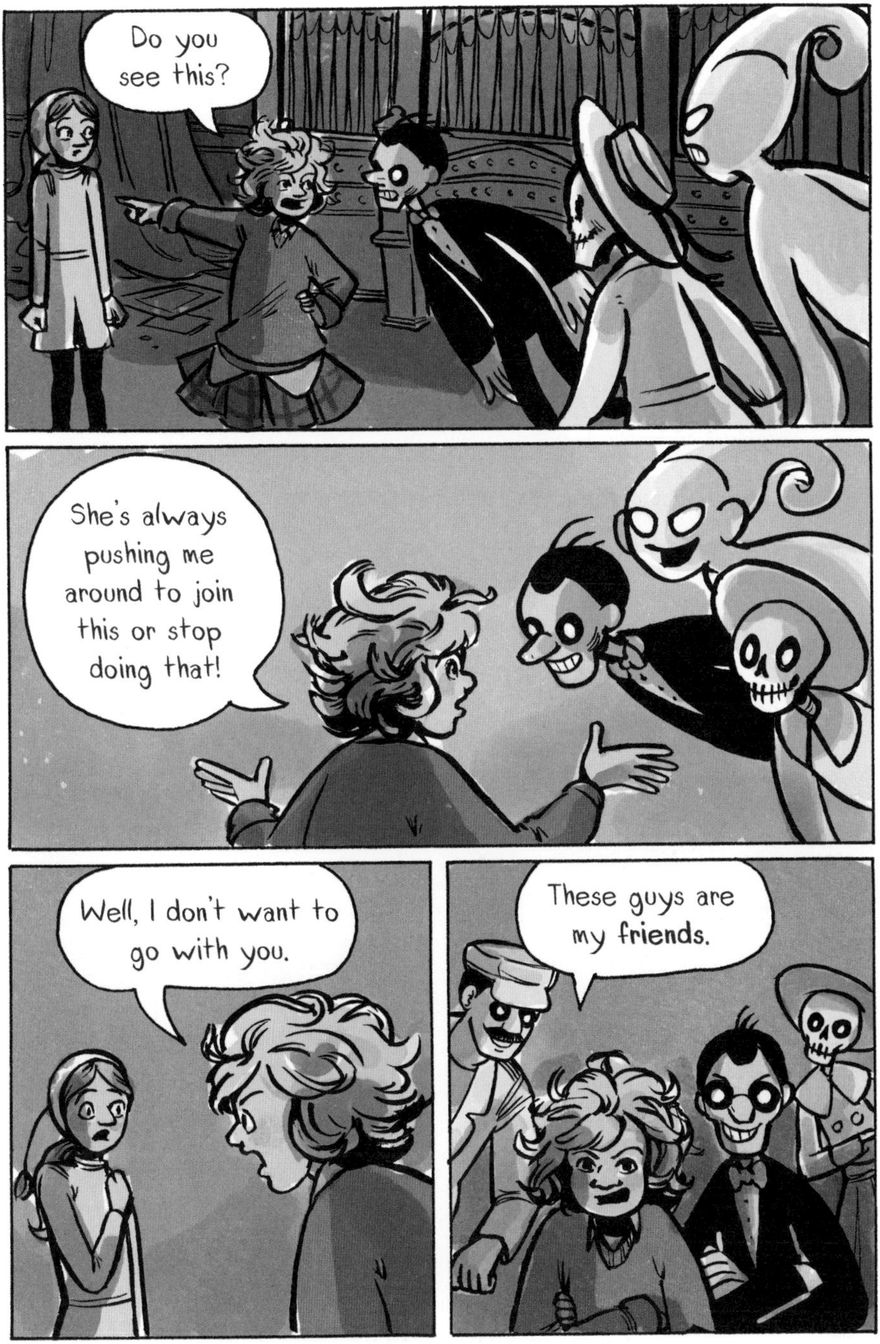
Do you see this?
She's always pushing me around to join this or stop doing that!
Well, I don't want to go with you.
These guys are my **friends.**

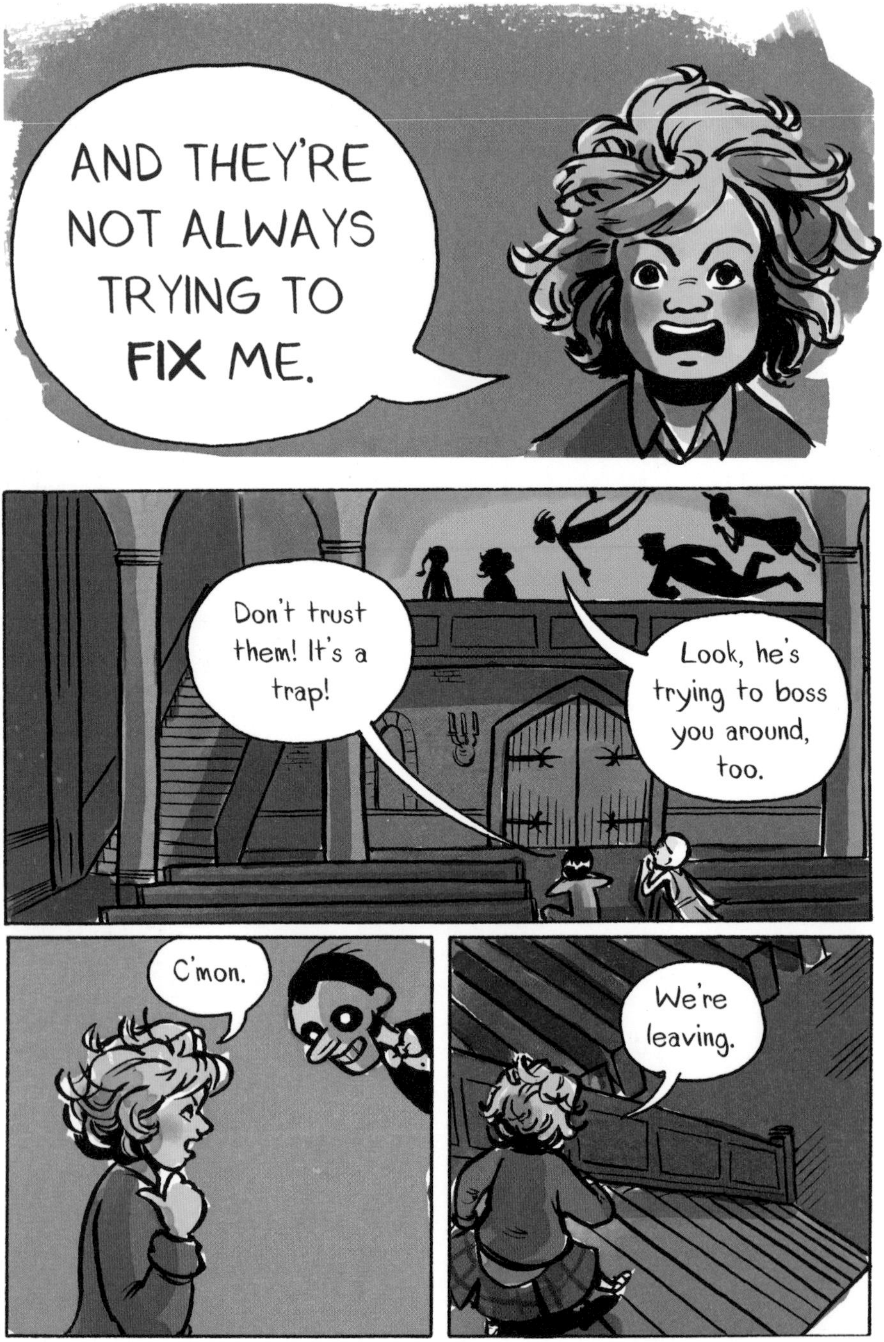
AND THEY'RE NOT ALWAYS TRYING TO **FIX** ME.
Don't trust them! It's a trap!
Look, he's trying to boss you around, too.
C'mon.
We're leaving.

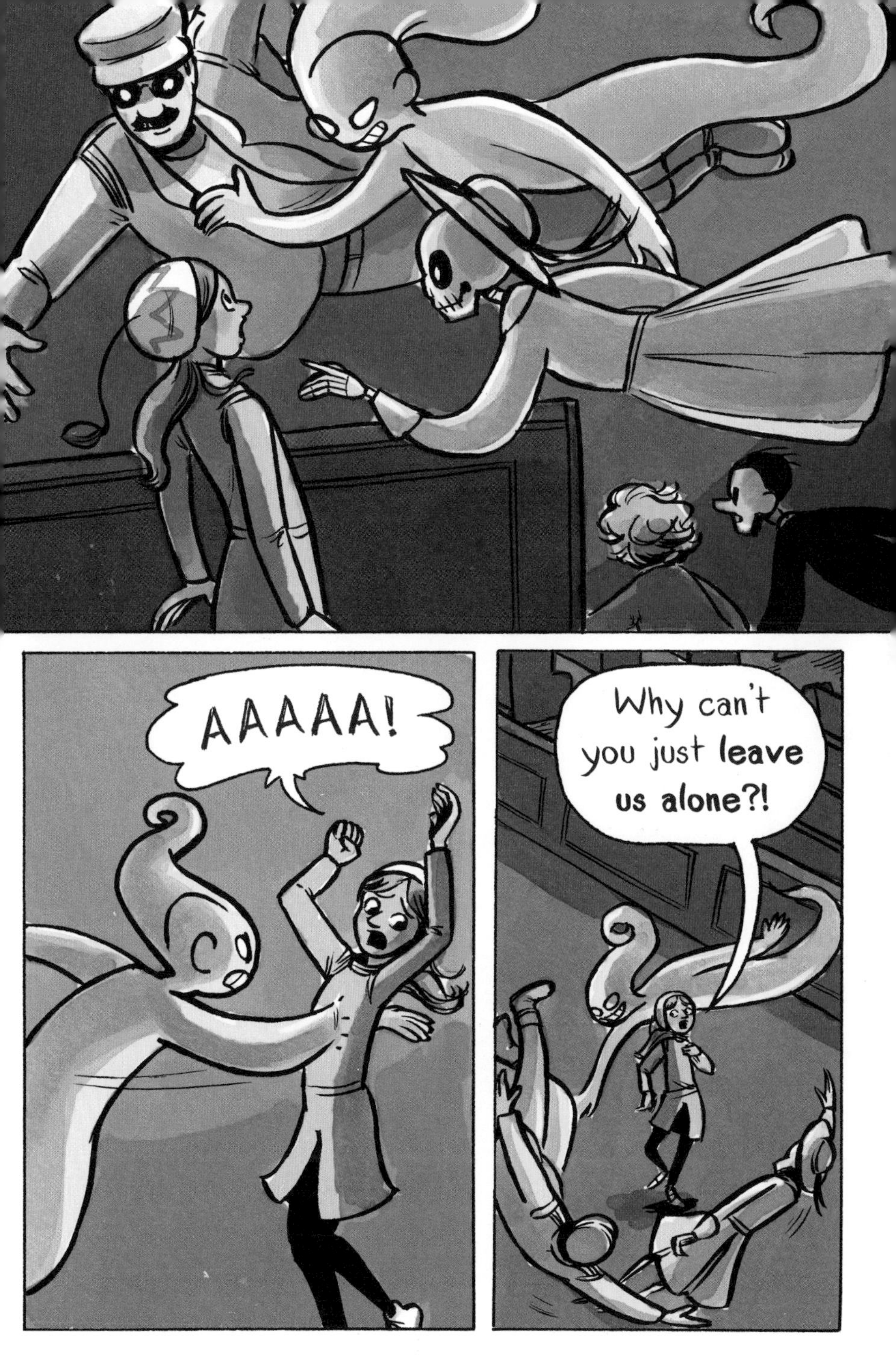
AAAAA!
Why can't you just **leave** **us alone?!**

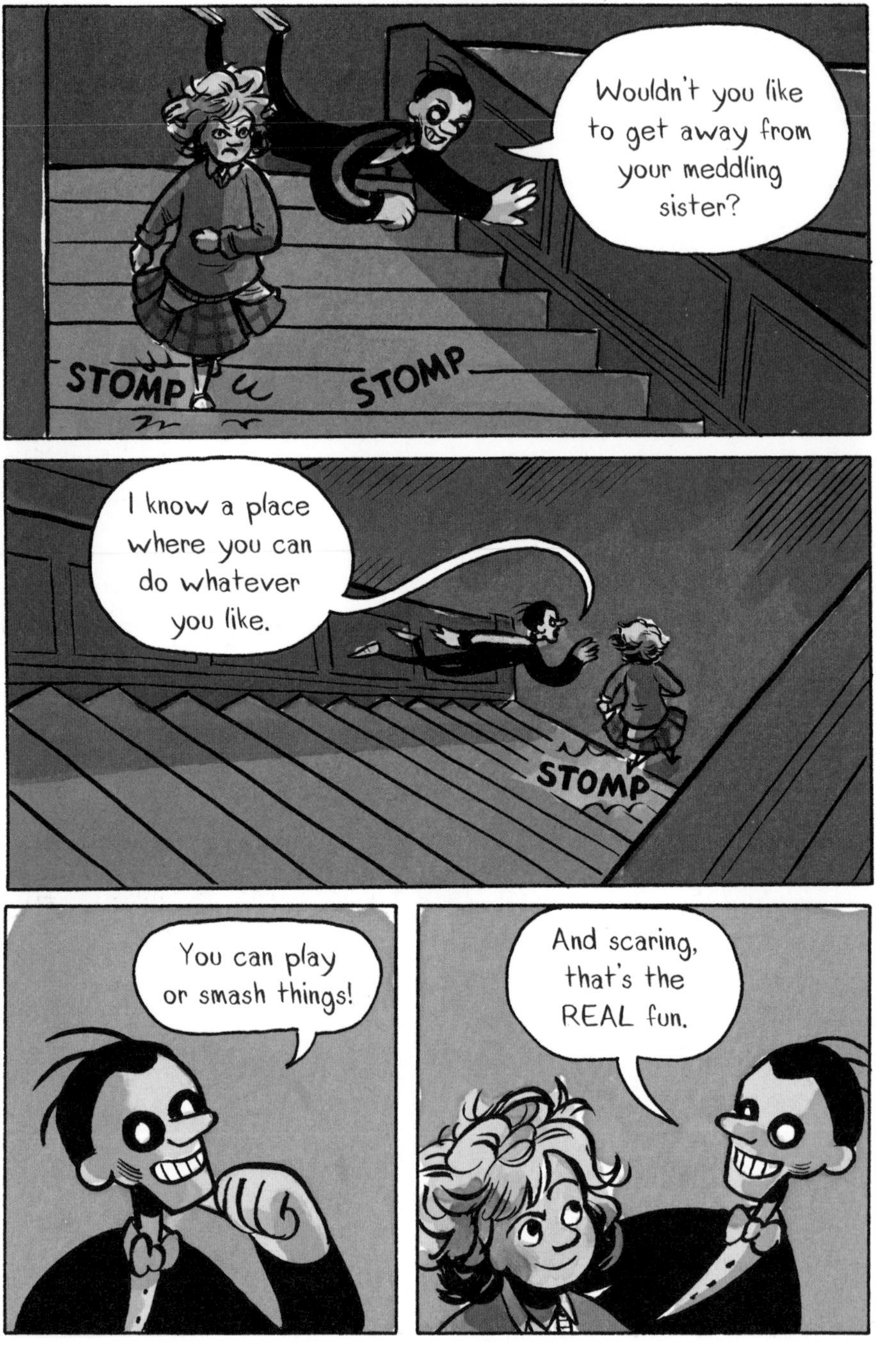
Wouldn't you like to get away from your meddling sister?
STOMP
STOMP
I know a place where you can do whatever you like.
STOMP
You can play or smash things!
And scaring, that's the REAL fun.

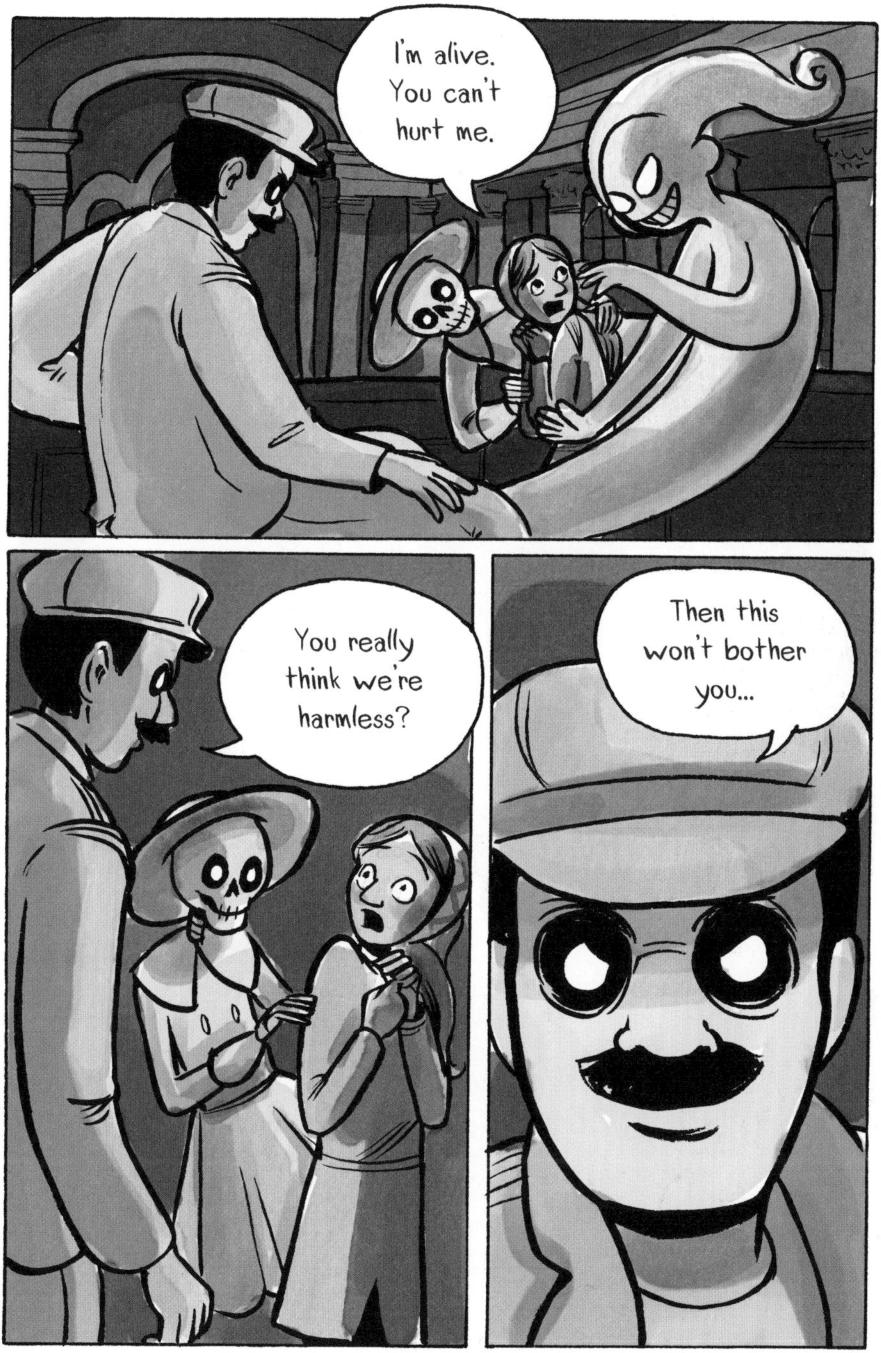
I'm alive. You can't hurt me.
You really think we're harmless?
Then this won't bother you...

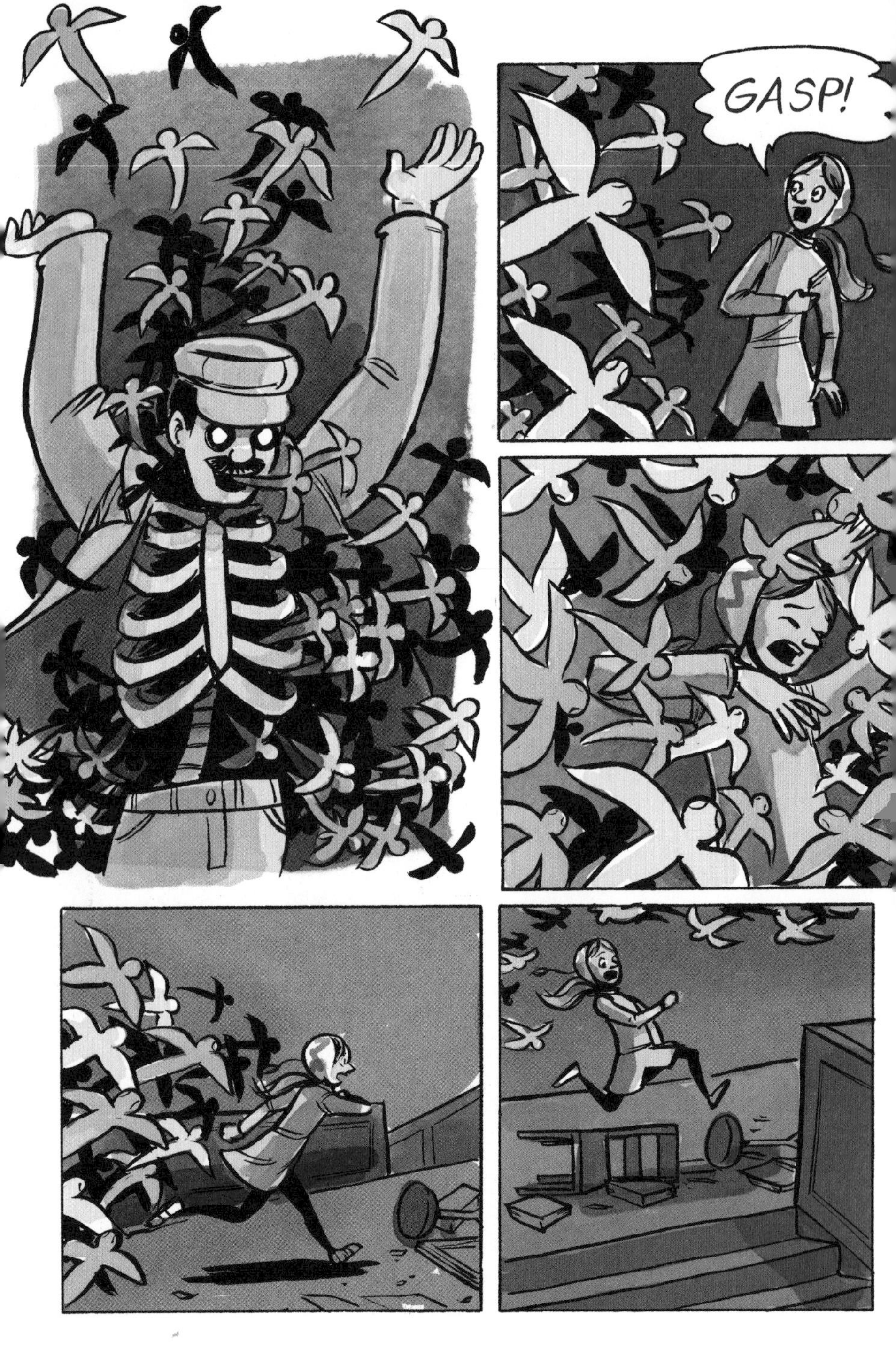
GASP!

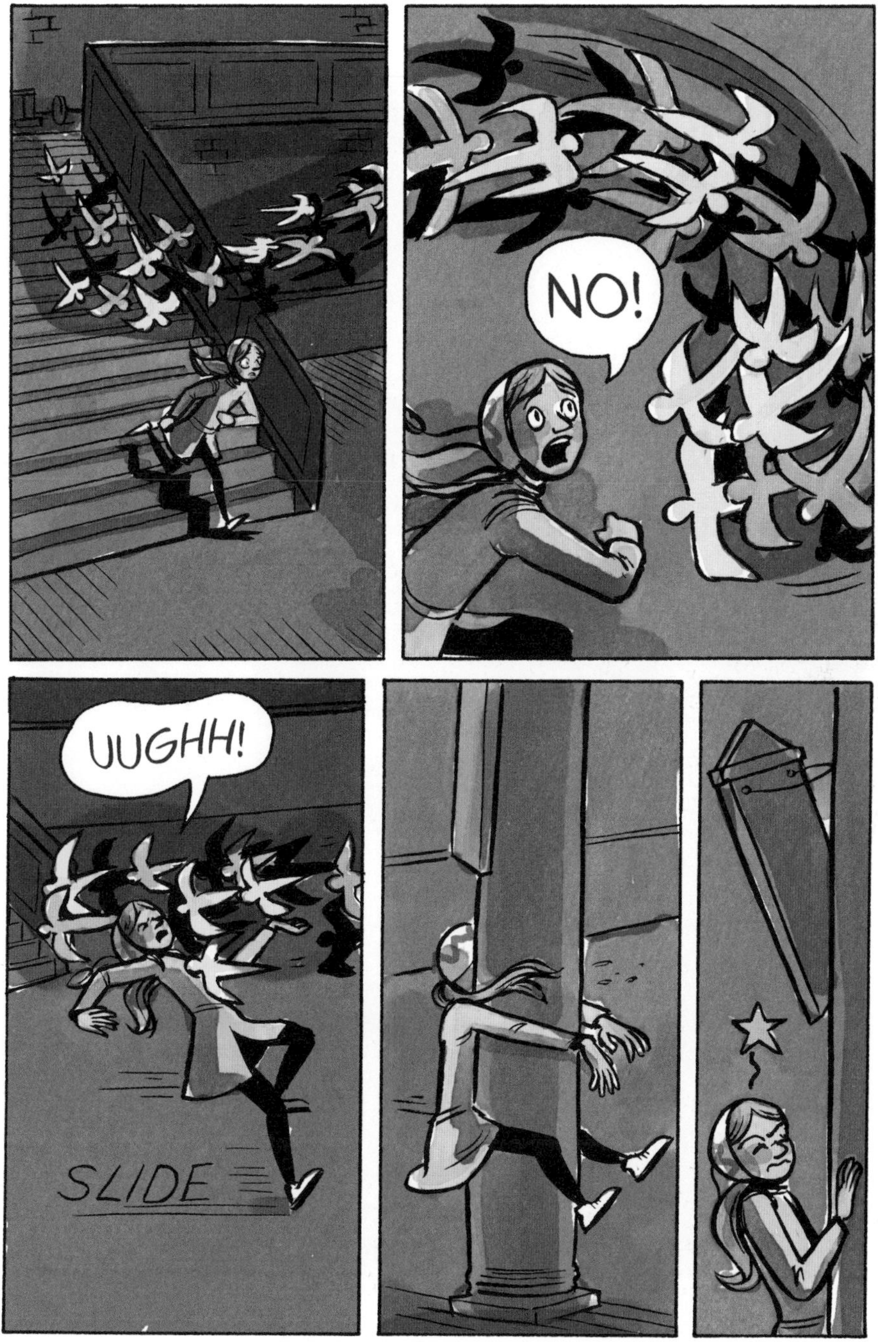
NO!
UUGHH!
SLIDE

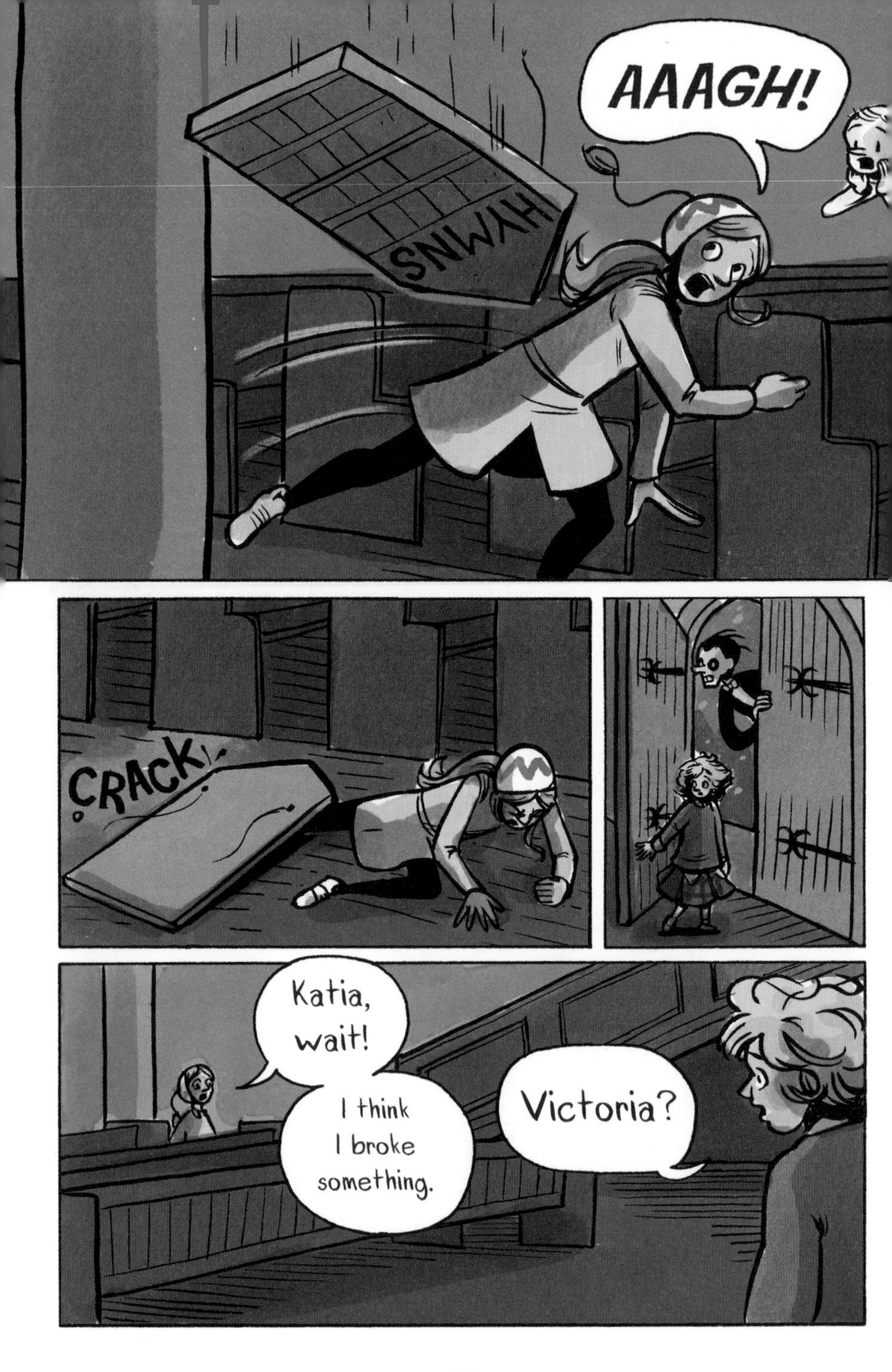
AAAGH!
HYMNS
CRACK
Katia, wait!
I think I broke something.
Victoria?

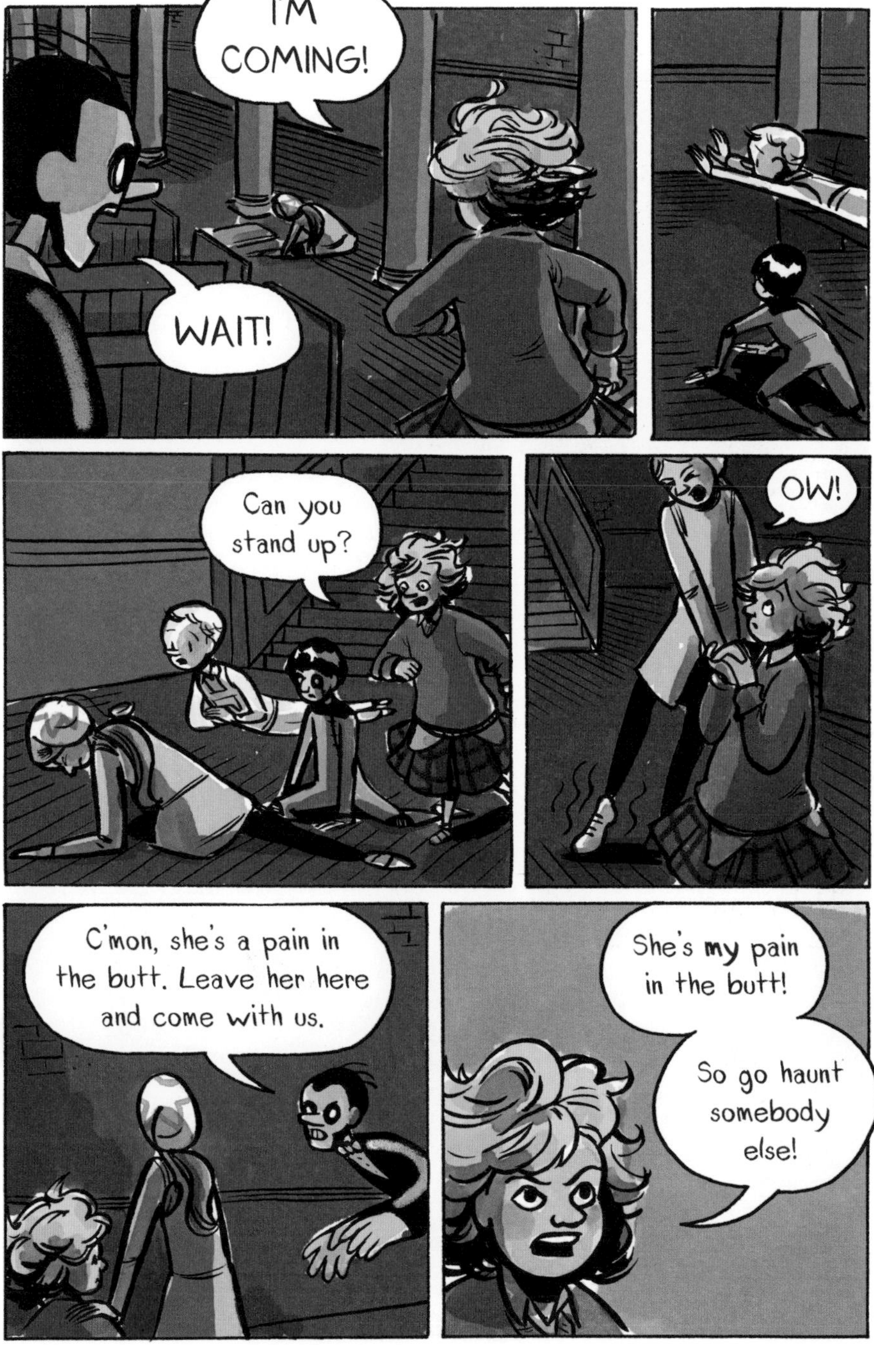
I'M COMING!
WAIT!
Can you stand up?
OW!
C'mon, she's a pain in the butt. Leave her here and come with us.
She's **my** pain in the butt!
So go haunt somebody else!

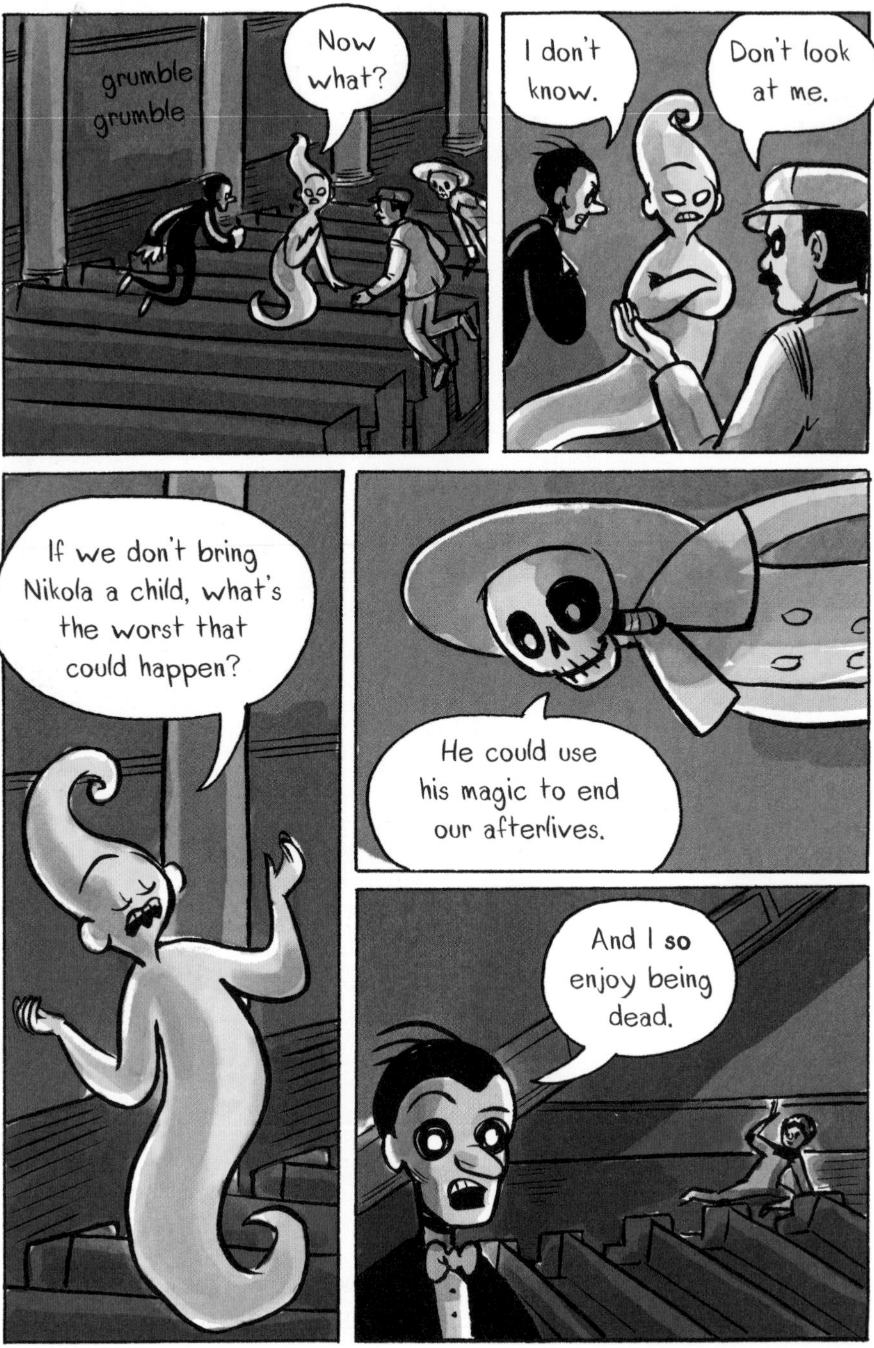
grumble grumble
Now what?
I don't know.
Don't look at me.
If we don't bring Nikola a child, what's the worst that could happen?
He could use his magic to end our afterlives.
And I **so** enjoy being dead.

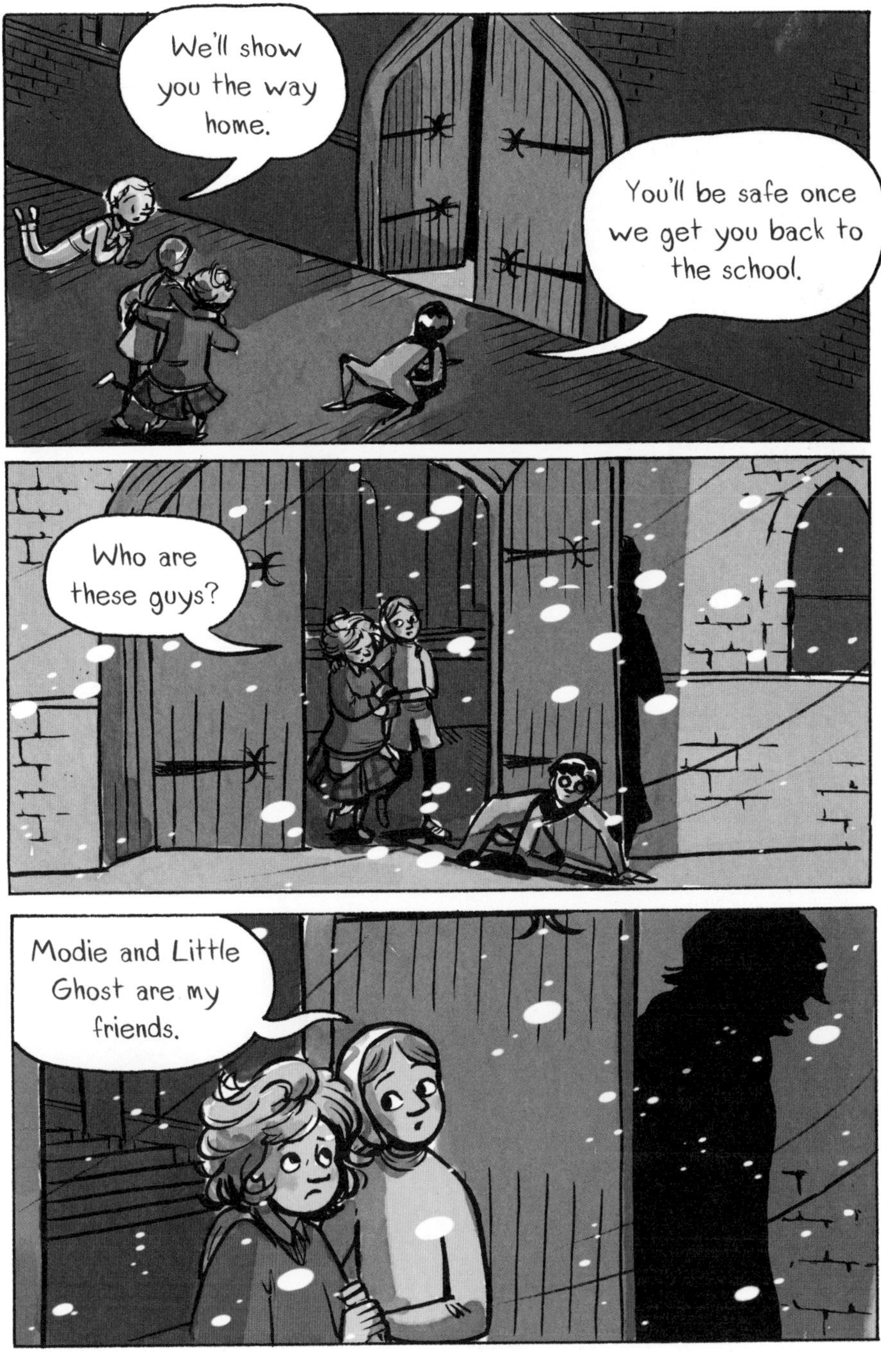
We'll show you the way home.
You'll be safe once we get you back to the school.
Who are these guys?
Modie and Little Ghost are my friends.

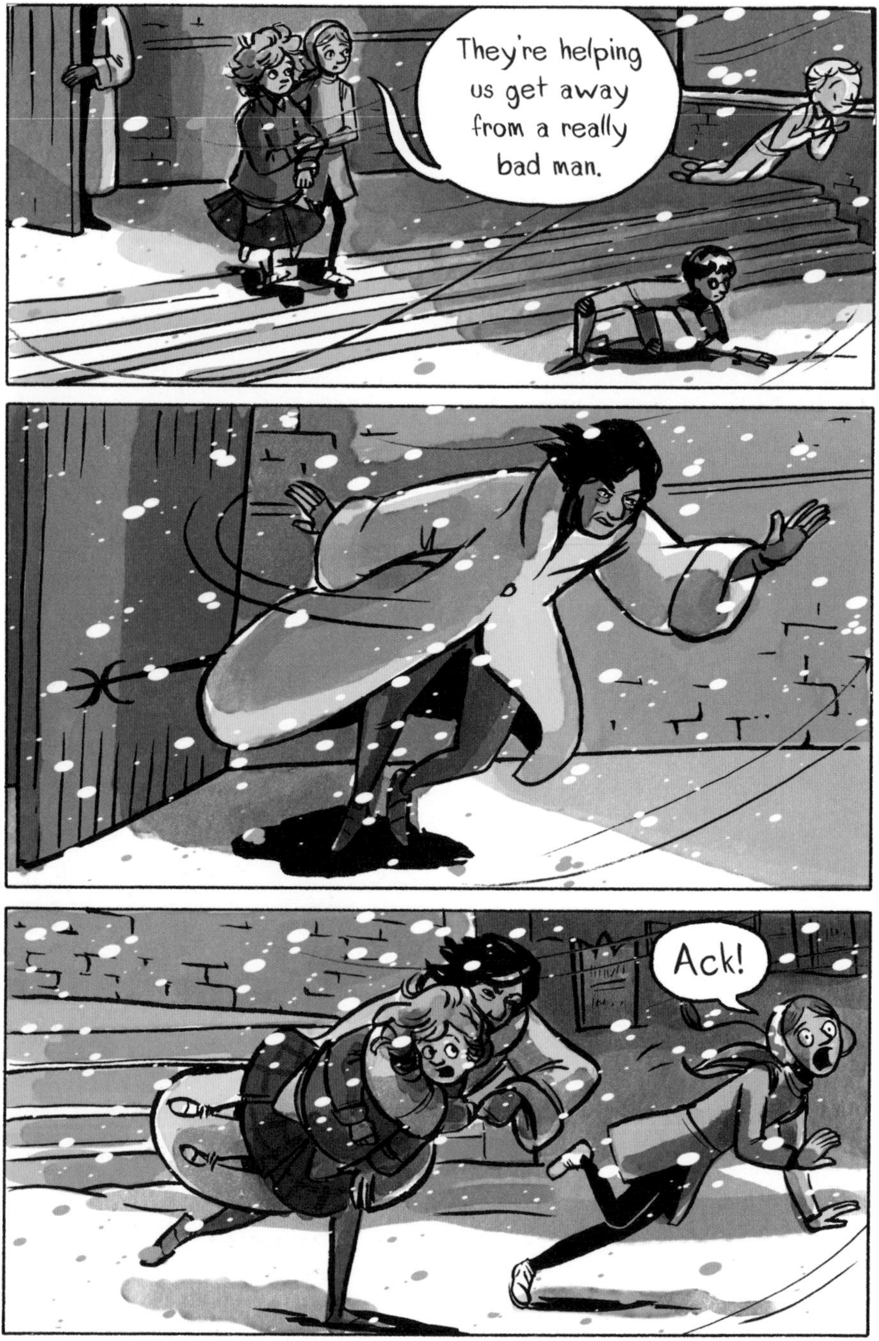
They're helping us get away from a really bad man.
Ack!

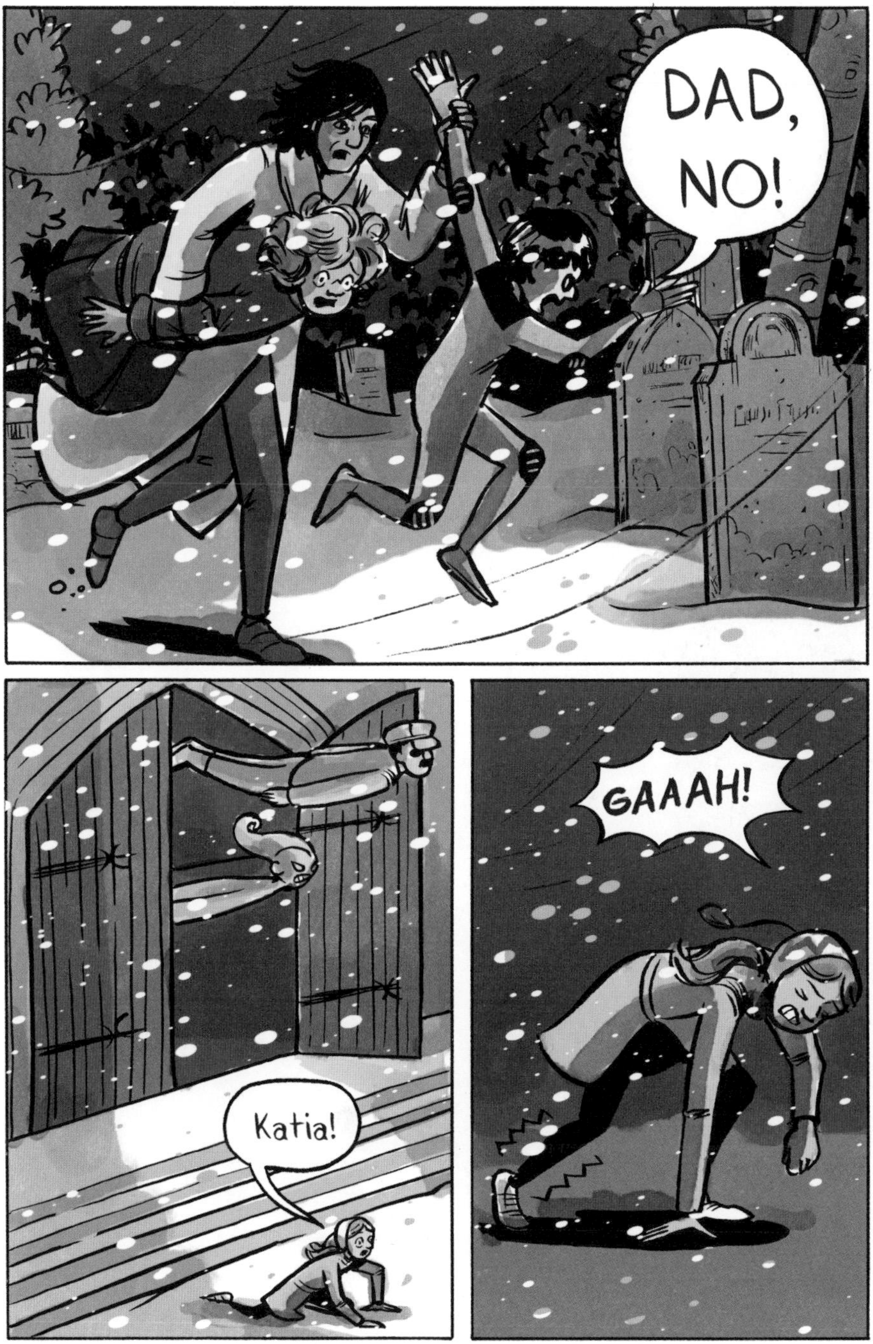
DAD, NO!
Katia!
GAAAH!

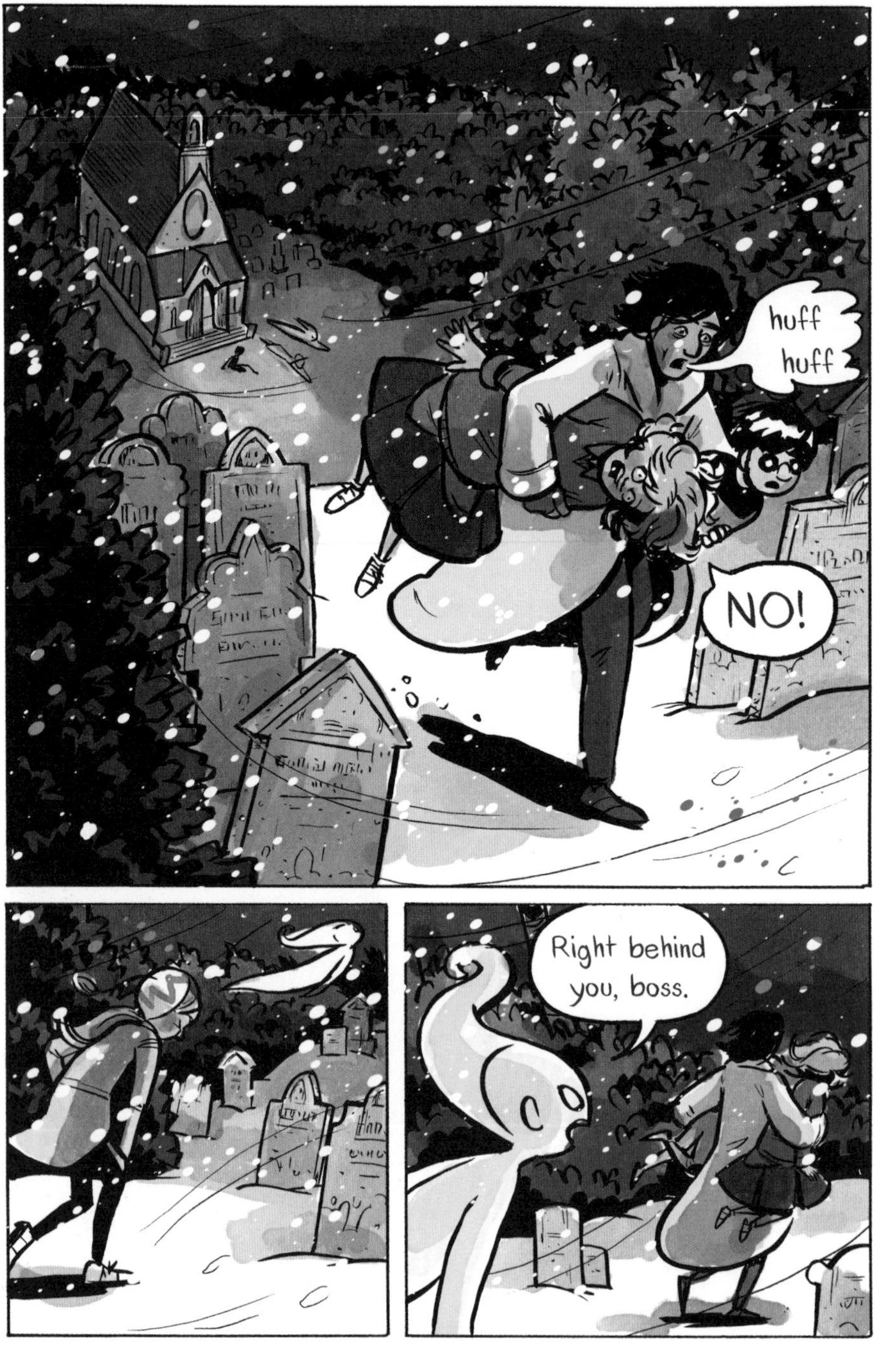
huff
huff
NO!
Right behind you, boss.

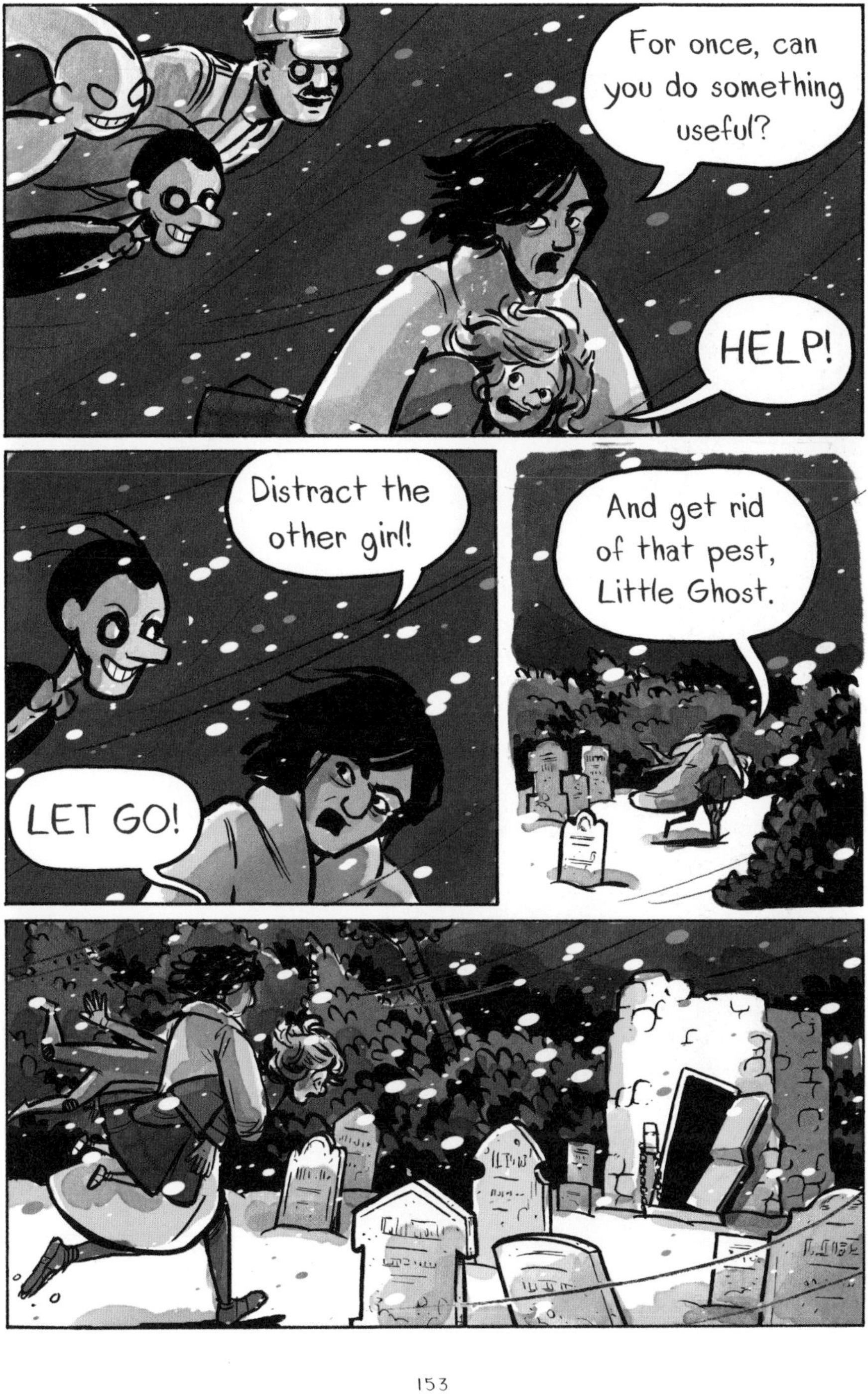
For once, can you do something useful?
HELP!
Distract the other girl!
LET GO!
And get rid of that pest, Little Ghost.

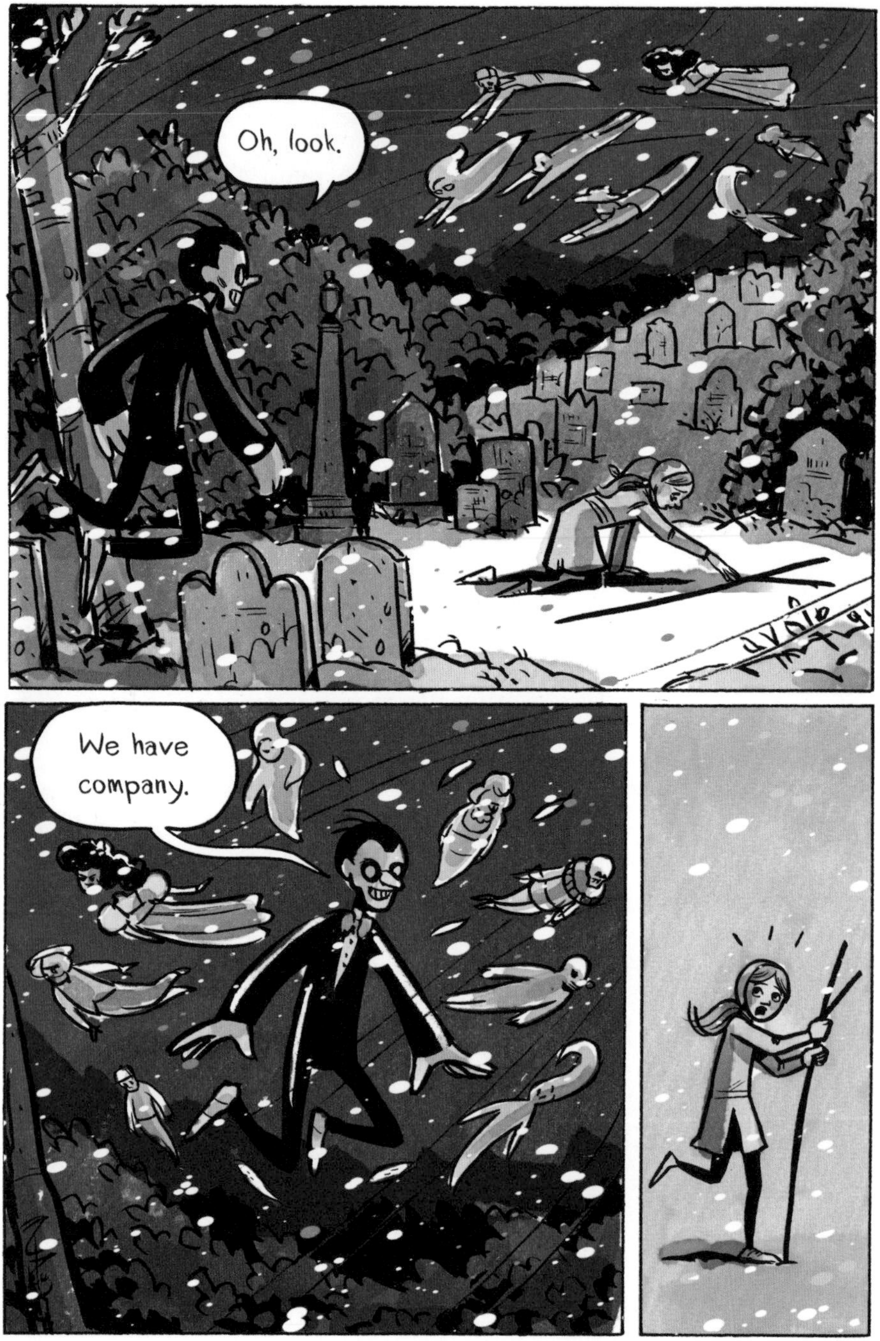
Oh, look.
We have company.

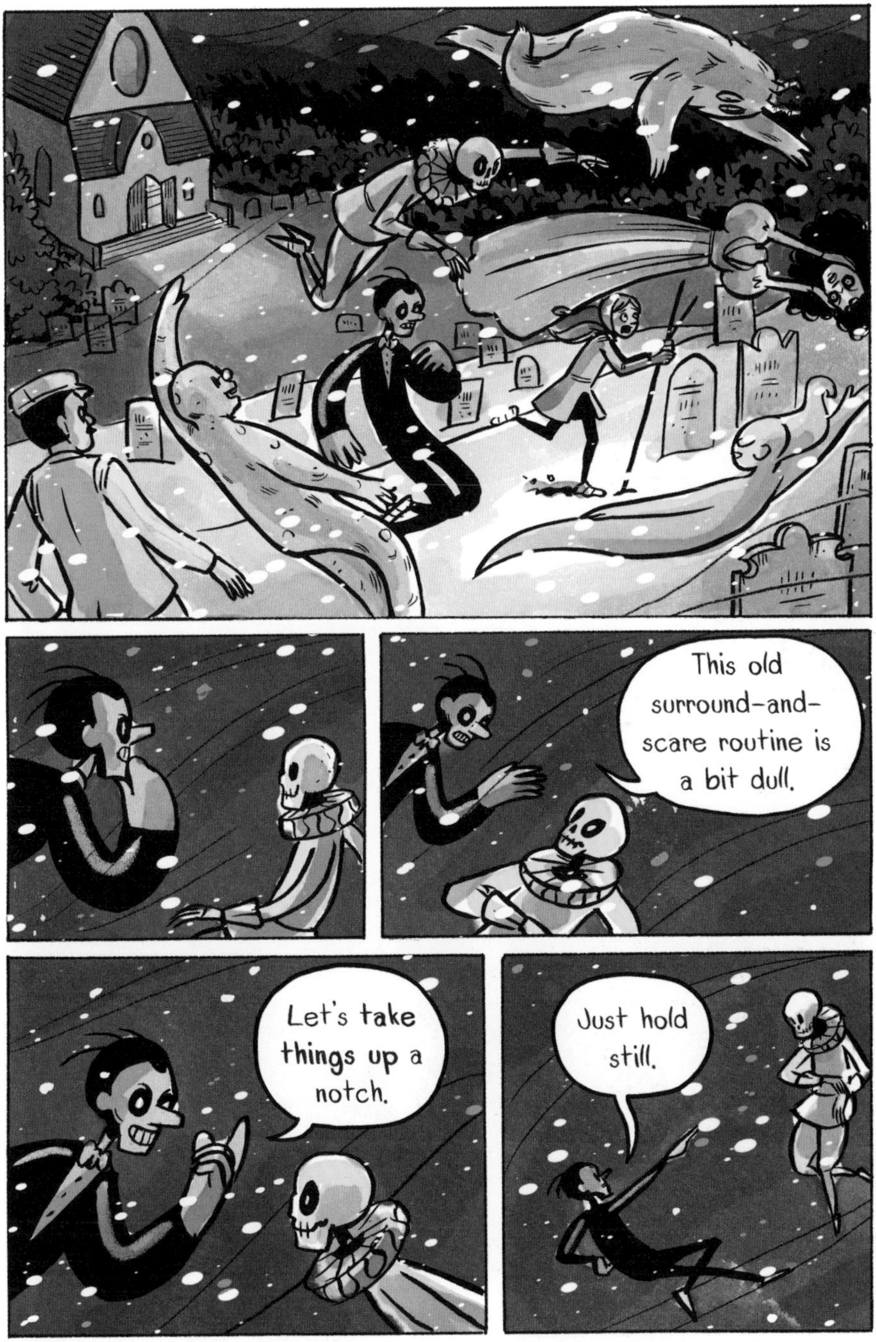
This old surround-and-scare routine is a bit dull.
Let's take things up a notch.
Just hold still.

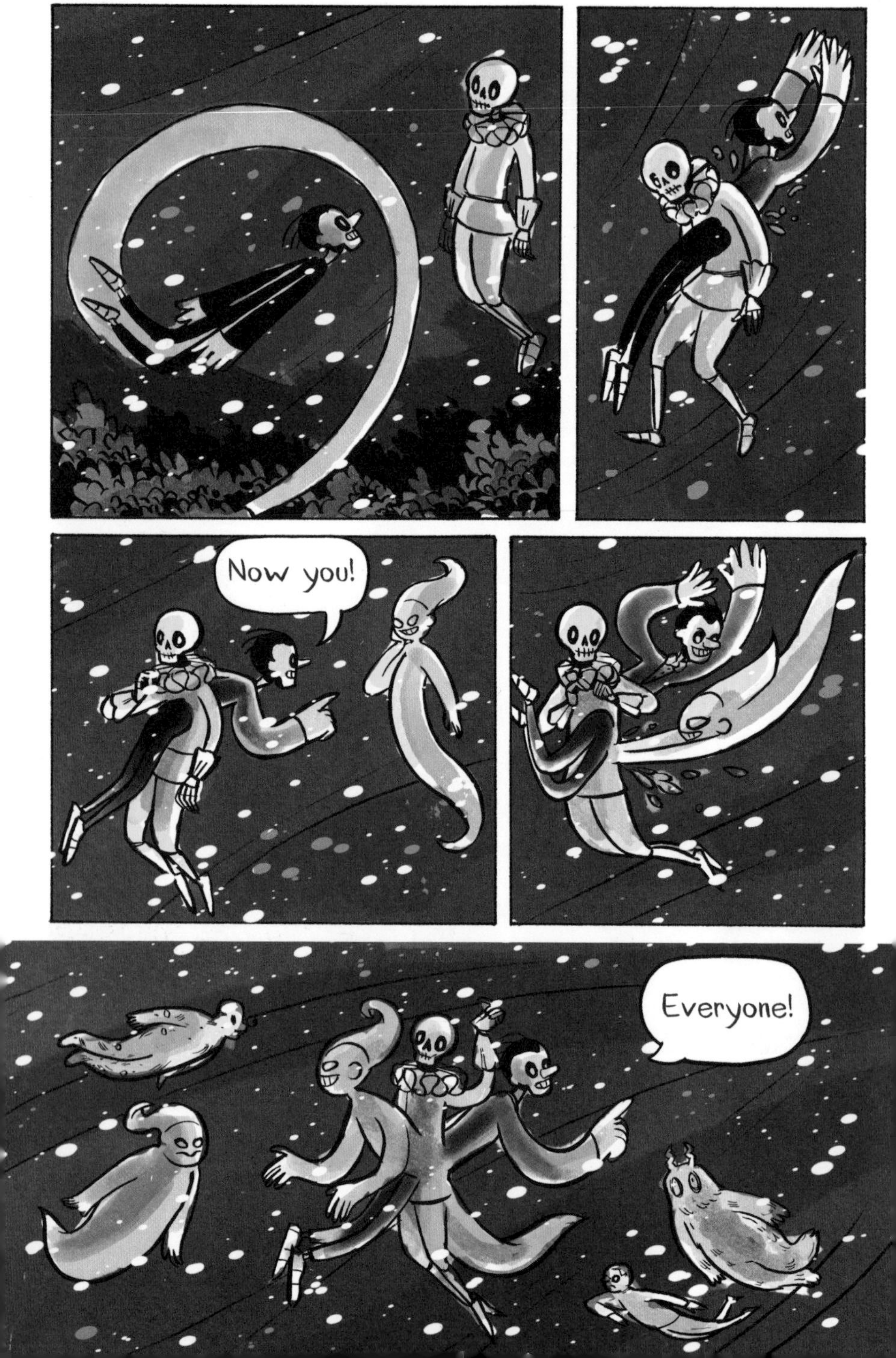
Now you!
Everyone!

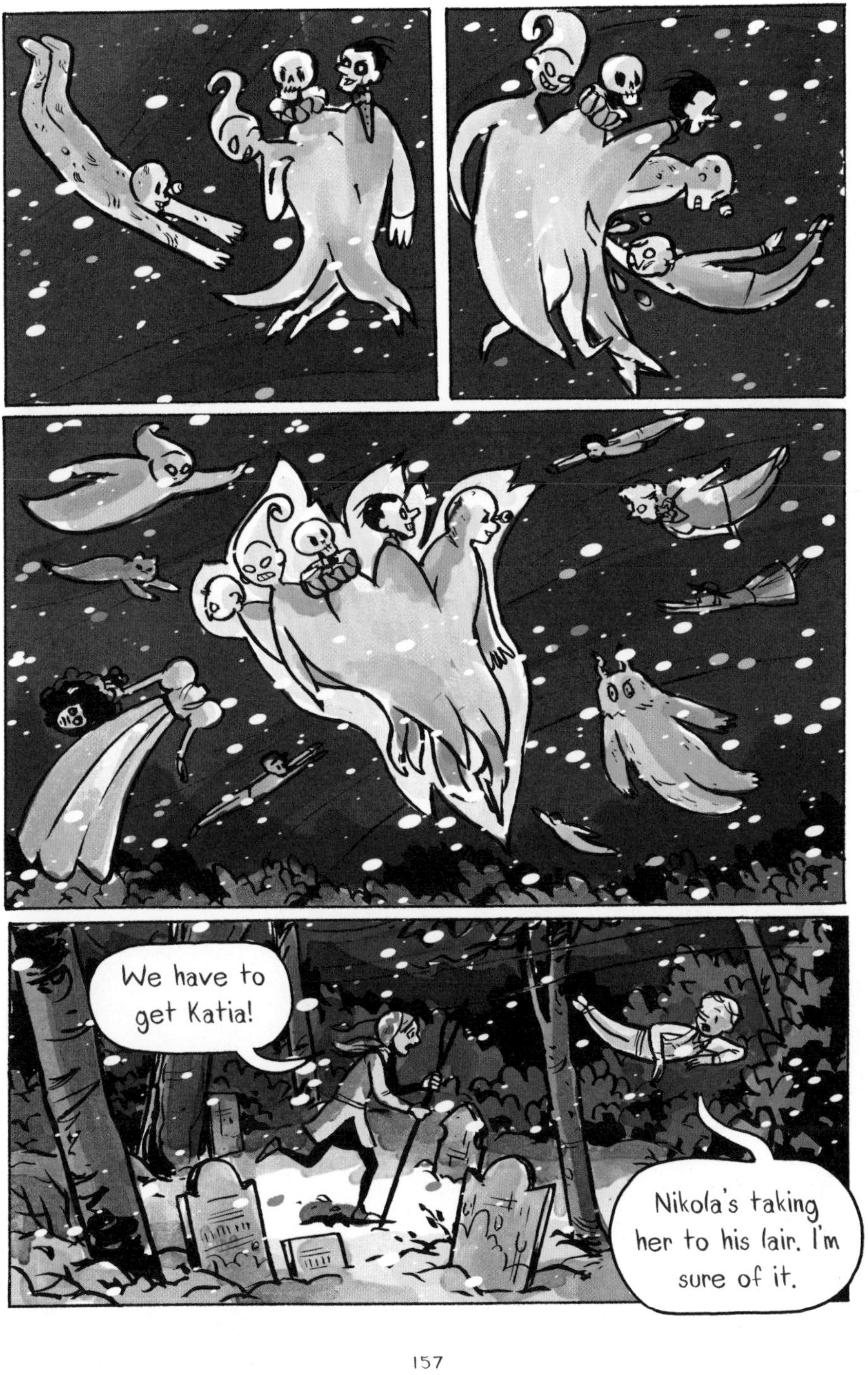
We have to get Katia!
Nikola's taking her to his lair. I'm sure of it.

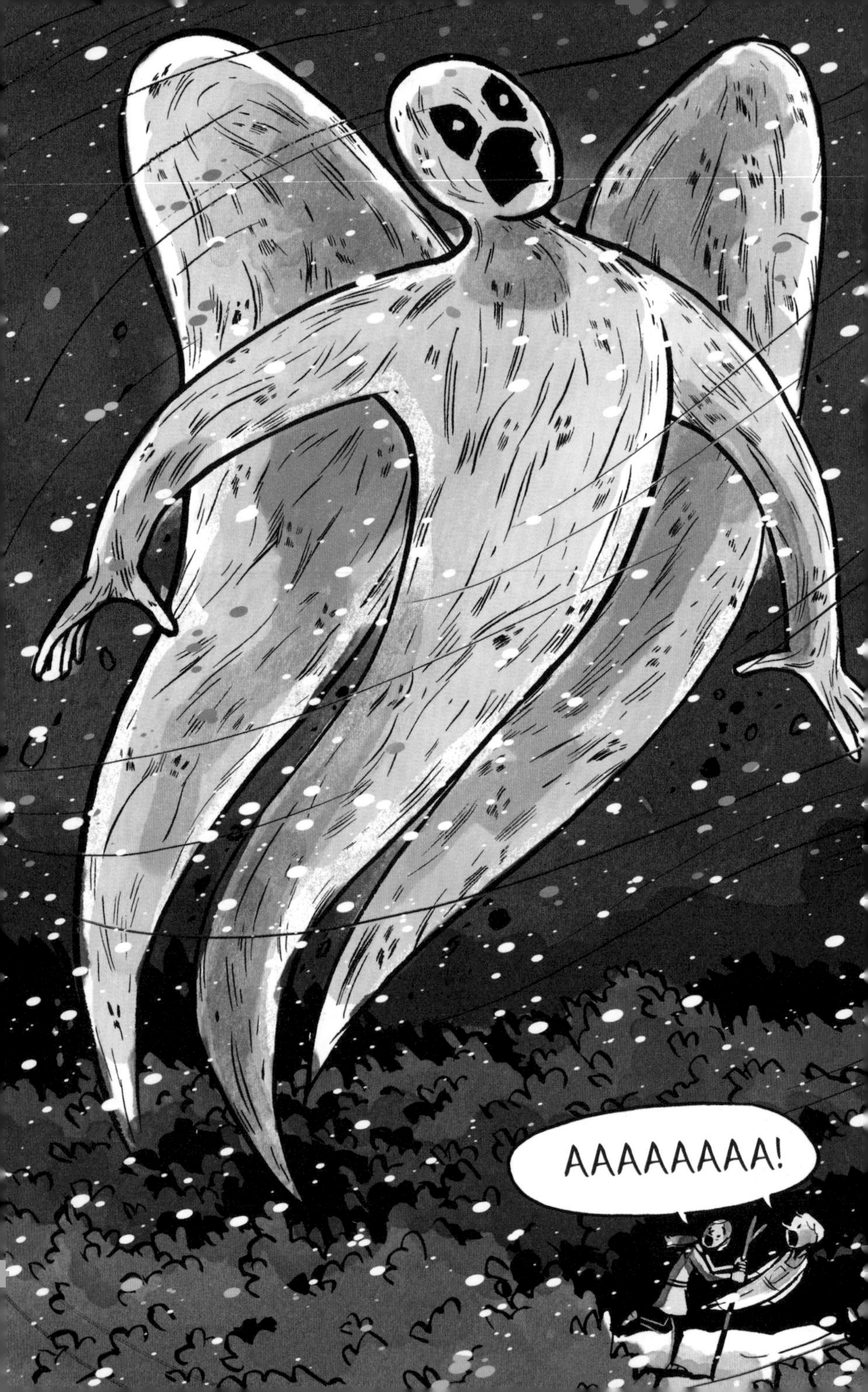
AAAAAAAA!

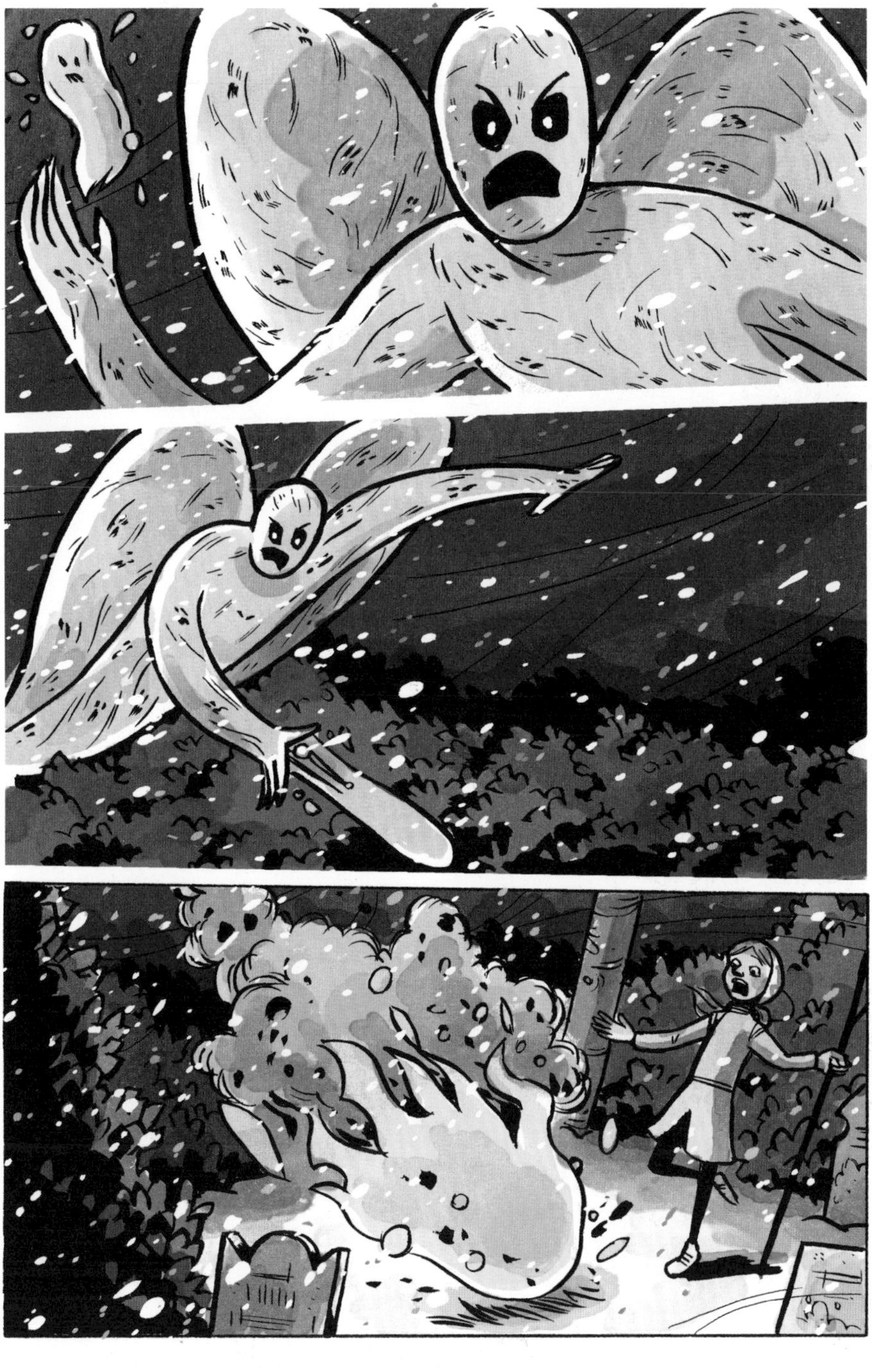

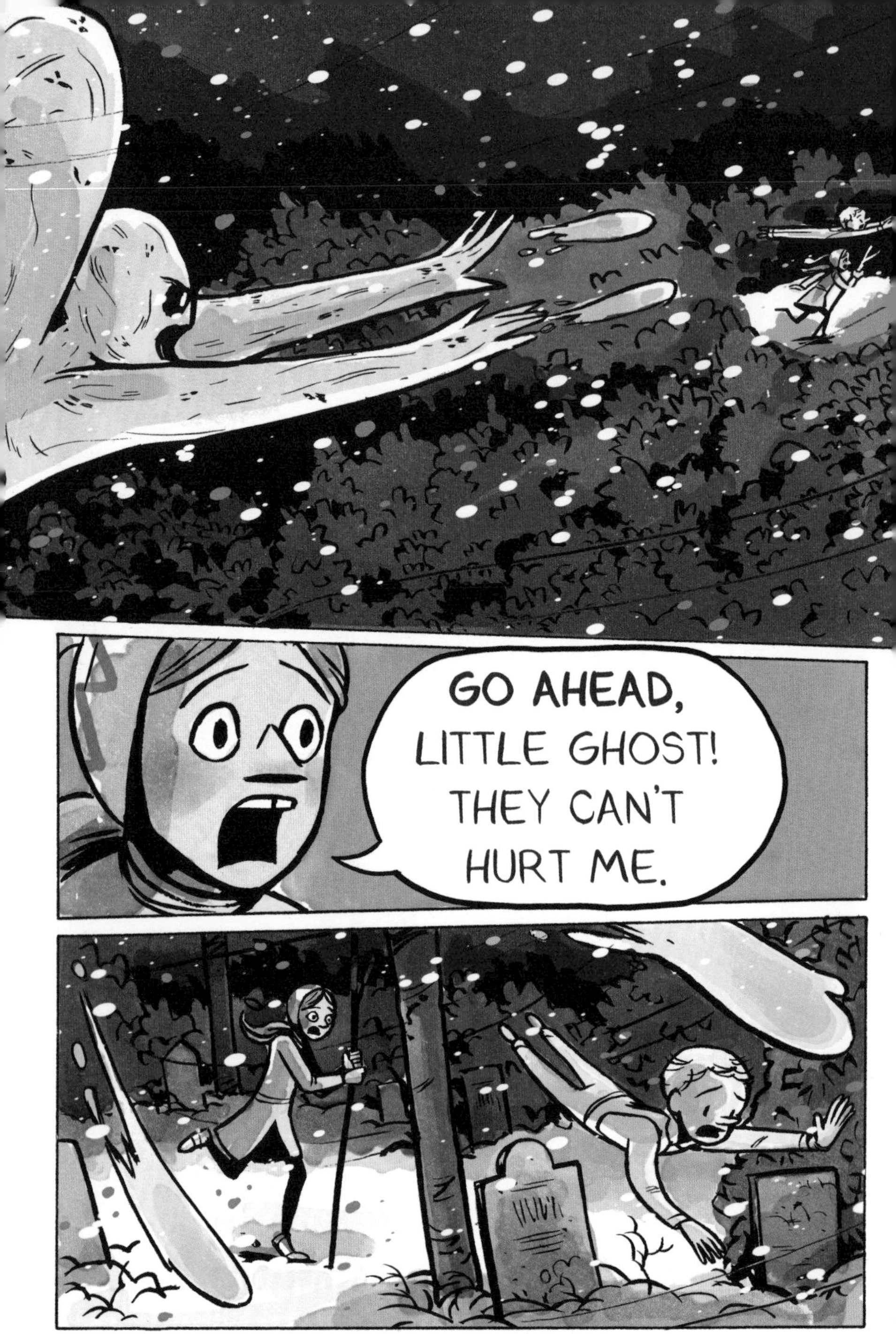
GO AHEAD, LITTLE GHOST! THEY CAN'T HURT ME.

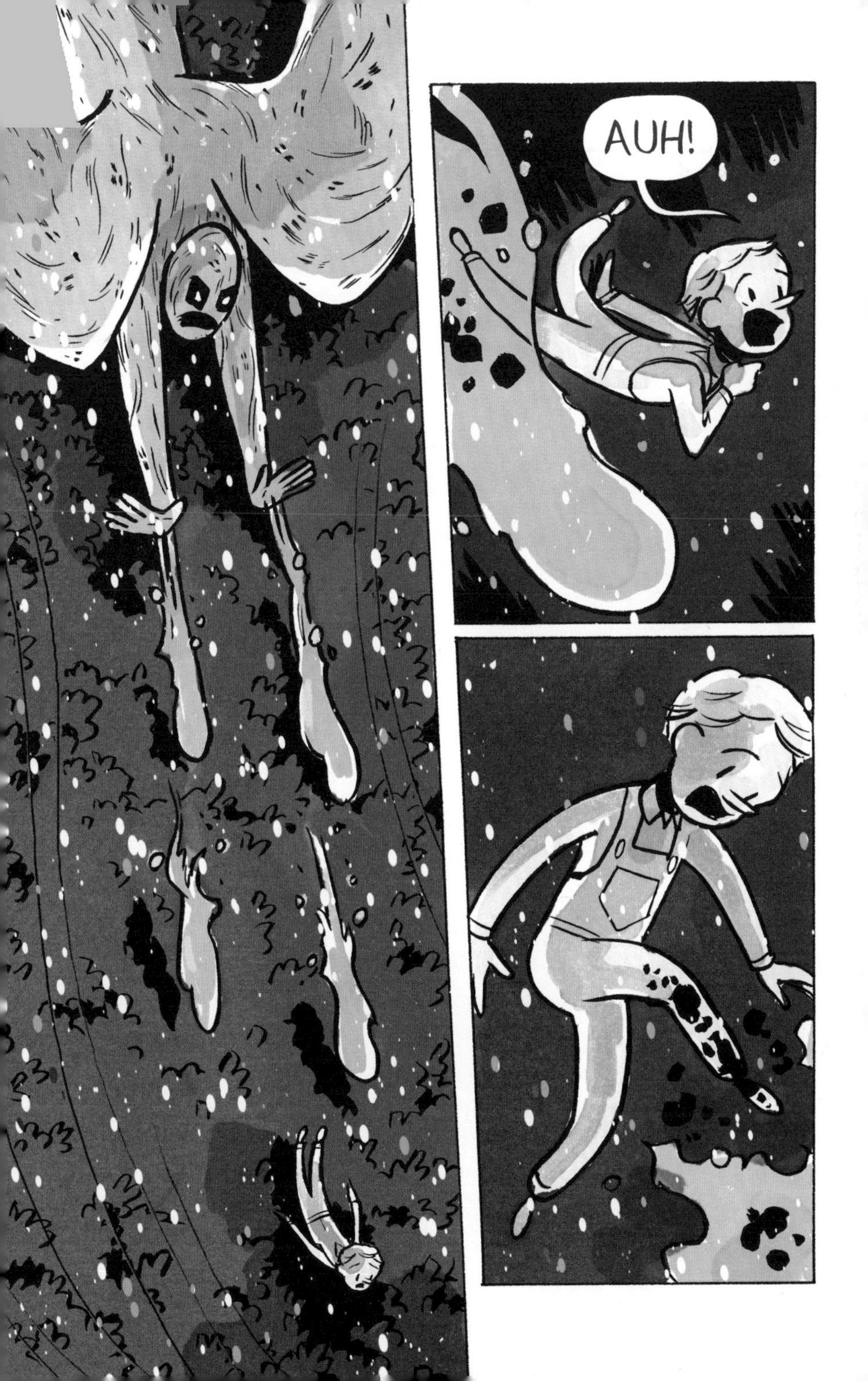
AUH!

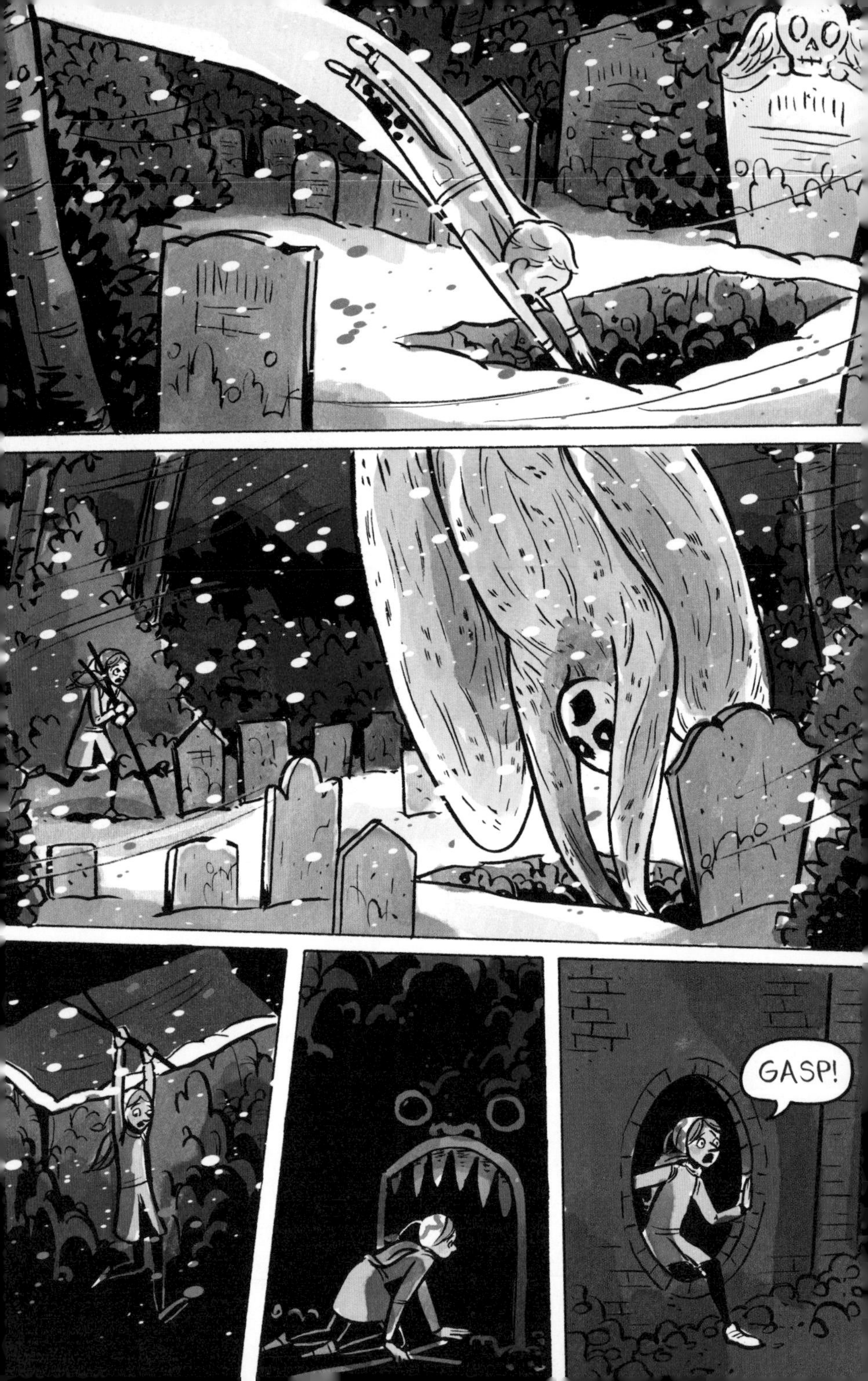
GASP!

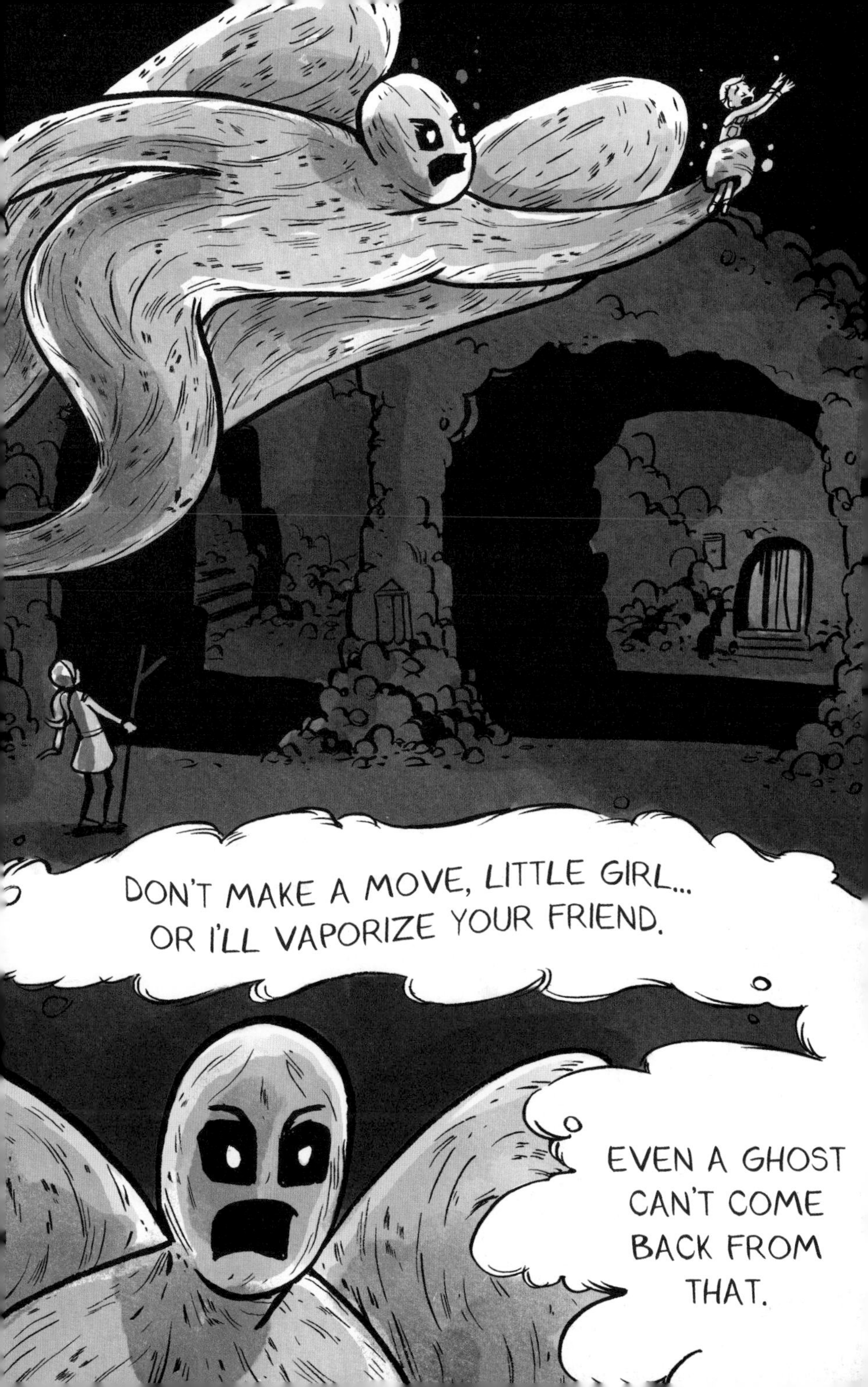
DON'T MAKE A MOVE, LITTLE GIRL... OR I'LL VAPORIZE YOUR FRIEND.
EVEN A GHOST CAN'T COME BACK FROM THAT.

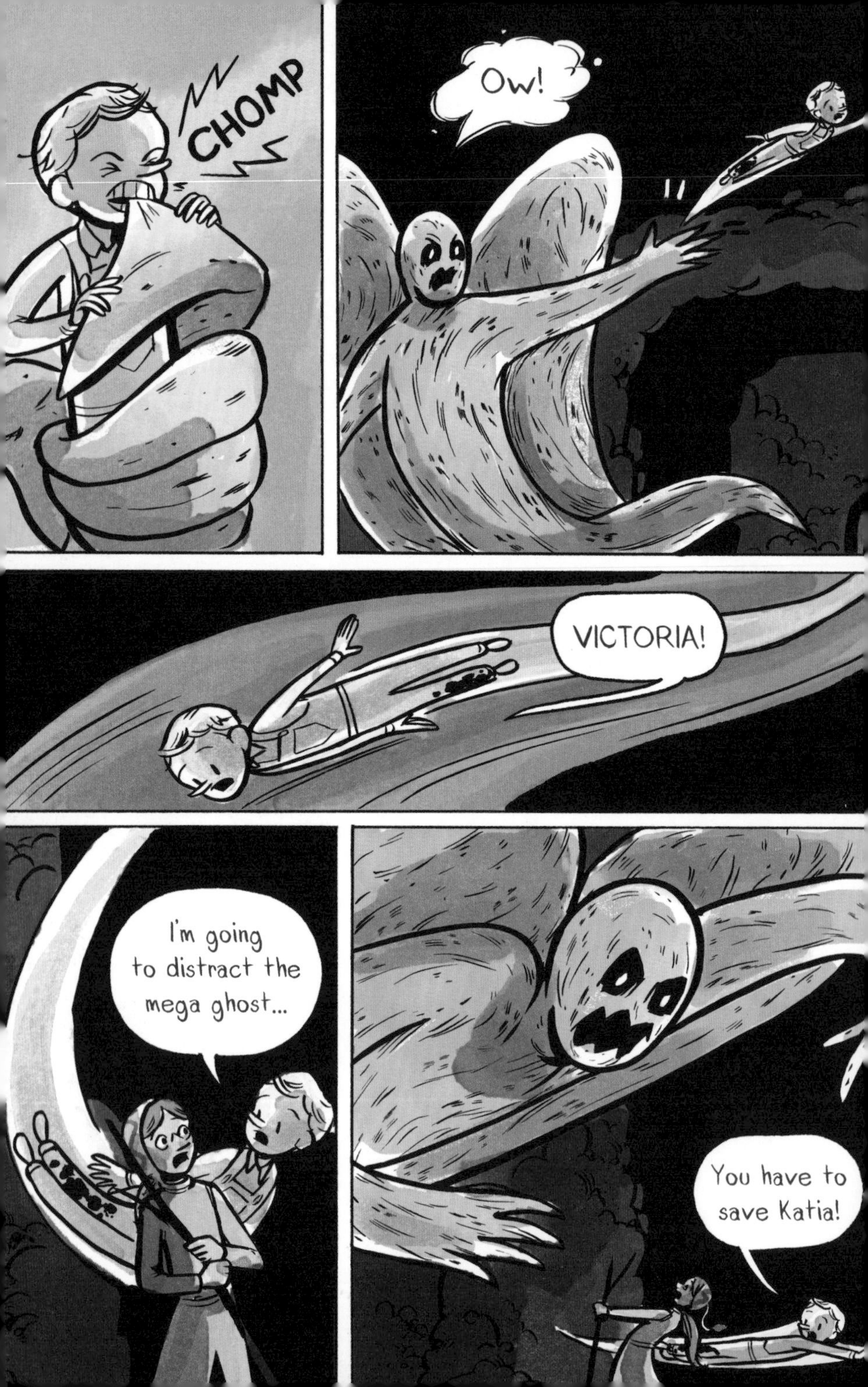
CHOMP
Ow!
VICTORIA!
I'm going to distract the mega ghost...
You have to save Katia!

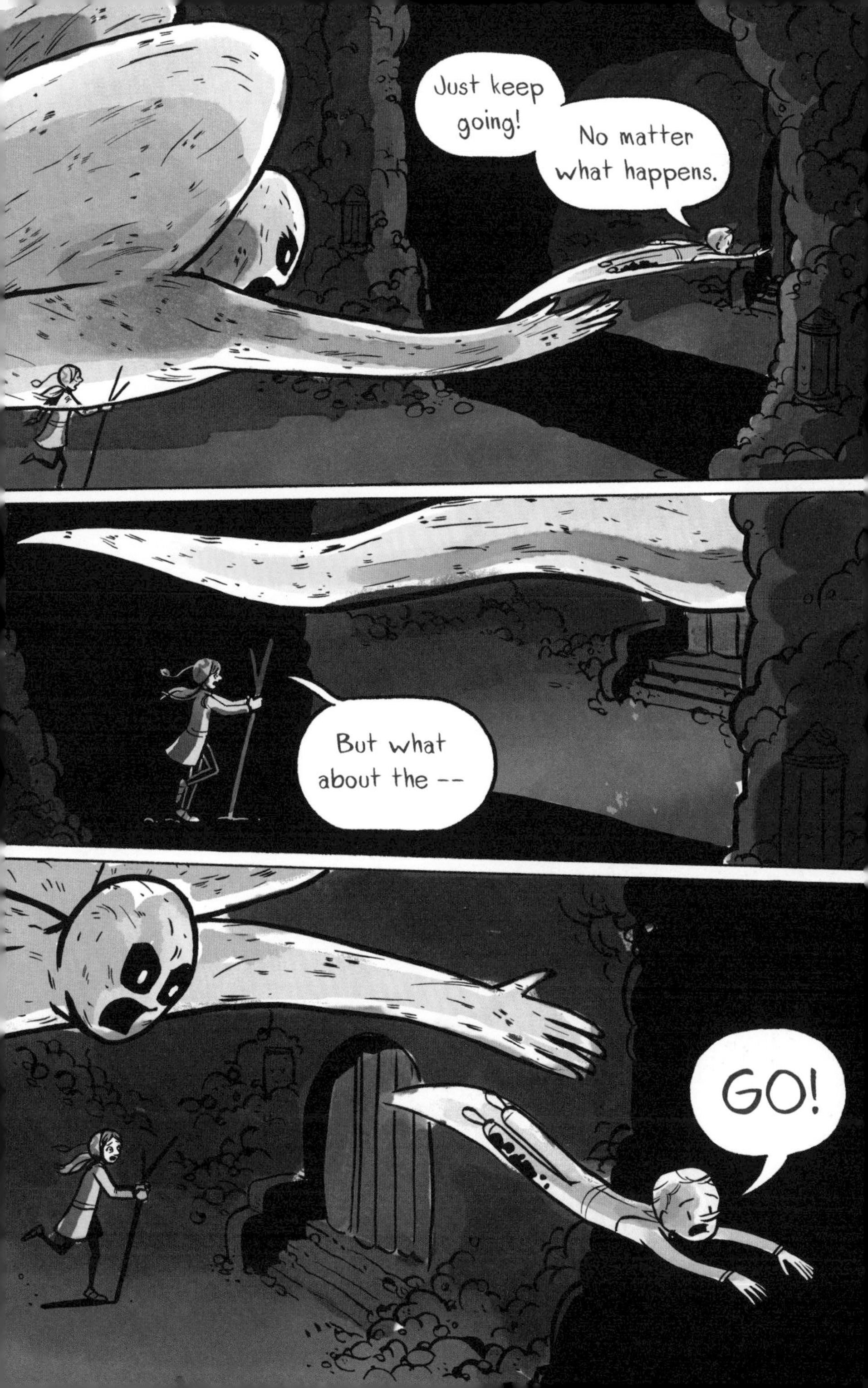
Just keep going!
No matter what happens.
But what about the --
GO!

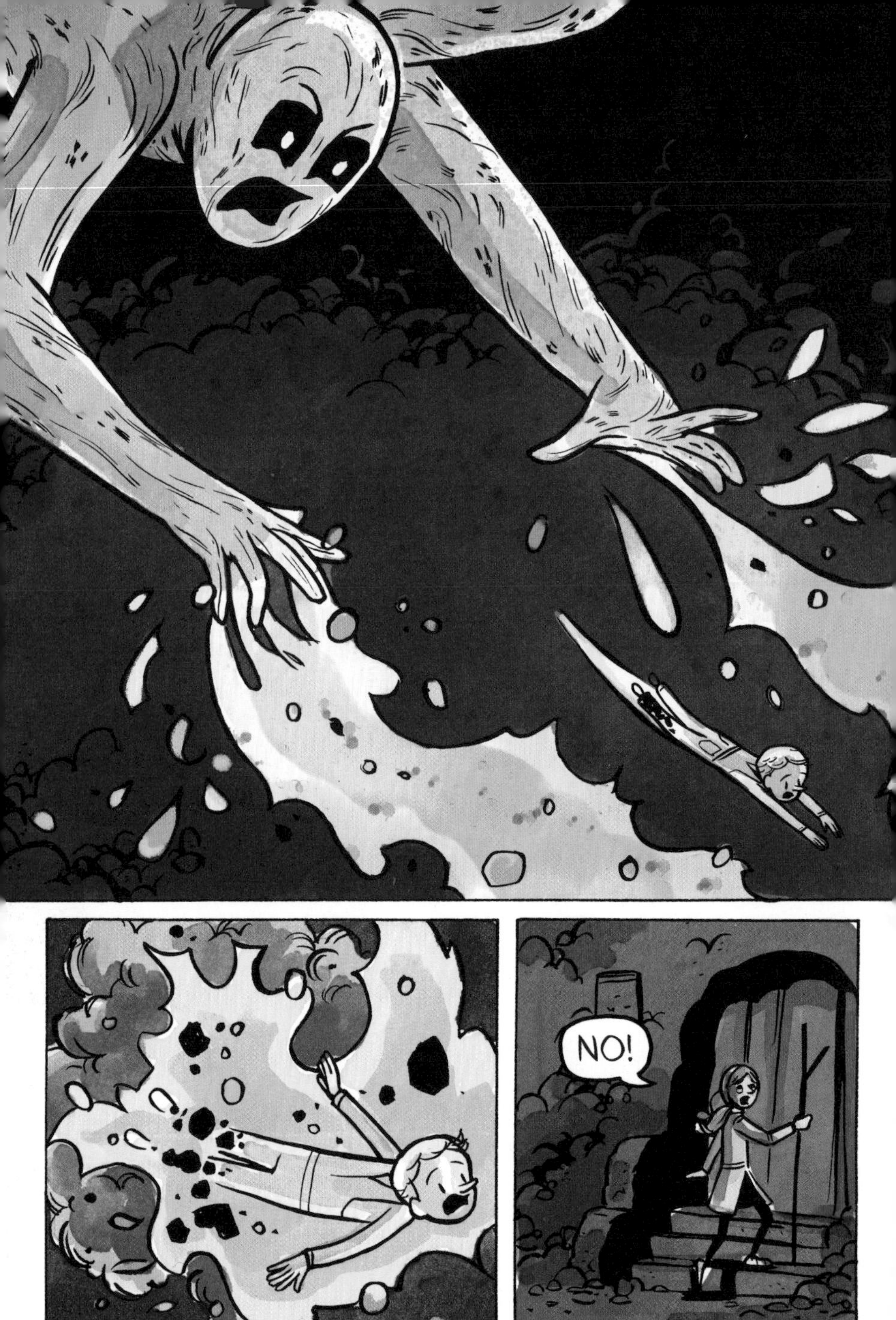
NO!

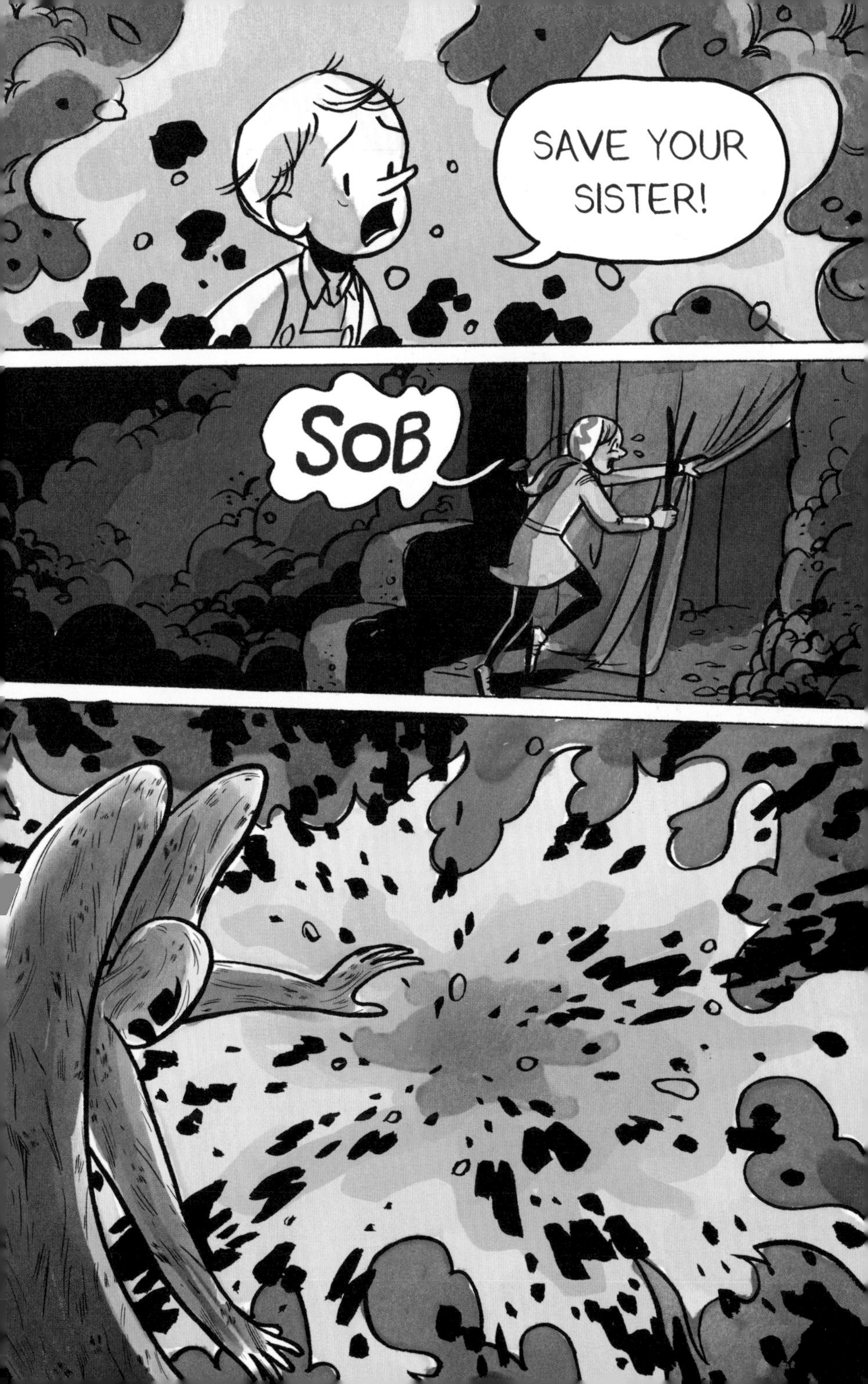
SAVE YOUR SISTER!
SOB

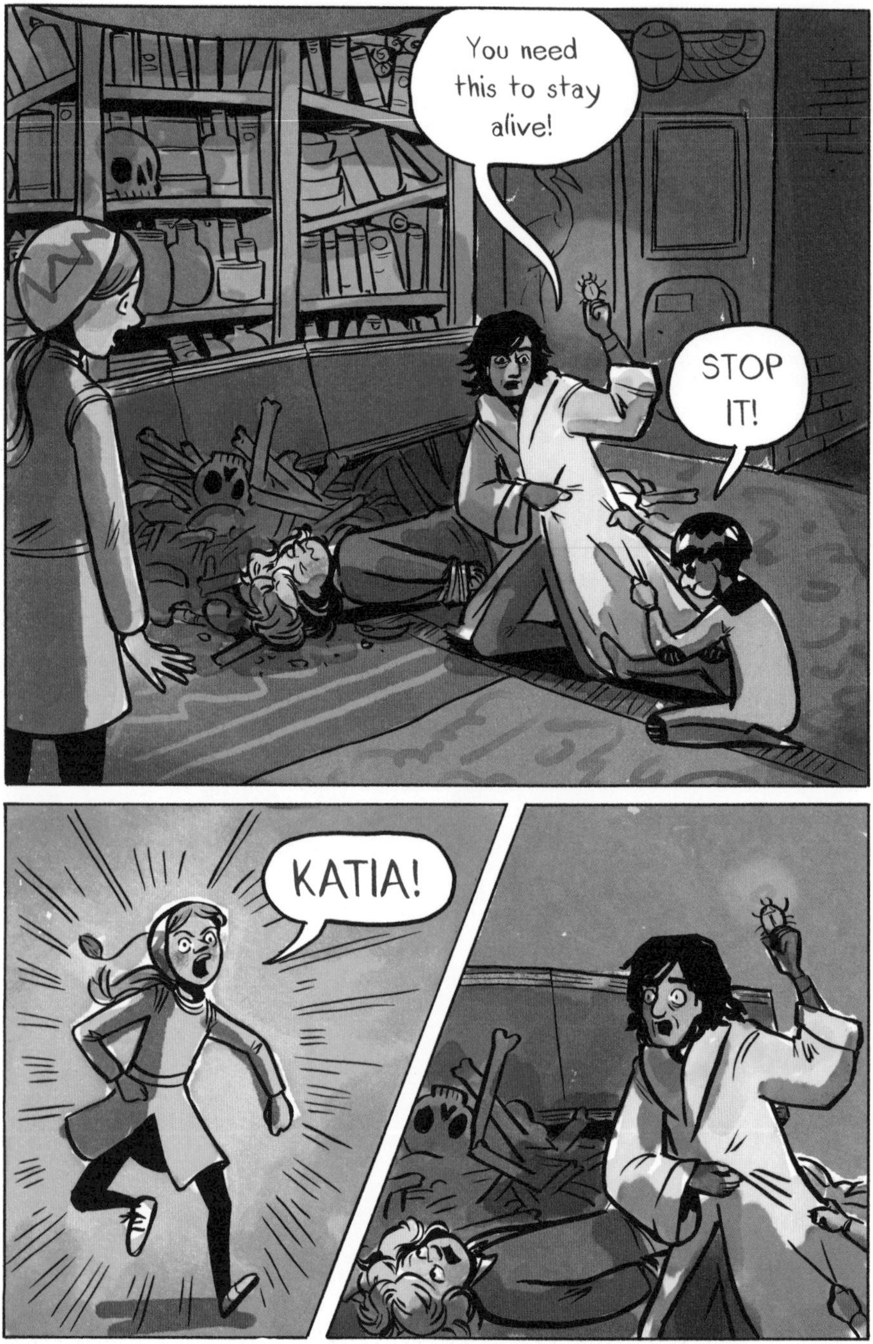
You need this to stay alive!
STOP IT!
KATIA!

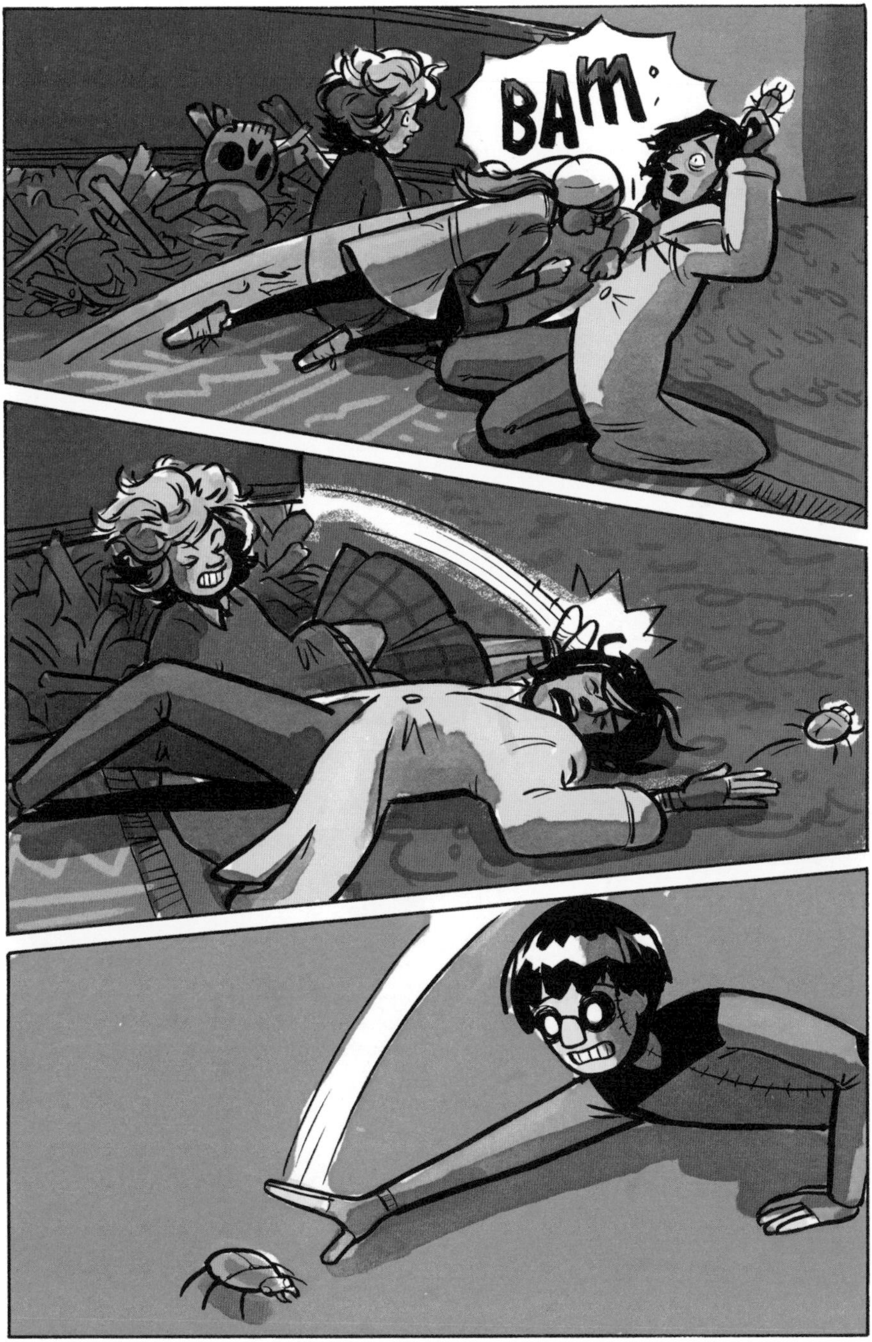
BAM

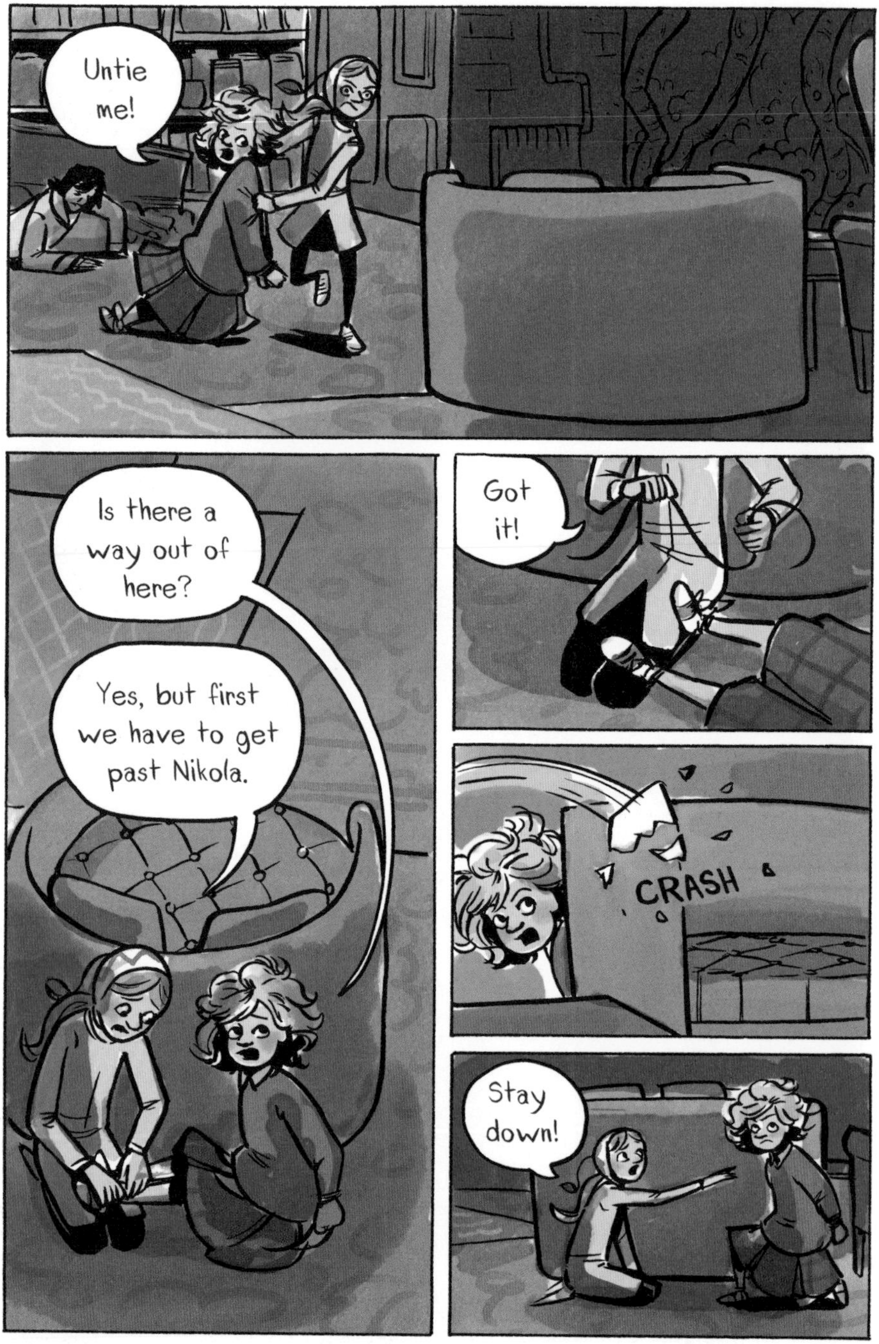
Untie me!
Is there a way out of here?
Yes, but first we have to get past Nikola.
Got it!
CRASH
Stay down!

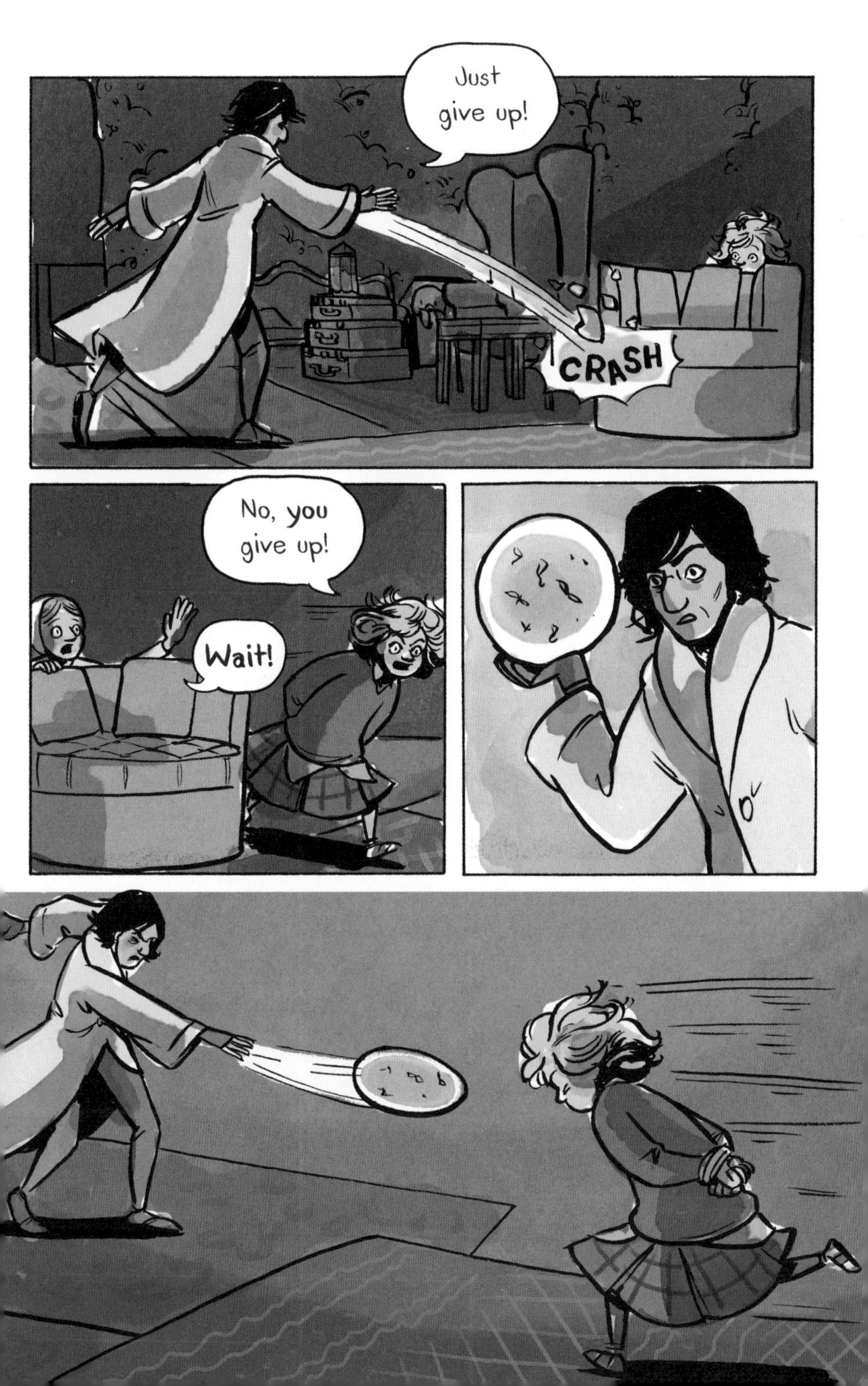
Just give up!
CRASH
No, you give up!
Wait!

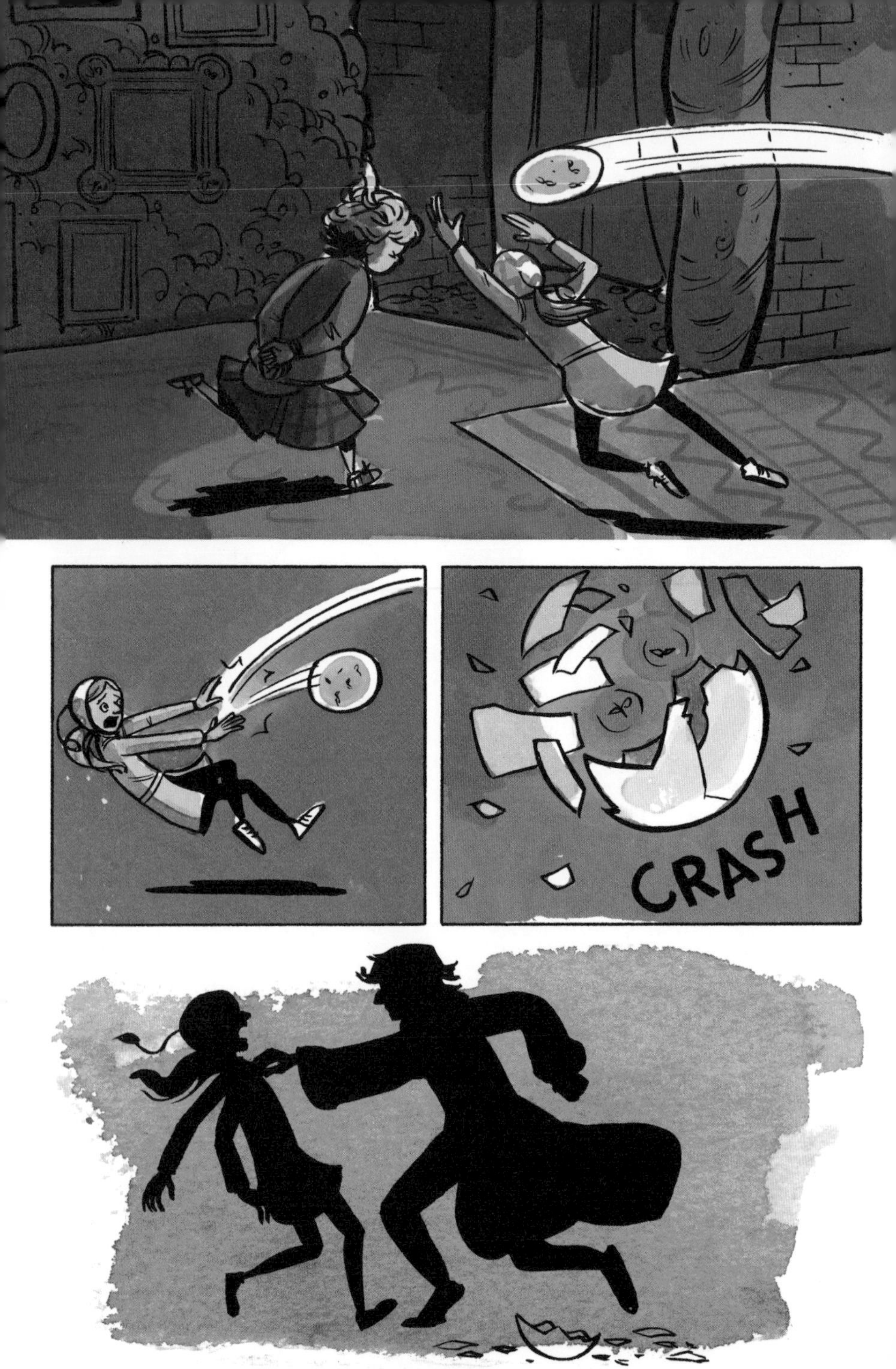
CRASH

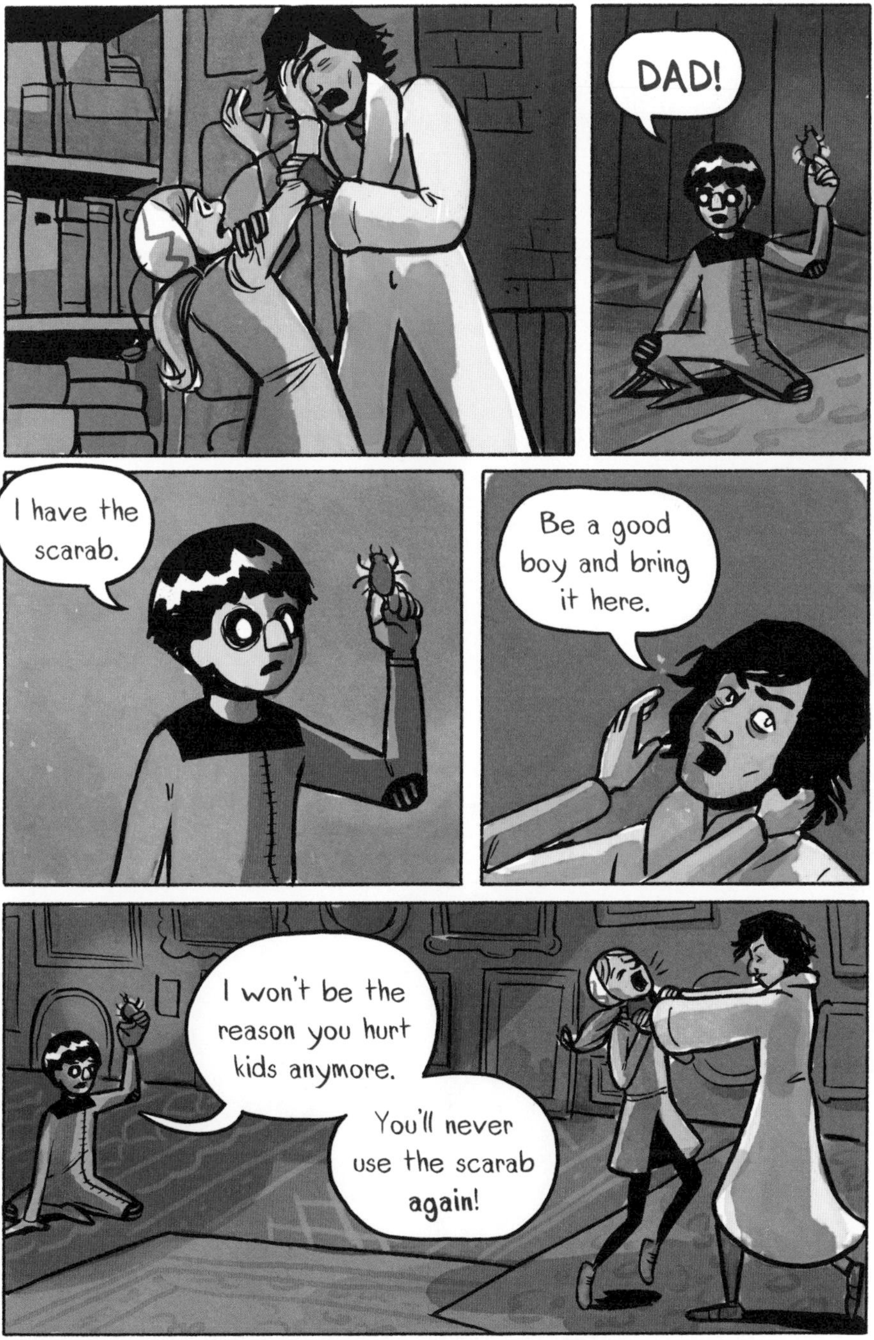
DAD!
I have the scarab.
Be a good boy and bring it here.
I won't be the reason you hurt kids anymore.
You'll never use the scarab **again**!

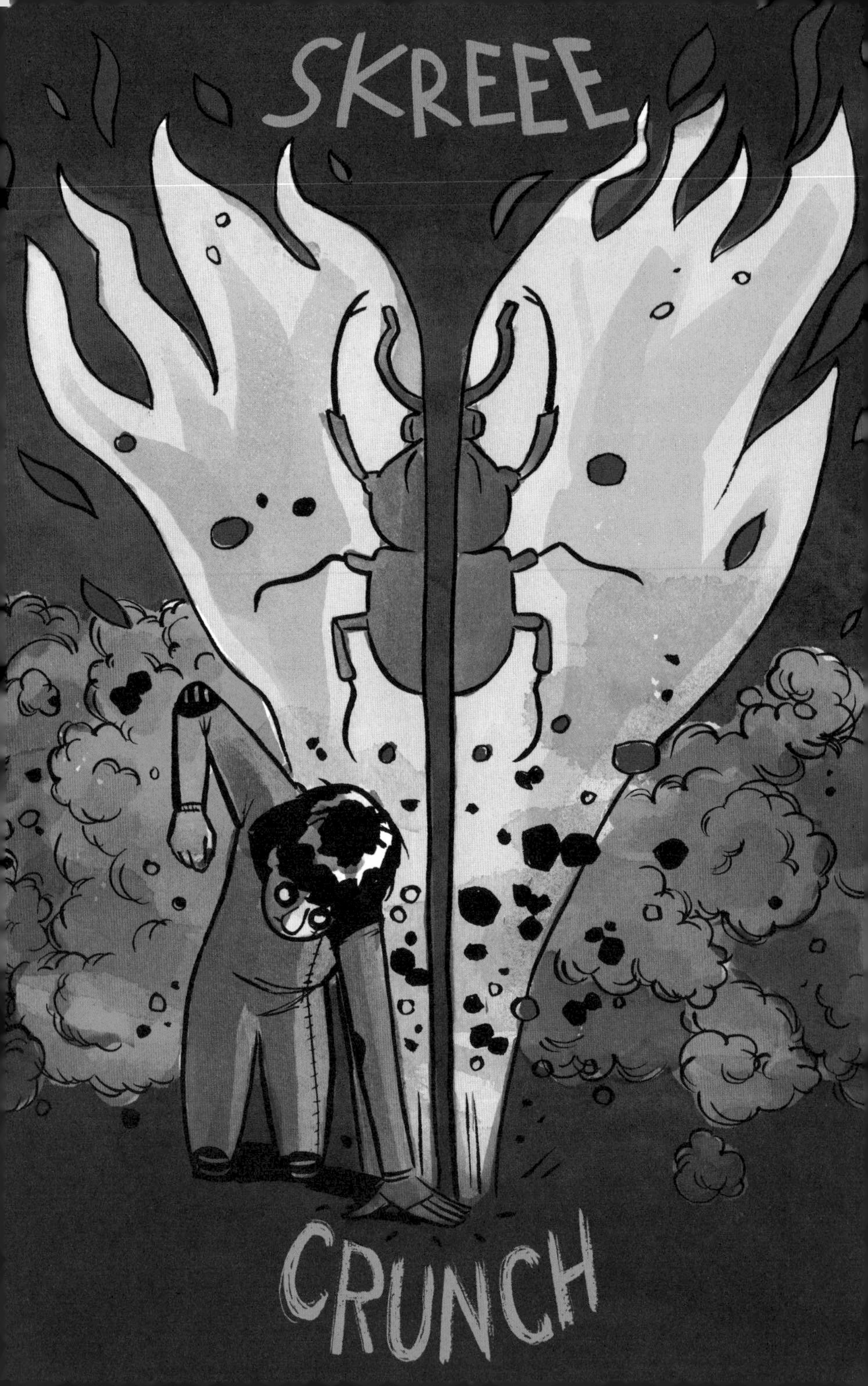
SKREEE
CRUNCH

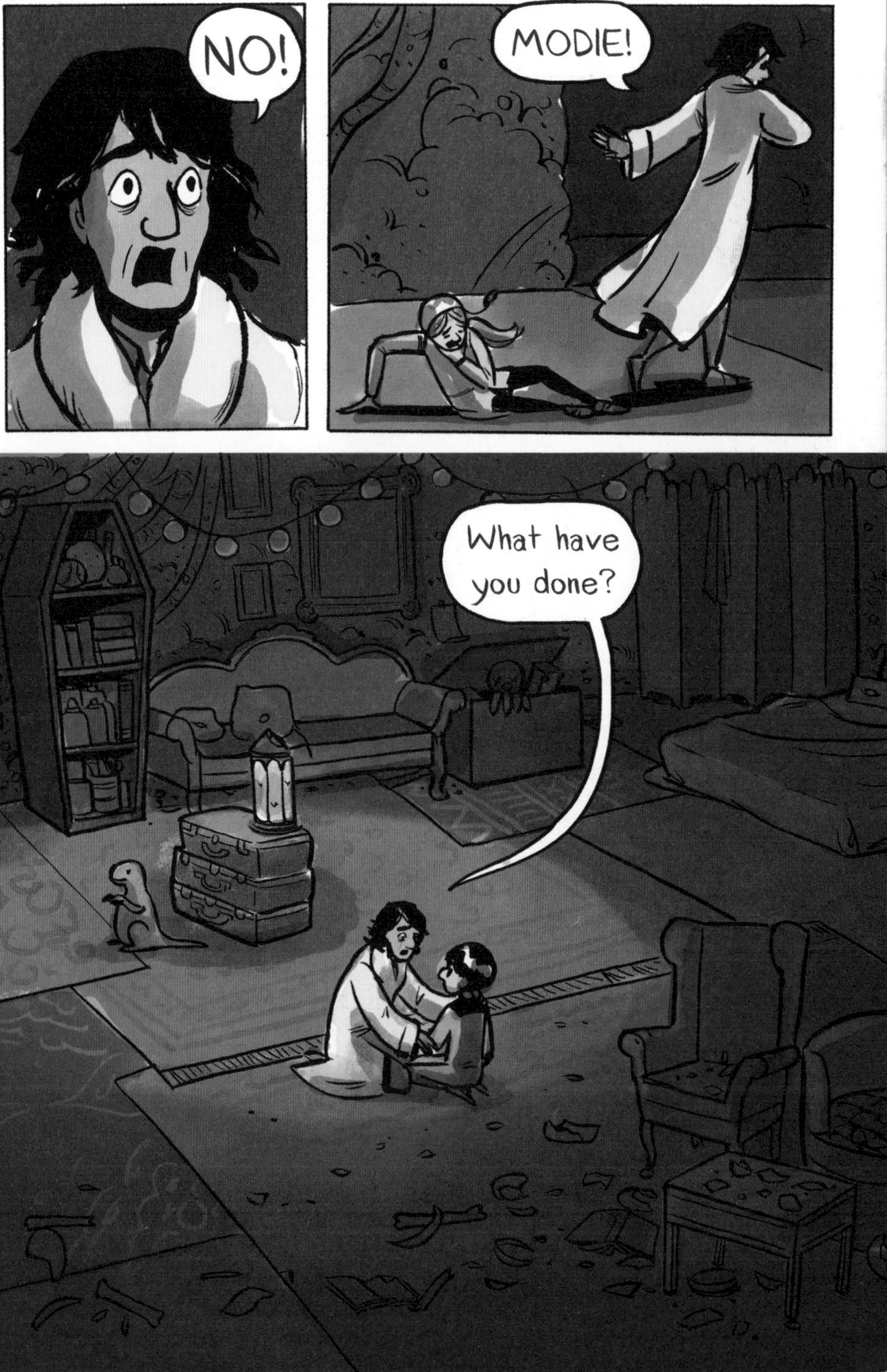
NO!
MODIE!
What have you done?

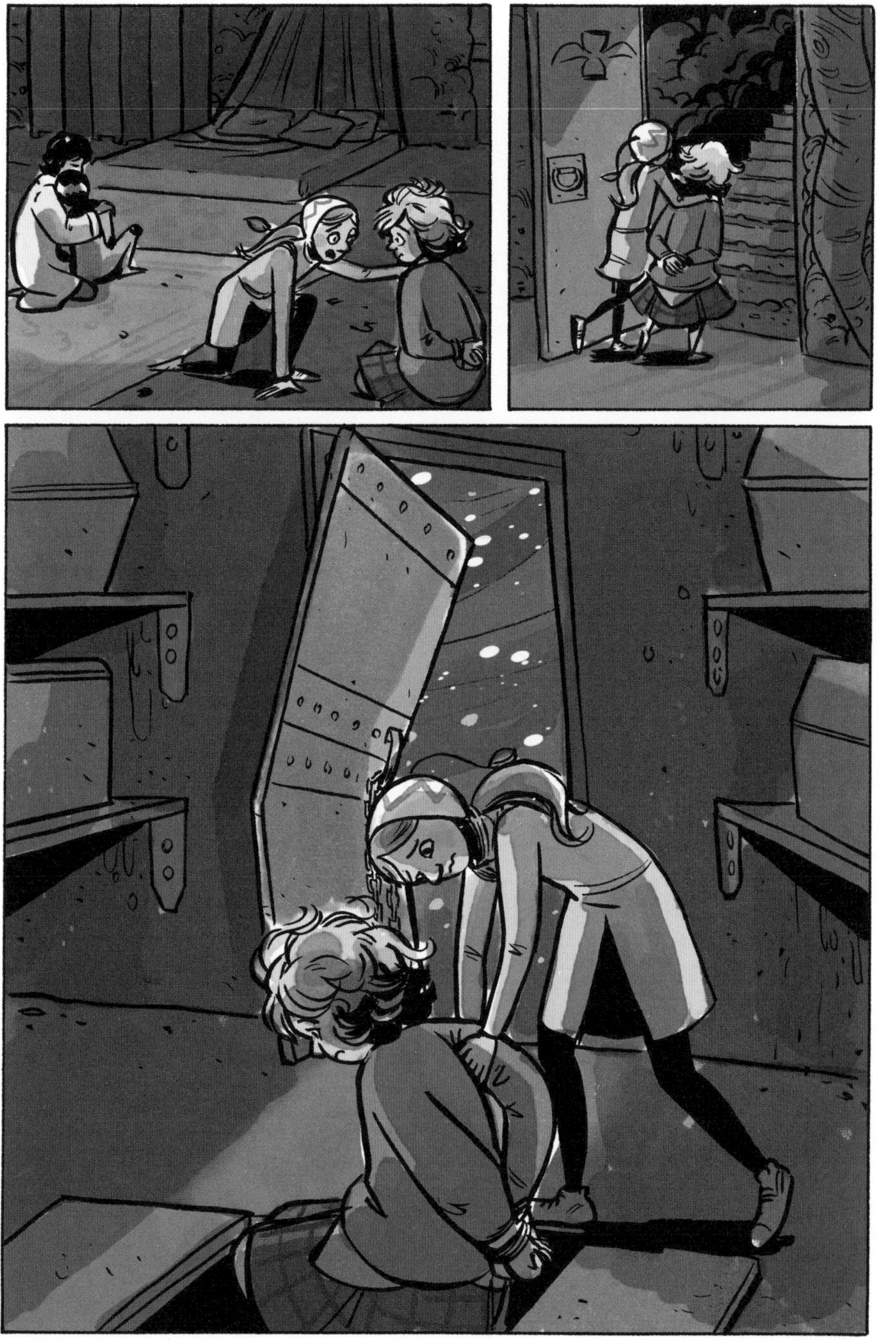

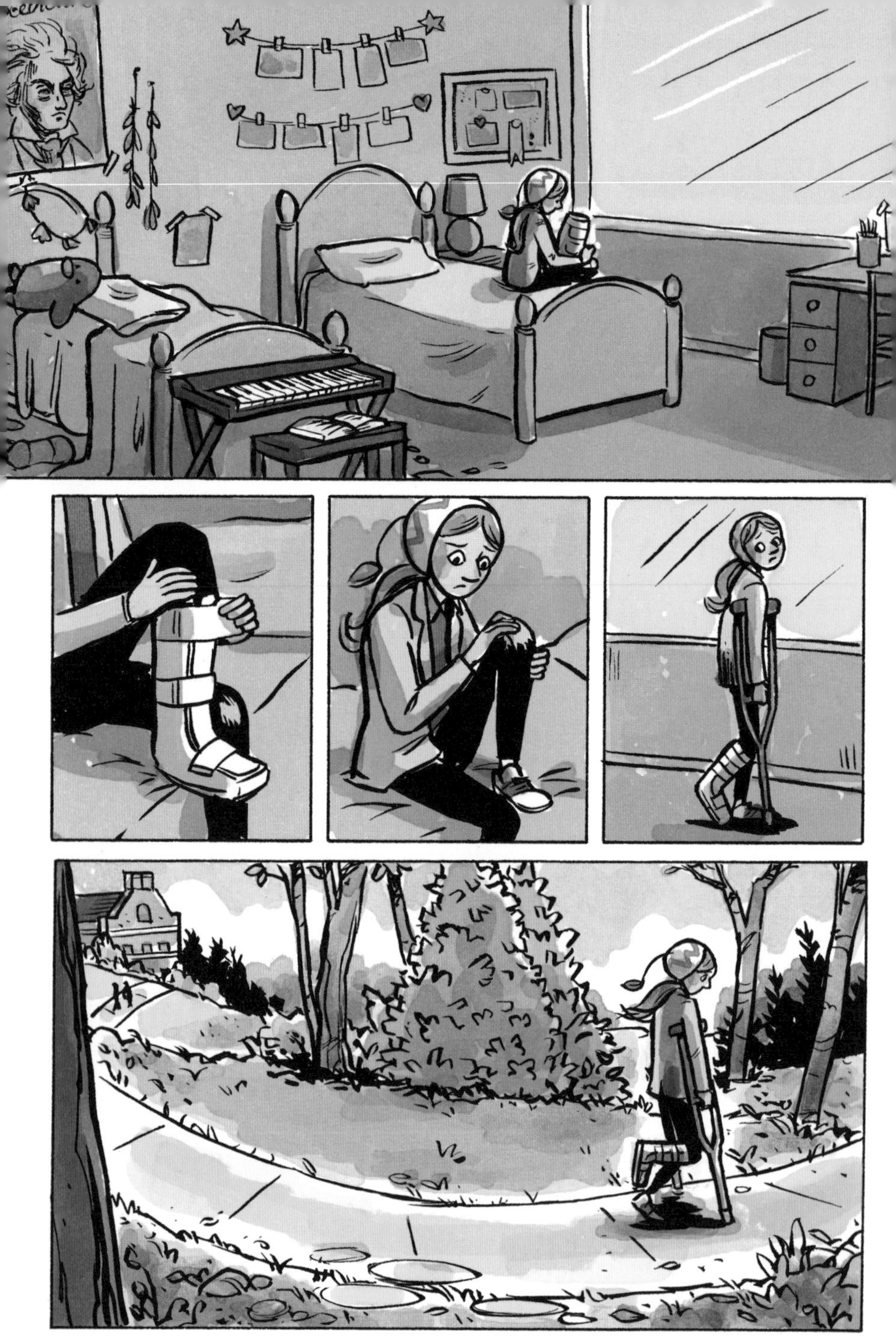

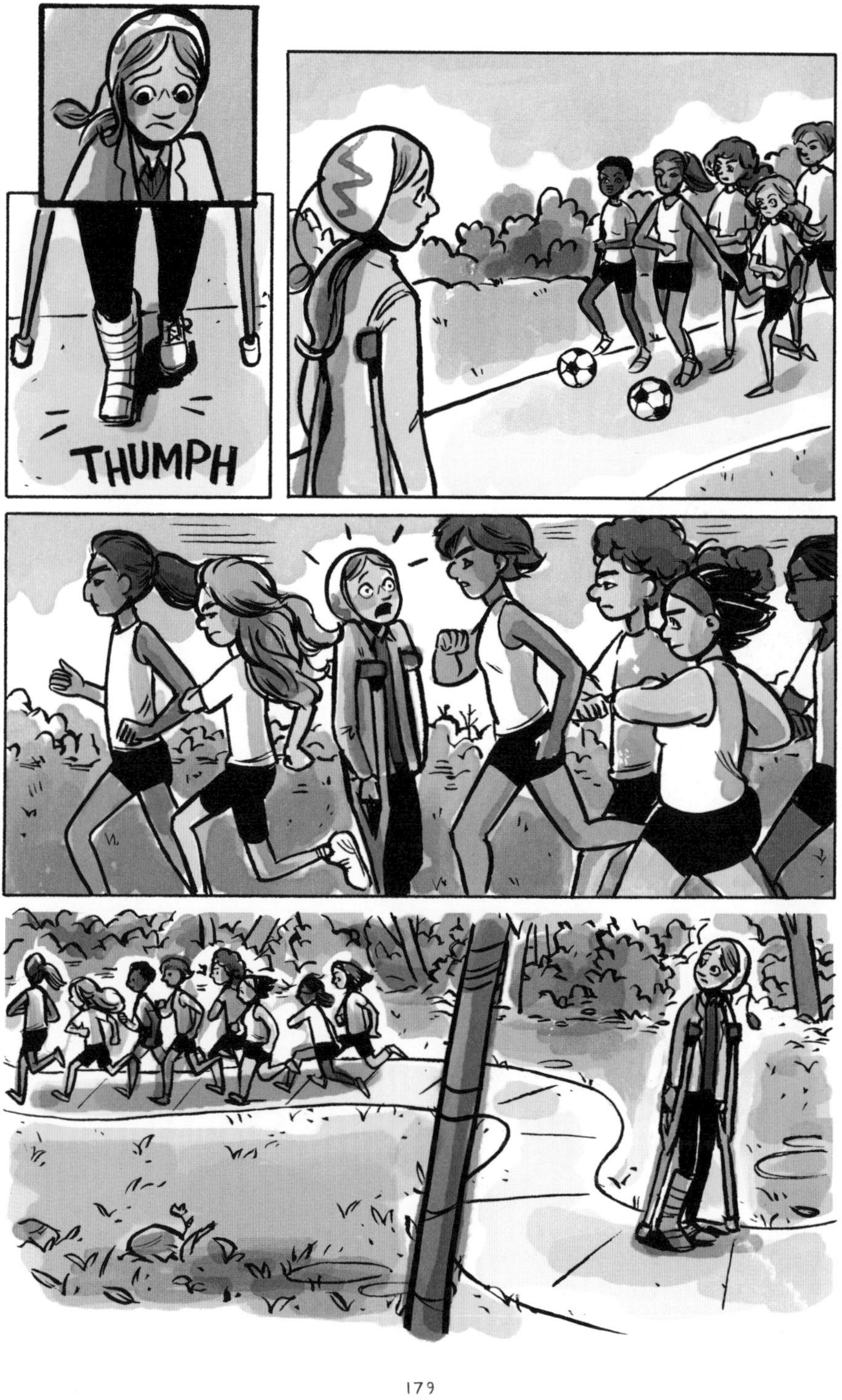
THUMPH

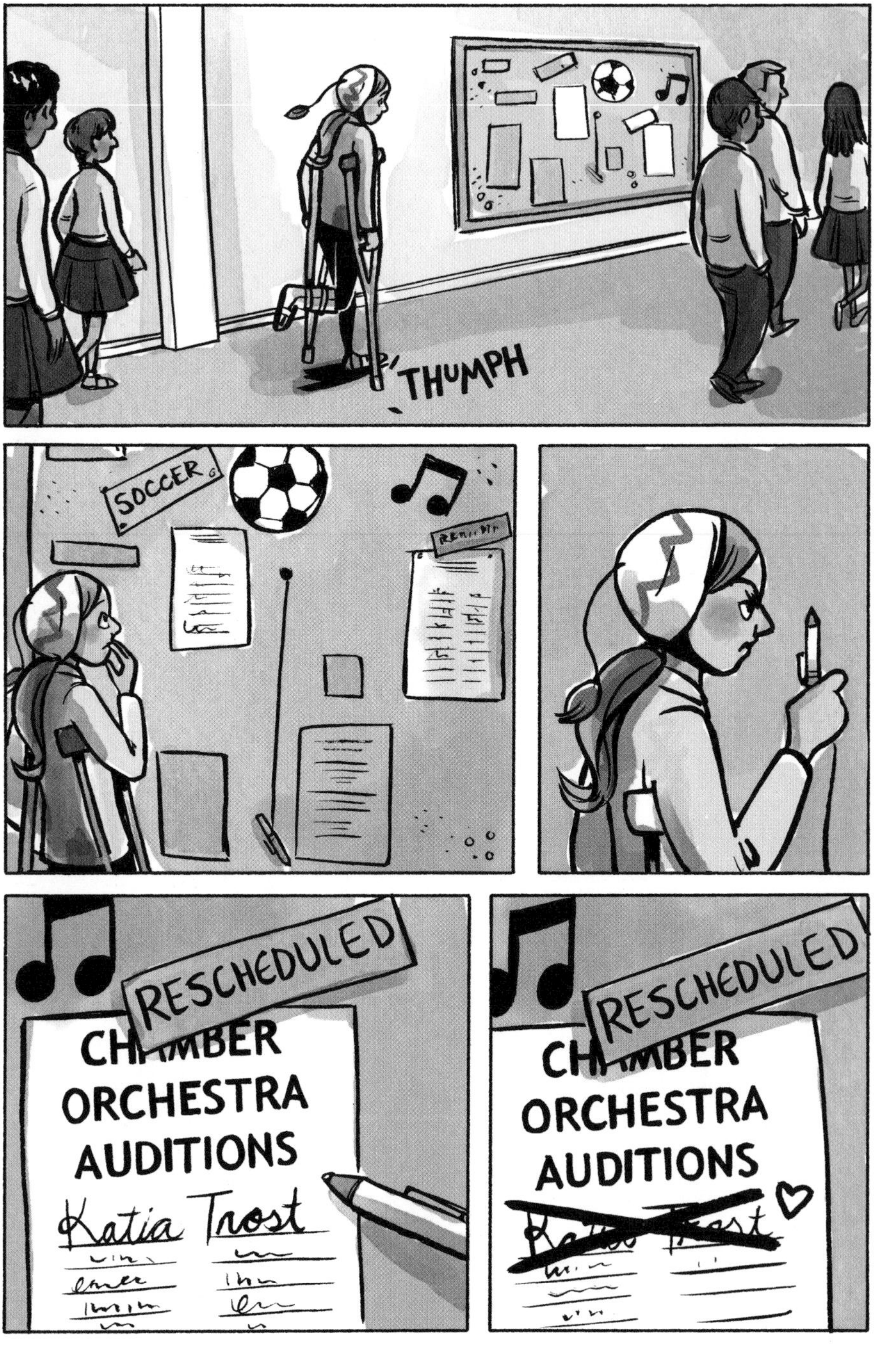
THUMPH
SOCCER
RESCHEDULED
CHAMBER ORCHESTRA AUDITIONS
Katia Trost
RESCHEDULED
CHAMBER ORCHESTRA AUDITIONS

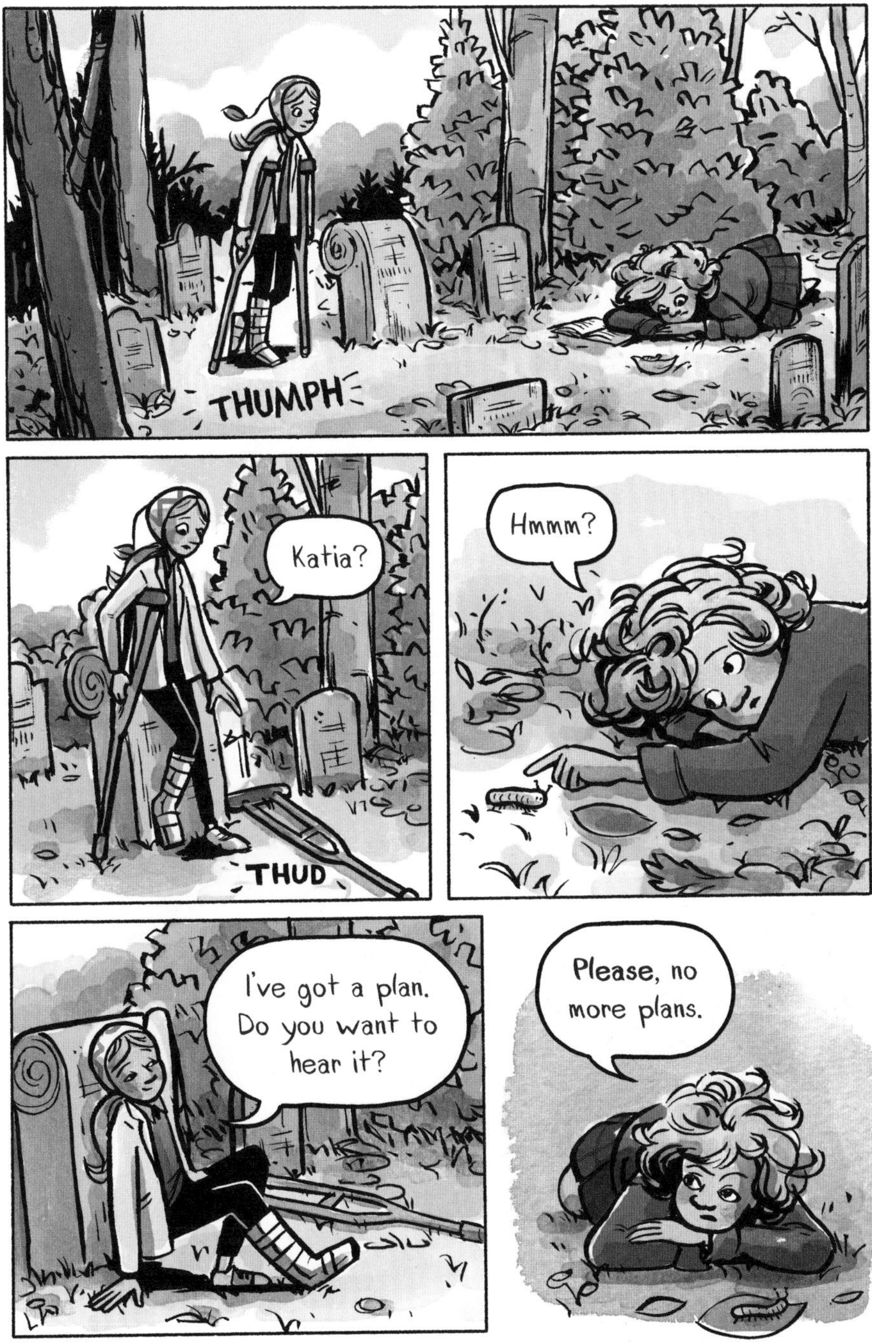
THUMPH
Katia?
THUD
Hmmm?
I've got a plan. Do you want to hear it?
Please, no more plans.

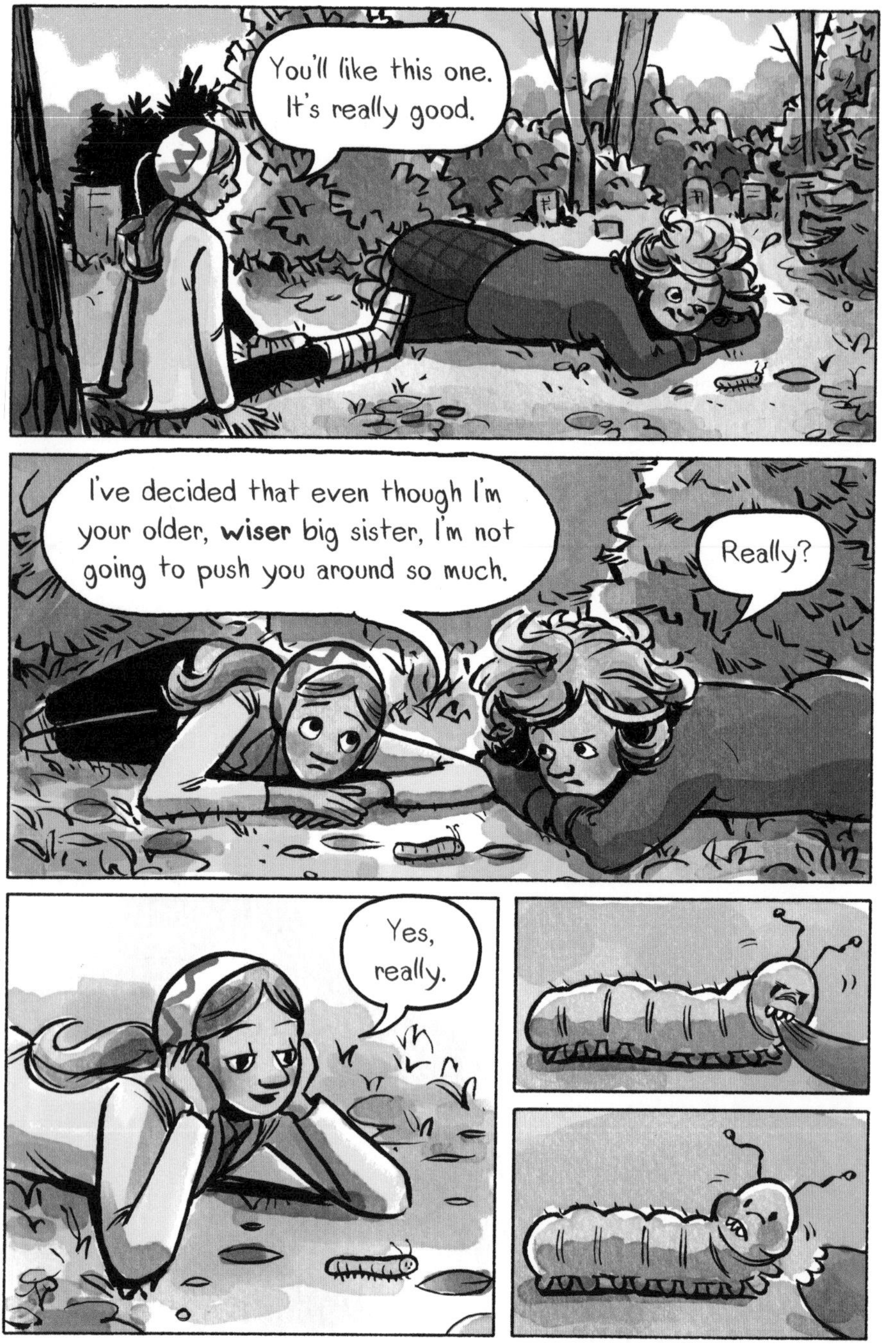
You'll like this one. It's really good.
I've decided that even though I'm your older, **wiser** big sister, I'm not going to push you around so much.
Really?
Yes, really.

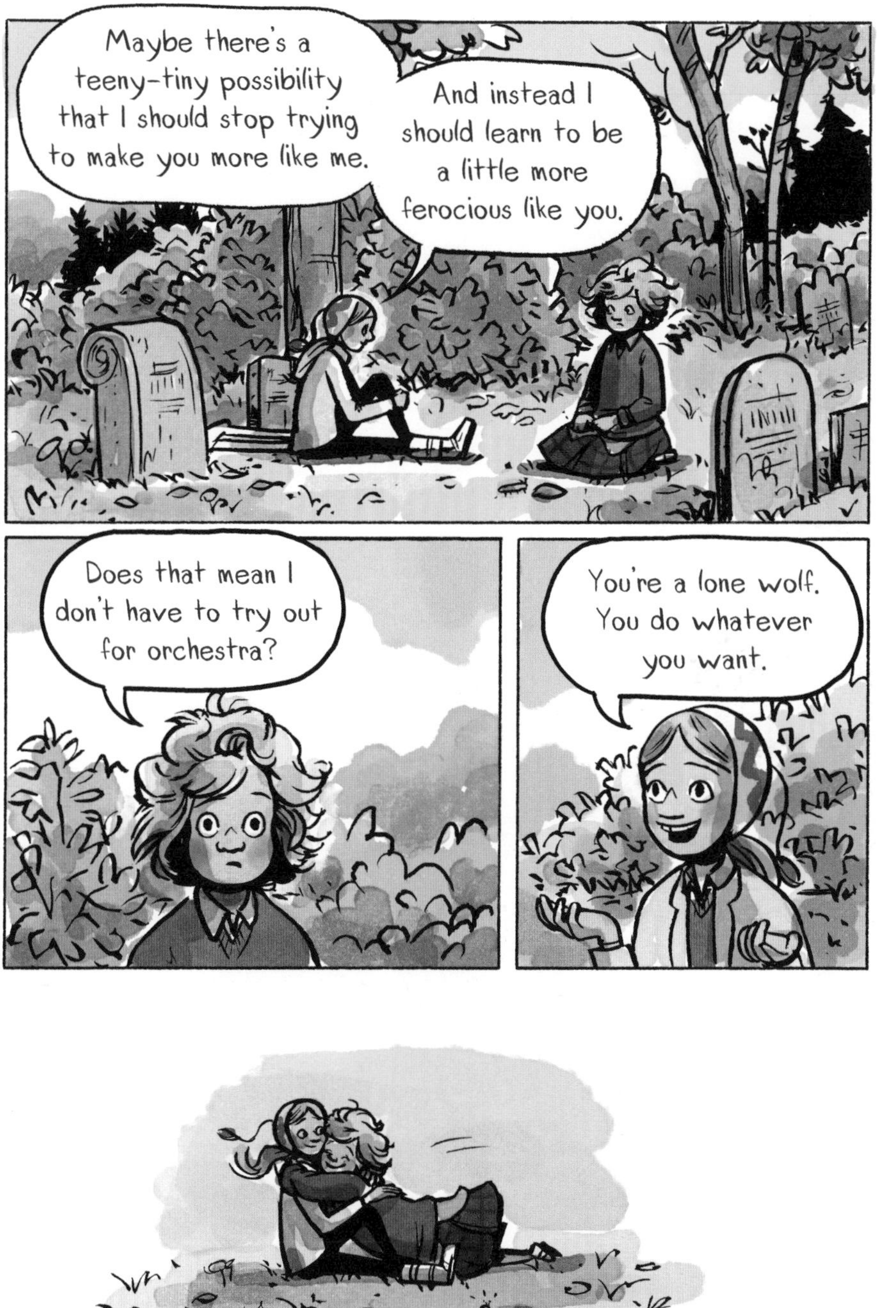
Maybe there's a teeny-tiny possibility that I should stop trying to make you more like me.
And instead I should learn to be a little more ferocious like you.
Does that mean I don't have to try out for orchestra?
You're a lone wolf. You do whatever you want.

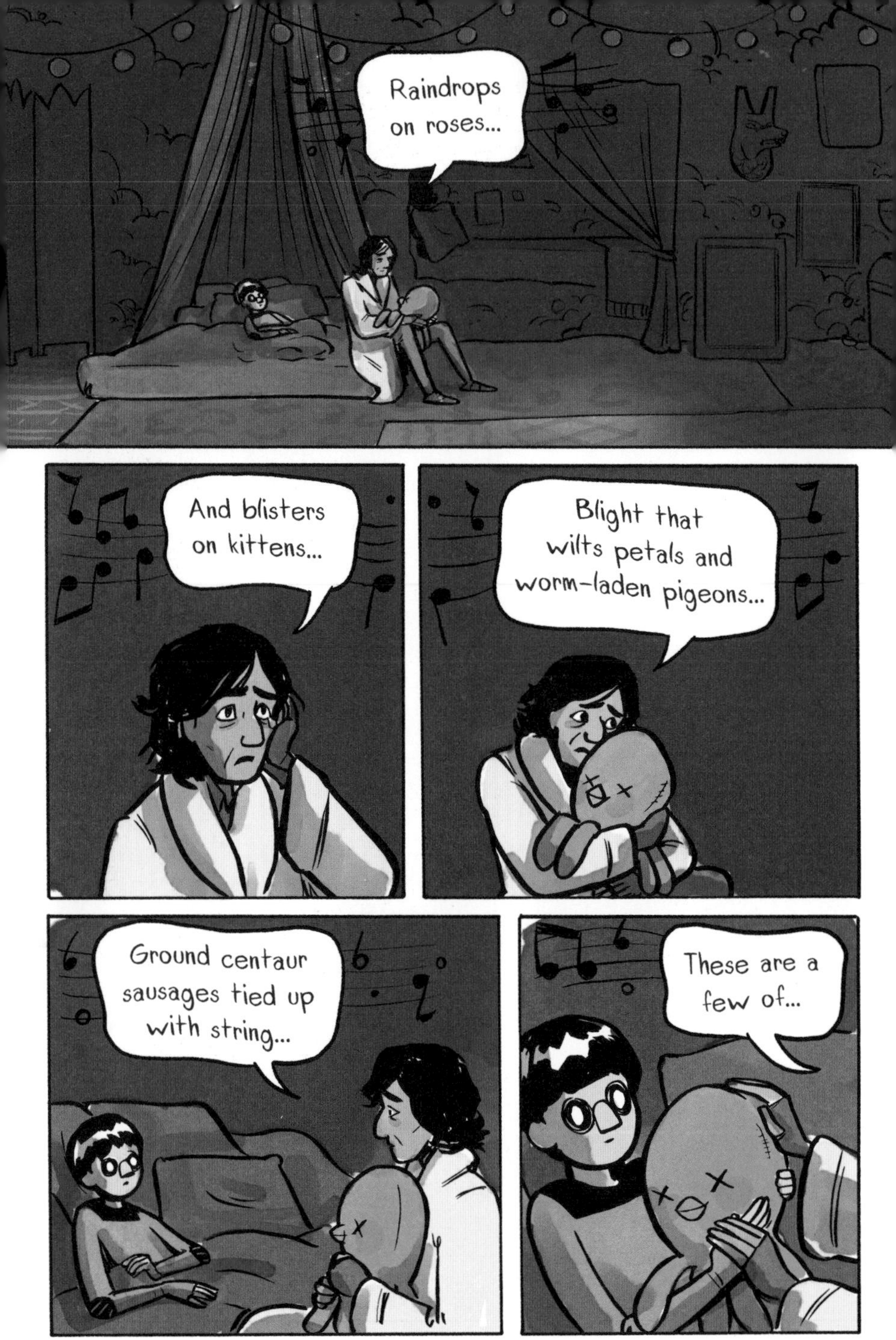
Raindrops on roses...
And blisters on kittens...
Blight that wilts petals and worm-laden pigeons...
Ground centaur sausages tied up with string...
These are a few of...

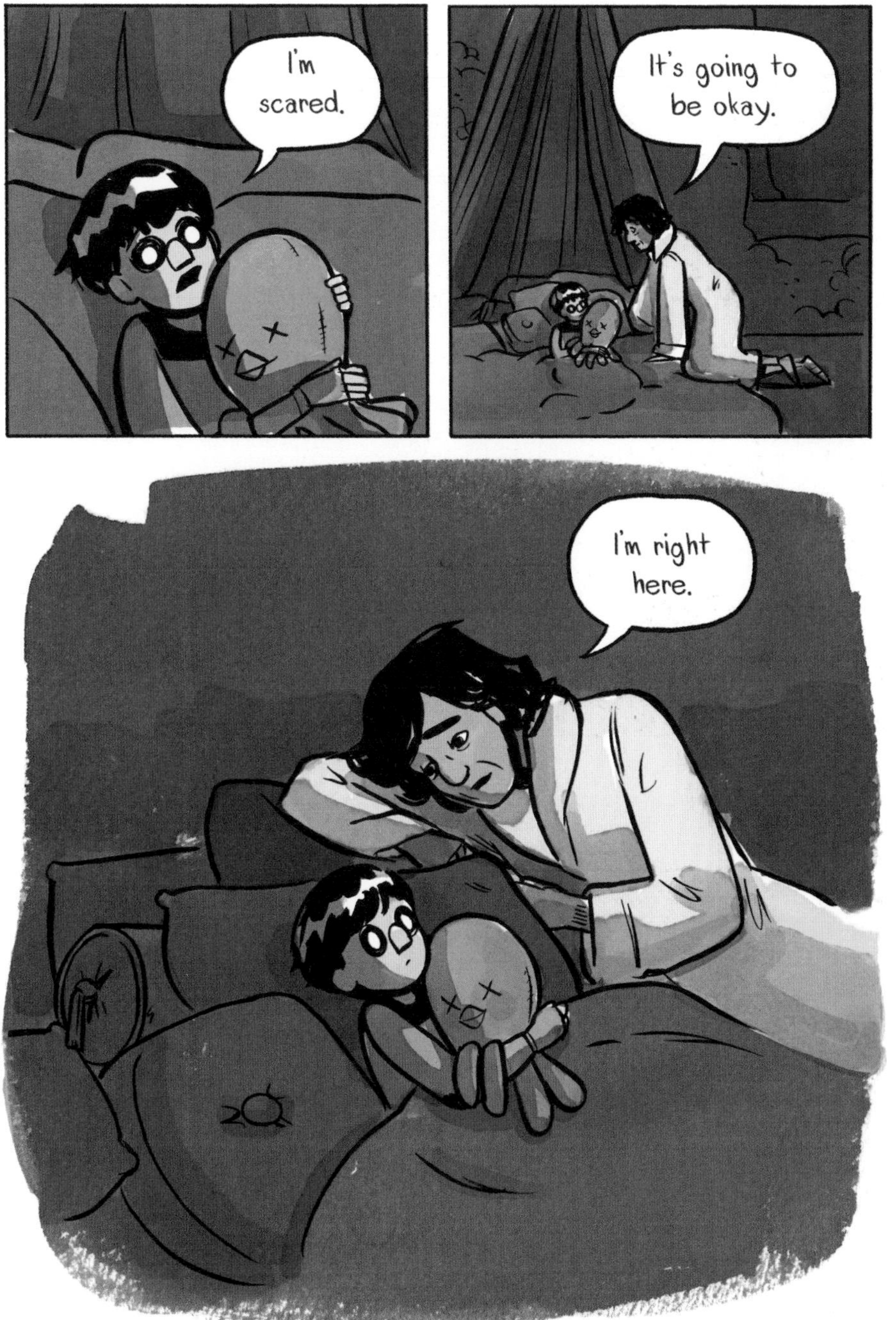
I'm scared.
It's going to be okay.
I'm right here.

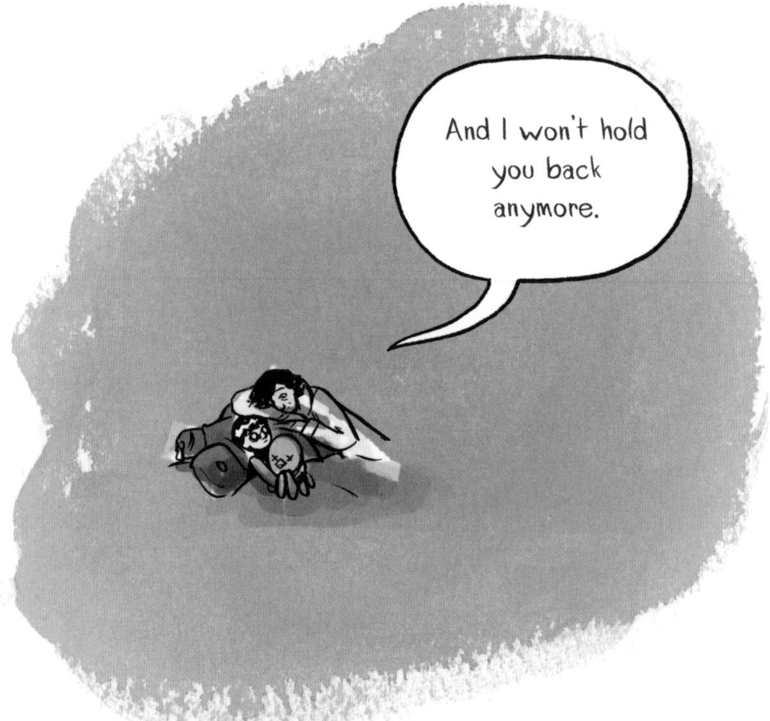
And I won't hold you back anymore.

Seven months later . . .

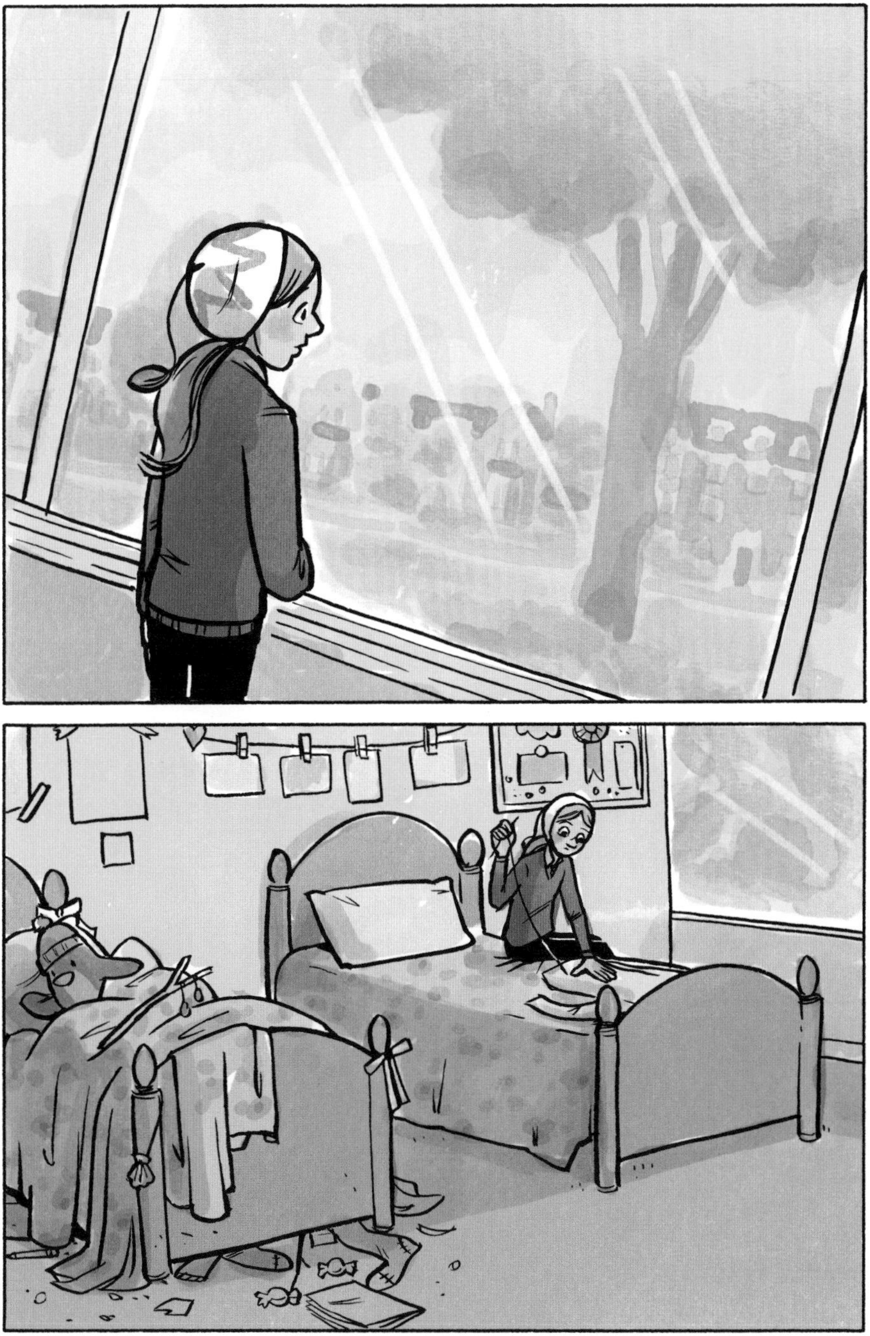

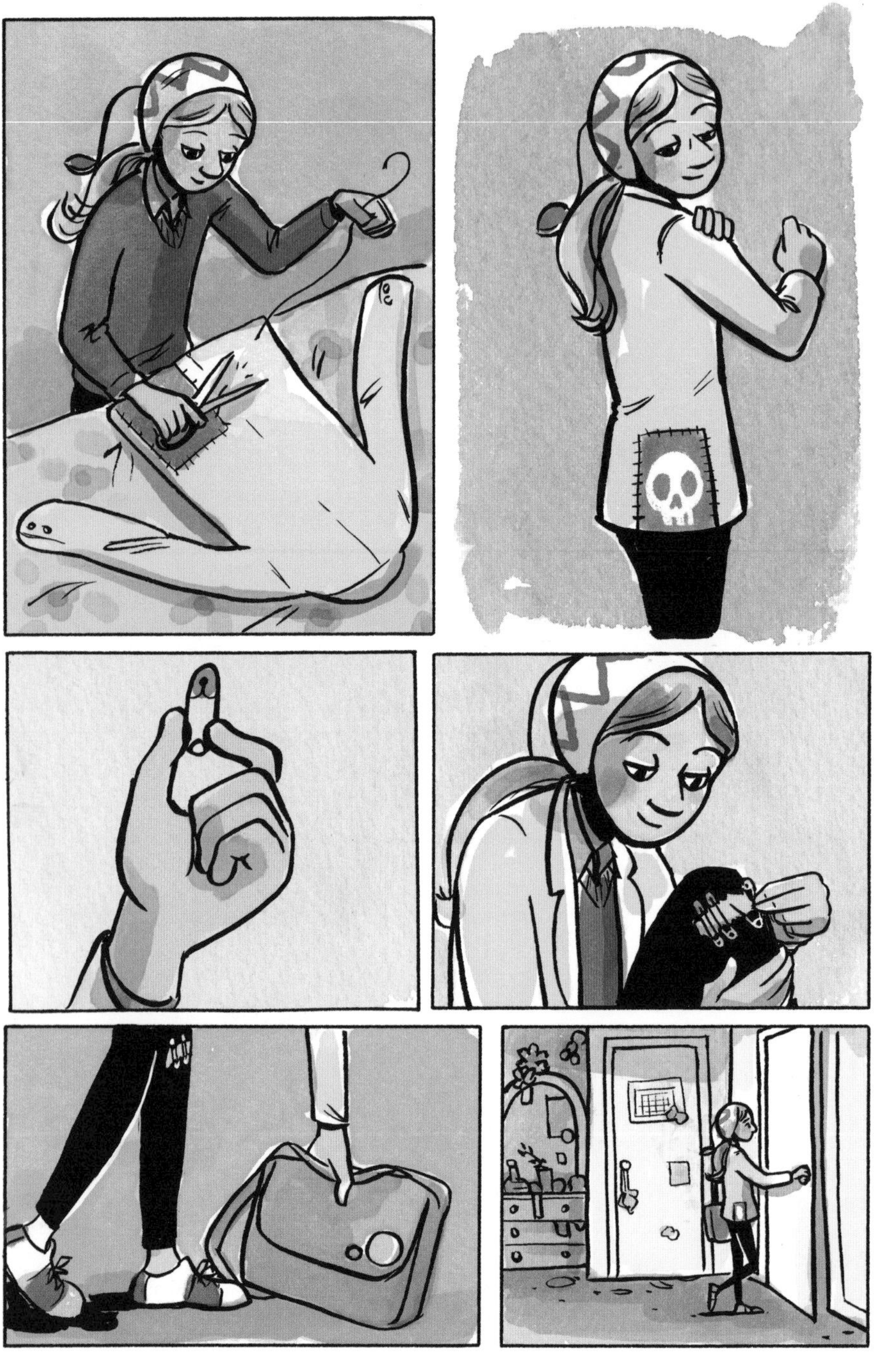

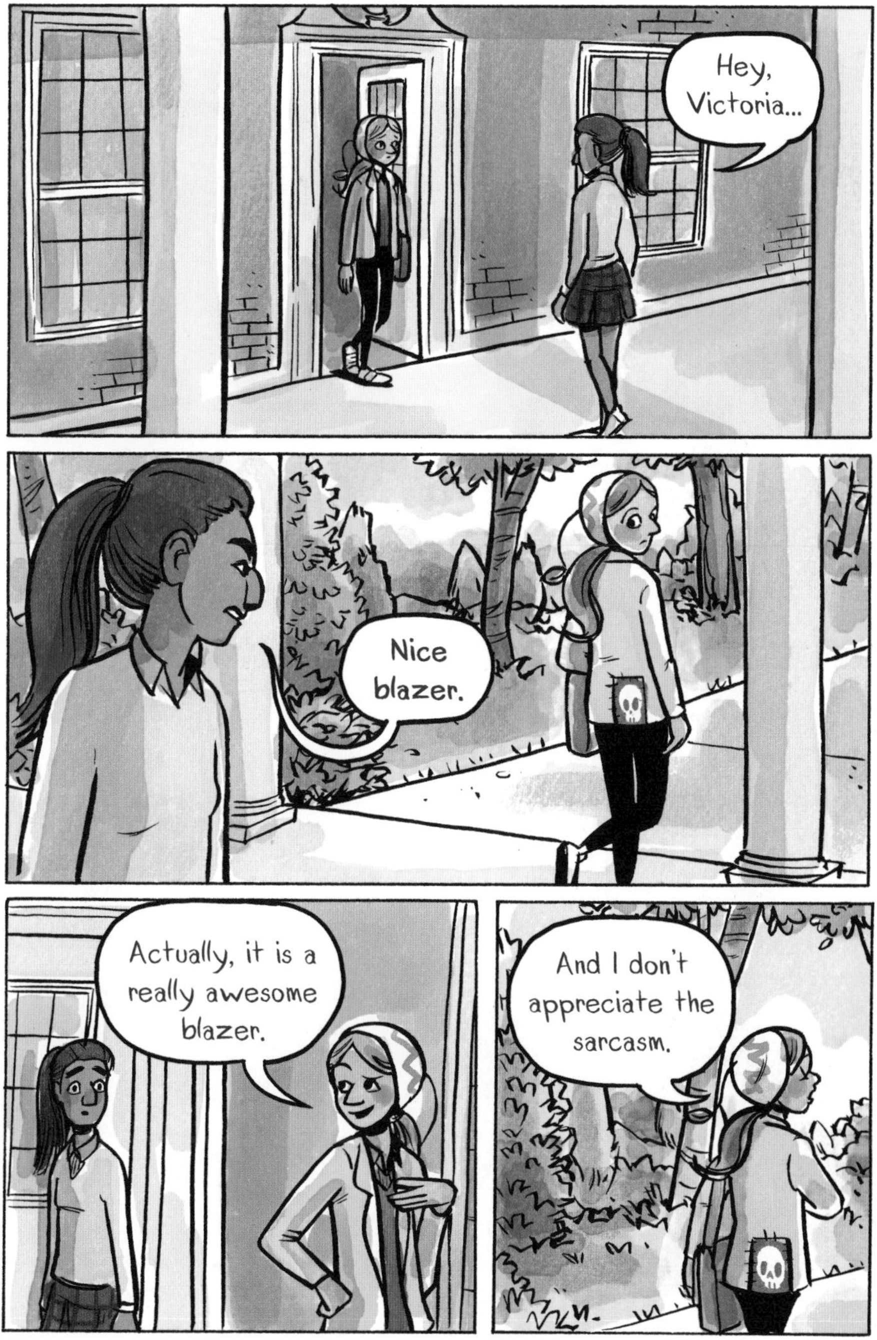
Hey, Victoria...
Nice blazer.
Actually, it is a really awesome blazer.
And I don't appreciate the sarcasm.

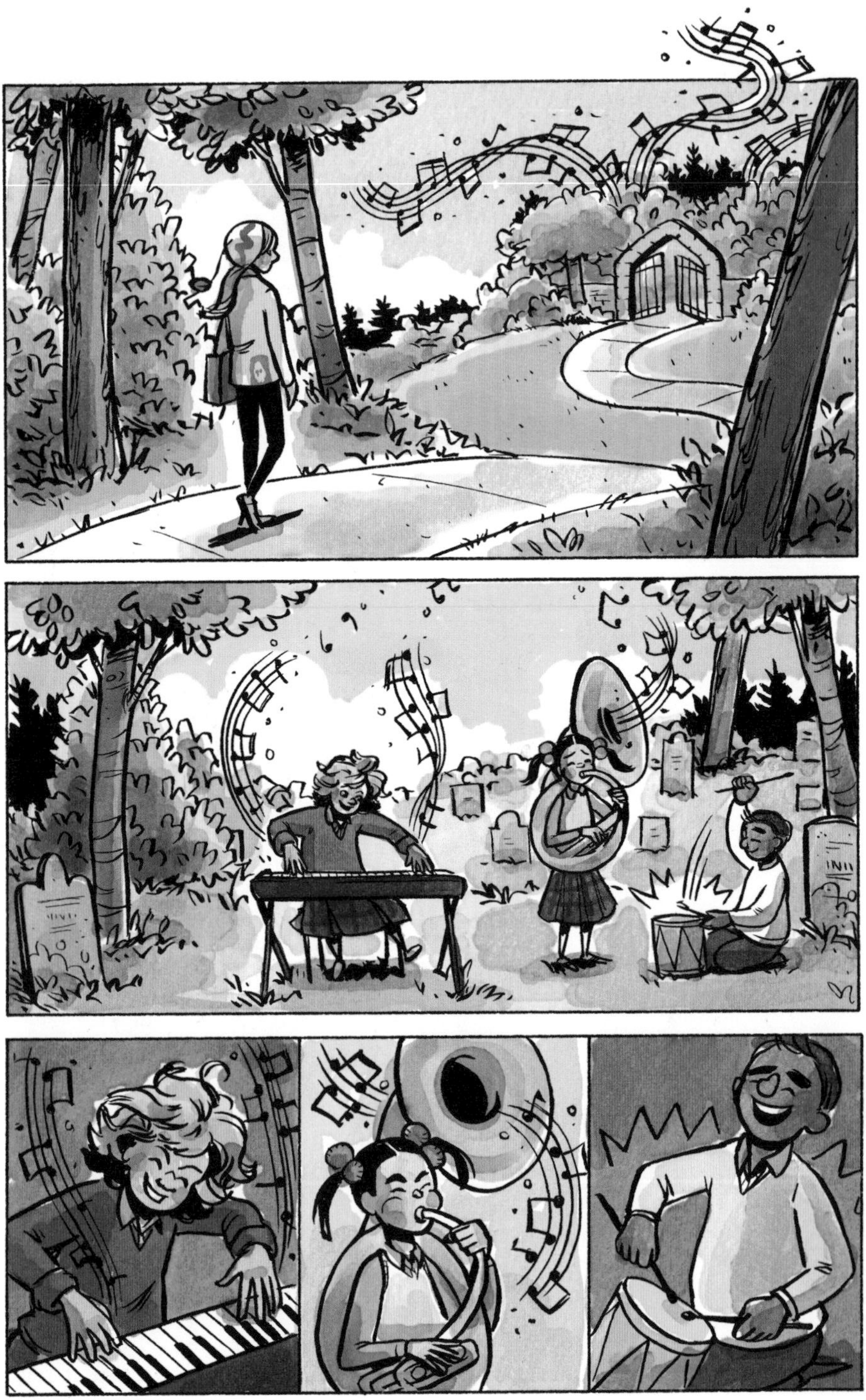

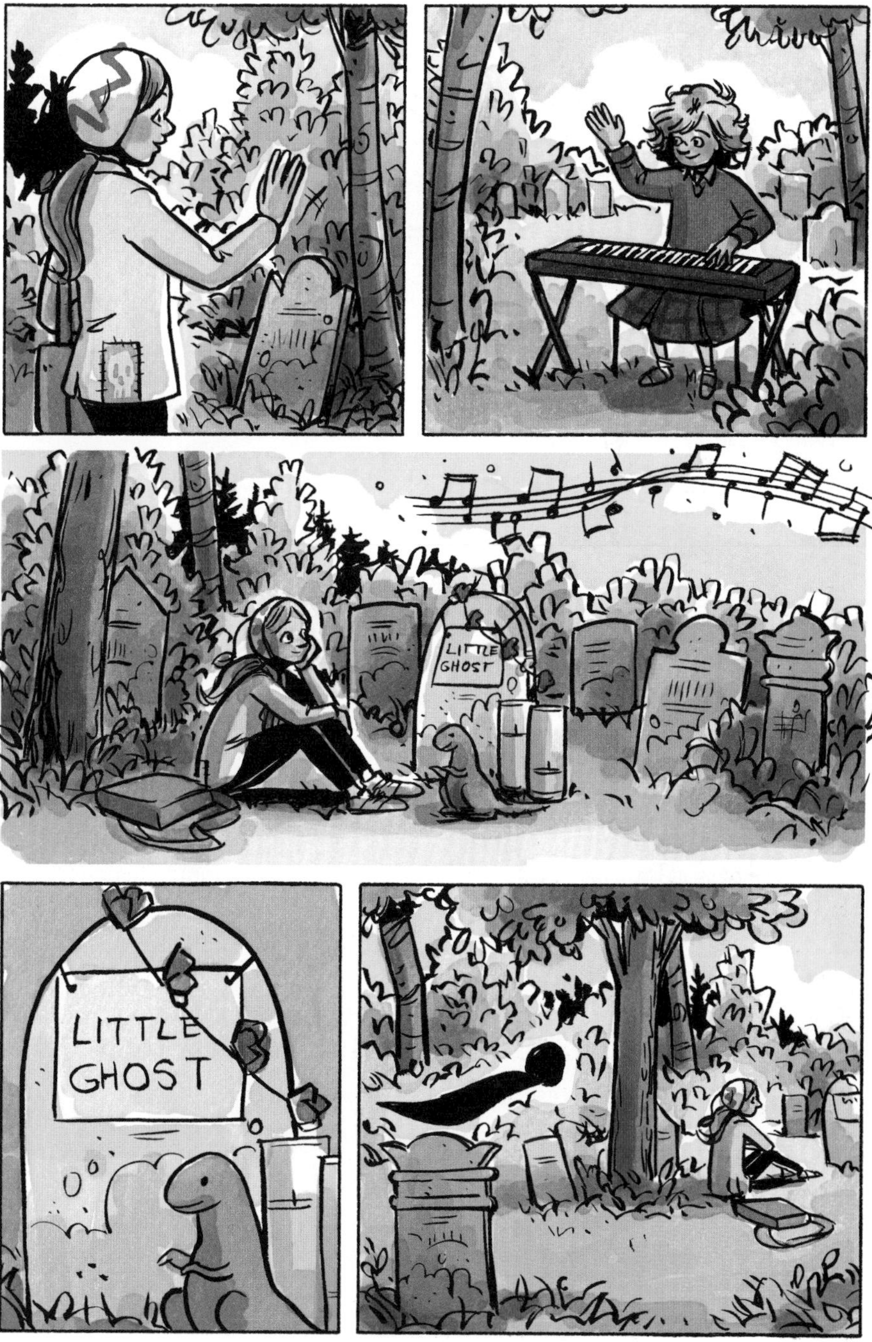
LITTLE GHOST
LITTLE GHOST

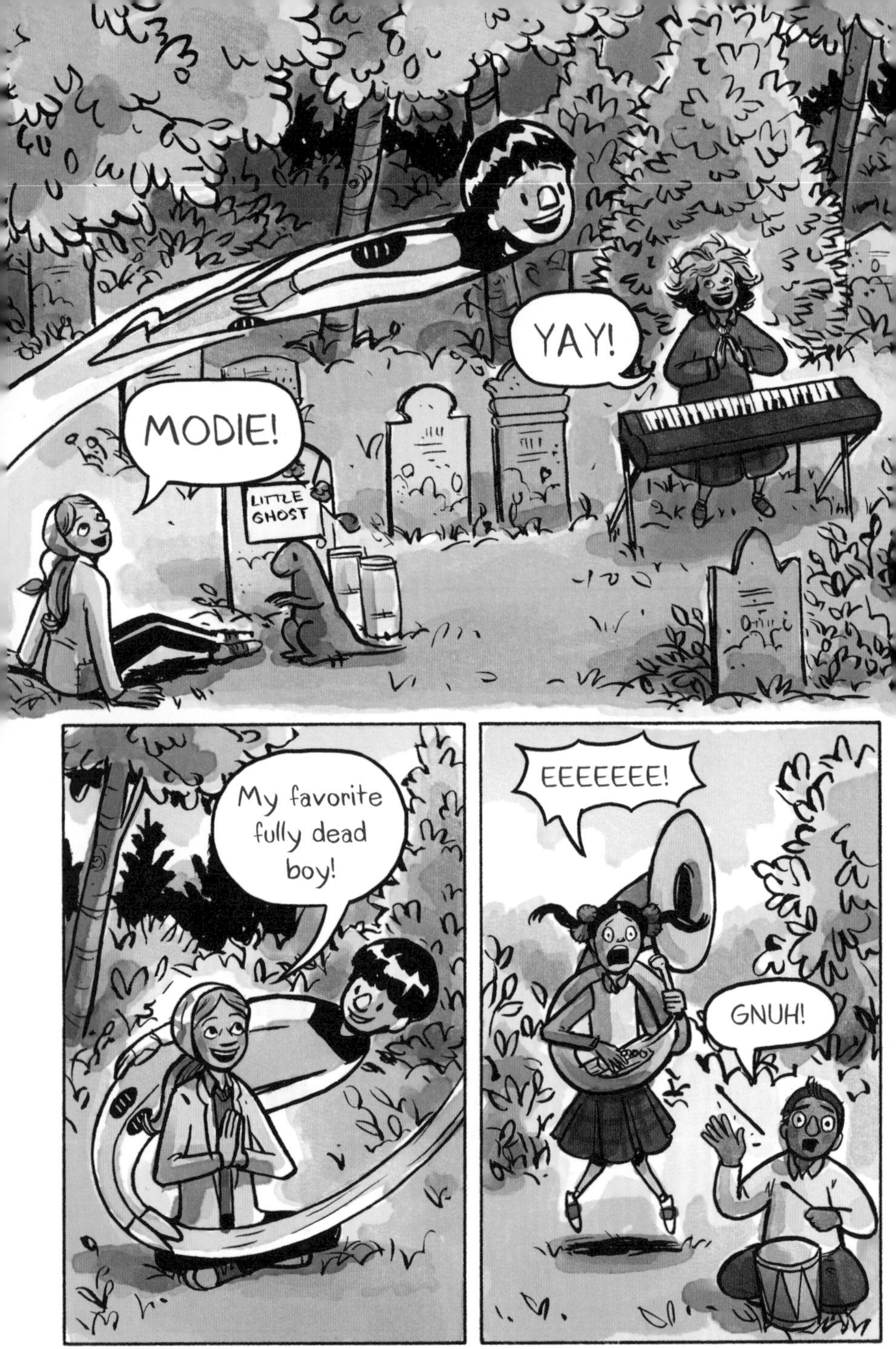
LITTLE GHOST
MODIE!
YAY!
My favorite fully dead boy!
EEEEEEE!
GNUH!

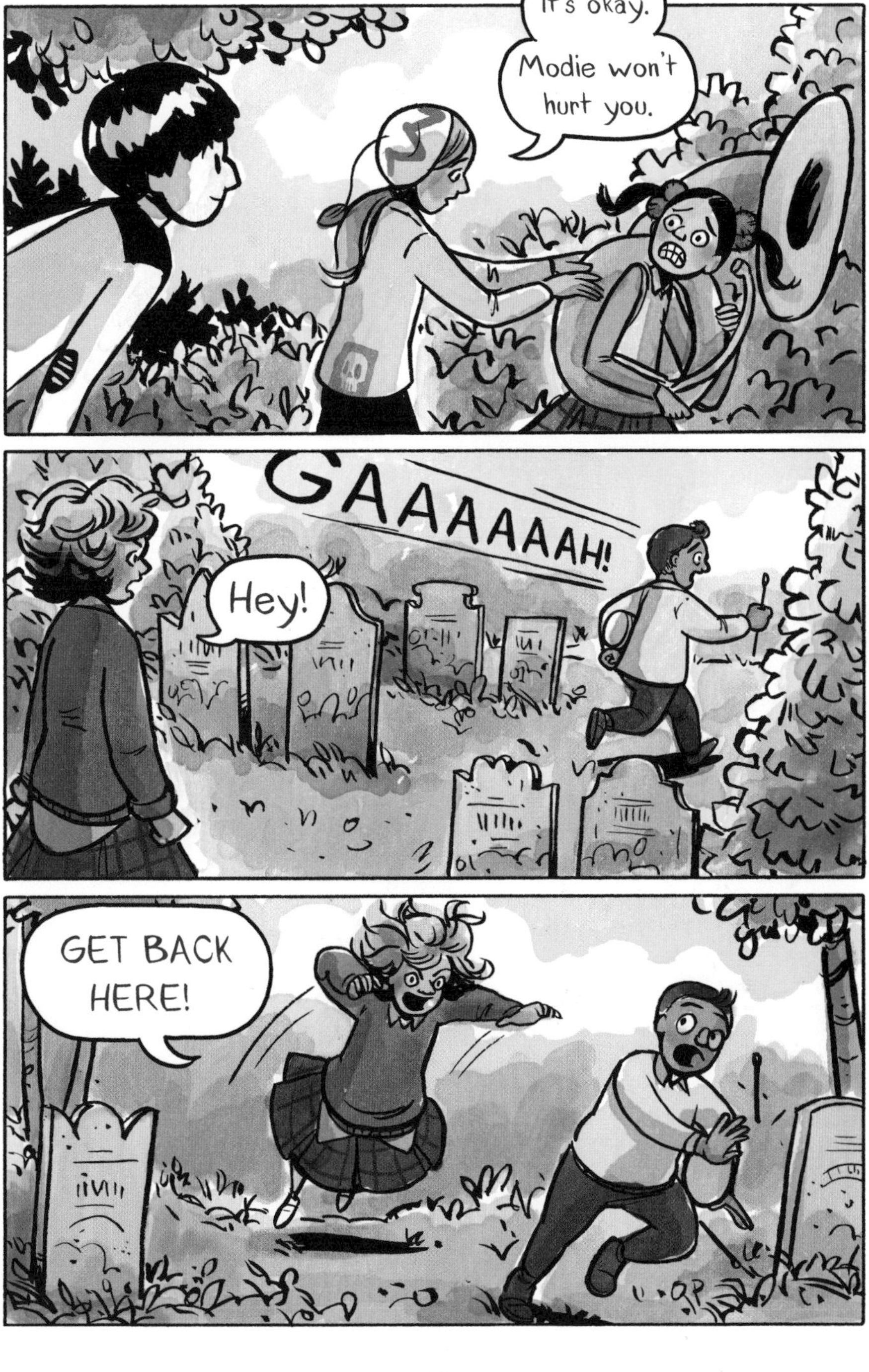
It's okay.
Modie won't hurt you.
GAAAAAAH!
Hey!
GET BACK HERE!

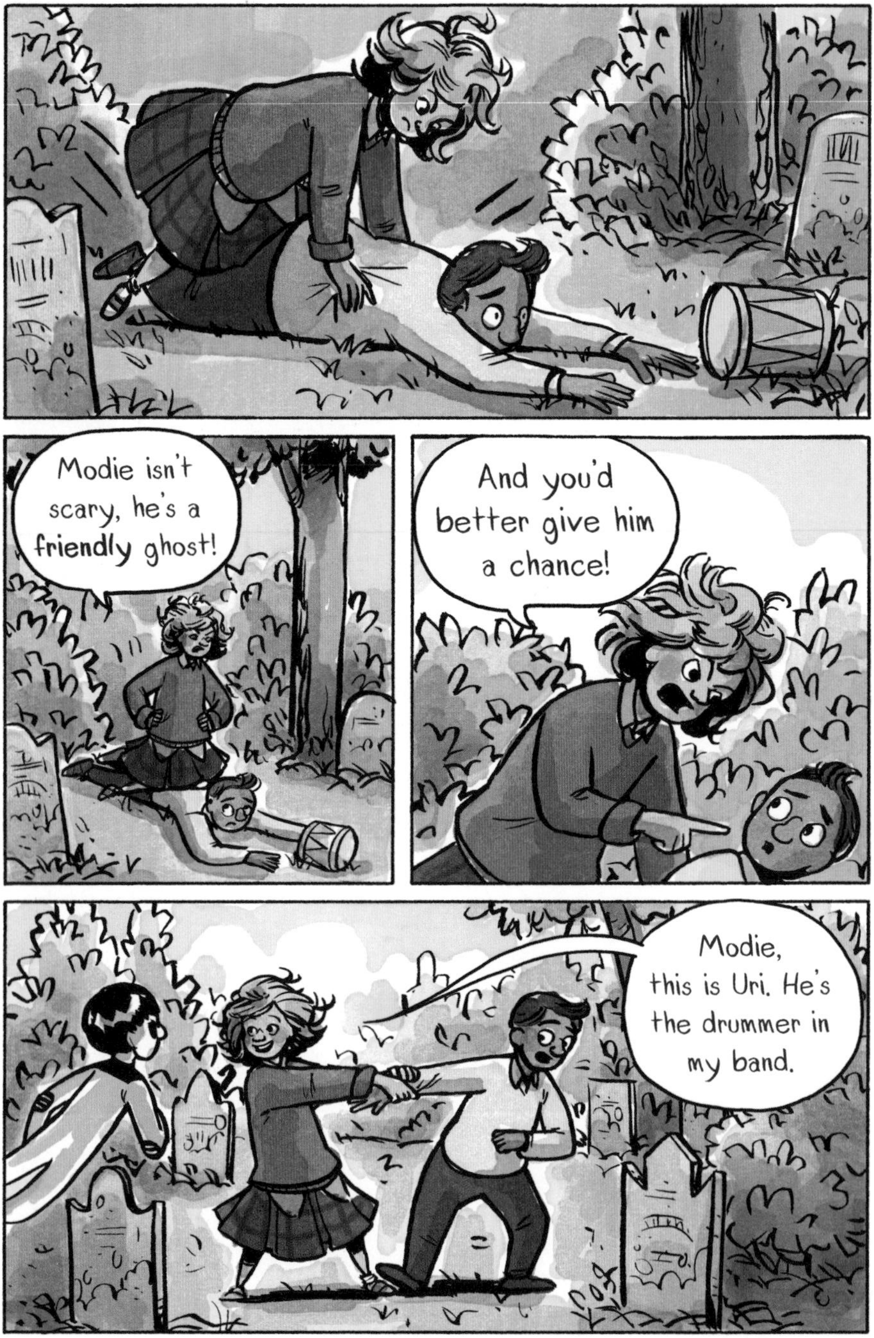
Modie isn't scary, he's a friendly ghost!
And you'd better give him a chance!
Modie, this is Uri. He's the drummer in my band.

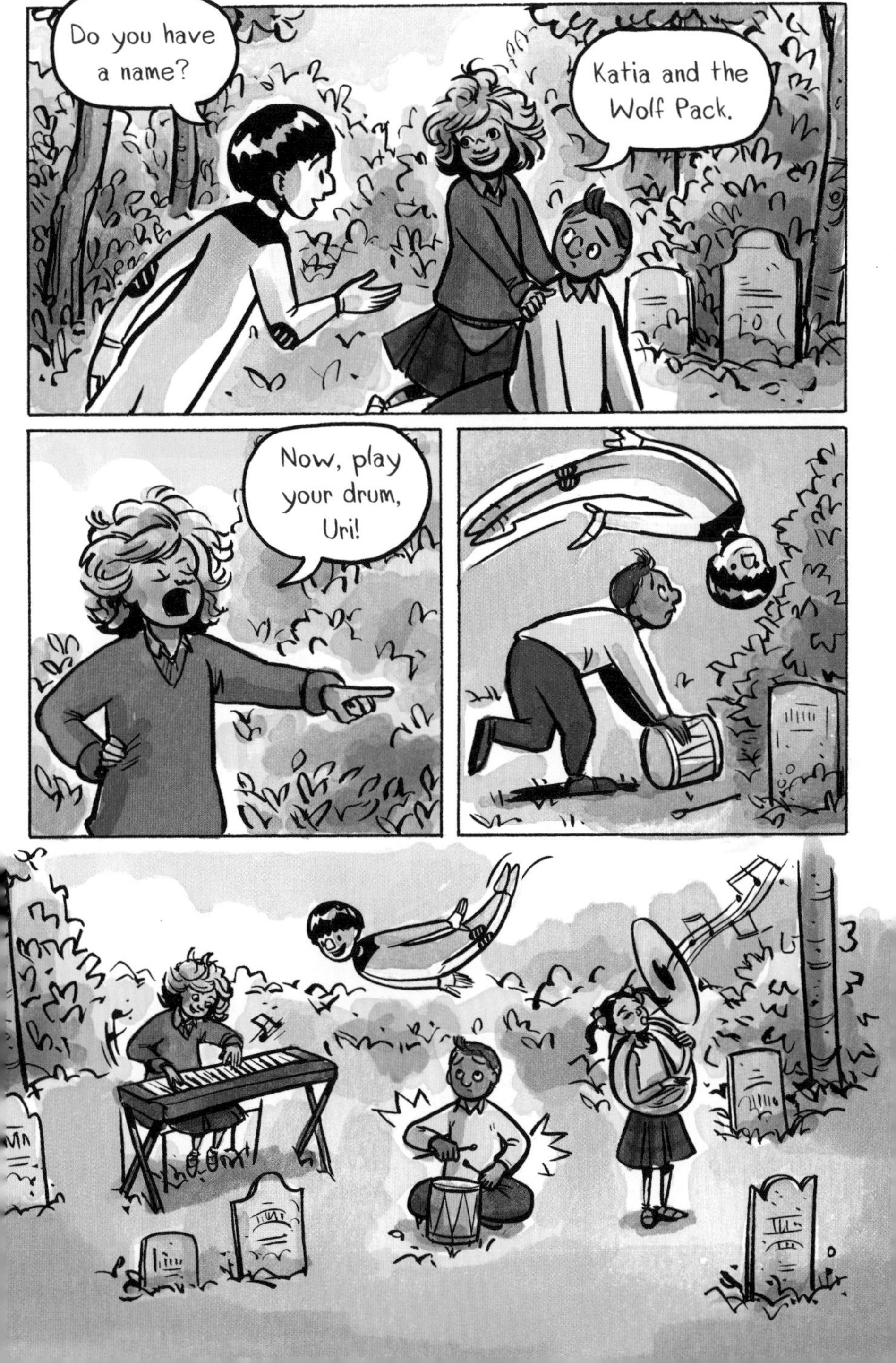
Do you have a name?
Katia and the Wolf Pack.
Now, play your drum, Uri!

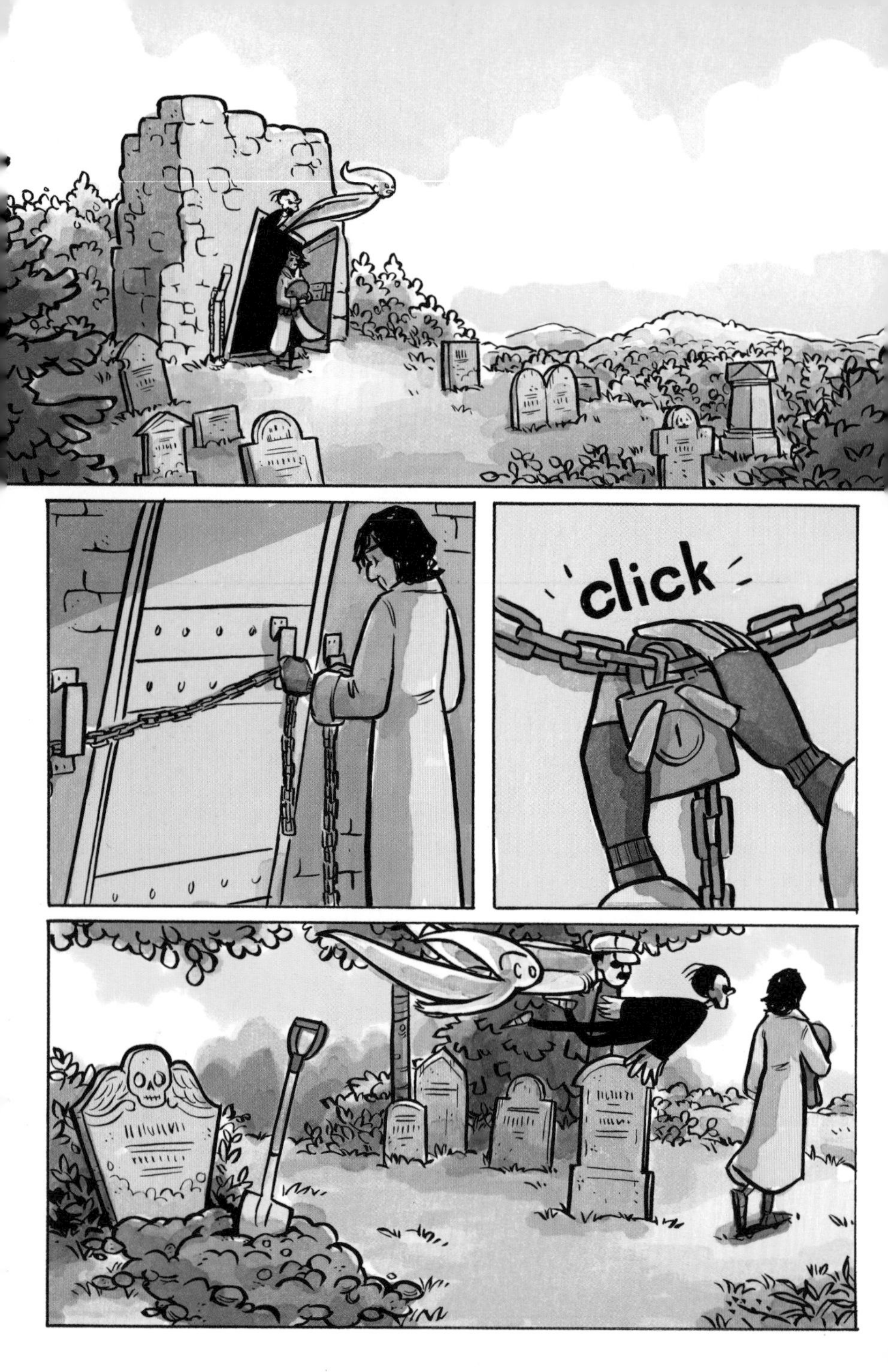
click

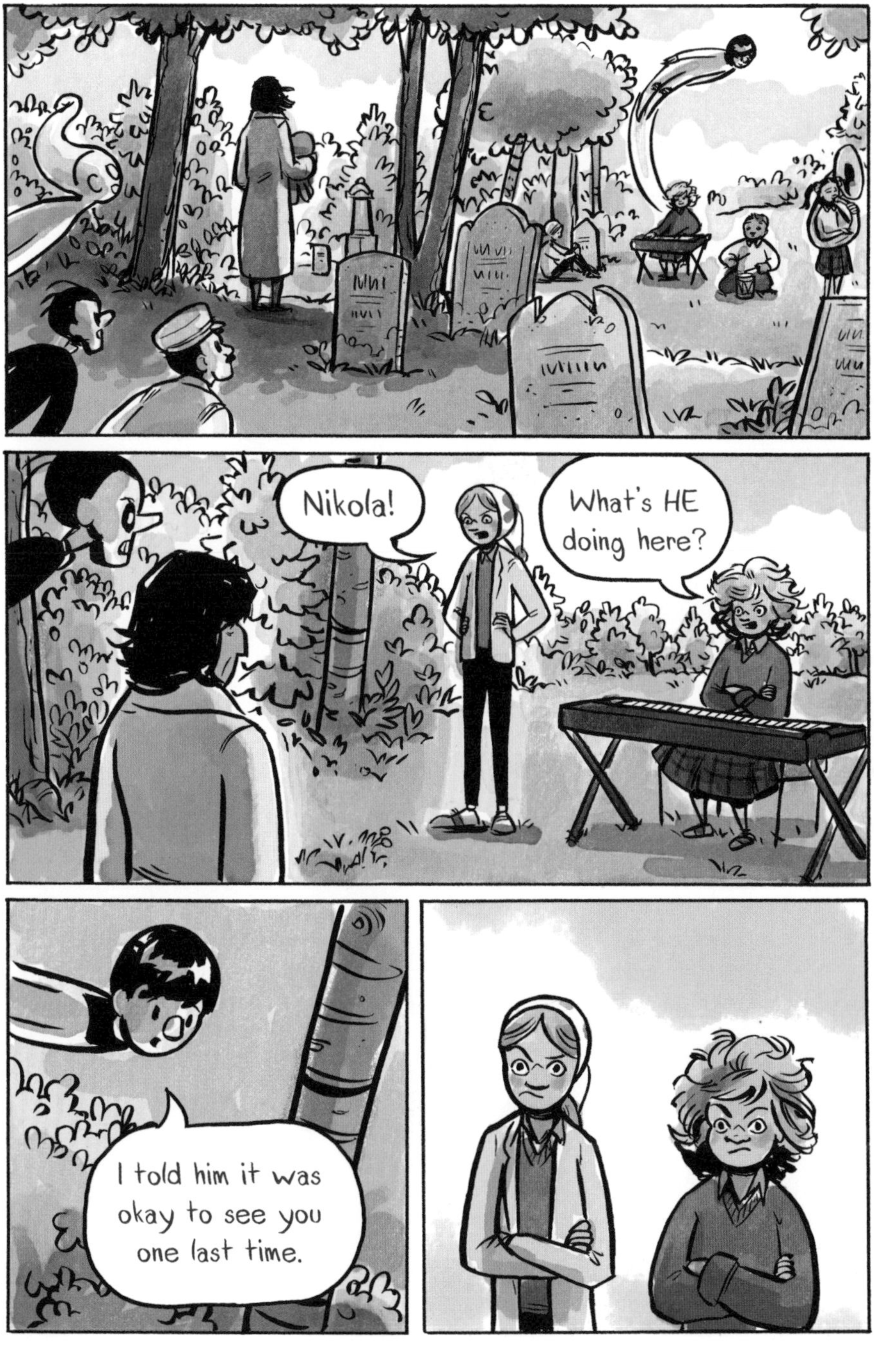
Nikola!
What's HE doing here?
I told him it was okay to see you one last time.

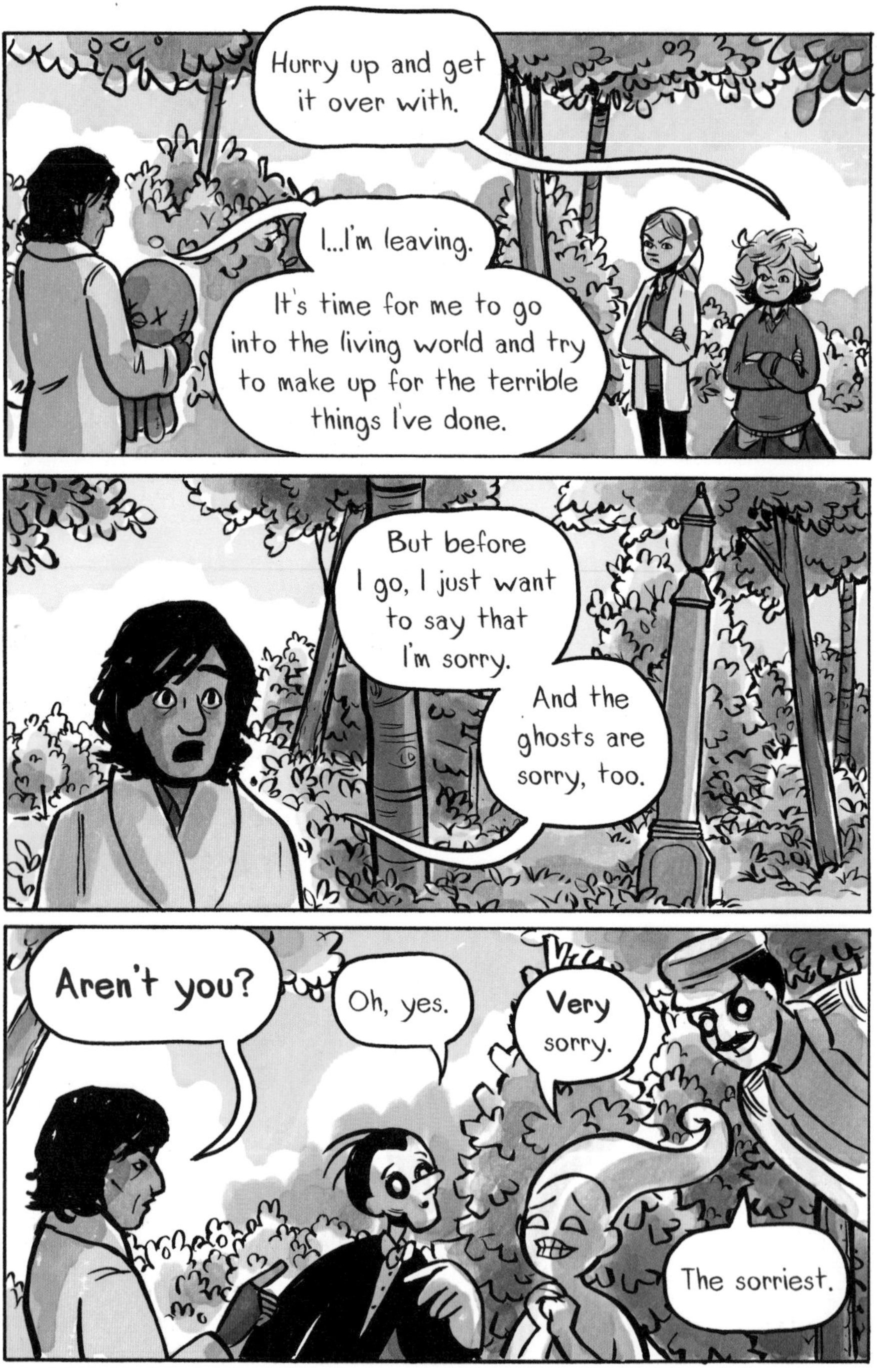
Hurry up and get it over with.
I...I'm leaving.
It's time for me to go into the living world and try to make up for the terrible things I've done.
But before I go, I just want to say that I'm sorry.
And the ghosts are sorry, too.
Aren't you?
Oh, yes.
Very sorry.
The sorriest.

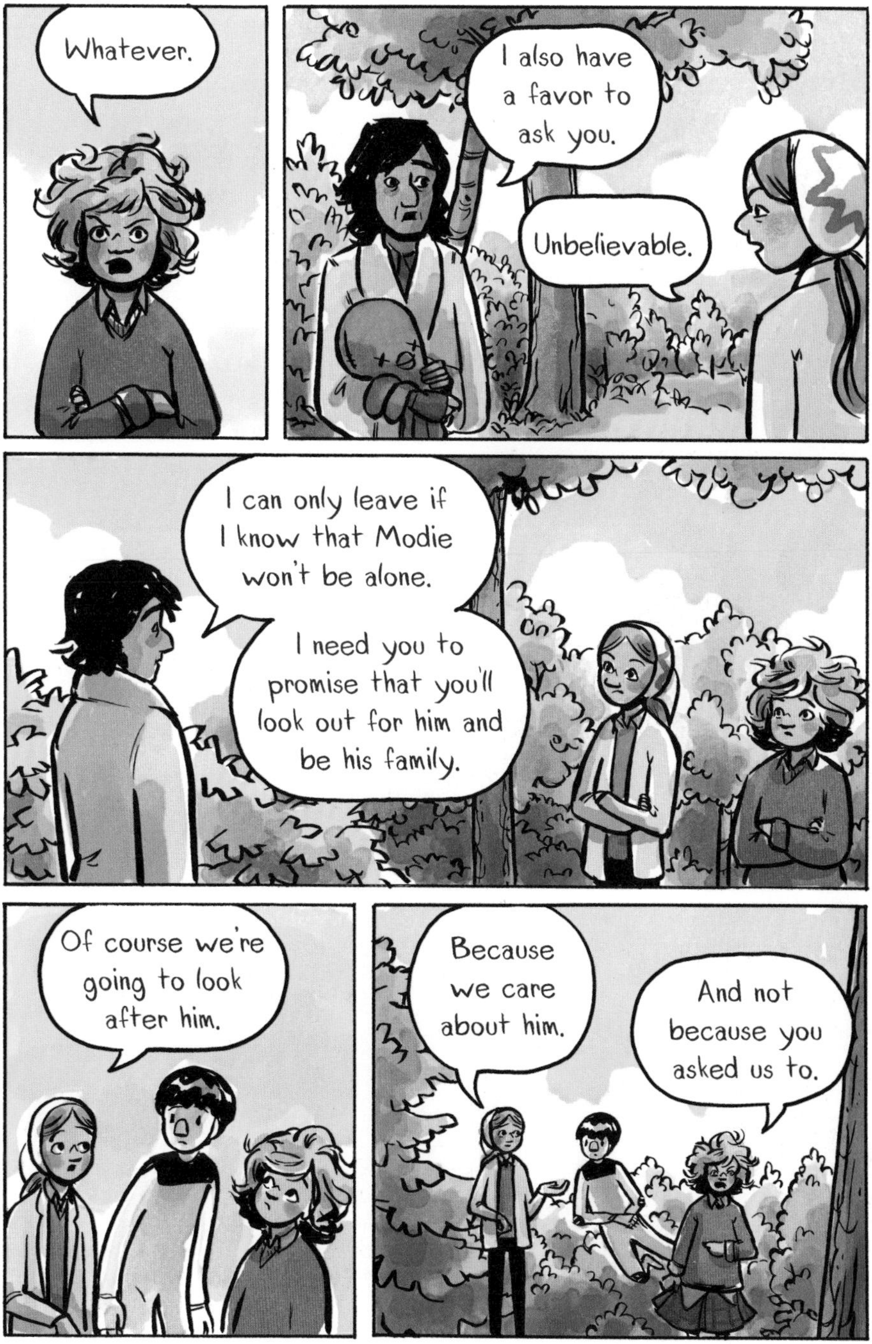
Whatever.
I also have a favor to ask you.
Unbelievable.
I can only leave if I know that Modie won't be alone.
I need you to promise that you'll look out for him and be his family.
Of course we're going to look after him.
Because we care about him.
And not because you asked us to.

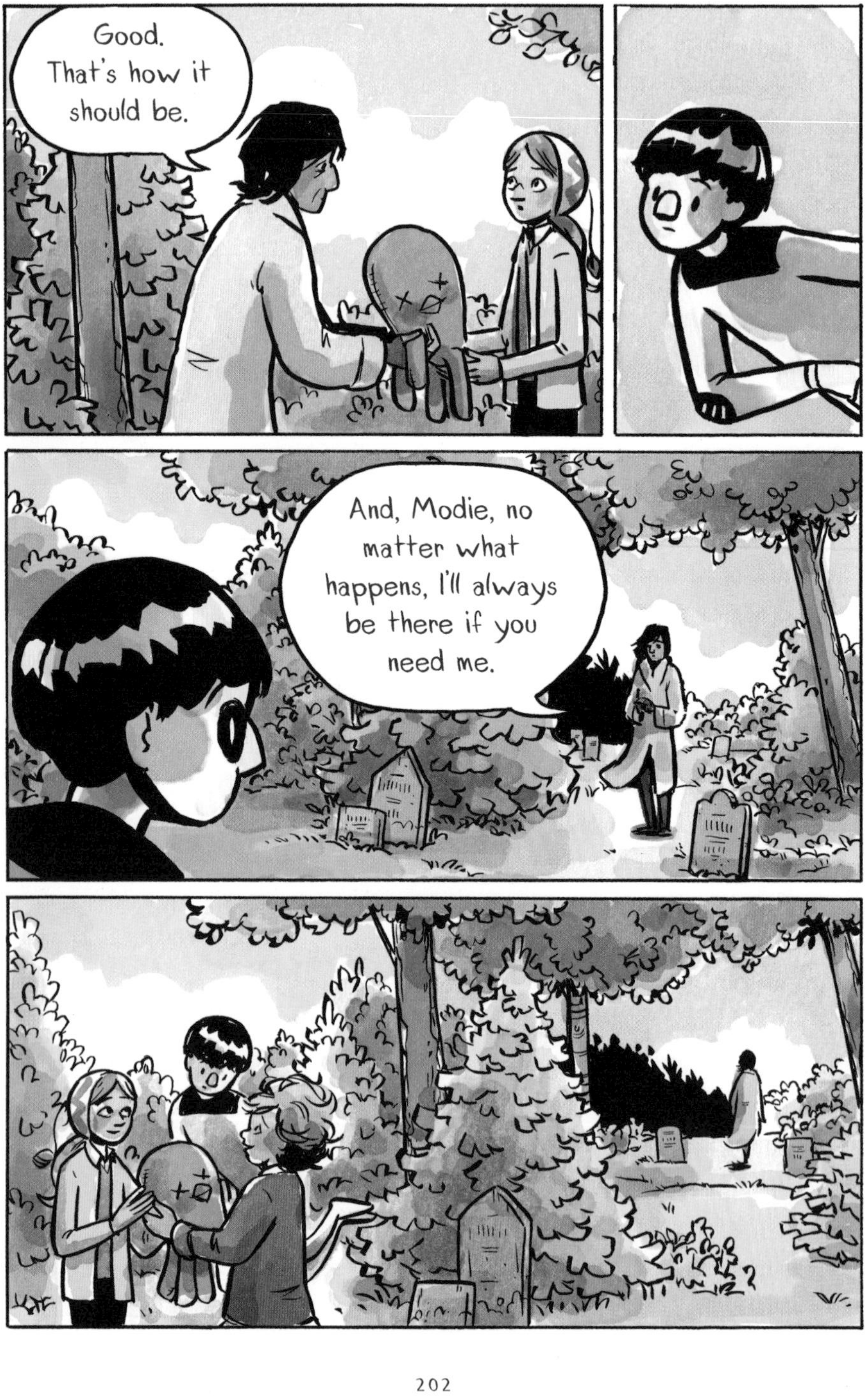
Good. That's how it should be.
And, Modie, no matter what happens, I'll always be there if you need me.

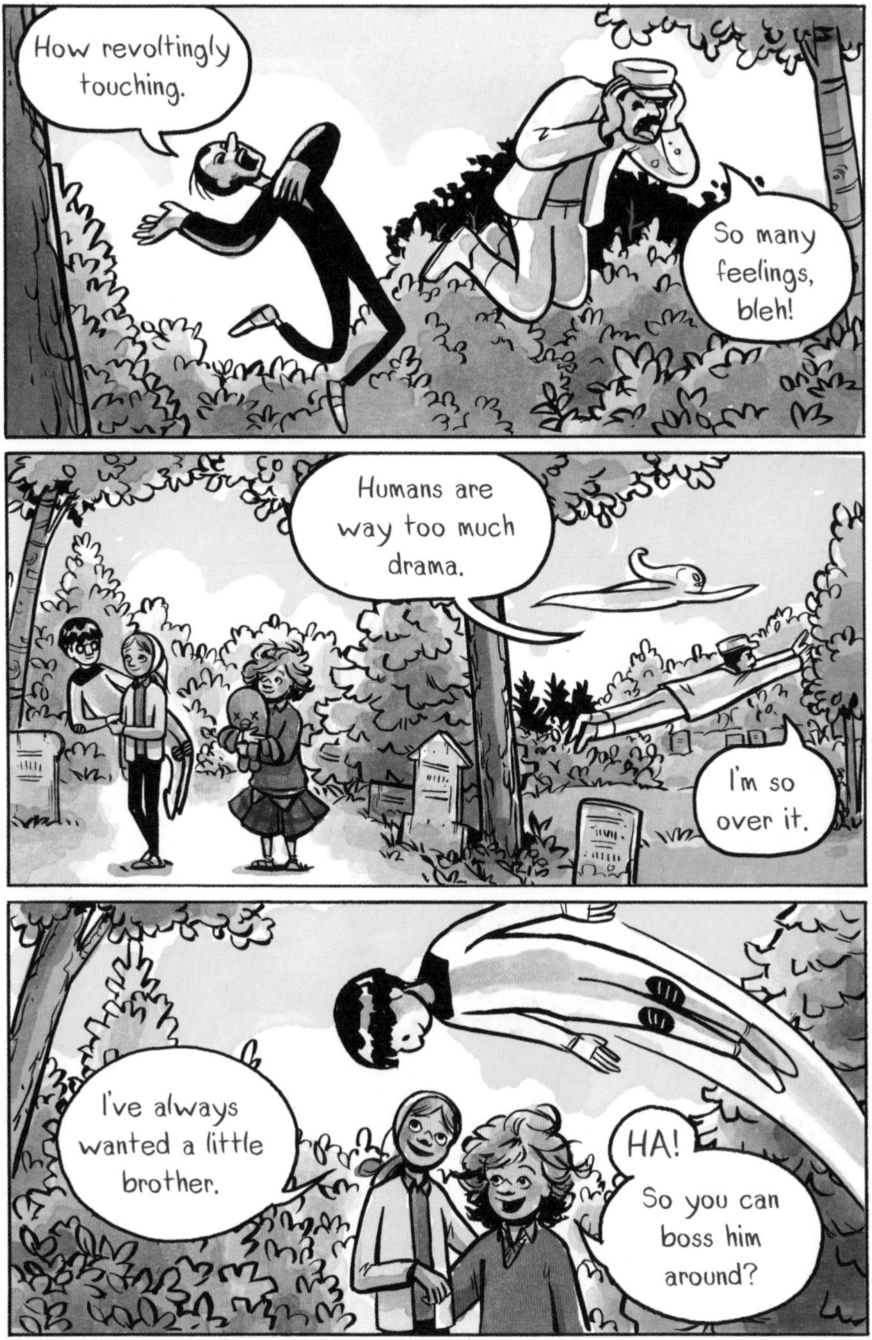
How revoltingly touching.
So many feelings, bleh!
Humans are way too much drama.
I'm so over it.
I've always wanted a little brother.
HA!
So you can boss him around?

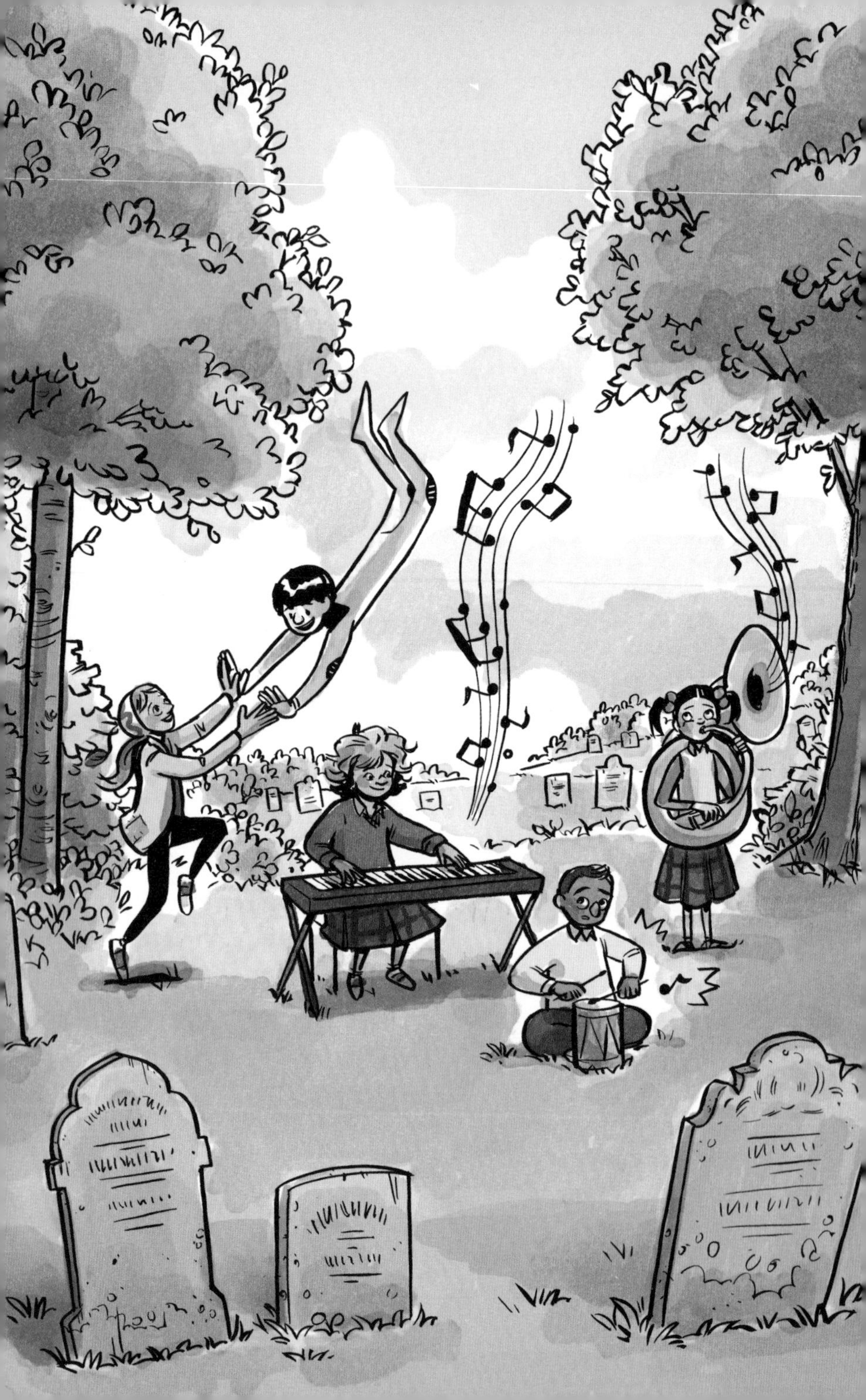

THANKS TO ...

My mother, father, and sister.

Cassandra Pelham, David Saylor, Phil Falco, and all the amazing people at Scholastic.

Bernadette Baker-Baughman, my brilliant agent.

Paul Karasik, my mentor, and Barbara Orlovsky, my hero.

My generous friends Jon Chad, Jay Edidin, Allie Kleber, Miriam Greenberg, Katherine Roy, Kenan Rubenstein, Veronica Agarwal, and Tim Stout.

The Center for Cartoon Studies and Michelle Ollie.

ABOUT THE AUTHOR

After a childhood misspent raising pigs, selling hot dogs, and drawing princesses, Laura Terry ran away to the relative splendor of an all-girls boarding school and wore many shades of plaid. She then graduated from both Pratt Institute and the Center for Cartoon Studies and self-published a number of minicomics. Now Laura spends her days living and working in Brooklyn with her poodle, Muffin. Visit her online at www.lauraterry.com.

Author photo by Andrew Frasz